W9-ABO-351

REMEMBER ME

ALSO BY MARY BALOGH

REMEMBER ME

A RAVENSWOOD NOVEL

MARY BALOGH

Berkley

New York

BERKLEY
An imprint of Penguin Random House LLC
penguinrandomhouse.com

Copyright © 2023 by Mary Balogh

BERKLEY and the BERKLEY & B colophon are registered trademarks of
Penguin Random House LLC.

Library of Congress Cataloging-in-Publication Data

Names: Balogh, Mary, author.
Title: Remember me : a Ravenswood novel / Mary Balogh.
Description: New York : Berkley, [2023] | Series: A Ravenswood novel ; 2
Identifiers: LCCN 2022043390 (print) | LCCN 2022043391 (ebook) |
ISBN 9780593438152 (hardcover) | ISBN 9780593438169 (ebook)
Subjects: LCGFT: Novels.
Classification: LCC PR6052.A465 R463 2023 (print) |
LCC PR6052.A465 (ebook) | DDC 823/.914—dc23/eng/20220909
LC record available at https://lccn.loc.gov/2022043390
LC ebook record available at https://lccn.loc.gov/2022043391

Printed in the United States of America
1st Printing

Book design by George Towne

REMEMBER ME

THE WARE FAMILY OF
RAVENSWOOD

Caleb Ware
Earl of Stratton
(1760–1812)

m.

Clarissa Greenfield
(b. 1768)

Marjorie Higgins m. Ben Ellis
(b. 1790)   (b. 1783)

Joy Ellis
(b. 1813)

Devlin Ware
Earl of Stratton
(b. 1786)
m.
Gwyneth Rhys
(b. 1790)

Major Nicholas Ware
(b. 1789)

Philippa Ware
(b. 1793)

Owen Ware
(b. 1796)

Stephanie Ware
(b. 1799)

CHAPTER ONE

Lucas Arden, Marquess of Roath, sank into one of the old brown leather armchairs in the library at Greystone Court in Worcestershire, a glass of after-dinner port in one hand, and looked around fondly at all the bookcases crammed with books. He would wager that his grandfather, the Duke of Wilby, had read most if not all of them. He had read a good many himself. The library here had always been his favorite room. He looked at the heavy oak desk before the south window, at the old furnishings and the Persian carpet, at the heavy brocade curtains and the painting of a hunting scene in a gilded frame hanging above the mantel. Nothing had been changed or renewed for as far back as he could remember. He hoped nothing ever would be.

His grandfather *had* changed quite noticeably, however, over the past couple of years or so. He was no longer just elderly. He was old. It was a distinction Lucas would be unable to explain in words, but he knew in his heart what it meant, and it saddened him. His Grace was standing now before the fire, his back to it, his feet apart, his hands resting palms out against his backside, warming before the blaze. He was a small man in both height and girth—and smaller now, surely, than he had once been—with a round head that had always seemed too large for his body. His grizzled, bushy hair, once as dark red as Lucas's was now, had thinned and even disappeared altogether from his temples and the crown of his head. His eyebrows, however, were as thick and shaggy as ever. He was dressed, as was usual for the evening, in tailed coat, embroidered waistcoat, old-fashioned knee breeches and stockings, and an elaborately folded neckcloth tied about high, starched shirt points even though there had been no outside guests for dinner—just the duke and duchess and their grandson and heir.

Lucas waited instead of making any attempt to initiate conversation. His grandfather had invited him to bring his port into the library rather than sit with it at the dining table as they usually did. His grandmother had already moved to the drawing room to leave them alone together. Obviously His Grace had something to say that was not for the ears of his butler or the footman who had waited upon them while they dined. He had probably been building to this moment since his grandson's arrival here two days ago, in fact. Lucas had been invited to spend a week or so over Easter. Though it had been more of a summons than an invitation. Jenny— Lady Jennifer Arden, Lucas's younger sister, that was, who lived with him at Amberwell in Leicestershire—had not been invited.

"I am an old man, Luc," his grandfather began now, his eyes, which had been gazing thoughtfully at the carpet, turning to regard his grandson keenly. "The Good Book allots us threescore years and ten if we are fortunate enough to dodge all the possible hazards along the way. I have outlived that allotment by nine years, going on ten. I cannot expect many more. Perhaps, indeed, not *any* more."

"Do you know something I do not, Grandpapa?" Lucas asked, feeling a twinge of alarm, though he knew, of course, that no one could live forever.

"Well, for one thing, I can still count," the duke told him. "And seventy-nine is a very advanced age. When I look around for acquaintances of my generation, I find very few of them still remaining. For another thing, that old quack of a physician I have been bringing here twice a year from London at considerable expense had the effrontery to inform me a few weeks ago that my heart is not what it used to be. I paid him his usual exorbitant fee to tell me what was as obvious as the nose on his face."

Lucas knew that Dr. Arnold, the duke's longtime physician, had come here recently on his semiannual visit to check upon the general health of the duke and the duchess. Lucas had written to his grandparents to ask what the report had been since he had not been here in person to question the doctor himself. The man would have given only the vaguest of answers anyway since he felt himself bound by professional ethics to respect the privacy of his patients. His usual response was that Their Graces were as well as could be expected. Which was the polite equivalent of saying nothing at all. The duke's answering letter had stated that he and the duchess were in cracking good health and it had been a waste of a small fortune to drag Arnold all the way to Greystone to tell them so and eat them out of house and home before deciding to take himself off back to London.

"It is a serious condition?" Lucas asked now. He dreaded the answer. He did not want to know.

"Serious or not," his grandfather said, "the fact is that I have an old heart in an old body, Luc. And another fact is that my only son is dead and he had only the one son. That is two facts. I am dearly fond of my daughter and my grandson of her line and of all my granddaughters, but none of them can carry on my name or my position no matter how many sons *they* produce. Only you can. I have an affection for my Cornish first cousin, but he is only three years my junior, and he complains with every letter he sends me that old age is for the hardy but hardiness deserted with his sixties. Besides, of the seven children he produced with his two wives, not one of them was a son. Not a single one. *Seven* daughters, Lord love them. They all married and produced sons as well as daughters, but much good those sons do me. Someone on high has been enjoying a jest at the expense of a few generations of my family and yours, Luc."

Lucas had met the Cornish cousins a few times when he was a boy and his father was still alive. But he could not say he knew any of them well. Those of his generation were third cousins and had never really felt like relatives.

"My Yorkshire cousin, on the other hand, was always a thorn in my side when we were boys," his grandfather said. "If you should die without male issue, Luc, then it is *his* grandson who would no doubt step into your shoes. And I recall how you felt about *him* during your own boyhood. Kingsley Arden would inherit the dukedom and Greystone and everything else that is entailed. I will be in my grave and thus be spared from having to witness his ascension to such lofty heights. You will be in *your* grave and spared too. But there will be plenty of our family still alive who *will* witness it and suffer the consequences but be powerless to prevent it. Even Amberwell would belong to him."

It was *not* a pleasant prospect.

Kingsley had been at school with Lucas for a few years, one class above him. He had tried constantly to bully his younger relative and had succeeded more than once in making his life miserable. The thought of his living here at Greystone was not a pleasant one. Even less pleasant was the prospect of his owning Amberwell one day. Amberwell was where Lucas had grown up until he was fifteen and where he lived again now. More important, it was where Jenny lived and probably always would—unless Kingsley became Duke of Wilby and turned her out, as he almost undoubtedly would. He had always despised Jenny even though he had never met her. He had liked to ask Lucas when other boys were around how his crippled sister was doing and how he felt about being burdened with her for the rest of his life.

"Then I will have to see to it that I live to your present age and beyond, Grandpapa," Lucas said now. "And that I father a dozen sons or more in the meanwhile."

His Grace moved away from the fire and lowered himself stiffly into the chair beside it. He was still stubbornly resistant to any suggestion that he use a cane. He gazed into the fire while Lucas got to his feet to put on some coal and poke it into more vigorous life.

"Your father died at the age of forty," the duke said after Lucas had resumed his seat and taken a sip of his port. "Less than a year after your mother died soon after she gave birth to your stillborn brother. The damned fool of a son of mine was always an excellent horseman and proud of it, but no one is immune to accident when he insists upon jumping a six-foot-high hedge. Especially when he does so while still engulfed by grief over the loss of his wife and son—the son who would have been his spare, born more than fourteen years after he had done his duty and produced the heir. You, that is. Life is an unpredictable business at best, Luc." He paused and transferred his gaze from the fire to his grandson. "Her Grace and I have made a decision."

And it was going to be something he did not like, Lucas could safely predict. His grandfather always invoked the name of Grandmama whenever he knew what he was about to say would be unwelcome. Like the time both grandparents had come to Amberwell after their son's death and informed Lucas that he would be leaving both school and home and returning to Greystone with them, where he would stay until he reached his majority—except for the scholastic terms he would spend at Oxford when the time came. At Greystone he would learn all he needed to know about his future role and duties as the Duke of Wilby.

Only Lucas was to go there, though. Aunt Kitty, the widowed Lady Catherine Emmett, his father's sister, would be moving to Amberwell to live with Jenny and make all the arrangements for the wedding of Charlotte, Lucas's older sister, to Sylvester Bonham, Viscount Mayberry. The nuptials had been delayed twice, first by their mother's death, then by their father's. They had finally wed two weeks after the year of mourning for their father was over. Poor Charlotte. It could not have been the wedding she had dreamed of. But the marriage was undoubtedly a happy one and had produced three children in the ten years since.

Lucas had fought and argued and sulked over that ducal decree, but his protests had been in vain. Two days after his father's funeral he had left for Greystone with his grandparents, leaving a tearful Jenny and Charlotte behind but refusing to weep himself with a fierce grinding of his teeth and fists so tightly curled into his palms that he had left behind the bloody marks of eight fingernails.

Despite himself he had come to love Greystone. And his grandparents too, of whom he had always been fond, but in a remote sort of way since he did not see them often.

It was pretty obvious, of course, what decision they had made now. Even though he was only—God damn it!—twenty-six years old. There was that missing generation. His father had died. From more than just a moment's recklessness on horseback, caused by debilitating grief over the loss of his wife and stillborn son, however.

No other living soul had an inkling of the full truth except Lucas. The heaviness of his secret knowledge had weighed him down for longer than a decade and probably would for the rest of his life. He had been in the wrong place at the wrong time one rainy afternoon during a school holiday, and his life had been drastically and forever blighted as a result.

"As soon as Easter is behind us," his grandfather said now, "we will be going to London, Her Grace and I. It is time I did my duty and showed my face in the House of Lords once more. I did not go at all last year or the year before, to my shame. And it is time your grandmother and I renewed our acquaintance with the *ton* in a place where almost the whole of it gathers for the spring Season. Perish the thought, but it is unavoidable. We will need to find out who is in town. Your grandmother is better at that than I am, of course. She will know within a day or two what might take me a whole week. There will be any number of young girls there, fresh out of the schoolroom and eager to make their mark upon society and reel in the most eligible of the bucks and marry them before the Season is over. There will be a positive frenzy among them all—not to mention their mamas and some of their papas too—when it becomes known that you are on hand at last, Luc. The Marquess of Roath, heir to the Duke of Wilby and Greystone Court and other properties and a vast fortune besides. The *very elderly* duke, that is."

He paused to gaze keenly at his grandson from beneath those shaggy brows. There was no point in attempting any protest or any reply at all, though. Lucas had learned his lessons well during the six years he had lived here before he turned twenty-one and returned to take up residence at Amberwell. He knew what his primary duty was.

It was to produce an heir and a spare or two, to put it bluntly.

"There will be pretty ones and alluring ones and ones you will fancy more than others," the duke continued when Lucas said nothing. "There will be wealthy ones and ones whose papas have pockets to let. There will be very few, however, who will be eligible in both birth and breeding to be the future Duchess of Wilby and mother of the next heir to the title. Very few. You will leave it to your grandmother and me to find out who they are."

"I am to have no choice in the matter, then?" Lucas asked.

"Well, I am no tyrant, Luc," his grandfather said, not at all truthfully. "I daresay there will be more than one. Maybe even as many as half a dozen if this is a good year. There is sure to be a beauty or two among them to please your young man's fancy. Not that looks mean everything. Your grandmother was not considered a particular beauty when my mother presented me to her. But it did not take me long to discover that she was beautiful to *me* and that there was no need to look further. Not that I would have been given the chance to do so anyway. When my mother had decided upon something, it would have been as easy to move the Rock of Gibraltar as to change her mind. I daresay I was in love with your grandmother within a fortnight and I have never yet fallen out of love. Despite her height."

The duchess was half a head taller than the duke—or that was the story the latter insisted upon. It was true too when His Grace was wearing his heaviest riding boots and his hair was at its bushiest.

"She admitted on our tenth wedding anniversary, when we were reminiscing," the duke added, gazing into the fire, "that it took her a whole year to fall in love with me. But she did it, by Jove. Despite my height."

"So I am to go to London after Easter to choose a bride," Lucas said, bringing his grandfather's attention back to the matter at hand.

"You are," the duke said. "It is not going to happen unless we give you a bit of a push, after all, is it? You are unfortunately a bit on the reclusive side, Luc. More than a bit. As though you had never heard of wild oats. Or of London and a wide world beyond the confines of Amberwell. Or of the spring Season and the great marriage mart. Or of all the young girls who come flocking to it each year."

Lucas was not a recluse. He was happy at Amberwell and had a wide circle of acquaintances as well as a few close friends there. He had an active social life. He loved living in the country and managing his farms along with his steward. He had made friends at Oxford too and remained in communication with a number of them. Some of them still visited him at Amberwell. He still visited them, sometimes for a couple of weeks at a time. There were even a few friends remaining from his school years, before he was fifteen. He had always valued and nurtured friendships.

He just did not like London. Not that he had ever spent much time there, it was true. Whenever he had, though, he had found it crowded and noisy and grimy, and he had craved fresh air and open spaces and a wider view of the sky. And silence. Not that silence was ever total in the country. But he craved birdsong and the chirping of insects, the lowing of cattle, the bleating of sheep. The sound of wind. The hooting of night owls.

He had always been uncomfortably aware of *who* he was whenever he was in town—heir to a dukedom and a fabulous fortune, that was. Men he did not know assumed a friendship with him upon very little acquaintance. Women with daughters of marriageable age fawned upon him with the slightest encouragement or even no encouragement at all. The daughters themselves simpered. Oh, all that was an exaggeration, of course. But not much of a one. He had always felt more like a commodity than a person when he was in town. He had often wished he were simply Lucas Arden, son and grandson of country gentlemen of no particular social significance.

His feelings about being in London no longer mattered, however. And he had always known this day would come. For while he remained at Amberwell, it was unlikely he would meet any young women who would rise to his grandparents' exacting standards for a future bride. He was not at all averse to marrying. It was virtually impossible, after all, to have any sort of personal friendship with a woman or—heaven help him—a liaison with one while he lived in the country, where everyone knew everyone else and everyone else's business. It was five years since being at Oxford had given him more sexual freedom, though even there he had not been exactly promiscuous, as many of his fellow students and even a few of his friends had been.

He rather liked the thought of marrying, not just for the obvious sexual satisfaction he might expect, but also for the close companionship a life partner might offer. He thought he would enjoy having children too—because a son would provide a much-needed heir for the next generation, of course. But not *just* for that reason. He would like to have children—plural. Sons and daughters. He always found his niece and nephews, Charlotte's children, to be great fun, though Sylvester, their father, claimed that his most frequent pastime these days was counting his gray hairs.

"A penny for them," his grandfather said abruptly, and Lucas looked at him and grinned.

"Are you quite sure you would *like* me to sow some wild oats, Grandpapa?" he asked.

"It is too late for them now," the duke said. "You have lost your chance. Your grandmother and I want you married before the summer is out, Luc. Preferably before the Season is over. St. George's on Hanover Square in London is the finest church for the wedding of a duke's heir to the daughter of someone of equal or nearly equal rank. We want to see a boy in your nursery before next summer. I will undertake to live long enough to hold him at his christening, that quack of a physician be damned."

Good God! Had Dr. Arnold really given his grandfather less than a year to live?

"I believe I can commit myself to the marriage," Lucas said. "Provided one of the ladies Grandmama chooses for me will have me, that is. I will do my best on the birth of a son."

But his stomach was rebelling a bit against the dinner he had eaten. For one thing, his grandfather was obviously dying, and the reality of that fact was beginning to hit home—as far as his stomach was concerned, anyway. Yet he was to be given no time to prepare himself emotionally for what lay ahead. With one's head one might know that the time left for an aging loved one was limited, but one's heart was more inclined to take refuge in denial. *Not just yet . . .*

Not just yet had become *soon*. And he was not nearly ready, damn it all.

He was *not* averse to marrying or to fathering a child within a year. But, devil take it, the prospect of marrying a stranger just because she was the daughter of some aristocrat and of a suitable age was more than a little . . . cold. He did not consider himself a romantic. He did not particularly believe in falling in love and walking about with his head among the stars or any of that poetic nonsense. But he *did* believe quite firmly in companionship and friendship and compatibility and some basic degree of attraction, both sexual and otherwise. He would have to be intimate with his wife very regularly, after all, at least until there were sons—plural— in his nursery. But ensuring all of that would require time in which to get to know his future bride and discover if all his reasonably modest requirements were going to be met. For her sake as well as his own. For whoever she turned out to be, she was a person, not just a female *breeding* entity who happened to have been born to nobility.

It was pointless, however, to wish he had got to work on finding just the right woman before now so that he could have a bride of his own choosing. It might not have worked anyway, for even then the Duke and Duchess of Wilby would have had no qualms about vetoing his choice if the woman did not suit them.

At the very least he must hope now that his grandmother would find more than just one or two suitable candidates in London after Easter. Let him at least have *some* choice. And a thought occurred to him. Were there young ladies of aristocratic birth even now awaiting their come-out Season in London and praying fervently that their parents would find *more than one or two* eligible candidates for a husband for them? So that they might hope for some degree of happiness with *one* of them?

This ordeal no doubt worked both ways.

Being rich and titled was not *all* wine and roses and endless freedom—not for men and not for women. Marriage for the privileged few was rarely about love and happiness and friendship and sexual attraction. But, like it or not, he was one of the rich and titled and privileged and there was no point in wishing otherwise.

"*If* one of the young ladies Her Grace chooses for you will have you?" his grandfather asked him, his eyebrows almost meeting for a moment across the bridge of his nose. "*If,* Lucas? *If?* Have I taught you nothing in the years since your father's death? There is no such word as *if* when you have decided that something will be so."

They were not questions that required any answer.

CHAPTER TWO

E aster was over for another year and members of the *ton* were beginning to gather in London in growing numbers, as they always did during the months of springtime. Soon both houses of Parliament would be in session again to occupy many of the men, especially those of the aristocracy, as they conducted the business of the nation. Men and women would fill every available hour of every day hosting or attending a dizzying number and variety of social entertainments—balls, soirees, concerts, garden parties, Venetian breakfasts, to name but a few. For spring in London was the time of the Season. It was also the venue of the great marriage mart, where young ladies fresh out of the schoolroom were brought by hopeful parents to be viewed and courted by gentlemen in search of brides, and the young of both genders vied for the most coveted matrimonial prizes in terms of looks, birth, and fortune.

Lady Philippa Ware, elder daughter of the late Earl of Stratton and sister of the present earl, was *not* fresh out of the schoolroom. She was twenty-two years old, an age at which some would consider her perilously close to being left on the shelf to gather dust. She feared it herself. Nevertheless, she was on her way to London for the first time and, therefore, for her very first Season. She was traveling with her mother, Clarissa Ware, Dowager Countess of Stratton, and her sister, Lady Stephanie Ware. Stephanie was sixteen years old and very definitely still *in* the schoolroom. Leaving her behind at Ravenswood Hall in Hampshire, however, would have meant leaving her alone there with Miss Field, her governess—as well as a houseful of servants, of course—since all her brothers were elsewhere.

Devlin Ware, Earl of Stratton, was currently in Wales to attend the wedding of his wife's brother before following his mother and sisters to town. Major Nicholas Ware was with his regiment somewhere in northern Europe, where the Duke of Wellington was gathering his armies again to deal with the renewed threat posed by Napoleon Bonaparte, who had recently escaped from exile on the island of Elba and was reputed to be raising a massive army again. Owen Ware was in the final term of his first year at Oxford. And Ben Ellis, their half brother, older than Devlin by more than three years, had gone for a few weeks with his two-year-old daughter to Penallen, a manor house on the Hampshire coast he had purchased from Devlin the year before and was having renovated before moving there permanently later in the year.

Philippa's mood fluctuated almost hourly between excitement over being *finally* on her way to London to meet and mingle with the *ton* and a stomach-churning anxiety that she was going to be a terrible failure there and perhaps even be openly scorned and rejected. She would see London for the first time, she would be presented at court and make her curtsy to the queen, and she would attend as many balls and parties as her mama deemed suitable—*if* she was invited to any at all, that was. She would perhaps make new friends. Maybe she would meet someone and fall in love, though she had no preconceived notion of what that someone would look like. He must, though, be kind and personable and honorable and without any great vices, like drinking or gambling to excess or . . . womanizing. That last was most important of all. He would not have to be extraordinarily handsome, only reasonably pleasant to look at.

She might also be spurned and ordered to leave London and never even *think* of returning. No amount of sensible reasoning would quite banish that unlikely possibility from her mind. Or the fear that she would be invited nowhere. Given the cold shoulder. The cut direct.

She was very much afraid that it was too late for her. She feared that any gentleman in search of a bride would look first at those who were younger than she and perhaps never look at her at all. She had voiced her concern to her mother yesterday, when their personal maids and Miss Field were leaving for London ahead of them, together with most of their baggage.

"Pippa!" her mother had exclaimed, laughing softly and drawing her daughter into a warm hug. "Have you taken a good look at yourself in your glass lately? It frequently amazes me that I actually gave birth to someone so beautiful in every way—in looks *and* nature. And have you remembered that you are the daughter and sister of *an earl*? You have a large dowry. And as for being *old,* well, you are just far enough past childhood to have developed poise to add to your youthful beauty. It would surprise me very much indeed if soon after Devlin joins us in London he does not find himself besieged daily by young gentlemen come to offer for your hand."

Philippa had laughed at the obvious exaggeration, though she had been reassured—for the moment. Perhaps she would not be a *total* wallflower. Gwyneth, her sister-in-law, had been *twenty-four* when she married Devlin just before Christmas last year, after all. Yet she was vividly beautiful and had been practically betrothed to a famous musician when Devlin had returned home from war in the early autumn after a six-year absence.

Philippa turned her eyes now to the carriage seat across from her own, where her sister sat gazing out through the window. Stephanie was looking forward to being in London, even though she was too young to attend any but the most informal of entertainments. She claimed that she had no desire *whatsoever*—she always emphasized the one word—to attend balls and parties. But she *did* want to see everything that was to be seen and believed she had convinced Miss Field that a visit to a gallery or museum or one of the famous churches was as important a part of her education as the conjugation of French verbs or learning to embroider in such a way that it was virtually impossible to distinguish the back of the stitches from the front. Uncle George Greenfield, their mama's brother, who always stayed a part of the Season at his bachelor rooms in London—though he was a widower, not a bachelor—had promised to take her to the Tower of London one day and show her all the most gruesome exhibits there, like axes that had been used for beheadings. The sorts of things Miss Field would surely keep her well away from lest they induce nightmares in her young pupil. Stephanie was thrilled.

Uncle George was with them now, riding his horse close by the carriage. He had brought forward his own planned journey to London by a week or so since he did not like the idea of his sister and nieces traveling without male escort. He had assured them all, winking at them as he handed them into the carriage outside the doors of Ravenswood early this morning, that even the most fierce of highwaymen would surely turn tail and run after taking one look at him.

Stephanie turned her head from the window and smiled at Philippa. She did not speak, though, after glancing at their mother.

She held a finger to her lips instead, and Philippa turned her head
to see that Mama had dozed off, her head propped on the corner
of the cushions behind and to one side of her. Philippa winked at
her sister, who resumed her perusal of the countryside passing the
window.

Poor Steph had a very low image of herself. She had been a
plump child, who had been assured by everyone, perhaps unwisely,
that she would soon grow out of her baby fat. She had given up
asking *when* that would happen by the time she was ten. Now she
was a large young lady with a round face and smooth, shiny cheeks.
She had very long golden blond hair, which she refused to have cut
or even trimmed and wore in thick, heavy braids wound over the
top of her head. To Philippa she had a beauty all her own—
wholesome and bright-eyed and genial. But in her own eyes Steph
was fat and ugly.

Ah, what we do to destroy ourselves, Philippa thought. *Yet so
many of us do it.*

She turned her head to look at her mother again. She was still
beautiful even though she was in her late forties by now. There was
no gray in her dark hair. She was dignified and charming and re-
spected, even loved, by all who knew her. Yet she must have spent
years of her life feeling unattractive and inadequate, believing that
she was not *enough*. When they were all young children, Mama had
stayed home with them during the spring while Papa went to London alone to do his duty as a peer of the realm and a member of the
House of Lords. For the rest of the year, when Papa was back home,
she had glowed as she worked tirelessly to organize and host all the
grand entertainments for the neighborhood he had loved. Yet, looking back, Philippa realized that he had done little or nothing to
help Mama with all the work. And then he had dishonored her in
the worst way possible. One summer he had brought a young mis-

tress to the village of Boscombe just outside the gates and across the
river from Ravenswood, and he had invited her to attend the summer fete in the park. There had been a horribly public scandal when
Devlin had discovered them in compromising circumstances together in the temple folly a short distance from the house during
the evening ball and had refused to keep quiet about it until the
next day, when he could have confronted their father alone. He had
denounced Papa in front of all their neighbors.

It had turned out—though it was never actually acknowledged
openly—that Mama had been fully aware of Papa's infidelities
through the years but had never spoken a word of them to anyone.
Perhaps not even to Papa himself. What must all that have done to
her confidence in herself? To her belief in her beauty and charm
and ability to attract love and lasting devotion?

Philippa sighed but smiled and shook her head when Stephanie
turned her face from the window and raised her eyebrows in inquiry.

Mama *had* gone to London with Papa for the three Seasons
following that scandal. Papa's sudden death of a heart seizure had
put a stop to any more. She knew enough people, though, she had
assured Philippa a few days ago, and was known well enough, to
introduce her daughter to the *ton* and ensure that she was invited
to all the most prestigious entertainments.

"I am, after all, the *Dowager Countess of Stratton*," she had reminded Philippa. "I am *somebody*. Just as you are—you are *Lady
Philippa Ware*. Devlin is the *Earl of Stratton*. *Now* will you relax,
you silly goose?"

Yet Philippa had refused a Season when she was eighteen and
again last year when she was twenty-one because she had feared
that the family's scandal of more than six years ago had spread to
the *ton* in general and that as Papa's daughter she would be ostra-

cized if she showed her face in London. It might seem to have been a foolish fear, but it had not been groundless.

Life at Ravenswood had changed after the scandal. She had been fifteen years old at the time, on the cusp of young womanhood, her head filled and bubbling over with dreams of an exciting future. They had been a close and happy family then, and they had been loved in the neighborhood. But the day after the scandal erupted Devlin left home, banished by Mama, and Ben went with him for reasons of his own. They went to the Peninsula, where war was raging against Napoleon Bonaparte, Devlin as an officer in a foot regiment, Ben as his supposed batman. Nicholas joined them there a month or so later though in a different regiment. Owen, twelve at the time, went off to school. Mama stopped entertaining, and the light seemed to go out of her. Papa continued as usual— cheerful, genial, gregarious. Yet there had seemed something hollow about his joviality, as though he were somehow playing a caricature of himself. Or so it had seemed to Philippa, who had suddenly found herself seeing him through newly opened eyes.

Stephanie, aged nine at the time, and Philippa had carried on as best they could. But nothing had been the same. They had no longer been the golden family, and Ravenswood had no longer been the center of the universe for all who lived within a five-mile radius of it.

"Did I fall asleep?" Mama asked now, her voice still sleepy. "I must have eaten too much luncheon. I am very poor company, girls, I am afraid."

"Steph and I are happily communing with our own thoughts in order not to disturb you," Philippa told her.

"I am busy watching the passing countryside," Stephanie said. "I am disappointed to see that the grass and trees are still green this far from home instead of orange or purple or checkered or something more interesting. And the houses and churches look much like those at home."

"Absurd," their mother murmured, and closed her eyes to sleep again.

The sisters exchanged a smile, and Philippa moved the side of her face close to the window to peer ahead. Surely London would come into view *soon*. A couple of times she had been deceived by a distant church spire, only to discover that the church was situated in a country village. But this time . . . Oh, surely that faint halo of smoke on the horizon was it, though doubtless it would take them another hour or two to get there. She felt as though butterflies were dancing in her stomach as she attracted Stephanie's attention and pointed. Her sister swiveled about in her seat to take a look behind her and then nodded and beamed happily. She clapped her hands silently, and they both laughed just as soundlessly.

Their uncle rode up beside the carriage as they were doing so and bent to peer through the window. He looked across at their mother, shook his head, and indicated to his nieces that they should look ahead. *London,* he mouthed at them. They nodded at him with smiling animation, though they did not attempt to lower the window and risk waking their mother. Uncle George nodded back and rode on ahead.

It was not the changes at Ravenswood, however, that had stopped Philippa from going to London at the age of eighteen with Mama and Papa for a come-out Season. It was something else entirely. She had been planning to go. Indeed, for several months she had waited with impatient excitement at the prospect of life turning bright and eventful again. She had dreamed of romance and love and happily ever after.

But then something had happened.

She had joined the local maypole dancing group just after

Christmas. They practiced one evening every second week in a large, rather elegant barn on Sidney Johnson's property. Philippa had joined them even though she would not be in the neighborhood on May Day but in London instead.

On this particular occasion, James Rutledge, middle son of Baron Hardington, their neighbor, had come too, bringing with him a friend from his years at Oxford who was visiting him for Easter. There had been a buzz of interest over the visitor, for they rarely saw strangers in the neighborhood. And he was a titled gentleman, a marquess, though someone had said it was only a courtesy title. What that meant, though, was that he must be heir to a *real* title. Philippa had been as curious and interested as everyone else. But she had forgotten all about the splendor of his prospects when she saw him. For he was quite the most gorgeous man she had ever set eyes upon—tall, long-legged, perfectly formed, and handsome as well. But it was his hair that was his most striking feature. It was both dark and red at the same time and thick and shining and expertly styled.

Philippa, with all the questionable maturity of an eighteen-year-old, had fallen headlong in love with him.

James had introduced him as the Marquess of Roath but had not presented him to everyone individually.

He had bowed to all of them a bit stiffly. Philippa had thought that perhaps he was on the haughty side. Or perhaps he was merely shy and feeling daunted at having so many strangers stare at him, dumbfounded for the first few moments.

The men had gathered in a group at one end of the barn, as they always did at the start of the evening, while the women had huddled and chattered and giggled closer to the maypole. There had been more chattering and giggling than usual, of course, but Philippa had not participated in it. She had been straining her ears to overhear what the men were talking about. It would have been far better for her if she had not done so, for she had succeeded all too well. Four years later the memory was still as raw as if it had happened yesterday.

The men had been urging the marquess to dance even though he protested that he knew absolutely *nothing* about maypole dancing and would be sure to make an utter ass of himself if he tried. And yes, he really had used the word *ass*, believing as he had that he was talking just to the men. He had said it moments before a burst of laughter from the women over an unrelated subject had drowned out the men's voices.

"Give it a try," Sidney Johnson had been urging the marquess when Philippa could hear them again. "Come on. I'll introduce you to one of the women and she will guide you through the steps and the patterns with the ribbon."

"If you could make it the blond beauty . . ." the marquess had said, and Philippa had looked away sharply so that she would not be caught staring. She was the only real blonde among the women. But . . . *blond beauty? Really?*

"Ah. You mean Pippa," she had heard James say. "*Lady Philippa* to you, Roath. The Earl of Stratton's daughter."

And then the Marquess of Roath had said the words that had seared themselves upon her mind and her memory and completely changed the course of her life. It was no exaggeration.

"*Stratton?*" he had said, sounding startled. "She is *Stratton's* daughter? I do not dance with soiled goods, Rutledge."

The words had been spoken a mere second before another burst of gleeful laughter from the women drowned out anything else he might have said—or anything the other men might have said in reply. By the time Philippa darted a look in their direction, both James and the marquess had disappeared. They had not returned.

But the damage had been done.

It had been painfully clear to Philippa that her father's infidelities—for she had never been in any real doubt since the night of that fete that they were plural—and Devlin's public exposure of them in the middle of a crowded ball had had a more far-reaching effect than she had realized. The whole of the *ton* had heard of it and been scandalized and disgusted by it. Disgusted not just with her papa but with the whole family. They were all *soiled goods.*

On the following morning she had informed her mama and papa that she would not be going to London after Easter. She had refused to give them any reason for the complete turnabout in her attitude but had remained adamant. *Obstinacy,* her father had called it as he had tried to wheedle her out of her doldrums. *A nervous collapse,* her mother had called it as she had tried to coax Philippa into believing that she would soon be cured if she would but go to London and start attending parties.

They had ended up going without her.

By the following year there had been no question of her making her come-out. Her father had died suddenly. And the year after that, just as they were leaving off their mourning for him, Grandmama Ware, his mother, had died. Last year she had simply said no when her mother has asked, halfheartedly it had seemed to Philippa, if she wished to go to London.

Then, early in the autumn, Devlin had come home at last. Devlin and Ben, and Ben's one-year-old daughter, Joy. His wife, whom he had married the year before, had died while the British battalions were crossing the Pyrenees into France before the Battle of Toulouse.

By then Philippa had been twenty-one years old, still single, and with almost no social life to speak of. She had been deeply depressed, though she had hardly realized it.

Until, that was, Devlin had sat down with her one afternoon while she was hiding out in the turret room at the top of the west wing at Ravenswood. And somehow he had wheedled the whole sorry story out of her—Devlin, who had come home after six years with what had seemed like a granite heart. She had resented him because he had not written to any of them after he was banished and because he had waited two whole years and a little longer after Papa's death before returning home. He had been her favorite brother before that even though she loved them all. He had come home not even realizing that he still loved them with a fierce passion deep within the frozen core of himself. At least, that was what Philippa had come to understand during those early weeks after his return and during that conversation he had had with her, when she had finally cracked and told him everything.

Everything.

The reason he had sought her out on that particular day was that there was to be a gathering that evening in Sidney Johnson's barn, but *not* to practice maypole dancing as usual. Sidney and Edwina Rutledge, who both occasionally spent time in London during the spring, were going to teach the steps of the waltz to anyone who was interested. It was the new dance that had come from Germany and was rapidly gaining in popularity in England. Devlin had agreed to go with Stephanie and Gwyneth Rhys, but Philippa had said no—more than once. She would not go. She had not even been sure she would go to the village assembly the following evening, though it was to be held in their own ballroom rather than the village inn for the first time in many years. But Devlin had challenged her after she had told her story. He had asked her if she was going to allow a man of such low, despicable character as the Marquess of Roath to blight the whole of the rest of her life.

And of course she was not going to allow any such thing.

Devlin had made her understand that she had been in hiding from her own life all that time, cowering at home, depressed and lethargic because she was afraid that if she took a step out into life she would be terribly hurt again. He had made her realize that the only person who was being hurt by her fears was herself. *Not* the man who had spoken with such cruel disregard for her feelings and reputation—though he had not realized, of course, that she had overheard him.

She had gone to that waltz lesson. And she had gone to the assembly the following evening—and danced every set, including the waltzes.

Now she was going to London. To do all the things she ought to have done when she was eighteen. Surely it was not too late. She was *only* twenty-two. She was not quite in her dotage. Perhaps the old dreams could be revived. Romance. Falling in love. Marriage. Happily ever after.

Well, perhaps not quite that last one, for it was something only children and very young persons could believe in. But happiness was surely possible. Just consider Devlin and Gwyneth, for example. They had fallen in love with each other at that infamous fete. Philippa was sure of it, though neither of them had said anything. Then they had been parted for six years and Gwyneth had almost married that Welsh musician. But she had wed Devlin instead just before Christmas in the presence of both their families. Philippa and Stephanie and Joy had been bridesmaids. And ever since there had been a quiet glow about the two of them. It seemed to Philippa that they were each other's best friend and a great deal more besides.

Perhaps she would meet someone in London with whom she could find happiness like that.

Perhaps the *ton* would have forgotten the old scandal by now.

Or perhaps there never had been any great outrage after all. Mama had spent three Seasons there and had never been driven home by vicious gossip.

"Good gracious," her mother said, sitting up and looking through the carriage window on her side. "We are almost there. I must have been sleeping for an hour or more. I am *so* sorry, girls. You have been very quiet. You must be terribly tired of communing with your own thoughts." She laughed and regarded both her daughters with open affection. "This is going to be an exciting time—for both of you."

"I know." Philippa stretched out her hand for her mother's and squeezed it, though she was not quite sure she spoke the truth. She felt suddenly anxious again. "Thank you for bringing me, Mama, even though I am sure you would a thousand times rather remain at home."

"Not a bit of it," her mother protested. "Not even nine hundred and ninety-nine times. This is one of the pleasurable duties of motherhood to which I have long looked forward, Pippa—introducing my daughters to London and the *ton* and watching them triumph and begin a happy life on their own account. You this year and Stephanie the year after next. But I shall do my best to see to it that you enjoy yourself even this year, Steph."

"This year, yes, but forget about the year after next, Mama," Stephanie said. "Oh, look. We really are here."

They had indeed arrived within the confines of London. Philippa turned her wide-eyed gaze to what was passing beyond the windows. Her uncle was in sight again. He turned his head to look into the carriage, nodding when he saw that his sister was awake and smiling as his nieces gazed at the wonder of London out the window.

CHAPTER THREE

Clarissa Ware, Dowager Countess of Stratton, had never particularly enjoyed London, except during the first two years of her marriage, when she had been young and in love and the whole world of the *ton* had been new and wondrous to her. It had not taken her long to become disillusioned, however, and to choose to remain at Ravenswood with her children during the spring months while her husband was fulfilling his duties in the House of Lords. She had, however, gone to London with him and stayed for the whole of three Seasons following the ghastly scandal that had ruined one of their annual summer fetes and damaged the warm relationship between the Wares of Ravenswood and their neighbors. Her own family and his had urged her to go in order to keep up appearances and exercise some restraining influence upon her husband—by which was meant making it near impossible for him to employ a mistress or to visit brothels or whatever it was he did when he was there alone.

She had smiled her way through those London Seasons, hosting dinners and soirees with her husband, paying and receiving after-noon calls without him, attending garden parties and balls and theater parties and dinners, sometimes with him, sometimes not, hating almost every moment until it was time to return home.

This year everything was different. Now she was here on her own account, to present her elder daughter to society, to see that she was invited everywhere, to make sure she had every opportunity to make suitable lady friends and meet eligible suitors. There was her presentation at court to arrange, possibly a grand ball at Stratton House to organize later, after her son and his wife arrived in London, a coveted voucher to Almack's assembly rooms to procure, a whole wardrobe of new clothes for all occasions to be ordered—among other things.

Pippa was all of twenty-two years old, and of course she was worried about being *too* old. It was absurd, as she would soon dis-cover for herself. She was even more lovely now than she had been at the age of eighteen when *something*—she had never said just what—had happened to cause her to change her mind about going to London. She had a greater poise and maturity now. The dowager countess felt no doubt whatsoever that her daughter would take well with the *ton*. But she desperately hoped Pippa would meet a man of honor who deserved her, not someone who was all flash and charm and very little substance.

Clarissa set to work with a will the day after they arrived in town, writing letters to acquaintances to let them know she was in London with her daughters.

Not that she was entirely alone, of course. George, her beloved younger brother, was in London too and was always available as an escort whenever he was needed—or as a companion or confidant anytime. Charles, the late earl's brother, would be here soon with his wife, Marian, and Angeline, their daughter, who was the same age as Pippa but had the advantage of four years of Seasons behind her and a recent betrothal to Ninian Fortescue to give her standing. He was a steady young man who had inherited a respectable fortune last year and a decently sized home near the Scottish border. Eloise Atkins, the late earl's sister, would be in town too with Vincent, her husband, and their son, Leonard, now thirty-four years old.

Pippa had settled happily. She was delighted with her room, which was next to Stephanie's on the second floor overlooking the back garden and the mews beyond it, where the horses were stabled and the carriages were kept on the lower level, while grooms and stable hands lived in the rooms above.

Stephanie had settled into the schoolroom and rearranged it to her liking. She had presented Miss Field with a lengthy list of places she wished to visit and made the case that all of those excursions would somehow be educational. Miss Field had confided to the dowager, her eyes twinkling, that she fully agreed with her pupil, though she had not said so. Stephanie would enjoy them far more if she felt she was getting away with something.

The first week was taken up largely with shopping. They spent hours on Bond Street and Oxford Street, purchasing everything from bonnets to dancing slippers, from fans to reticules, from silk stockings to kid gloves, from handkerchiefs to jewelry—to mention but a few essential items. Stephanie accompanied them only once before declaring that shopping must be the most fatiguing and tedious activity ever invented. She spent most of her month's allowance on that one occasion on pretty clothes and toys to send to Joy at Penallen.

Pippa spent long hours posing for the modiste the dowager countess always patronized when in town, being measured and fitted, and sitting on a delicate chair with brocaded cushions and gilded arms and feet, looking through a pile of fashion plates to choose designs she liked for ball gowns, morning and afternoon dresses, and walking and riding and carriage dresses. It amazed her that she needed all of them and more, and in large numbers.

They took out a subscription at Hookham's Library on Bond Street and relaxed over tea and cakes at fashionable tearooms and even consumed ices at Gunter's. They strolled in Hyde Park and visited several galleries. They went to St. Paul's Cathedral, and Pippa and Stephanie insisted upon climbing all the steps to the Whispering Gallery high above the nave while their mother chose rather to sit quietly in one of the pews below to replenish her store of energy.

After a few days, invitations began to arrive by post and private messenger. One of them in particular gratified Clarissa. It was from Lady Catherine Emmett, a friend she had made during her own first Season, when she had been newly married to Caleb. She told her daughters about both the invitation and the friend, interrupting them at the breakfast table as Stephanie was reading a letter from Ben and Pippa was reading one Gwyneth had sent from Wales.

"Kitty was newly married too that year," their mother explained. "In fact, we discovered the very first time we met that we had celebrated our weddings on the same day and at exactly the same hour. We became firm friends during that spring and the next and have written to each other regularly ever since. We have not met often, however. She came here with her husband during the years when I did not. And then, by the time I returned here, she was already widowed and had taken on the charge of her niece, who is unfortunately crippled and in delicate health. But this year we are both here. She has brought her niece to town."

"I am glad for your sake she is here, Mama," Pippa said.

"Kitty is quite delightful," Clarissa told them. "You will both like her. Sir Matthew Emmett, her husband, was never a robust man, sadly. He died ten or more years ago, leaving her with a son and daughter. Her daughter is married to an Irish nobleman. Her son must be in his middle twenties and is still single, I believe. At least, she has not told me he is married, and she surely would have done if he were. He is a baronet." She looked speculatively at Philippa. "Kitty derives her own title—*Lady* Catherine—from her father, who is a duke."

"And she has invited us to tea?" Philippa said. "All of us? That will be delightful, Mama."

"She is at the duke's town residence," the dowager explained. "Her niece cannot go out as much as she would like, I suppose. The tea is probably for her benefit. Kitty does say that Stephanie will be very welcome to go too, though she asks me to warn her that there will be no one else there below the age of eighteen and that she may find the whole thing a bit tedious."

Stephanie laughed. "She is very tactful, Mama," she said. "I will not go, of course. And you must not feel you are neglecting me whenever you and Pippa go off to all the various entertainments for which you have come here. I do not even *wish* to attend any of them. Miss Field and I will go to Westminster Abbey instead of the tea. She wants me to see Poets' Corner. I want to see *everything*."

"I will look forward to making the acquaintance of Lady Catherine and her niece, Mama," Philippa said. And then, with a slight blush and a twinkle in her eye, "And that of her son if he is there too."

"Fortunately, a few of your new afternoon gowns have already been delivered," her mother said. "Including the sprigged muslin, which I know is your favorite. I will return an acceptance, then, for you and me?"

"Yes, indeed, Mama," Pippa said. And she looked as though excitement were bubbling up inside her. It was lovely to see after the depths of depression into which she had sunk and remained for a number of years after that wretched fete.

"It is *so* good to see you with a smile on your face, Pippa," Clarissa told her.

"Remember," Stephanie said, "that I insist upon being a bridesmaid at your wedding, Pippa."

Lady Catherine Emmett, Kitty to her family and close acquaintances, had had a happy marriage, which had ended far too soon with the premature death of her husband. She had brought out her daughter, Beatrice, at the age of eighteen and had seen her married before the end of her first Season to a man of whom she thoroughly approved except that he lived quite inconveniently in Ireland. They now had two healthy, energetic sons.

Sir Gerald Emmett, Lady Catherine's son, had settled contentedly on his late father's estate. He had implemented a series of improvements on the land, all of which had increased its prosperity. Kitty would like to see him happily married too with children, but he was only twenty-eight years old and could be trusted to manage his own affairs in his own time.

Lady Catherine liked to be busy, and she liked to feel needed. Eleven years ago, soon after Beatrice married, her brother broke his neck and died when he tried unsuccessfully to jump his horse over an impossibly high hedge. Poor Franklin had not been in his right mind at the time, of course, having lost his wife in premature childbed less than a year before. The child, who would have been a second son and the all-important spare to Lucas, had never drawn breath. It had been a ghastly couple of years for the whole family, for Franklin had been their father's only son and heir, their father being the Duke of Wilby. Lucas had become the duke's heir at the tender age of fifteen and had been whisked off to Greystone to be educated for his future role.

Meanwhile Frank's daughters had remained at Amberwell, their home in Leicestershire. Charlotte had been betrothed to Sylvester Bonham, Viscount Mayberry, at the time. Jennifer had been twelve years old then. If she had been a normal child, both she and Charlotte would almost undoubtedly have gone to Greystone with their brother. She was *not* normal, however. She had suffered a debilitating illness at the age of five and for a year or more had not even been expected to live. Her legs had suffered first, with numbness and tingling, and then pain and paralysis. The illness had spread upward until for weeks on end even breathing had been difficult for her, poor thing. She had survived, though, and even recovered to a large degree. But the illness had left her thin and pale and unable to walk except very short distances with the aid of crutches. Her right leg, thinner than the left, was twisted out of shape. And sometimes she suffered relapses and a return of the pain and weakness in muscles all over her body.

The Duke of Wilby had decreed that Jenny should remain in the familiar surroundings of Amberwell, where she had always lived. Kitty, he had decided, with nothing much to do with her time now that her daughter was married and her son no longer needed her, would move in with her nieces to look after Jenny and arrange a wedding for Charlotte.

Kitty might have refused to comply with such a high-handed demand. She was, after all, no longer under her father's authority. She was a widow of independent means. Her father was right about one thing, however. She did not have much to do with her time except visit her daughter and her grandsons as often as she could persuade herself to get into a boat bound for Ireland and allow it to transport her over open water that would never remain obligingly still beneath the vessel. Besides, she had always had a soft spot for Frank's girls, especially Jenny, who had endured the difficult years of her childhood and girlhood with cheerful and uncomplaining courage.

In apparent obedience to her father, whom, by the way, she adored, Kitty had descended upon Amberwell to console her nieces in their grief, which was considerable, and smother them with love and loving care. They might have resented her if she had not been wise enough to admit to her own grief and occasionally weep with them before rallying them and explaining that life was far from over for them despite the loss of their mama and papa and brother. And despite the fact that their living brother had been spirited away to Greystone just when they were most in need of him themselves.

Jenny had usually smiled cheerfully after these rallying talks, while Charlotte had sighed and complained that she sometimes feared her wedding day would *never* come. And then as like as not she would start weeping at the realization that her papa would not be there to give her away when the day *did* come. Or her mama to help her don her wedding clothes.

Those early days really had *not* been easy for any of them.

By now, however, Charlotte was contentedly married with children of her own, and Jenny was no longer a girl. She was twenty-three years old. She still needed the company of her aunt, though, for she could not expect ever to marry despite the fact that she was the granddaughter of a duke. Unless, that was, some fortune hunter was prepared to make the sacrifice in order to get his hands on her money—and there were always plenty of such men lurking on the outer fringes of the *ton* and sometimes indeed at its very heart. Both Kitty and Jenny were alert to that particular danger.

Jenny accepted that she was not likely to marry. She really did not intend to become a recluse, however, a fact that pleased her aunt, for Kitty still loved to mingle with society. Amberwell was a lovely home in a pleasant neighborhood, and it offered some amiable and genteel company—but not nearly enough to satisfy all the social needs of either lady.

They had been to London for a part of two Seasons after Jenny turned eighteen. They had always stayed at Arden House, the duke's town house on Berkeley Square. Jenny had been presented to the queen during their first visit. She had attended several parties with her aunt and had gone a number of times to the theater and the opera. She had seen Hyde Park and Kew Gardens from an open barouche, in which she had ridden with her aunt. Mostly, however, her social life had been confined to Arden House itself, where there was not all the bother of lifting her in and out of conveyances and in and out of her heavy and cumbersome wheeled chair. There were soirees and afternoon teas and card parties and one literary evening at Arden House. Kitty loved hosting parties, and she knew that her niece enjoyed them. The duke and duchess, both elderly now, rarely came to London themselves, and Lucas never did.

This year aunt and niece had come to London again. And she would begin their Season, Kitty told Jenny the day after their arrival, with an afternoon tea, to which they would invite as many of their acquaintances as they could expect to be already in town— perhaps as many as thirty, even possibly more.

"For there will be some who cannot attend for one reason or another," she explained. "And we do not want it to be said that our very first entertainment here was sadly thin on numbers."

"You would become a social pariah, Aunt Kitty," Jenny said, laughing. "I will help you make a list and write the invitations."

It was a task Kitty enjoyed, especially the making of a list. She always aimed for a careful balance—roughly equal numbers of ladies and gentlemen, and people of all ages and interests and character types. In particular, she liked to invite young people who would be company for Jenny.

"At the very head of the list will be the Countess of Stratton and her daughter," Kitty said. "Actually, Clarissa was my dearest friend a lifetime ago, when both of us were newly married and here in London for the Season. We have remained close friends even though we are both now widows and very rarely have a chance to see each other. But this year I am here with you, and she is here with her two daughters—Lady Philippa Ware is close to you in age, Jenny, though this is to be her first Season. Perhaps you will be friends. And there is also Lady Stephanie Ware, who is still in the schoolroom, though she is not a child."

"I will look forward to making their acquaintance," Jenny said. "They will indeed go at the head of the list, Aunt Kitty. Lady Stephanie too, do you think? I believe she ought to be invited. Now all we need is twenty-seven more names. Or more, so that we will be sure to have at least thirty actually here."

Chapter Four

Philippa was absurdly excited as the carriage conveyed her and her mother the short distance from Grosvenor Square to Berkeley Square. It was only a private tea to which they had been invited, but it was her first social event in London, and it was at the home of a duke. She was wearing her new sprigged muslin afternoon dress, the one her mother had rightly dubbed her favorite. It was fashionably high-waisted with a slightly scooped neckline and short, puffed sleeves over long, close-fitting sleeves that extended to her wrists. It felt light and summery. Her hair was knotted high on her head, with far more curls and fine ringlets than usual trailing over her neck and ears.

Her mother was looking her usual elegant, poised self in dark blue. She also looked happy. She seemed genuinely delighted to be in London with her two daughters, just the three of them together until Devlin came with Gwyneth.

"Do you think there will be many other guests?" Philippa

asked. She was nervous as well as excited. She was certainly not behaving like a poised twenty-two-year-old.

"I am not privy to Kitty's guest list," her mother said, smiling at her and patting her knee. "But I doubt she would have sent a formal invitation card with her letter to me if all she had planned was a small gathering of close friends. I would expect anywhere from twenty to forty fellow guests. I do look forward to seeing her again. She was such a . . . Oh, what is the word I am searching for? Such a *fun* companion when we were both young brides and little more than girls. There was no starch in her even though she was the daughter of the Duke of Wilby."

"Will he be there too today, do you think?" Philippa asked. "Is there a duchess?"

"There is certainly a duchess," her mother said. "At least, I have not heard of anything having happened to her, though both she and the duke must be very elderly by now. Perhaps a little older even than Grandmama and Grandpapa Greenfield. I do not know if they are in town this year, though I doubt it." The carriage rocked to a halt as she was speaking. "Here we are, Pippa, and soon all your questions will be answered. I am so looking forward to launching you upon society at last. Just enjoy yourself. It is all I ask. It is all I have ever wanted for any of my children—that they be happy."

Twenty to forty people, her mother had predicted. There must be all of forty, probably more, in the large drawing room to which they were admitted a few minutes later after the Duke of Wilby's butler had announced them. Philippa felt flutters in her stomach, inhaled slowly and deeply, and smiled as she let the breath out. Young and old and everything in between, she thought, and surely an equal number of men and women. One of the women, a lady about her mother's age, with regal bearing and a welcoming smile and twinkling eyes, detached herself from one group and hurried toward them, arms wide.

"Clarissa!" she cried. "Here you are and looking not a day older than when we first met. Well, perhaps *one* day older."

"Kitty!" Philippa's mother said as they hugged each other at some length, laughing as they did so. "What a delight it is to see you again."

"And this must be Philippa," Lady Catherine Emmett said, withdrawing from the hug, still smiling. "How perfectly beautiful you are, Phil— Oh, *may* I call you Pippa, as I know your mama does?" She took Philippa's hands in hers and squeezed them. "I am so sorry that the passing of your dear papa and then your grandmama delayed your appearance in society. It must have been *very* provoking for you even while you grieved. However, all that is behind you now and I can confidently predict without even having to use a crystal ball that you are about to take the *ton* by storm. Your poor mama will be sweeping an overflow of suitors from your doorstep within days."

"Never, Kitty," Philippa's mother said. "I have servants to do that for me."

And the two older women went off into peals of girlish laughter over the silly joke, drawing looks and smiles their way from other guests. Philippa chuckled with them, already feeling more relaxed. She could understand why her mother liked her friend so much.

"I would have been delighted if Lady Stephanie had come too," Lady Catherine said. "But I can perfectly well understand why she declined the invitation. She would doubtless have found the party stuffy. But come, both of you." She took Philippa by the hand. "Let me introduce you to a few people. You probably know most of my guests already, Clarissa, but I doubt Pippa knows anyone. She soon will, though. It will all be very bewildering at first, my dear, facing roomful after roomful of fashionable persons, but you will find after a short while that you see many of the same people wherever you go. Before long, faces will become familiar and then names. The tricky part, of course, will be putting the right name to each face."

She laughed with delight over her own dire warning.

It was not going to be easy, Philippa agreed over the next fifteen minutes or so as she was introduced to what seemed like a very large number of people. She found herself in conversation with men and women who had known her father or who knew her mother or who just chose to be amiable to a stranger newly descended upon the *ton*. All she had to do in return was smile and answer questions and pose a few of her own. Her upbringing, after all, had prepared her to do that without either cowering or becoming tongue-tied.

Soon she began actually to enjoy herself.

Small tables had been arranged about the perimeter of the room and set for tea with crisp white linen cloths and what must be the very best china, crystal, and silver. Each table had a vase of flowers at its center. Very few people were seated awaiting their tea, however. Most were standing in groups or circulating about the room, conversing with friends and acquaintances, greeting the few people they did not know.

Philippa found herself after a while in conversation with Sir Gerald Emmett, Lady Catherine's son. He must be about Devlin's age, she guessed. He had polished manners and was very charming. He was good-looking too. Philippa was aware of his mother giving a little nod of satisfaction as she moved away and left them alone together after introducing them.

"This is your first Season, Lady Philippa?" he asked her.

"It is," she said. "Even though I am ancient."

He drew his head back a few inches and looked her over critically from head to foot—but with a twinkle in his eye. "Ah," he said. "Then I must ask you to peel off the mask of youth, if you please, and reveal yourself in all your ancientness. If there is such a word."

She laughed. "*Ancient* was perhaps an exaggeration," she said.

"I would call it an outright whopper of an untruth," he told her. "My mother has told me about the family losses that kept you at home and in mourning for a couple of years or more. I am sorry about those but delighted that you are here now. Have you met my cousin Jenny?"

"I have not," she said, "though I have met a lot of other people."

"Bewildering, is it not?" he said. "I remember my first visit to London. I once sent a groom to fetch my horse as I prepared to leave a garden party and discovered after he had brought it that he was not only a gentleman but also a viscount *and* my host. That gaffe will haunt me for the rest of my life, I daresay, for there are a number of persons who were witness to it and will see that I do not forget."

"Oh no!" Philippa said, and laughed again. "But I do believe you may be telling a bouncer of your own, sir."

"Not a bit of it," he assured her. "I have never uttered a lie in my life. Well, no more than a dozen times, anyway. Let me take you to Jenny."

He was very attractive, Philippa thought as she followed him across the room. And personable and good-humored. And the grandson of a duke, and a baronet in his own right. She smiled with amusement as she realized she was already looking with speculation at the young men in the room.

He stopped in front of one of the few guests who were seated, and Philippa saw a young woman who must be close to her in age.

She was thin and pale complexioned, a fact that was somehow accentuated by the dark red of her hair. She was not pretty, but there was something distinguished about her narrow face with its high cheekbones, very straight nose, and slightly upward curving top lip. Her eyes were dark and large. She was smiling at the two people with whom she was conversing. They were all seated in armchairs by the fireplace.

"Jenny," Sir Gerald said, bending over her. "I have brought Lady Philippa Ware to meet you. She is the daughter of the lady Mama was telling me about yesterday when I called here."

"The dear friend and partner in crime of her youth? Lady Stratton?" Lady Jennifer spoke in a low, musical voice, holding out one thin hand toward Philippa and smiling up at her.

"Lady Jennifer Arden," Sir Gerald said, completing the introduction. "My cousin and a granddaughter of the Duke of Wilby, Lady Philippa. You must not learn only names while you are in town, you need to understand, but also titles and relationships. And at the end of the Season there will be a test to decide if you qualify to return here next year."

"Take no notice of him, Lady Philippa," his cousin said as Philippa took her hand. "He is an incurable tease. Will you not be seated? And do call me Jenny."

The two people who had been talking to her had moved away and Philippa took the chair vacated by one of them.

"Then you must call me Pippa," she said.

"It must appear to you that I am sitting here holding court when I ought to be on my feet mingling with my aunt's guests," Jenny said. "I would do so with great pleasure if I could, but alas, I cannot. I am crippled."

"I am sorry," Philippa said.

"You need not be," Jenny told her. "I have been more or less crippled since I was five years old and have adjusted my life accordingly. I do *not* bore friends and acquaintances with details, but I do like to explain to those who do not know me so they will not think me lazy and horribly bad-mannered. This is your first visit to town? And your first Season? That is what Aunt Kitty says. What was your very first impression of London?"

"That it is not as magnificent as I had expected," Philippa said. "The streets are not paved with gold. What a colossal disappointment *that* was. My second impression somewhat contradicted the first, however, for it turned out that Stratton House is not after all a house but a mansion, just as this is."

"You have probably not seen a great deal of London yet," Jenny said. "I especially love visiting the galleries and the grandest of the churches. But I enjoy the social life too—going to the theater and parties at which I can be in company with others. I enjoy it all for just a few weeks at a time, however. I am always glad to return to the country afterward. I am comfortable with my neighbors and friends there and my books. Enough about me, however. Tell me about yourself. Tell me about your family. You have brothers and sisters? Indeed, I know you have one younger sister here in town with you."

"Stephanie," Philippa said. "She is sixteen years old and caught in that frustrating middle land between childhood and womanhood. Though fortunately she is not jealous of me, or even envious, I believe. She is enjoying London but claims to be *very* glad she will not be expected to waste her time at parties. I have three older brothers and one younger. And I have one niece. Oh, and one sister-in-law since Christmas. Gwyneth. She and my brother Devlin will be coming to London soon."

They continued talking about their families and homes after Sir Gerald had moved away with someone who had approached to shake his hand.

"You must not feel obliged to remain here with me indefinitely when I am sure you must wish to meet everyone else, Pippa," Jenny said after a while. "I will not be left alone if you step away, you know. People are very kind, and since most of them know I cannot go to them, *they* come to *me*. I am truly delighted to have made your acquaintance, though, and hope quite sincerely that we will be friends."

"I would like that very much," Philippa said in all honesty. She had felt comfortable with Jenny from the first moment. She should probably take the hint, however, and move on to another group. It was what happened at parties, and there were many people yet to meet. Jenny should be left to receive more of her aunt's guests.

Before she could get to her feet, however, Jenny spoke again. Her eyes were fixed upon the door, and her face had lit up with surprise and pleasure.

"Oh," she said. "Luc has come."

Philippa turned her head to see the person at whom her new friend was gazing. A tall man stood in the doorway, looking around the room. Her first impression was not only that he was immaculately and fashionably dressed but also that he was extraordinarily handsome and indeed physically perfect in every way. But in the very next moment she felt herself turn cold, as though all the blood had drained from her head. Jenny's voice seemed to come from far away.

"My brother," she was explaining. "We were not expecting him in town yet." She raised one thin arm to attract his attention, and he looked toward them and smiled.

He had hair like his sister's but a shade darker—thick, shining red hair that would have drawn admiring attention even without his perfect physique and handsome face.

He also happened to be the Marquess of Roath.

He strode toward them, his eyes moving between his sister and Philippa. And lingering admiringly on her. There was not a glimmer of recognition in his face.

"Luc," Jenny cried as he bent over her and drew her into a close hug. "You are here."

"Well, I am definitely not *there*," he said, causing his sister to sputter with laughter. "I arrived an hour ago to discover there was a party in progress. Aunt Kitty's doing, no doubt? How are you, Jenny? But before you answer, present me, if you please."

She should have hurried away while she had the chance, Philippa thought as he straightened up and looked at her with open appreciation. Where, though? It was too late now anyway. But how could he *not have recognized her*?

"My brother Lucas, Marquess of Roath, Pippa," Jenny said. "Lady Philippa Ware, Luc."

Philippa waited for realization to dawn. But none did. He extended a hand for hers.

"This is a great pleasure, Lady Philippa," he said.

Lucas had been surprised to learn a few years ago, when his sister went to London for several weeks of the Season with their aunt, that she actually enjoyed herself there. She loved the galleries and museums, the theaters and the busy round of parties and receptions, despite the difficulties she had moving about. She had made a number of acquaintances she looked forward to seeing again. She had corresponded regularly with several of them after she returned to Amberwell. And she had gone back a few times since. She was quite determined not to be a recluse even if her condition did confine her to home most of the time.

She was very different from him. If it were up to Lucas, he would be content to spend the whole of the rest of his life at Amberwell, with occasional visits to his elder sister and brother-in-law and to his grandparents and some of the friends he had made over the years. Alas, it was not up to him, and he was going to be compelled to spend all of this particular spring—his favorite season in the country—in London, courting one of the prospective brides his grandmother would pick out for him. Pray God he would at least have some choice and find that one of her picks appealed to him. And this year he had better get used to being in town, mingling with the *ton,* of which he was a member. At some time in the not-so-distant future, he was going to have to go there every spring as a peer of the realm. As a duke he would have to take his place in the House of Lords for the spring session. He hoped that day would not be very soon, but his grandfather was an old man, and he had clearly been given bad news by his physician.

When Lucas returned home from Greystone after Easter, he found that Jenny and Aunt Kitty had already departed for London and decided that he would follow them there without delay. There was no point in dragging his feet until he heard that his grandparents had arrived there too. There would be no point either in trying to hide away once he was in town. Indeed, if he went immediately, perhaps he could attend a few functions with his aunt and sister and begin meeting people he ought to have met years ago. If he was very fortunate, perhaps he would even meet someone before his grandparents arrived, someone female, that was, who was both eligible and congenial to him. Someone to whom he was equally congenial.

And—in a perfect world—someone of whom his grandparents would approve.

There was no harm in dreaming, was there?

He left for London a mere two days after returning to Amberwell, made good time on the road, and arrived at Arden House in the middle of an afternoon, fully expecting that his aunt and sister would be out or at least sitting quietly at home and he would have an hour or two in which to relax before dinner.

What he found instead was a party in full progress. According to the butler, who received him with unruffled calm as though he had been expecting him any moment, there were forty-two guests.

Forty-two.

Even from the hall one floor below, Lucas could hear the cheerful hum of conversation and a few louder peals of laughter coming from the drawing room.

He could have crept up to his room, preferably via the servants' stairs beyond the green baize door, in order to avoid being seen by any of the forty-two—forty-four, presumably, with Jenny and Aunt Kitty—who might have strayed from where they were supposed to be. He could have remained in his room until the house was quiet again. He was not even averse to lying down for an hour or two and catching up on a bit of sleep. There was nothing quite as wearying as traveling in a carriage over British roads, and even the best of inns and the most exclusive of rooms within them seemed quite unable to provide a comfortable mattress for their guests.

He did go up to his room—via the main staircase—and glanced into his dressing room, where his valet had already set out his shaving gear and was busy unpacking clothes suitable for formal afternoon wear. Lucas might have closed the dressing room door, hauled off his boots unassisted, and collapsed onto the bed in all the wrinkles and dust of his traveling clothes. His valet would have taken the hint. The temptation was almost irresistible. He was not expected downstairs, after all. No one, except probably every ser-

vant in the house, even knew he was here. But if he followed inclination, he would miss the perfect opportunity to put his resolutions
into practice.

He heaved a sigh and stepped into the dressing room, drawing
his valet's attention.

Twenty-five minutes later, Lucas was standing in the doorway
of the drawing room, which he understood to be used only for entertaining unless His Grace was in residence, its vast size making it
impractical and a little cheerless for daily use by the family. He had
always thought, on the few occasions when he had seen it, that it
might more accurately be called a ballroom. Indeed, it was occasionally used for that exact purpose, though usually then no doubt
the folding doors into the music room were thrown back to extend
its size still further. With forty-four people inside it now, it looked
full but not stuffed to an uncomfortable degree. Nevertheless, almost all his aunt's guests were strangers to him. That was hardly
surprising, of course, since he rarely set foot in London.

He looked around in those few blessed moments before he was
noticed. His aunt had always been a superlatively accomplished
hostess. He would guess that there was an almost exactly equal
number of men and women, and they spanned all age groups so
that the elderly would not feel like fossils and the very young would
not be bored beyond endurance. Though tables had been set for tea
and footmen were beginning to carry in food and drinks to place
upon them, most of the guests were standing in groups and in what
appeared to be animated conversation with one another. There were
no wallflowers. And no one, at least at this particular moment, was
holding the floor, dominating the conversation and drawing all attention to himself—or herself. That could always pose a challenge
to a hostess less accomplished than his aunt.

It took a few moments for him to see her in the crowd. But

there she was, in the midst of a largish group, half turned from him, her arm linked through that of a handsome, dark-haired lady in blue, whom Lucas did not know—of course. But before he could make his way toward her, he was distracted by movement close to the fireplace and saw that Jenny was sitting there, smiling brightly and waving one arm to attract his attention.

Even she was not a wallflower—as she had assured him she never was when she was in town. She was seated in an armchair rather than in her wheeled chair, another young lady beside her, also seated, and a few other people standing close by and looking fondly down upon her as though to make sure she did not lack for company. She looked pretty today in a peach-colored muslin dress he had not seen before. Her hair was drawn back from her face in a style that lent a certain elegance to her face. He felt instantly that ache of love he always felt for her, that impotent desire to make her whole so that she could live the life she deserved, that helpless feeling of not being able to wave any magic wand to restore her to perfect health.

But even before he began to cross the room toward her, a good part of his attention was being diverted to her companion. She was blond and slender and shapely and so purely beautiful in every way that he inhaled sharply and held the breath before releasing it more slowly. She was looking back at him, and he would swear her eyes were clear blue even though he was still some distance away. Interestingly, her attention appeared to be as riveted upon him as his was upon her.

He hugged his sister warmly but gently so he would not accidentally hurt her, joked with her a little, asked her how she did, and in the same breath asked to be introduced to the lady beside her. She was even more breathtakingly lovely when seen close up. Her eyes were indeed blue and fringed with lashes several shades darker than her hair. He did not even try to hide his admiration as he gazed at her. It was unusual for him, though. He usually behaved in a reserved manner with women he did not know. Partly it was due to an annoying sort of shyness—what if they did not like *him*? Mostly, though, it was out of an awareness of his eligibility as a matrimonial prize. So why was he not exercising his usual caution now? Could this be that foolishness known as love at first sight?

The thought amused him as Jenny introduced them, and he smiled down at Lady Philippa Ware and extended a hand for hers instead of acknowledging her, as he normally would have done, with a polite bow.

"This is a great pleasure, Lady Philippa," he said.

As indeed it was in more ways than one. If she was *Lady* Philippa, she must be the daughter of a peer and therefore surely within the very exacting range of eligibility requirements his grandparents had set for him. She was not married—he had glanced at her left hand, which was bare of rings. If he was very fortunate, she was not betrothed either or involved in any sort of romantic attachment. It might be almost too much to hope for, though. She was stunning.

She gazed at him wide-eyed and smiling as she set her hand in his, though surely she looked a little pale and the smile almost forced. Was she as shy as he was at heart? It was an endearing possibility. Her hand was soft and smooth-skinned. Unmistakably feminine. He released it reluctantly, having rejected the idea of raising it to his lips. That would be just too much.

"I trust you are enjoying yourself?" he said. "I see the food is being brought in and the guests are beginning to take their places. It seems I timed my arrival perfectly. Jenny, may I—?"

But before he could offer either to carry her to a chair at one of the tables or fetch her wheeled chair, which would be more comfortable for her, his aunt appeared beside him.

"Luc!" she cried, drawing him into a warm hug. "What an absolutely splendid surprise. We were not expecting you for a while yet."

"I am sorry to have arrived unexpectedly at your party, Aunt Kitty," he said, hugging her back. "I hope I have not thrown your numbers out of balance. I shall leave immediately if I have and sulk in my room for the rest of the day. Unless I can smuggle a few pastries out with me, that is."

"Absurd boy," she said, laughing. "I am delighted you did not feel obliged to hide somewhere until everyone had left. I wish you had appeared a little sooner, however, before it was time to sit down to tea. I would have taken you about to show you off to all my guests. I do not suppose you know many of them at all, do you? Let me at least introduce you to the dearest friend of my heedless youth." She turned to the woman in blue with whom she had been arm in arm when he saw her earlier. "My nephew, Lucas, Marquess of Roath, Clarissa. The Countess of Stratton, Luc."

He was already in the act of making her a bow, smiling as he did so. He somehow completed the action, though something inside him froze. *That name!* He felt a slight buzzing in his head.

"Ma'am," he said.

"Make that the *dowager* countess, if you please," she said, smiling at him in return. "My daughter-in-law has been the countess since she married my son before Christmas. I am pleased to make your acquaintance, Lord Roath."

He smiled and nodded, but his mind was still frozen in shock.

"I see you have already met Clarissa's daughter, Luc," his aunt said. "I do hope you are enjoying yourself, Pippa."

Good God! Ware. *Ware.* Had he known that was the family name of the man who must now be the *late* Earl of Stratton if this woman was the *dowager* countess? He had not heard of the man's death. Because he had not *wanted* to hear anything about him at all. For years he had kept his distance from the *ton* and from London during the spring months very largely because he did not want to meet or know anything that might pertain to the *Earl of Stratton.*

"Will you mind if I remain here to have my tea, Aunt Kitty?" Jenny asked. "And if Luc draws up a chair and sits with me? I have a thousand and one questions to ask him about Grandmama and Grandpapa and his visit to Greystone. Perhaps Pippa will agree to stay with us also if it is not too much of an imposition when she has already been kind enough to sit with me for all of the past ten or fifteen minutes."

Cousin Gerald had approached while Jenny was speaking. "How do you do, Luc?" he said, grinning at him and shaking his hand. "You were able to find London, then, were you, without going astray? Have you even been here before?"

"My coachman found it," Lucas told him. "Fortunately he did not blink at the wrong moment and drive the horses right on by. Happy to see you, Gerald."

This was absurd, he was thinking as he digested the fact that during his first appearance in London in years he found himself in company with Stratton's widow and Stratton's daughter. He had not even had to set foot outside the house. He told himself determinedly that he had no quarrel with *them.* And Stratton himself was dead. When had it happened? And how? It did not matter, though. Or it *should* not matter. He was going to have to think about it afterward and decide to let the whole thing go at last and set himself free.

But what colossal ill fortune that Lady Philippa Ware had been sent his way on his very first day in London. He was even going to have to sit with her for tea. In his grandfather's drawing room.

"But of course, Jenny," their aunt was saying. "That is a good idea. Gerald, would you like to join your cousins and Pippa and have your tea here?"

Pippa. It sounded like the name of a very young girl.

She was not very young. He would guess her to be in her twenties. She was still smiling.

The smile still looked a bit forced.

CHAPTER FIVE

No one *knew,* except Devlin, but he was still in Wales with Gwyneth. Even her mother did not know. Philippa had never told her, or anyone else until her brother had coaxed it out of her last year. It had been her deepest, darkest secret for years before that. It had eaten away at her youth and happiness and her confidence in herself. It had killed her dreams.

I do not dance with soiled goods.

James Rutledge and Sidney Johnson and a few other men who had been there that night had heard his words, of course. But none of them had realized she had heard too. She could remember smiling and dancing her way through the rest of that ghastly evening after the marquess had gone away with James and the practice had started. Those men, with the possible exception of James, had surely forgotten the whole thing by now, four years later.

He had forgotten too.

The Marquess of Roath had just looked at her with appreciative eyes and taken her hand and told her it was a great pleasure to make her acquaintance. There had not been a glimmering of recognition on his face, even when Jenny had told him her name.

Philippa stayed where she was, quelling every instinct to jump to her feet and run. Run *anywhere.* Just away from *him.* It would have been unkind to Jenny, though, even to insist upon going to join a different group for tea when she had been specifically invited to stay here as part of this intimate group of four. But how was she going to be able to relax when *he* drew up a chair facing hers while Sir Gerald Emmett sat across from Jenny and a footman set a low table in the middle? How was she going to eat anything? Or drink the tea that Jenny was even now pouring for her? She was not at all sure her hand would be steady enough to lift the cup to her lips without spilling its contents. She set a cucumber sandwich and a slice of fruit cake on her plate. And smiled.

The Marquess of Roath assured his sister and his cousin when they asked that the Duke and Duchess of Wilby were as well as could be expected and did indeed intend to come to town within the next week or so. Then the conversation turned to memories the three of them had of their grandparents, mostly humorous anecdotes. They were all polite enough, however, to include Philippa in the conversation by enlarging upon some of the details for her benefit. There was the time, for example, when their grandfather had taken the two boys fishing and had spent a whole afternoon instructing them on safe and correct techniques while they yawned in the boat. Then he had caught a fish and reeled it in, ostentatious about doing so in the correct manner. He had disengaged the hook from its mouth with careful precision, pronounced to the boys that *that* was the way to be a successful fisherman, and promptly fallen backward into the water.

Philippa laughed with them.

"I remember," Jenny said. "Poor Grandpapa was dripping wet

when you arrived home, and he was bristling with fury because
someone had rocked the boat and the fish had swum away while he
was swallowing half the river."

"It was Luc who rocked the boat."

"Gerald was the one who rocked the boat."

The two men spoke simultaneously and pointed an accusing
finger at each other, as though they were still those mischie-
vous boys.

"You must have stories to tell of your own family, Lady
Philippa," Sir Gerald said. "Do you have grandparents still living?"

"I do," she said. "My grandmama and grandpapa Greenfield,
my mother's parents. I remember sitting on Grandmama's knee one
day when I was four or five and playing with her necklace though
my mother told me *twice* not to lest I break it. The string broke and
beads went cascading to the floor and rolled everywhere. I remember Grandpapa on his knees, crawling about among the furniture
legs to retrieve them all and pick them up while I ran to a corner in
tears. My mother scolded me and Grandmama assured me that I
had a silly grandpapa, who seemed to have forgotten that there was
a houseful of servants with knees far younger than his own."

It was a foolish, trivial story, and Philippa felt embarrassed even
while they all laughed.

"Greenfield," Sir Gerald said. "Is George Greenfield related to
them? And to you?"

"He is my uncle," she told him.

"A thoroughly decent fellow," he said. "He rescued me from a
ticklish situation when I made my first appearance in London at the
age of twenty-one. I was a raw new member of White's Club, shaking in my boots with terror that I would do something wrong and
enrage the entire membership. But I went there alone one morning,
having decided to take my courage in both hands. I strode into the

reading room as though I owned the whole building, hailing everyone in sight with hearty good cheer. I daresay there was no one in there under the age of sixty. I was glared at by one half of them and shushed by the other half. Both groups looked murderous. I heard someone call me an impudent young puppy. My membership in the club and my very career as a gentleman seemed to teeter on the brink of extinction. But George Greenfield, whom I would not have known from Adam at the time, strolled in from outside the door, bade me a very civil good morning, shook my hand, slapped me on the shoulder, and led me away to have luncheon with him—all within half a minute. Speaking aloud in the reading room, he explained to me, is a cardinal sin at the club. Not quite a capital offense, but perilously close."

Yes, Philippa thought, that sounded like Uncle George.

Voices hummed all around them and glass and china clinked as the other guests feasted upon the sumptuous tea set out before them. Spoons scraped upon dishes of fruit trifle. Philippa glanced down at her plate and was surprised to see that the cucumber sandwich had disappeared. She even had the taste of it in her mouth.

But would this tea, to which she had looked forward with such eager anticipation, *never* be over? She felt as though she were suffocating.

"I have just realized to my shame that I have not yet spoken with at least one-third of our guests," Jenny said as she set her napkin down on the table. "I was so absorbed in my conversation with Pippa before you arrived, Luc, that I neglected everyone else. And I kept you from mingling too, Pippa, though I know you have very few acquaintances in London and came here to make some. I do apologize."

"We can put your first concern to rest without further delay, Jenny," Sir Gerald said, getting to his feet. "I see your wheeled chair in the corner here beside the mantel. Let me get you into it, and we will move about together from table to table, greeting people we have not already spoken with."

He was fetching the chair as he spoke. He bent over his cousin and, with what was obviously practiced ease, lifted her into it.

"That is kind of you, Gerald," Jenny said. "But now I am abandoning Pippa after begging her to stay with me. Luc, will you be so good as to give her your company until everyone begins to move about again?"

"It will be my pleasure," he said while Philippa smiled and her heart thumped uncomfortably and she felt robbed of breath.

The Marquess of Roath was on his feet, moving his chair out of the way so the wheeled chair could pass behind it, and bending to tuck the hem of his sister's dress about her ankles so it would not catch beneath a wheel.

When he sat down again, he did not move his chair back to where it had been. It was now closer to Philippa than before. She was aware again of the voices around them, seeming to enclose them in a cocoon of silence, which neither of them broke for a few moments. Their eyes met. His were brown, but not very dark. There were hints of green in them. He opened his mouth to speak, but she forestalled him. She had learned something in the last seven or eight months, since Devlin's return home from the wars. She had learned the importance of speaking truth rather than suppressing it and living with the illusion that all would be well in her world if only she kept quiet about what was *not* well.

"Remember me?" she said.

The sound of many voices talking at once had grown louder as more of the guests finished eating. A few had risen from their places and were moving about to talk with fellow guests at other tables. Lady Philippa Ware had spoken quietly. Lucas was not quite sure he had heard her correctly.

But all through tea, while the four of them had chatted amiably and shared family anecdotes and laughed over them—his and Jenny's and Gerald's on the one hand, Lady Philippa's on the other— he had been dragging up a distant memory from that place in the mind where one stuffs away gaffes one would dearly love to obliterate altogether if only it were possible. It was a memory from four or five years ago of going to spend Easter with James Rutledge, a friend from his Oxford years. James lived with his parents and siblings somewhere close to the village of . . . Boscombe? Lucas thought that was the name. It was in Hampshire anyway. When he had accepted the invitation, he had had no idea that the Earl of Stratton lived at Ravenswood Hall, a mere stone's throw from the village. He had discovered it within a day or two of his arrival, however. James had taken him—because he had thought it would amuse Lucas—to watch a crowd of his neighbors practice maypole dancing in someone's large barn, or what was supposedly a barn. It had clearly not seen either animals or hay for many a year, if ever.

Lady Philippa was not going to speak again, it seemed, until he did. But her eyes—those large, very blue eyes—did not waver from his own. And though she had spoken quietly, she had also spoken quite distinctly. He did not need to have her repeat the words.

Remember me?

"Have we met before, Lady Philippa?" he asked. But he had the ghastly feeling that they had.

Literally they had not—if she was the person he thought she must be, that was. They had certainly not been introduced to each other. *He,* as the stranger in their midst, had been introduced, but he seemed to recall James explaining to everyone gathered in that barn that there were too many to present to him individually—he would never remember their names. Someone, surely as a joke, had then suggested that he join the dancers and try his skill at one of the ribbons dangling, bright and intimidating, from the maypole. He, in the spirit of the joke, he supposed, had suggested that he was willing to give it a try if he could dance with . . . *the blonde.* There had been only one pure blonde in the group of girls and young women gathered in a cluster closer to the maypole some distance away from the men. He had not seen any of them close up, including the blonde herself, though he had been given the impression that she was the prettiest girl among them.

It was surprising sometimes how clear certain memories could be even when one had buried them deep and not brought them out into one's conscious mind since the events happened.

Totally unexpectedly he had learned that Stratton—the Earl of Stratton—lived nearby. His name had been mentioned as something of a joke—a warning that the blonde was not just anybody. She was *Lady* Someone-or-other, *daughter of the Earl of Stratton.* He had not danced, with either the blonde or anyone else. Nor had he stayed to watch the others dancing. He could not remember leaving the barn, but he *did* remember very clearly, now that the memory was in the forefront of his mind, that the normally mild-mannered James Rutledge had been furious with him. He had told Lucas that he would have planted him a facer as a prelude to pounding him to a bloody pulp if Luc were not a guest at his father's home. He had settled for a blistering verbal assault instead, and Lucas had taken himself off early the next morning before the family was even up. He had neither seen nor heard from Rutledge since, though he did recall sending a carefully worded letter of thanks to Lady Hardington, James's mother, for her kind hospitality, and some sort of fictitious and surely unconvincing explanation for his abrupt departure before Easter had even arrived.

He was quite sure they had never spoken to each other, he and Lady Philippa Ware. They had never been within twenty feet or so of each other. Not until today, that was. How was he supposed to remember her? He had the uneasy feeling that there was more to those two words than polite inquiry, though—*Remember me?*

"Was that *you?*" he asked her, just as if he expected that she had been following his train of thought.

Her chin jutted and her lips thinned, but she still spoke softly.

"It was," she said.

Good God! But why was she so angry? She very obviously *was.*

"By my recollection we were not personally introduced," he said, "though I believe I was generally presented to the whole gathering. It was a large barn and the lighting was dim and flickering. I left with James Rutledge before the dancing even began. I was afraid of being coaxed into participating and making an idiot of myself before strangers. I do beg your pardon if you were offended that I did not stay and dance with you or any of your friends. I am sure I did not intend any insult. And it was a long time ago. I was twenty-one or -two, I would guess. You must have been a mere girl."

"I was eighteen," she said. "Do you really believe, Lord Roath, that you left early that evening only because you did not wish to be persuaded into dancing? Would not a simple *no* have sufficed if that had been the case?"

He was sitting closer to her than he had been earlier, he realized suddenly. He had not moved his chair back after Jenny passed behind him. And he was leaning forward, his forearms across his knees. Their faces were uncomfortably close despite the low table between them. But he resisted the impulse to move back now despite the fact that he felt a certain dread of what she might be about to say. Some of the details of that particular memory, doubtless the worst ones, had not yet surfaced in his mind. She was about to help that process along, speaking in her quiet, distinct voice.

"You left, Lord Roath," she said, "because you *did not choose to dance with soiled goods.*" She even put particular emphasis upon the final words, as though she were directly quoting him. And good God, he believed she really might be.

It felt as though the blood were draining from his head. "Did I say that?" he asked her. But even if he had—*and he knew he must have*—how could she possibly have heard? The girls and women had been some distance away in a chattering, giggling group. Had one of the men told her afterward? But that seemed highly unlikely. Good God!

"You did," she told him, and she was half smiling, though it was obvious she did not feel anything resembling amusement. "You said it as soon as you were told who my father was. It was because of your reaction and your words that I knew his disgrace was not after all a purely local matter, but that the whole of the *ton* had been scandalized and disgusted—to such a degree, in fact, that no member of his family would ever again be welcome in polite society. I ought to thank you for alerting me to that reality. You saved me from a ghastly fate. I was about to go to London with my parents for my come-out Season, you see. Needless to say, I did not go."

His disgrace? Her father's? What the devil was she talking about?

He stretched out a hand toward her, though he did not actually touch her. He saw her arm tense, and she flinched back an inch or two in her chair.

"Four years later," she said, "I have defied the *ton* to do its worst, and here I am." She smiled again that smile that was not really a smile.

Do its worst? About what?

Four years. She must be twenty-two now. She had hidden away in the country all this time when she might have taken her place in society here in London as other young ladies of her birth and standing did as soon as they quit the schoolroom? When she might have been courted and married and be living happily with a husband and perhaps a child or two by now? And all because of words *he* had spoken? Words that made no real sense to him now even if they had at the time. Why should she be soiled goods merely because she was Stratton's daughter? He had obviously not been thinking straight when he spoke.

"Lady Philippa," he said. "You misunderstood. Yet the misunderstanding was entirely my fault. There was no disgrace or public scandal that I knew of. Had something terrible happened, news of which you feared had spread to London and the *ton* at large? Something concerning your father? I am sorry for your sake that whatever it was happened, but I do assure you I knew—and know—nothing of it. I have never spent a great deal of time in London. Almost none, in fact. I probably do not know many more members of polite society than you do. I hear almost no gossip either. I read the London papers for events about which I feel I ought to be informed. I avoid the society pages. I find them distasteful and actually uninteresting. I prefer to concern myself with local matters from my own neighborhood in the country."

He paused, but she was tight-lipped and not about to agree that yes, she must have misunderstood. He plowed onward.

"But I do know that gossip here in London, even outright scandal, rarely lasts for long," he said. "Gossips always crave what is new and quickly grow bored with what is more than a few days old. The *ton,* I have also heard, is rather tolerant of its members, provided they act with discretion when they stray from strict propriety. You misunderstood what you overheard."

He realized even as he was speaking that he was probably just making matters even worse. What if she were to ask what he *had* meant, then?

"Then in what way was—or *am*—I soiled goods, Lord Roath?" she asked him even as he was thinking it.

He gazed at her, not knowing what on earth he was going to say. Good God, this was his first day in London in a number of years, yet he found himself in company with surely the only person who could make a nightmare of his coming. It was her first Season in London *ever*. Yet right at the very beginning of it she had had the misfortune to meet *him*, the very man who had blighted the last four years and perhaps ruined her life. That might not even be an exaggeration. What the devil could he say?

He was rescued—at least temporarily—from having to say anything at all, however. His aunt appeared beside him again and set a hand on his shoulder.

"Do you not think, Luc, that you have monopolized Pippa's company for long enough?" she asked, smiling from one to the other of them. "What *will* she think of your manners and of my skill as a hostess?" She did not wait for him to reply. They had been rhetorical questions anyway. "Do come along with me, Pippa. There are a number of my guests who have not been introduced to you yet but very much wish to be. I have been delighted to observe you enjoying the company of my son and my niece and nephew, but it would be very selfish of me to try keeping you just for my own family. And, Luc, I have been hearing from a staggeringly large number of my guests that they have never yet made your acquaintance. Yet how old *are* you? Do get up and begin to mingle, my dear boy, though I know your reserved nature makes it painful for you."

She had linked an arm through Lady Philippa's while she spoke and bore her off now across the room without waiting for him to answer.

He would like nothing better than to slink off to his own room and stay there until he was quite sure every guest had left the house. It could not be done, however. He had made the decision when he arrived earlier to attend his aunt's party, to begin to mingle with his peers among the *ton* and establish himself in their midst, as he ought to have done years ago and could no longer avoid doing. Now he must remain at the party until the bitter end. Time enough to lick his wounds later.

He could feel the beginning of a headache pricking at his temples as he rose from his chair and turned to offer his hand to a man who was approaching him purposefully at the head of a small group of smiling guests.

"Lucas Arden," he said, returning the smiles. "I was fortunate enough to arrive in London in time to discover that my aunt was entertaining here."

CHAPTER SIX

Philippa went downstairs to the library after divesting herself of her bonnet and gloves in her dressing room and washing her hands and doing a few minor repairs to her hair without bothering to call her maid. She hoped she would have the library to herself for a while so that she could consider what had happened this afternoon and compose herself before having to be sociable again. It was not to be, however. Her mother was seated at the escritoire, an open letter in one hand. She was seated sideways on her chair, listening to Stephanie, who had apparently just returned from an excursion to Hampton Court Palace with Cousin Angeline Ware and Ninian Fortescue, her betrothed. The educational tour of Westminster Abbey with Miss Field had been postponed to another day.

"You had a good time, then, Steph?" Philippa asked her.

"Oh, I did," her sister assured her. "We went by boat on the river Thames, but Mr. Fortescue hired a carriage for our return because Angeline felt a bit queasy on the water. I wish visitors were permitted to go inside the palace, but just walking in the grounds and sensing all the history around us was marvelous. They made me feel very welcome."

"Well, of course they did," Philippa said. "They particularly invited you."

"Charles sent a note home with Stephanie," their mother told Philippa, holding up a sheet of paper. "He and Marian have invited you and me to join them in their box at the theater tomorrow evening, Pippa. Angeline and Ninian will be with them, and they have invited George and Leonard too."

George was Mama's brother. Cousin Leonard Atkins was the son of Uncle Vincent and Aunt Eloise, Papa's sister.

"That will be something exciting to look forward to," Philippa said, seating herself close to Stephanie.

"I will write to inform them that we will meet them there, then," her mother said, getting to her feet and picking up the glass of wine she had set on the desk. She went to the sideboard to pour wine for Philippa too and lemonade for Stephanie and brought them their drinks before sitting down in an armchair with her own.

"No matter how much I enjoy myself in town," she said, "I do find that being in a crowd of people and feeling obliged to mingle and converse and smile can be very wearying. How lovely it is to sit quietly here with just my two girls."

"Did you find it tiring to entertain, Mama?" Stephanie asked. "Back in the days when you organized and then hosted all those lavish events at Ravenswood, I mean. Like the Valentine's treasure hunt and the summer fete."

"Oh goodness, yes, I did." Her mother laughed. "On each occasion I would be utterly exhausted by the time I waved the last of our guests on their way. And quite convinced that I could not possibly *ever* do any such thing again."

"I loved those times," Stephanie said. "Even though I was just a little girl at the time and could not participate in many of the entertainments. I loved all the busy preparations and the anticipation. I used to attach myself to Dev, whether he wanted me or not, and insist upon helping. He always found something for me to do, even though I realize now that he could have done whatever it was much faster on his own. Ben used to find things for me to do too. They were such happy days."

Yes, they had been, Philippa thought. For them anyway—for the children. Not so much for her mother, apparently. How strange that they could look upon those days from such vastly different perspectives.

She wondered why her mother had done it all. Apparently Grandmama Ware had not entertained nearly as elaborately when she was the countess. It must have been because Papa had wanted it. He had been a man of extraordinary congeniality and charm. He had loved to entertain his neighbors and friends, to play the part of generous, welcoming host and lord of the manor. But he had done almost none of the huge amount of work that preparing such events entailed. Mama had done it all, with the help of her children and the servants. Yet Philippa had always thought her papa perfect in every conceivable way—until she had not.

"I always saw you as indefatigable and infallible, Mama," she said. "And unshakable. Like the Rock of Gibraltar."

Her mother laughed again. "I suppose children always think that of their mothers," she said. "It is what they *ought* to think until they are old enough to deal with the fact that no one is perfect and nothing lasts forever."

"Oh," Stephanie said, looking stricken. "Do you mean that you are *not* perfect after all, Mama?" Then she grinned cheekily. "Pippa, Mama was just telling me that you both had a lovely time at Lady Catherine Emmett's tea this afternoon. She says you met a large number of people, including several young and handsome gentlemen who appeared quite smitten with you."

"I did not use the word *smitten,* Steph," their mother protested. "But Pippa was much admired—in a perfectly well-bred way. Kitty would never entertain any gentleman ill-bred enough to *ogle* a lady."

"Were you smitten with any of them, Pippa?" her sister asked. "Or rather, did you *admire* any of them? Do tell."

"I was pleased to meet everyone to whom I was introduced," Philippa told her. "In particular I believe I may have made a friend of Lady Jennifer Arden, Lady Catherine's niece. She is much to be admired. She cannot walk, but she will not allow her affliction to render her helpless. She loves entertaining and goes out quite frequently. She is cheerful and interesting. I very much liked Lady Catherine's son, Sir Gerald Emmett, too. He has easy manners and a good sense of humor as well as a kind regard for his cousin."

"And you must not forget the Marquess of Roath, Pippa," her mother added. "Lady Jenny's brother, Steph, who arrived in London while the party was in progress and changed his clothes and came down to the drawing room, though I daresay he was weary from his journey. He seemed quite taken with Pippa."

"Because I happened to be sitting with Jenny when he came into the room," Philippa said. "He joined us for tea. So did Sir Gerald."

Stephanie sighed as she set down her empty glass. "So all your fears of the past month or so have been groundless, Pippa," she said. "Just as I predicted they would be. You are going to have so many marriage offers before the Season is over that I will run out of fingers to keep count and will have to start on my toes."

"Absurd." Philippa laughed.

"Oh, I think not," her mother said. "I was proud of you this afternoon at your very first event of the Season, Pippa. You behaved just as you ought. And of course you looked like an angel. *Not* that I am biased. Now I am going upstairs. Perhaps there will be just enough time for a lie-down before I dress for dinner."

Philippa set down her half-empty glass of wine and picked up a cushion to hug to her bosom as her mother left the room.

"Do you think Mama is happy?" Stephanie asked after the door had shut.

"Do you think she is not?" Philippa looked curiously at her sister, her eyebrows raised.

"I keep thinking of the fact that she was seventeen when she married Papa," Stephanie said. "Only a year older than I am now. Years younger than *you* are now. They were almost neighbors and had been acquainted with each other since childhood. She had no Season in London, no chance to meet anyone else. It must have seemed a splendid match for her, of course. I daresay Grandmama and Grandpapa Greenfield encouraged it. The prospect of having their daughter become the Countess of Stratton would have been a dizzying one. And Papa must have been terribly handsome in those days, even more so than I remember his being years after. And always so charming and outgoing. I suppose she fell in love with him."

"I suppose she did," Philippa agreed.

"Do you think it was a terrible blow to her when she learned of Ben's existence after his mother died?" Stephanie asked. "When she discovered that Papa had had a mistress before he married *her* and had actually had a son with her?"

"Mama has always genuinely loved Ben," Philippa said.

"That is not the point, though, is it?" Stephanie said. "Do you think that by then she suspected he had other mistresses too? Or even *knew* for a fact that he did? Do you think that was why she never came to London with him during the spring after Ben was brought to Ravenswood to live? Because she did not want to come face-to-face every day with the humiliation of knowing that every-one else knew too? Do you think she stopped loving Papa early in their marriage?"

"Oh, Steph," Philippa said with a sigh. "How could she *not* have suspected and even *known*? And how could she have continued lov-ing him when he had done *that* to her? Yet she kept it all bottled up inside for years and years before Devlin forced everything out into the open over that ghastly incident with Mrs. Shaw at the fete. Yet Mama was always warm and charming and apparently happily married. The thought of the reality of it is difficult to bear, is it not? For she made very sure we all grew up with the happy illusion that we were the perfect family. Oh, I think she *must* have been desper-ately unhappy for most of her life after the age of seventeen until Papa died. And since then? Was she suddenly happy again once he died? I do not suppose happiness quite works that way. I sometimes think I would gladly devote the rest of my life to staying with her and making her happy, but it is impossible, of course. She has to find her own happiness—or not. I think we could both help her somehow, though, if we can show her that we will not make the same mistake she made. Though how could she have *known*? There was no one more charming and affectionate than Papa."

Philippa *knew* why her mother had kept everything bottled up inside. It was the innate compulsion some people—particularly women?—felt not to make a fuss, not to display their suffering and humiliation to the whole world or even to those who are nearest and dearest to them. Perhaps especially to those people. Just as she herself had never said anything about what had happened when the Marquess of Roath came to the maypole dancing practice with James Rutledge. For very pride's sake she had kept quiet about the humiliation that had ravaged her life. There was all the horror of being pitied if one spoke out.

She rested her chin on top of the cushion she held and gazed through the window at a few small clouds that scudded by against a backdrop of blue sky.

But at long last, after Devlin had returned home, she had told *him*. And a burden had been lifted from her shoulders and a determination had been born to cast aside her depression and never again allow anyone the power to destroy her sense of self-worth. Yet she still guarded her secrets. Only Devlin knew that deepest one of all, and she hoped to keep it that way.

She had begun the life she was determined to live. She was here in London. She had just attended her first social event of her first Season, and, modest though it had been, she could count it a definite success. No one had pointed a finger at her and accused her of being soiled goods. No one had turned away from her as soon as they learned her identity. Quite the contrary, in fact. She had met young ladies who had greeted her as though they would like to be her friends and young gentlemen who had looked upon her with admiration, even speculative interest in a few cases. She had met older people who knew her mother and were delighted to make her acquaintance. She had not found it at all difficult to make conversation and feel that she belonged.

She believed Jenny Arden would definitely pursue a friendship with her and that Lady Catherine Emmett would gladly promote it. She knew too that when she attended other, larger entertainments in the coming weeks, she would find that she already had a base of acquaintances upon which to build. Lady Catherine had predicted that she would take the *ton* by storm. That was surely an exaggeration, but at least she felt confident that she would not be a total wallflower. And certainly not a pariah. *He* had said that to his knowledge there never had been any scandal in London, and that even if there had been, it would have been forgotten within a very short while.

There had been no real unpleasantness in London or among the *ton,* then. Yet upon hearing her father's name on that infamous evening, the Marquess of Roath had recoiled in horror and looked upon *her,* the Earl of Stratton's daughter, with revulsion and called her soiled goods. He had refused to dance with her, had abruptly left the barn before the practice had even begun, and had quit the neighborhood the very next day.

His words and his behavior had changed the course of her life. It was not too exaggerated a claim. Her confidence had already taken a hard hit after what had happened when she was fifteen. The future to which she had so looked forward had no longer seemed as bright and certain as it had always been. There had no longer been any glittering social events at Ravenswood—at just the time when she was old enough to start participating in them. Her three older brothers, all of whom she adored, had gone away. She had been trying to continue with her life nevertheless as though nothing had happened—except that she had been less sure of being loved and accepted wherever she went. There had been that one upsetting incident, for example, soon after the fete, when she had not been invited to a birthday party of a supposed friend and had found out about it quite by accident. But despite the setbacks, she had believed that once she turned eighteen and was taken to London for her come-out Season, all would be well again and she would live happily ever after.

Then he—the Marquess of Roath—had killed all her hopes and fragile dreams as well as her sense of self-worth with one short sentence.

But *why?*

If there had been no real scandal among the *ton,* and if he had been unaware of the local scandal, which had happened three years previous to his visit, why had he said what he had? Until moments before he said it he had apparently not even known that Papa lived close by, so it could not have been that someone had been telling him about that old upset.

"You have gone into one of your dreams, Pippa," Stephanie said. "I hope it is a happy one. You will not make Mama's mistake. You are older and wiser than she was, and you do not have parents pushing you into what seems an advantageous match. You will have the opportunity to meet more people than Mama ever did. More men. And you have enough good sense and enough experience of the dangers of choosing without due consideration to decide wisely whom you will marry."

Philippa smiled warmly at her. "You have such faith in me," she said. "I will try not to let you down, Steph."

Having to smile at *him* this afternoon and actually *set her hand in his,* and then having to sit near him during tea while doing her best to participate in the conversation and laugh with the others, had been nothing short of torture. Talking to him tête-à-tête after Sir Gerald Emmett had pushed Jenny away in her wheeled chair had been the stuff of nightmares. He had been sitting uncomfortably close and gazing directly into her eyes as he spoke earnestly to her, trying to explain his behavior of four years ago without explaining it at all. Indeed, he had raised more questions than he had answered. He had not answered *any.* And she had been compelled all the while to contain her anger, to speak softly, even occasionally to smile, for they had been surrounded by other people, any number of whom might have been observing them.

She could never, ever forgive him no matter how earnestly he tried to convince her now that she had *misunderstood*. What was there to misunderstand in *I do not dance with soiled goods*?

Was that you? he had asked her. He had ruined years of her life, yet he had not even *recognized* her this afternoon. Not even her *name*.

It was too much to hope that she would not see him again for the rest of the Season, of course. Indeed, even before she came to London she had accepted the possibility that he might be here too. But now they had not only met. They had been introduced to each other. Lady Catherine, who was one of Mama's oldest and dearest friends, was his aunt. Jenny Arden, with whom Philippa had already begun a friendship, was his *sister*. She had sat to take tea in a very small group that included the marquess. They had talked tête-à-tête together for what must have been all of ten minutes after their two companions moved away. Everyone in the room would have noticed. They were both young and new to London, after all, and they were both very eligible.

It would be almost impossible now to ignore him when they met again. She could only hope that they could avoid each other as much as possible without being too obvious about it.

"You could never let me down whatever you did, Pippa," Stephanie said. "You are my sister."

Sometimes it was hard not to shed tears.

T he following morning, Lucas offered to take Jenny to call upon Charlotte, their older sister, who was also in town with her husband and children. Gerald had already made arrangements to take her and his mother to Hookham's library, however. So he went alone.

Both Charlotte and Sylvester, Viscount Mayberry, were in the nursery with their children. Sylvester was constructing an elaborate-looking kite with the aid of Timothy, aged nine, and Susan, aged five. Charlotte sat wedged into a chair with Raymond, their seven-year-old, as he read her a story he had written the day before while his parents were attending what Charlotte described as a stuffy afternoon gathering of literary and political types.

"But we felt compelled to go," she told her brother as she turned her face so he could kiss her cheek. "It was being hosted by close neighbors of Sylvester's when he was growing up. I daresay you had a far more jolly time at Aunt Kitty's tea. I would have very much preferred to be there. But what a delightful surprise this is, Luc. We knew you were coming to town—Grandmama wrote to tell me so. But we had a wager on, Sylvester and I, over how long you would drag your feet before actually getting here. Neither of us came even close. A pity. I had plans for my five guineas."

"Uncle Luc," Raymond cried as though he were speaking to someone in the next room, "do you want to hear my story?"

"Is it full of blood and mayhem and monsters with red eyes and three rows of pointy teeth?" Lucas asked, frowning.

"Uncle Luc!" Susan screeched. "Come and see my kite."

"*Your* kite?" Timothy sputtered. "Papa, tell her—"

"How do you do, Lucas?" Sylvester said, grinning. "Welcome to our usual tranquil, happy abode."

Lucas listened to the story, which he had been assured would not give him nightmares, and admired the kite. He listened attentively to a lengthy, technical description of its intricacies given by Susan and the frequent interruptions by Timothy to correct her. He declined to return later to help paint the kite on the grounds that he might splash paint on his boots and his valet would scold him and might even quit his service. He accepted an invitation, however, to attend its maiden flight in Hyde Park on the first day there was enough wind to hold it aloft but not so much that it would be whipped out of their hands and blown away to kingdom come.

"I will send you a letter to tell you when, Uncle Luc," Raymond promised.

"Why should *you?*" Susan demanded to know. "*You* did not make the kite."

"Then *you* can write it," her brother said, smiling falsely to display most of his teeth. "Everyone knows you get half your letters backward and could not write in a straight line if your life depended on it."

"Perhaps," Lucas suggested to his niece, "you will write *Dear Uncle Luc* at the top of the page and *Love, Susan* at the bottom, and Raymond will fill in the rest of the page with a formal invitation to come view the maiden flight of his brother and sister's kite."

"What about me?" Sylvester bleated, and picked up Susan and wrestled her to the floor in a heap of flailing arms and legs and giggles while Timothy warned them to mind the kite.

"You will think we are a family of barbarians, Luc," Charlotte said, clucking her tongue. "Once upon a time I used to be perfectly sane."

Actually, Lucas always found them rather delightful, though admittedly he only ever had to endure small doses of his niece and nephews.

He went with Sylvester to White's Club, where he was greeted by a few men to whom he had been introduced at his aunt's tea party yesterday, and one university friend he had not seen for a few years. Sylvester introduced him to a number of other members, and the two of them joined a group for luncheon. Lucas had been a member of the club since he turned twenty-one but had rarely been there.

His brother-in-law would have taken him to Jackson's boxing saloon later to take out a membership, but Lucas had other plans for the afternoon and reluctantly declined. He must not be distracted from what he really ought to do today. He did *not* look forward to it one little bit, and of course there was every chance the ladies would not be at home anyway. But he must at least try. He would leave his card with the butler if nothing else.

He went home to change his clothes and sent word for his curricle to be brought to the door—he had brought it with him from the country, as well as his carriage. He stopped on the way to Grosvenor Square to buy a posy of flowers from a street vendor, and found himself wondering if the Dowager Countess of Stratton knew of that incident four years ago at the maypole dancing. Surely if she did, though, she would have given him the cut direct yesterday afternoon instead of greeting him with warmth and charm.

Had Lady Philippa Ware told *anyone* in her family? Had James Rutledge or any of the other men told anyone else? He would wager James had not. He would have been too ashamed of the guest he had invited into the neighborhood. Had she held it all inside, then, until she saw him again yesterday? It hardly bore thinking of.

He almost lost his courage after turning his curricle into Grosvenor Square and stopping outside Stratton House, but it was too late. He had been seen. The doors had opened and a footman was hurrying down the steps to take the ribbons and hold his horses' heads while he descended from his perch.

The ladies were there, though the butler who met him at the door with stiff formality did not admit as much. He invited Lucas to wait a moment in the hall while he checked to see if her ladyship was at home. Less than five minutes later Lucas was being ushered into a library rather than the drawing room. It was a cozy room. He always loved libraries. It had something to do with the smell of books and leather, he supposed, though he did not dwell upon the subject at the moment. The dowager countess was rising from a chair before an elegant escritoire. Her daughter was seated by the fireplace, one finger holding her place in a book she had already closed. Another very young lady sat near her. She was looking up from what appeared to be a letter in her hand.

He bowed. "Ma'am?" he said, addressing the dowager. "I hope I am not inconveniencing you by coming here unannounced."

"Not at all, Lord Roath," she said, smiling as warmly at him today as she had yesterday. She indicated a chair. "Do come and sit down. Meet Stephanie, my younger daughter. May I pour you a glass of wine?"

"Thank you," he said, and nodded to Lady Stephanie Ware, a plump, moon-faced, pleasant-looking girl, who was regarding him with open curiosity.

"Lady Stephanie," he said.

"The Marquess of Roath," she said. "Mama and Pippa met you yesterday at Lady Catherine Emmett's tea."

"She is my aunt," he said before turning his gaze upon her sister. She was dressed today in pale blue—a slightly faded blue, perhaps. Her blond hair, smooth over the crown of her head, was twisted into a simple knot at her neck. Yesterday's glamour was absent, but to his eyes she looked even more stunningly lovely today, if that was possible. Hers was a beauty that did not need embellishment.

"Lady Philippa?" he said, and was about to sit down when he noticed the posy of spring flowers clutched in his hand. He smiled and held them toward her, feeling like a bit of an idiot, though he was not sure why.

She looked at them, withdrew her finger from her book and set the volume down on a table beside her, got to her feet to pull the bell rope beside the mantel, and finally took the posy from him.

"Thank you," she said, looking up into his eyes at last, not even a suggestion of a smile in her own.

The butler must have remained outside the door after admitting him. He came almost immediately, and she held out the flowers to him.

"Will you have these put in water, if you please, Mr. Richards?" she asked, and he crossed the room to take them from her.

She resumed her seat and Lucas sat down while Lady Stratton set a glass of wine on the small table beside him. He wished he were somewhere else far away. Almost *anywhere* else would do.

"My aunt was pleased with the success of her tea party yesterday," he said. "I hope you enjoyed it, Lady Stratton? Lady Philippa?" Asinine words. How could they possibly say anything other than that they had?

"It was lovely to see Kitty again," the dowager told him. "It had been quite a long time. We were very close friends when we were young and have corresponded regularly ever since. It was a delight too to meet Sir Gerald, her son, whom I have not seen since he was a boy, and to be introduced to her niece, your sister."

"Jenny was pleased to make your acquaintance too, ma'am," he said. "She is quite hoping she has made a friend of Lady Philippa."

"I like her," that young lady said, but she did not elaborate.

"She lives at Amberwell with Kitty and you?" her mother asked.

He waited while the butler, who had reentered the room with a round crystal bowl holding his posy of flowers, set it in the middle of a chest of drawers close to the window, stood back a moment, adjusted it more to his liking, and then withdrew.

"She does," Lucas said. "Though for several years after my father's passing I was obliged to live at Greystone Court with my grandparents. I was the only remaining heir of the direct line, and it was important to my grandfather that I be trained for the ducal role I will hold one day—though I fervently hope it will not be very soon. I am dearly fond of both grandparents."

"You are a duke's heir?" Lady Stephanie asked.

"The Duke of Wilby is my grandfather," he told her. "My father, his only son, is deceased."

"Kitty informed me yesterday," Lady Stratton said, "that the duke and duchess are expected at Arden House within the next week or so."

"My grandfather feels he really ought to put in an appearance at the House of Lords after not having done so last year or the year before," he told her. "My grandmother is eager to renew her acquaintance with people she has not seen in just as long a while. I might have pointed out to them both when I saw them at Easter that at their age they have surely earned a rest from obligations they have fulfilled quite diligently all their adult lives, but I knew I would be wasting my breath. I hesitate to say that my grandfather is the most stubborn person I know, for that might well be my grandmother. They are a formidable pair."

She laughed. "I believe I met them a long time ago," she said. "Though for many years I spent no more than a week or two in London each spring. My children were growing up and I preferred to remain with them in the country."

"They were fortunate children, then, ma'am," he said.

"We were," Lady Stephanie agreed, beaming at him. "I am the youngest."

He thought of his sister and brother-in-law, who brought their children to town with them for a month or so each spring and took them to a wide variety of places, partly for their entertainment, even more for their education. There could not be many places in the world so full of history and art and culture in all its variety of forms as London. And even science.

He was very aware of the silent Lady Philippa Ware. He did not believe she was particularly shy. Nor did he believe that she simply lacked conversation. Jenny had told him that before his arrival yesterday they had talked for a long time without stopping and that, before she joined Jenny, Lady Philippa had been chatting at her ease with Gerald. Besides, she was a *lady*. Ladies were taught to make polite conversation even if they *had* spent all their lives in the country.

"Lady Philippa," he said, turning his attention to her. "I have my curricle outside your door. I wonder if you would like to come with me for a drive in Hyde Park?"

He knew from the way she looked back at him that it was something she most definitely would *not* like. She opened her mouth to say so—he was sure of it.

"We have been enjoying a quiet afternoon after a busy morning and before what we expect to be a busy evening," her mother said. "My brother- and sister-in-law have invited Pippa and me to join them and a few other family members in their box at the theater tonight. But a short drive in the park and some fresh air would surely be just the thing for Pippa. It is kind of you to have come to invite her, Lord Roath."

"It is my pleasure, ma'am," he assured her. "But if Lady Philippa would prefer to remain at home to rest, I can—"

"No," she said, getting to her feet. "Thank you, Lord Roath. That would be delightful. If you will give me ten minutes, I will go and change into something more appropriate."

Left alone with her mother and sister, Lucas smiled. "I believe I heard you say yesterday," he said, addressing the dowager, "that you are expecting the earl, your eldest son, to arrive here soon?"

"He is in Wales with his wife," she told him. "They went for her brother's wedding after Easter. Idris is our neighbor. His parents,

Sir Ifor and Lady Rhys, own the estate adjoining Ravenswood. Gwyneth lived there too, of course, until she married Devlin just before Christmas. Yes, they will be here any day now."

"I can hardly wait," Stephanie said. "Dev has always been my favorite brother, though I would never say that in the hearing of any of the others, for one is not supposed to have favorites. And I do love them all dearly. I am terribly worried about Nicholas, for he is with his regiment somewhere in northern Europe and there is sure to be war again now that Napoleon Bonaparte has escaped from Elba. I was *so* thankful last year when it really seemed that the wars were over and Devlin and Ben came home. Now I am cross because someone was careless and allowed Bonaparte to escape. From an *island*."

Lucas spoke with her while he waited. At the same time, though, he wondered why he was doing this. Surely the best thing he could have done was remove himself completely and permanently from Lady Philippa Ware's life. He was just not sure it would be possible, however. She had come to London to make her debut in society at last. He had come because his grandfather had told him he must and duty decreed that he obey. Almost daily for the next few months they were going to be moving in the same circles and attending many of the same social functions. He could not simply do what might seem the honorable thing and go home to Amberwell while she enjoyed her Season here and found an eligible husband.

For honor also dictated that he remain here and find a bride. Not only find her but *marry* her.

Sometimes life was just . . . complicated.

CHAPTER SEVEN

By the time Philippa reentered the library dressed smartly for a drive in the park, she was so angry, she had a hard time holding a smile on her face for her mother's sake. Mama had *no idea*, and after four years it was far too late to tell her now. Stephanie, of course, was delighted. She was probably dreaming of being a bridesmaid again.

"I am ready," Philippa said unnecessarily as both her mother and the Marquess of Roath rose to their feet. How dared he come here to force her into this? And how dared he be so tall and handsome and such a . . . *perfect* physical specimen.

How dared he!

Her mother came to stand at the top of the steps outside the front doors while they descended and crossed the pavement to his curricle. Philippa had no real choice then but to set her gloved hand in his in order to ascend to the high seat. It was not a very wide seat, she noticed, an impression that was confirmed when he took his place beside her and gathered the ribbons in his hands.

Mama was smiling warmly at them. She was pleased. As why should she not be? They had been in London for just a very short while, they had attended only one really quite modest entertainment, yet here was her daughter already being singled out for attention by possibly the most eligible bachelor in town, or even all England, the heir to a dukedom, a handsome, distinguished, personable young man. *Seemingly* personable, except when he was crushing the hopes and dreams of young girls with vicious insults. He had come calling today, without an invitation, no doubt confident of being received with eager, open arms. He had come, flowers in hand, to make himself agreeable to all three ladies. And he had succeeded all too easily with two of them. He had behaved charmingly, even with Steph, whom many men would have ignored as totally without importance since she was still officially a child. He had wooed her mother and younger sister before getting to the main point of his visit and inviting Philippa to go driving in Hyde Park with him.

Where they were almost certain to be seen together by at least *someone.* Probably by a whole lot of someones actually. It was quite insufferable.

And more than a bit incomprehensible.

Yet it must all look very promising indeed to Mama, whose spirits must be soaring. She might already be imagining a grand wedding at St. George's on Hanover Square, half the *ton* in attendance. Mama had brought her here, after all, to enjoy a Season with people of her own class and to find a husband.

Just the thought of how her mother must be viewing all this made Philippa's anger boil hotter. Could anything boil *hotter*? Or *hottest*? And why did the mind grapple with such questions at the most inappropriate moments?

This was all happening as a consequence of keeping silent!

Philippa had gone home after that maypole dancing practice, assured Papa when he had asked that yes, indeed, she had enjoyed herself, and found herself quite unable to tell him or Mama what had happened to take the fun right out of her evening. She had carefully hidden the agonies of pain and humiliation she was suffering. She had not fully realized at the time, of course, that *fun* had disappeared from her life for years to come.

The road between Grosvenor Square and Hyde Park was crowded, and the marquess needed to give his full attention to maneuvering his curricle past other conveyances, including a few slow-moving carts and one ridiculously flimsy high-perch phaeton driven at unrealistic speed by an impatient dandy, who was coming the other way and expected all and sundry to scatter before him. His efforts—and his appearance—were being met with caustic wit and considerable verbal abuse, much of it *very* colorful, and a flat refusal to scatter. It was *not* the time to begin any sort of serious conversation. Philippa held her peace and tried without any real success to stop her arm from brushing against his. It was suffocating. It was intolerable.

Once they turned toward the park and passed through the gates, however, everything changed. The park seemed vast and rural and almost quiet in contrast to the noisy bustle of the streets outside.

"Lord Roath," she said, aware even as she spoke that he was turning his head, about to say something to *her*. "This is insufferable."

"Yes, it is," he agreed. "On a certain occasion four years ago, I spoke impulsively and ill-advisedly to a friend of mine in the hearing of a group of other men who were strangers to me. What I said was quite unpardonable, and it weighed upon my conscience for some time afterward. My only consolation was that neither you nor any of the other ladies present had heard what I said and that out of respect for you neither James nor his neighbors who *did* hear me were likely to repeat my words. However, yesterday I made the discovery that in fact you *did* overhear and that the effect upon you was such that the whole course of your life from that moment to this was changed. Quite blighted, in fact. I cannot express quite how appalled I have been since learning the power those careless, cruel words had upon you."

"So let me understand you," she said. "What appalled you was not that you considered me soiled goods but that you said so loudly enough that I overheard you from some distance away and am holding you to account now?"

He glanced at her briefly before turning the curricle rather abruptly onto a path that was narrower than the broad avenue they had been on.

"It seems that I am not clever with words at all, Lady Philippa," he said. "I do not know where that phrase—*soiled goods*—came from. It was never justified. I would be tempted to believe you must have misheard except that I remember James Rutledge's fury after we had left that barn."

"Why did you come to Stratton House this afternoon?" she asked him. "Why did you invite me here? Did you—*do* you— intend to make me an apology? I will save you the trouble. It is rejected. I believe you should take me home now. There is nothing more you can say that will interest me, and there is nothing more I choose to say."

"Take you home and leave you to explain to your mother and sister why you are back so soon?" he asked her. "You did not tell your mother that evening what had happened, did you? She still does not know. She would hardly have received me as she did this afternoon if she was aware of how I once insulted her daughter and hurt her beyond measure."

He turned his head to look fully at her when she did not answer immediately, and oh goodness, he was close. She could see the green in his predominantly brown eyes. She could see the firmness of his lips and jaw. Villains really ought not to be good-looking. Or smell so good from some shaving cream or cologne. It was not fair.

"A person does not go home and tell her father and mother that she has just been horribly insulted by the man they know to be a guest in the home of their friends and neighbors—and all because he had just heard that the Earl of Stratton lived close by," she said. "My father would not have taken kindly to his daughter's being called soiled goods. There would have been fuss and mayhem and an eruption of renewed scandal just when memories of the old scandal were fading. Besides, we were never a family for open, frank discussion of any uncomfortable topic that touched us. It would not have soothed me to go home and tell, Lord Roath. Quite the opposite, in fact. I said nothing."

They did not speak while he slowed for a sharp bend in the path and turned cautiously lest something be coming the other way. Nothing was, however. Philippa glanced at his profile. And she was aware that if that incident had not occurred four years ago, she would very possibly be looking upon him quite differently now and enjoying herself enormously. But if it had not occurred, he would not have called upon her this afternoon, would he? Or invited her to come driving. If it had not occurred, this would not even be her first Season. The point was that if one were to change one small detail of history, one must also change a whole host of other details that had happened—or *not* happened—afterward.

She wished it were Sir Gerald Emmett who was seated beside her, or one of the other young men who had seemed pleased to meet her yesterday. Someone with whom she had no history at all.

He sighed audibly as he drove them between trees on both sides, and it was easy to forget that they were in the middle of one of the busiest and most densely populated places in the world. "This is the situation as I see it, Lady Philippa," he said. "We are both here for the Season. In all probability we will encounter each other with some frequency at the myriad social functions that will occupy the *ton* during the coming months. It would be remarked upon if we were to cut each other's acquaintance after we were seen together yesterday and again today by a few people. One never wants to provide the *ton* or the society columns of the morning papers with food for gossip, and it does not take much. My aunt and your mother have been close friends for years. My younger sister means to pursue a friendship with you. She spoke of you last evening and again at breakfast this morning. She plans to invite you and your sister to take tea with her. We cannot ignore each other, then, without arousing comment. May we agree at least to behave civilly toward each other when we do find ourselves in company together?"

"I believe I know what good manners are, Lord Roath," she said stiffly. "I have always done my best to practice them in my dealings with other people. I am not the one who uttered an unfounded insult in the hearing of other people, mostly strangers. And in the hearing of the person who was being insulted."

"No," he agreed. "Neither of us will ever forget that I am the villain of this piece."

He turned the curricle again, onto a wider path this time, one with trees on one side and a wide stretch of rolling grassland on the other. Philippa could see the Serpentine some distance ahead of them.

He seemed genuinely distressed by what had happened, she thought. Yet somehow that realization only annoyed her the more.

A villain ought to be villainous through to his black heart. She was *not* going to forgive him, but she wished he would say something to make that an easier decision.

"Lord Roath," she said after neither of them had spoken for a minute or two. "Why did hearing my father's name shock you so much that night?"

His head turned sharply her way. "I . . . suppose I had heard something about him of which I disapproved," he said. "I beg your pardon. I—"

"You had heard of his philandering ways when he came to town each spring for the parliamentary session, leaving my mother and us behind in the country?" she asked.

"Y-yes," he said.

"And you had heard that he brought scandal home with him to Ravenswood one year and caused considerable embarrassment to his family and the whole neighborhood?" she asked.

"Yes," he said again.

Very unconvincingly.

"Then you lied yesterday?" she asked him.

"I— Did I?" He was looking decidedly uncomfortable. "I forget what I said yesterday."

Liars really ought to spend some time sharpening their memories.

"You told me," she reminded him, "that you had not even heard of the local scandal, which had seemed so catastrophic to us. You told me that to your knowledge there had been no great scandal here in London, that Papa's . . . *behavior* would not even be frowned upon to any marked degree here provided he was always discreet. You told me that anyway you have never spent much time here. Or indulged in the reading of the gossip columns of the newspapers. Were you lying yesterday? Or are you lying now?"

He slowed the carriage to a walking pace and kept his eyes on the path ahead.

"Did you know my father?" she asked.

"No." He sighed audibly again. "I never met the late Earl of Stratton."

"Then why on earth did his name come as such a shock to you that it provoked you into calling his daughter soiled goods in the hearing of a number of her neighbors at Ravenswood?" she asked him.

He turned to face her after pulling the horses to a full stop. He was looking a bit white about the mouth, she saw. His eyes were troubled. She felt not one iota of pity for him.

"I had heard he was a . . . an unsavory character," he said. "When I was at Oxford, perhaps? It is hard to remember. I was very young, very righteous, very judgmental in those days. It disturbed me to learn when I visited a friend for Easter that the infamous earl I had heard of lived close by. I do beg your pardon for the whole sorry episode, though I know you cannot forgive me."

He was still lying. She was quite certain of it. His explanations were as full of holes as a tea strainer. But he was clearly not going to tell her the truth. There was no point in pressing the matter further.

"I wish to go home," she said.

"Yes," he said. "I will take you."

They moved off again along the path and soon came to the wider avenue they had left several minutes before. There were pedestrians and horsemen and other carriages in sight now, including an open barouche in which a man and a woman sat facing the horses and three children sat opposite them, two boys with a girl sandwiched between.

"Uncle Luc!" the older boy cried, waving an arm when he spied the Marquess of Roath. "I am going to sail my boat on the Serpentine."

Both conveyances stopped.

"And I am going to sail my duck," the little girl said.

"You don't *sail* a *duck*, idiot," the younger boy said. "I am going to sit on the bank and read my book, Uncle Luc. I have twelve pages left."

"Did my ears deceive me?" the man asked. "Did you just call your sister an *idiot*, Raymond? I believe an apology may be in order."

The woman smiled serenely at the marquess before transferring her gaze to Philippa as the boy was muttering a grudging apology to his sister. "I believe all of our manners have gone begging," she said. "Present us, if you please, Luc."

"I have the honor of presenting Lady Philippa Ware, sister of the Earl of Stratton," he said. "My sister Charlotte, Lady Philippa, and her husband, Sylvester, Viscount Mayberry. Their children, Timothy, Raymond, and Susan, in descending order of age."

They all exchanged greetings. Lady Mayberry beamed at Philippa. So did Susan.

"I made Lady Philippa's acquaintance at Aunt Kitty's tea party yesterday," Lord Roath explained.

"I was sorry to miss it," the viscountess said, addressing Philippa. "Alas, we were obliged to attend another . . . Hmm. I hesitate to call it a party. Most of the people there were political types and spent almost the whole afternoon talking ad nauseam about that annoying little man Napoleon Bonaparte and his escape from Elba. It was one giant yawn, Lady Philippa, I promise you. I heard so many ridiculous theories about how and why that escape came about that I had a hard time remaining civil. I suppose it will mean war again, though, since it would appear the French are still besotted with their former emperor and are flocking to his banner. I do hope you enjoyed Aunt Kitty's tea. Her entertainments are usually jolly affairs."

"I did," Philippa said. "I particularly enjoyed talking with your sister."

"Jenny refuses to mope in the country," the viscountess said, "though she would have every excuse for doing so. She loves to come to town when she can. I greatly admire her spirit."

"Mama-a-a," the little girl said pointedly.

"We have a duck here that is desperate to get into the water and be sailed," her father said, smiling at Philippa.

"Will you come with us, Uncle Luc?" the girl asked politely. "You can bring Lady Philippa with you."

"I must beg to decline your kind invitation on both our behalves, Susan," he said. "Lady Philippa needs to go home. She is going to watch a play tonight and must not be late. Everyone in the theater would boo and hiss at her, and perhaps even the actors too. I will very definitely attend the launch of your kite, however, as I promised this morning. I would not miss it for worlds."

"Lady Philippa can come to that too," Timothy, the older brother, said with boyish eagerness. "It is a super kite. I made it myself with Papa's help and a bit of help from Susan. She is going to paint it. We are going to fly it here on the first windy day. Do say you will come with Uncle Luc. It will be jolly."

"We are going to invite Aunt Jenny and Great-Aunt Kitty too," Susan said, bouncing in her seat. "They are sure to want to come."

"We will send you a written invitation to make it official," Raymond offered. "Though we will have to do a bit of guessing about the wind when we choose a day. Do say you will come, Lady Philippa."

"I may have to have a grandstand built to accommodate all our guests," Viscount Mayberry said cheerfully. "My own side of the family is to be invited too. They will be suitably thrilled. But this kite launch is sure to be a sight to behold, Lady Philippa. Something to tell your grandchildren about one day. We can only hope the contraption will be beheld in the sky and not languishing forlornly on the grass."

"Please, *please* say you will come," Susan said. "I am going to paint it orange. And green and blue."

"I will have to see if I am free that day," Philippa said evasively. "But I do know the thrill of seeing a kite up in the sky. I remember once watching my brother Nicholas fly one while running along the crest of the hills at the edge of our property. His was homemade too. He made it with the help of Ben, our eldest brother. I was about your age at the time, Susan, and thought it about the most awe-inspiring sight I had ever seen."

What had she done now? Philippa wondered as the barouche drove off toward the Serpentine for a toy boat and duck to sail upon and the marquess turned the curricle in the direction of the gates. She hoped those children were not counting upon her coming with their uncle to see them launch their new kite. It was simply not going to happen. But it was so difficult to disappoint children when they were excited about something that was very important to them. Perhaps if they really did send her a written invitation she would come here on foot. Stephanie would probably be happy to accompany her. They could keep their distance from the family spectators yet also make sure the children knew they were there.

Viscountess Mayberry, she thought with an inward sigh, had looked at her while they were being introduced in almost the exact way Mama had looked at her earlier. With pleased speculation, that was. And with a hopeful question in her eyes: Was there a romance in the wind?

There was *not*. Oh good heavens, there most decidedly was not. It was a horrible irony, though, that she liked every one of his family she had met so far. And they all seemed to like her.

"If your brother Devlin Ware is now the Earl of Stratton," the marquess said as they were turning back onto the street beyond the park gates, "how is it, Lady Philippa, that your eldest brother is *Ben*?"

"He was born before my father married my mother," she explained. "His own mother died when he was three years old, and he grew up with us. Presumably his mother had no family or else they were unwilling to give him a home. Papa brought him to Ravenswood before I was born. His name is Ben Ellis. He is my half brother, but I have always loved him as dearly as I do my other brothers and my sister. He could not inherit the title, of course, for he was born out of wedlock. But he always knew that. So did Devlin. I do not believe it caused any hard feeling between them. They are the closest of friends."

He said no more. They had both run out of conversation, it seemed. They rode home in silence.

Two mornings later a written note was delivered to Stratton House, inviting Philippa and Stephanie to take tea that afternoon with Lady Jennifer at Arden House. The letter to Philippa continued:

> *After I hoarded your company to myself for far too long at*
> *Aunt Kitty's party, I hope you will not consider this invitation*
> *a dreadful imposition on yet more of your time. Perhaps you*
> *have another engagement. Perhaps you plan to go walking*
> *or driving somewhere pretty and rural since the weather*

promises to be unseasonably warm later. But if you can persuade yourself to do without the "spacious" part, then I can provide prettiness in the form of the garden behind the house here. We can sit outside and take tea at our leisure and talk to our hearts' content.

I am twenty-three, but I remember just what it feels like to be sixteen and neither a child nor an adult, just someone living in a no-man's-land between and filled to the eyebrows with dreams. Do please assure Lady Stephanie that she has not just been tacked onto this invitation because I felt obliged to include her. I will be more than delighted to make her acquaintance and perhaps coax her into sharing some of her dreams. Do come if you will.

With my best regards,
Jenny

If you will. Yet again it seemed to Philippa a cruel thing that the lady with whom she had felt most affinity of all those she had met since she came to London also happened to be *his* sister. Going to Arden House would put her in danger of coming face-to-face with him again. Though, as he himself had pointed out in Hyde Park, that was bound to happen over and over again anyway during the Season. She must not start trying to avoid all the places where he might be. Staying shut up inside Stratton House until summer came and it was time to return to Ravenswood was neither sensible nor an option.

Besides, Stephanie was delighted by the invitation, and so was their mother, who professed herself quite ready for a quiet afternoon at home alone.

The garden behind Arden House was indeed pretty. It was bor-

dered on opposite ends by the house and the mews and on the sides
by high rustic fences covered with ivy and other climbing plants,
including roses, though they were not blooming yet, of course. But
other flowers were. Flower beds were bright with spring blooms,
and the grass, lovingly tended, was lush and very green. Sunshine
poured down, and the sheltering walls and fences captured the heat
and made it seem more like summer than spring.

Jenny, already seated in her wheeled chair, beamed happily at
Philippa and held out both hands to her sister. "You must be Stephanie," she said. "I am *so* pleased you have come with Pippa. And just
look at your *hair*. You are both blond, but you are all gold while she
is all silver. Those braids about your head are *thick*. Your hair must
reach below your waist when it is brushed out. How long *is* it?"

"Well, it covers my— It is very long," Stephanie said, flushing.
"Miss Field, my governess, and Mama's maid keep trying to persuade me to have it cut, but I do not wish to."

"Dismiss them immediately," Jenny said, smiling brightly to
indicate that she was not serious. "How dare they? Your hair is your
own property. It is part of your person. You ought to be able to do
with it whatever you like. And in your case it is almost literally your
crowning glory. But now that I have incited you to insurrection—
with your sister as a witness—let me invite you to sit down."

Stephanie was beaming. Her heart had clearly been won. Soon
the three of them were conversing with great animation on a wide
variety of topics, and Philippa was enjoying herself, more than ever
convinced that Jenny would remain her friend for a long time to
come, even after they had both returned home to the country. Just
like her mother and Lady Catherine Emmett a generation ago.

"Luc took me to call upon our sister this morning," Jenny told
them as she poured a second cup of tea for them all. "She is almost
seven years older than I am, Stephanie. She and Sylvester have three

children whom both Luc and I adore, though Sylvester declares they will surely turn his hair white before he turns forty if, indeed, they do not first render him bald. Susan insisted upon brushing out my hair even though my poor maid had spent almost half an hour styling it before I left here. My niece lamented the fact that her mama had not inherited the family hair color but is simply dark-haired, as my mother was. She was sad too that *she* has even lighter-colored hair, just like her papa."

"Susan is a very pretty child," Philippa said. "I have met her."

"Of course she is," Jenny said. "Have either of you heard about The Kite?" She widened her eyes and spoke the words as though they ought to be written with capital letters. "It has been con-structed by my brother-in-law, though Susan and Timothy are ready to swear that he merely lent them the occasional helping hand. It is to be tested out soon in Hyde Park, and we have all been invited to witness it—Aunt Kitty, Luc, and I believe Sylvester's relatives too."

"Oh yes," Philippa said. "I was given a verbal invitation when I met them in Hyde Park the day before yesterday and was promised a more formal written one when the time comes. They have prob-ably forgotten, however. I am, after all, no more than a stranger to them."

"*Forgotten?*" Jenny said, laughing. "A prospective witness to their genius? Never. You would not even suggest such a thing if you knew my niece and nephews better. You must come in the barouche with Aunt Kitty and me. Both of you. It will be fun, I daresay, though I will have all my fingers crossed that the kite does indeed take to the skies. Kites can be temperamental."

"Oh, I would love to see it," Stephanie said. "I will persuade Miss Field to let me go on the grounds that it is educational, that I am making a study of how birds fly."

They all laughed. And the house door opened and the Marquess of Roath stepped out onto the terrace where they sat.

"What a perfect day for tea outdoors," he said, bending over the wheeled chair to kiss his sister on the cheek. "Lady Philippa? Lady Stephanie?"

He smiled at them with an ease of manner Philippa hoped she was matching. He must have known they were here. He might easily have avoided them.

"Do pull up a chair," Jenny said. "I will have another cup and saucer and plate brought out for you." She reached a hand to the little silver bell beside her plate, but her brother stayed her with a gesture of his own hand.

"I merely came to pay my respects," he said. "Far be it from me to insert myself into a gathering of ladies."

Stephanie, who had wanted to know the day before yesterday when Philippa returned from the park what Lord Roath had said to her, how he had *looked* at her, how she *felt* about him, smiled warmly at him.

"Pippa and I have been invited to go with Lady Jenny and Lady Catherine Emmett to watch your niece and nephews fly their kite in Hyde Park," she told him. "Will you be there too, Lord Roath?"

"I believe," he said, "the nephews and niece, together with their mama and papa, would expel me from the family and have me cast into outer darkness if I failed to put in an appearance." His eyes twinkled at her.

"I shall greatly look forward to it," Stephanie said, clasping her hands to her bosom. "So will Pippa."

And he turned his eyes, no longer quite twinkling, upon her and held her gaze for an uncomfortable moment.

"I will leave you ladies to your conversation," he said then, and returned to the house and shut the door behind him.

"I believe he *likes* you, Pippa," Stephanie said.

Philippa raised her clasped hands to her mouth and thought she might well die of embarrassment.

"You and I are going to get along famously, Stephanie," Jenny said. "I absolutely agree with you. But we must not embarrass your sister further. Tell me the names of those books you said you borrowed from the library this morning. You are a voracious reader, by the sound of it."

"I *have* embarrassed you, Pippa," Stephanie said, her voice full of contrition. "I am so sorry. Mama would look sorrowfully at me, and Miss Field would scold and remind me that a lady *always* considers the effect her words may have upon her listeners *before* she utters them."

"The names of the books?" Jenny asked with a smile.

If they only knew, Philippa thought.

CHAPTER EIGHT

T he crystal ball that lives on the top shelf of the toy cupboard
in the nursery, gathering dust and never leaving London,"
Sylvester, Viscount Mayberry, explained to his brother-in-law at
White's three days later, "predicts sunshine and moderate winds for
tomorrow after the two days of drizzle and nary a breath of a breeze
we have suffered through for the past couple of days. Formal letters
of invitation have gone out for the viewing of a kite launch in Hyde
Park. Yours should be awaiting you when you return to Berkeley
Square. We can rely upon your coming, it is to be hoped?"

"I would not miss it for worlds," Lucas said with a grin. And it
was perfectly true. He would not. He doted upon those children.
And at least he would not be facing the dilemma of whether he
should offer to escort Lady Philippa Ware. Her sister had told him
they were to go with Aunt Kitty and Jenny.

He had not gone out of his way to avoid Lady Philippa in the
last several days. Indeed, he had even stepped out onto the terrace
that one afternoon to pay his respects for fear Jenny and his aunt

might remark upon it if he did not. Apart from that they had been able to avoid any close encounter with each other.

He had learned from his aunt at dinner last evening that Lady Philippa had made her court appearance and been presented to the queen. She could therefore be considered officially *out*. That meant she would now be attending the larger, more glittering entertainments of the Season, some of the grander of the balls in particular. But it was news he had been expecting. It made no difference to anything, not for him at least.

It was time he started going to more of the grand balls too, though. The only one he had attended so far had not been particularly memorable except for the fact that he had been introduced to one of the *ton*'s grand dames, Lady Rochester, who had looked at him through her long-handled lorgnette as though he were a worm but had deigned nevertheless to present him to her great-niece, Lady Morgan Bedwyn, who was without a doubt one of the most eligible young ladies on the market this year, if not *the* most. She was the younger sister of the Duke of Bewcastle, who was reputed to be the haughtiest of all British aristocrats. Lady Morgan was a handsome, dark-haired young lady—*very* young, in fact—but she had looked at him, after nodding an acknowledgment of his existence, as though she already knew he was going to be a great bore. She had looked the same way at every other man who made his bow to her, though, Lucas had observed afterward with some amusement. Now, *there* was surely a young woman who had no interest whatsoever in choosing a husband just yet. He did not ask for the honor of a dance with her—or with anyone else either, to his shame. He had made his escape as soon as he decently could after an hour had passed and his hostess's back was turned.

He was going to have to do better in the future.

His invitation to the kite launch was indeed awaiting him at Arden House. Apparently his aunt and his sister had received one too. As he himself had suggested, the greeting and the closing were in the large handwriting of a five-year-old who reversed a few of the letters and mixed capitals indiscriminately with lowercase letters. The body had been written with painstaking neatness by his younger nephew.

"*The pleasure of our company,*" Aunt Kitty said, chuckling as she quoted some of her own letter. "That boy is eight years old going on thirty-eight."

"He read me one of his stories a couple of days ago," Jenny said. "It was remarkably good for a child his age. It had a beginning, a middle, and an end and did not let go of the suspense until the last possible moment. I was quite terrified that the villain was going to vanquish the hero, but of course he did not. There was no heroine, alas. Susan remarked upon it, but Raymond merely rolled his eyes and asked why there *would* be a heroine when it was an *adventure* story. Alas for the bland fate of women, who are not allowed to have adventures or participate in anyone else's."

"Pippa and Stephanie Ware are going to come with us," Aunt Kitty said. "Clarissa too if I can persuade her to change her mind. I am sure the children would welcome her. It was very sweet of them to include Pippa's sister in her invitation after Jenny had suggested it to them."

"They would be delighted if the Prince Regent were to put in an appearance," Lucas said. "It would not surprise me to hear they had sent him an invitation."

"Well," Aunt Kitty said, laughing, "I just hope for the children's sake that tomorrow does not turn out to be one of those still days that will not even flutter a feather in one's bonnet. How disappointed they would be. I hope too it is not so windy that all the feathers would blow completely *out* of one's bonnet and away to the ends of the earth. And rain would be something of a disaster."

"Sylvester has assured me," Lucas told them, "that the crystal ball from their toy cupboard forecasts sunshine and just the right amount of wind."

"Well, that is settled, then," Aunt Kitty said. "One cannot argue with a crystal ball."

So they would be part of the same small gathering tomorrow, Lucas thought, he and Lady Philippa Ware. But at least it would be outdoors in some large open space in Hyde Park, where it ought to be possible for them to keep some distance between them. Indeed, by now he should be able to put the whole embarrassment behind him and treat her as he would any other casual acquaintance.

Perhaps it *would* be easy, or easier, if she were not so staggeringly beautiful. But that was shallow of him. Her looks ought not to weigh with him at all. He had done her a cruel and lasting wrong four years ago, and she was unwilling either to forgive or to forget.

He could not blame her. But he could never properly beg her pardon because he could never explain to her why he had reacted as he had that night. He could never explain to *anyone*. Sometimes the burden of a dark and secret knowledge was almost too heavy to bear.

The following morning was sunny and breezy and really quite warm again after a few chilly, damp days—the perfect weather for kite flying. Philippa was in good spirits as she stepped out of the house with Stephanie. Lady Catherine and Jenny awaited them in an open barouche. Sir Gerald Emmett was dismounting from horseback and coming around the carriage to hand them in.

He was an ever-cheerful, very good-looking man, and Philippa felt a flutter of interest in him, as she had with several young men to whom she had been presented since her arrival in London. She introduced him to Stephanie, took the seat across from Jenny, and made room for her sister.

Their mother called good morning from the top step and waited to wave them on their way.

"We can still make room for you if you wish to run for a bonnet, Clarissa," Lady Catherine said, raising her voice.

But Mama, though she thought the whole idea of the outing quite charming and was delighted that her daughters had been included in it, had nevertheless chosen to keep a coveted appointment with her modiste.

"I shall see you tomorrow at Lady Abingdon's ball, Kitty," she called. "Do enjoy yourselves."

"It is not every day one has the opportunity to witness the maiden voyage of a kite," Sir Gerald said a minute or two later as he rode alongside the barouche while it made its way toward Hyde Park. "I have not been officially invited, Lady Philippa, but my mother assures me I am unlikely to be expelled from the park on that account."

"I believe Charlotte's children will be proud that you *wanted* to come, Gerald," Jenny assured them.

"I expect this to be great fun," Stephanie said. "Pippa can remember our brother Nicholas having a kite, but I do not. I must have been very young."

A long stretch of grass not far from the Serpentine had been chosen for the kite flying. It was half past nine in the morning, a time when many members of the *ton* would still be in bed recovering from last night's revelries. But here a cluster of people was already gathered about a hollow oval, upon which the kite itself was stretched. They included Viscount and Viscountess Mayberry, another young couple Philippa had not seen before, an older couple, also strangers to her, and the Marquess of Roath. There were five children, all of whom were fairly bouncing with suppressed energy, and one older boy, neither child nor man.

They all turned to watch the barouche being maneuvered into position behind a line of empty carriages. A few people raised a hand in greeting. Susan came racing across the grass toward them, hand in hand with a little boy about her own age.

"Great-Aunt Kitty! Aunt Jenny!" she shrieked as she approached. "I was terribly afraid you would not come, but Mama kept saying you were not even late yet. And you have brought Lady Philippa! I bet this is Lady Stephanie. Aunt Jenny told us about you and said you might enjoy seeing our kite flying, so we added your name to the invitation. Mama had to help Raymond with the spelling. *Thank you* for coming. And you have come too, Cousin Gerald, even though we did not send an invitation. Mama said you would be busy with other things and we had better not subject you to having to think up a good excuse. But she was wrong and you have come anyway. This is my cousin Matthew, Lady Philippa and Lady Stephanie. Everyone always says we are the same age, but I am actually the elder by three weeks and four days."

"Gracious!" Lady Catherine said as Sir Gerald dismounted from his horse and opened the door of the barouche to hand her down. "I do believe you said all of that in one breath, Susan. How do you do, Matthew? Oh, you wish to hold my hand to escort me over to the others, do you? How very gentlemanly of you."

"Not only did I have nothing else of any great importance to do today, Susan," Sir Gerald told her, "but I was also so excited about coming here this morning that I could scarcely sleep last night."

"You are funning me," Susan said, taking Lady Catherine's

other hand and pulling her toward the kite. "You always joke more than you are serious, Cousin Gerald. I bet you snored all night long."

"We managed to get closer than I expected," Sir Gerald said, turning his attention back to his cousin in the barouche. "You are going to have an excellent view from here, Jenny. I shall escort the ladies to join the others and then come and keep you company."

"There is really no need—" Jenny began.

But Philippa was already moving to take Lady Catherine's place beside Jenny. "I intend to stay here," she said. "But not just to give Jenny my company. I can also see that we will have the best and most comfortable seats in the house." She would also be able to remain some distance away from the Marquess of Roath.

Sir Gerald turned his smile upon Stephanie and offered his hand to help her descend.

"Oh," she said. "Perhaps I ought . . ." And she turned an uncertain look upon Philippa.

"Do go and join the fun, Stephanie," Jenny said. "The children will love having you close by."

Sir Gerald helped her down and then offered his arm.

Within moments, it seemed to Philippa, he was talking to her sister and Stephanie was chatting back and beaming happily.

"She is very sweet," Jenny said. "I like her exceedingly."

"She was genuinely excited about coming here this morning," Philippa said. "Especially as we were coming with you."

"We would have needed an extra gig to bring my wheeled chair," Jenny explained. "I would not hear of it, though Luc was very willing to bring it himself. You need not feel obliged, though, Pippa, to—"

"Hush!" Philippa patted her hand firmly. "It is no sacrifice to sit here with you. How lovely the park looks today, and what a beautiful morning it is after the rain. Even the wind is tolerable because it will be necessary to fly that kite."

"It is obviously not quite ready to be launched just yet, however," Jenny said, nodding in the direction of young Raymond, who had detached himself from the group and was skipping toward the barouche.

"Did you read my invitations?" he called before he was quite up to them. "Did you, Aunt Jenny? Did *you*, Lady Philippa? I wrote the message out on some old paper first and checked the spelling of a few words in the dictionary rather than ask Papa. It would not have been fair—would it?—when I could find out for myself. I did ask Mama to make sure I had put the full stops and commas in the right places, but I had. And I also asked Mama if *Stephanie* was spelled with one *f* or two and it turned out to be neither but a *ph* instead."

"It was an extremely well-written letter," Philippa assured him. "I was honored to receive a formal invitation in addition to the verbal one I had from you last week. My sister may already have told you that she was very excited that you thought to invite her too."

The Marquess of Roath was strolling up behind his nephew. "The demonstration is about to begin, Raymond, barring any more unexpected delays," he said. "I do not suppose you want to miss it." He touched the brim of his hat to the ladies. "Good morning, Lady Philippa. It was good of you to come. You are warm enough, are you, Jenny? The wind is a bit brisk."

He had set his hands on the boy's shoulders, Philippa noticed, and was kneading them lightly close to his neck. It was a gesture of affection, probably unconscious. It also sent slight shivers along her own neck and caused her to hunch her shoulders until she realized what she was doing.

"We are perfectly cozy here, thank you," Jenny assured him. "Go back quickly now with Uncle Luc, Raymond. Everyone is waiting for you."

And sure enough, several people had turned their heads to look toward the barouche. Lady Mayberry was beckoning. The older lady Philippa did not know called a greeting to Jenny. Raymond bounded back to join them, while his uncle walked more sedately. What a bizarre coincidence it was, Philippa thought, not for the first time, as she gazed after him, that the very first friend she had made in London also happened to be the Marquess of Roath's sister. And that she and her mother and sister were fast getting tangled up with his family.

"The older couple are Sylvester's mother and stepfather," Jenny explained. "Lord and Lady Patterson. The younger couple are Sylvester's brother, Jeremy Bonham, and his wife, Laura. Their children are Patty—short for Patricia—and Matthew, who is never known as Matt and will tell you so if you try it. The older boy is Roger Quick, Lord Patterson's grandson from his first marriage. Poor Pippa. More names to remember."

It was a family affair indeed, Philippa thought. She and Stephanie were the only outsiders, in fact. It looked, though, as if everyone was being kind to Steph. Sir Gerald had a protective hand against the small of her back, while Raymond seemed to be explaining something to her about the wind with exaggerated arm movements and Roger Quick gazed at her with wary interest. Steph was animated and attentive.

"Ah. At last," Jenny said, reaching across the seat to pat Philippa's hand. "Here we go."

Everyone had moved back from the kite and from Viscount Mayberry, who was down on one knee making a last-minute adjustment. Timothy hovered behind him and Susan stood at his side.

Timothy was given the first run with the kite, his father loping along beside him and Susan dashing after them both, holding her skirts high. The other children cheered loudly, and several of the adults, including Jenny, clapped their hands. And please, *please,* Philippa thought, let it fly. Children's emotions were such delicate things. This morning's venture was bound to end in either euphoria or despair, with no possibilities between those extremes. But childhood should be filled with far more triumph and happiness than disappointment. Children should be allowed to believe that all their dreams would fly if only they worked hard at them.

The kite flew.

It lifted from the ground behind Timothy, bobbed and weaved giddily, dipped and came perilously close to crashing back to earth, and then rose sharply and caught the wind. The boy turned and maneuvered the reel about which the string was wound, his father at his side. The child's face was bright with joyous concentration as he watched his kite and kept it aloft. Susan bounced and shrieked at his other side. The cheers of the other children had also turned to shrieks, and the adults shouted encouragement and applauded more loudly. Stephanie had the fingers of both hands pressed to her mouth, her eyes bright above them. Lord Patterson whistled piercingly, two fingers between his lips. A number of strangers within sight had paused to watch, some of them pointing skyward for the benefit of those who had not yet noticed the kite.

Perhaps, Philippa thought, flight was the ultimate dream for young and old alike. And how wonderful this moment was, she thought, her eyes welling with tears as for no apparent reason she remembered the years of her terrible depression, when joy and exuberance and hope had seemed things of the past, gone forever.

"Oh. *Careful,* Susan," Jenny murmured from beside her.

Timothy had handed the reel very carefully to his sister, and the kite had instantly threatened to dive earthward. But their father was there, his hands over hers, reeling in some of the string and running her backward until the wind caught the kite again and lifted it back into the sky. He removed his hands gently from hers but hovered close in case he was needed again. Even from some distance away Philippa could see the beaming happiness on the little girl's face.

And it occurred to Philippa that her father, whom she had fairly worshipped until she was fifteen, had never done anything like this with any of them. He had always praised their accomplishments, often without having witnessed them, and smiled genially at them. He had definitely *loved* them. But it was Ben and Devlin, and Nicholas too when he was old enough, who had given practical help and unswerving encouragement when they saw the need in a younger sibling.

These were foolish thoughts to be having at this precise moment, however.

"This is such *fun*," she said. "For everyone, not just the children. It is all quite unlike anything I expected of London."

Jenny turned her head to smile at her. "What did you expect?" she asked.

Philippa thought about it. "Excitement," she said. "Lots of busy activity. Balls and parties. Shopping. Seeing famous buildings and visiting galleries. Making new friends. Perhaps falling in love. But I did not expect to watch a kite flying in Hyde Park. Or to see children so exuberant and so much the focus of adult attention. To see the warmth of . . . of *family*. I suppose I thought that could be experienced only in the country. Perhaps it is because we—my brothers and my sister and I—were never brought to London in the springtime. Mama always stayed home with us while Papa came alone to carry out his duties in the House of Lords."

"Did you have a happy childhood?" Jenny asked.

"Yes," Philippa said without hesitation. "But I think perhaps we also missed something in never coming here. What about you?"

"My illness kept me at home," Jenny told her. "But like you I had much happiness in my childhood. Both my mother and my father nursed me tirelessly through my illness. I woke up many a night to find my papa at my bedside instead of my nurse. It made me feel very safe to see him there. I never doubted that I would live. Charlotte used to read to me. Luc had endless patience with me too. Whenever he was home from school he would spend a few hours every day entertaining me or simply listening to my chatter. He would carry me outside on good days and take me all over the park either in the gig or in my wheeled chair after I had it. He refused to let me molder in the nursery, as he used to put it, when all the bother of being transported made me plead to remain there. I missed him dreadfully after Mama and Papa died within a year of each other. Grandpapa took him off to Greystone to train him to be a duke one day. I missed my parents too, more even than I missed my brother. Life changed so suddenly and so irrevocably. But I do not mean to complain. I still had Charlotte until she married Sylvester, and Aunt Kitty came to live with us. I soon came to adore her and understand that though she could never take Mama's place, she was very precious indeed."

Life changed so suddenly and so irrevocably . . .

Sometimes, Philippa thought, a person could become very self-absorbed and imagine that no one else suffered quite as badly as oneself. Jenny's sufferings were undoubtedly worse than her own had ever been, for Jenny would never be done with the illness that had laid her low when she was still just a child. She would never run free.

"Do you ever resent being . . . confined to a chair?" she asked before it could occur to her that perhaps it was something she ought not to say aloud. But Jenny turned her head briefly again to smile at her.

"When I see that kite," she said, "I feel a great yearning to fly up there close to the clouds. But I would not be able to even if I had the full use of my legs. No one can fly. I suppose it is human nature to long for what is just beyond our reach. To envy birds. As for being confined to a chair, it has been a reality for me for so long, Pippa, that I hardly remember anything different. And I can jerk along with great inelegance whenever I want, you know, with the crutches that have been specially made for me. It is sometimes a pleasure to see the world on a level with the people around me."

While they talked, they watched the kite flying. The other children, including Raymond and Roger, took their turns with it with varying degrees of success. But the kite seemed to have been constructed with some considerable skill. Even after it had crashed to the ground from a great height twice in a row under Patty Bonham's guidance, it was still found to be undamaged. Lord Mayberry's brother helped a sobbing Patty and her little brother fly it with more success, Philippa noticed. He seemed to have just as much patience with his children as Viscount Mayberry had with his.

After less than an hour, though, the children were all satisfied and the viscount picked up the kite and carried it to his carriage. Everyone else drifted after him but veered off to come to the barouche to assure themselves that the two ladies had had a good view. Jenny introduced her brother-in-law's relatives to Philippa.

"It went so quickly," Susan said with a sigh. "I am not ready to go home yet, Mama."

"Then it is a good thing our cook has baked lots of her special small cakes and piled them to twice their height with creamy icing that is all colors of the rainbow," the Marquess of Roath said. "They are the sort of things mamas and papas everywhere regard with horror because the icing finds its way all over hands and mouths and clothes and even onto the ends of noses. Cook is also making a very large jug of lemonade to wash the cakes down. Perhaps you would all like to come to Arden House to help us eat them and celebrate the successful launch of the kite."

The young children all cheered. Their parents looked a bit reproachful. Someone muttered about appetites for luncheon being ruined.

"How splendid it was of you to have had the forethought to arrange it, Luc," Lady Catherine said, beaming at him. "I ought to have thought of it for myself. I daresay we were all feeling a bit anticlimactic a moment ago, just as Susan was. But if we had decided upon the spur of the moment to go en masse to a tearoom to celebrate, the proprietors would surely have had an apoplexy when they saw our numbers—and heard the volume of our conversation."

Everyone dispersed to their various carriages—with the exception of Stephanie, who, after one inquiring glance at Philippa, disappeared into a carriage with Lord and Lady Patterson, young Roger Quick, and Patty Bonham. Sir Gerald Emmett handed his mother into the barouche and mounted his horse.

"No, no," she said when Philippa would have moved back to her original seat. "Do stay where you are, Pippa. It is no great hardship to sit with my back to the horses. I must admit that I came here for the children's sake. But there is something of the child in all of us when we see a kite fluttering away in the sky, is there not?"

Philippa was perhaps the only one in the whole party who was feeling a bit awkward. She was not a member of this family, a fact that would not perhaps have been bothersome if the family concerned had not been the Marquess of Roath's. However, she could not now suggest being taken back to Grosvenor Square instead of Arden House. For Stephanie had gone with someone else.

She hoped the Marquess of Roath would not be annoyed that she had failed to make an excuse to avoid his cream cakes and lemonade feast. He had even glanced at her while issuing his invitation, but it had been impossible to interpret what his look had meant—if it had meant anything at all.

Why could he not have chosen to stay away from London this year? Or if he must be here, why could he not be a member of a family with whom she had no acquaintance at all?

CHAPTER NINE

Lucas was enjoying being in London far more than he had expected. He had made several new acquaintances and become reacquainted with some old ones. He had become involved in activities not available to him in the country, like boxing and fencing, and had attended a number of social events, including one ball. But it was family he was enjoying most—his sisters and nephews and niece, his aunt and cousin, his brother-in-law's family. It was rare for them all to be together in one place instead of scattered across England.

It always felt very good to belong.

Today he had thoroughly enjoyed being with them all as they watched the children fly their kite in Hyde Park. They were all seated now about the round table in the breakfast parlor, which had been chosen over the drawing room since there was bound to be at least one mishap with an iced cake. The youngest children had large linen napkins tucked in beneath their chins and spread down over their laps. So of course it was the eldest, Timothy, who upended the top half of his cake onto his unprotected lap while he tried to eat the bottom, less interesting half first. His napkin meanwhile lay untouched in its crisp folds on the table beside his plate.

"Ha!" Lord Patterson said in his hearty, booming voice. "I was about to try the same thing, lad, but now maybe I had better not. Your grandmama may scold. I never could understand, though, why a person is expected to eat the cake when the icing looks so much more inviting."

Sylvester and Charlotte meanwhile cleaned up Timothy as best they could with a couple of spare napkins, and the conversation proceeded as cheerfully and noisily as before, with a number of voices speaking at once and the children's merry voices rising above them all.

There was only one discordant note as far as Lucas was concerned, though *discordant* was an unfair word to use even in his own mind. There was nothing discordant about Lady Philippa Ware. Jenny was glowing with the delight of having a new friend who did not condescend to her or continually fuss over her. Gerald was clearly taken with her—he had sat beside her. Everyone else was careful to draw both her and her sister into the conversation, and she made it easy for them by smiling and responding just as she ought. She scarcely glanced his way, though she did not pointedly ignore him either. He behaved the same way toward her.

If only he could think of her as the children's guest or Aunt Kitty's or Jenny's, then perhaps . . .

But no. It would make no difference.

He wished to *God* he had not gone into the country with James Rutledge for Easter that time. How differently he would be looking upon Lady Philippa Ware now if he had not done so. It was a pointless thought, though. If he had *not* gone, she would have had her debut Season four years ago and would without any doubt be married by now with a few children of her own.

His eyes met hers briefly across the table, and he felt the now-familiar sinking feeling of guilt. For her eyes were the most expressive part of her face, and for that brief moment there was a soft wistfulness in them, a trace of sadness. Or perhaps he was just imagining it, for a moment later she was laughing over something Sylvester had said, her eyes twinkling with merriment. Hers was a delicate beauty. Her face was heart shaped, Lucas decided. Her complexion made him think of peaches and cream. Her eyes were as blue as an early summer sky, her hair pure blond. Her teeth were white and even.

She was the sort of woman a man instinctively wanted to honor and cherish and protect. But what *he* had done was call her soiled goods.

"And our next plan," Susan announced to the whole table, "is to make a hot-air balloon. Timothy is going to make it, and I am going to help him. And Papa, of course."

"Of course," Sylvester said meekly.

Lucas caught Charlotte's eye and she shook her head and tossed her glance at the ceiling.

"And I am going to ride in a big basket beneath it," Matthew cried. "I am going to fly to America or to Richmond Park."

"Lord love us," his mother murmured.

The door of the breakfast parlor opened abruptly at that moment and a small, elderly man, dressed for travel in a greatcoat that still swayed about his booted ankles, stood framed in the doorway and looked about the gathering with a frown upon his face.

An instant silence fell upon the room, until it was broken by three voices speaking simultaneously

"Grandpapa!" Charlotte cried.

"Papa!" Aunt Kitty exclaimed, getting to her feet.

"Great-Grandpapa!" Susan shrieked.

Lucas also got to his feet, scraping back his chair as he did so. There was a swell of sound, though it died within moments. The Duke of

Wilby was not the sort of man one mobbed or smothered with greetings or peppered with questions before he had had his say. He was also not the sort of man to use a butler to announce him in his own house.

"I see you have left me a cream cake," he said, frowning at the table. "It is to be hoped you left one for Her Grace too."

The duchess, wearing an enormous plumed bonnet, hovered behind him, looking over him from her superior height.

"There is another plateful on the sideboard, Grandpapa," Jenny said, laughing. "You will not have to share the last one with Grandmama. Do come inside the room so that she can come in too."

Everyone else took their cue from her, and there followed a great deal of noise and bustle as greetings were called, hugs exchanged, and space made for two more chairs at the table—though his grandparents looked more ready for their beds than for a celebration, Lucas thought. The butler appeared from somewhere, looking unruffled despite the fact that he had had to give chase to his employers instead of leading the way in orderly, stately fashion. He relieved the duke of his greatcoat and the duchess of her bonnet and gloves. His Grace sat down after Gerald had seated Grandmama, took one look at the cake Raymond had placed on a plate for him, pushed it away with an ungrateful harrumph, and demanded cold cuts of meat with some bread and butter. Aunt Kitty passed the message to the butler despite the fact that he had been standing a mere few feet away while His Grace spoke.

Someone asked about their journey.

"It is over," the duke said. "That is all that needs to be reported."

"It was really quite comfortable, thank you, Laura," the duchess added, smiling at Sylvester's sister-in-law.

The children, all speaking at once until their parents intervened, told the story of the kite launch. One of them explained how Uncle Luc had arranged for cakes and lemonade to be served here because he had feared they would all be tossed out of a tearoom if they turned up there unannounced and maybe get locked up in a dungeon somewhere.

Jenny assured her grandmother when asked that she was feeling well and was very much enjoying being in town. Gerald told his grandfather when asked that no, he was not staying here at Arden House but at his usual bachelor rooms on St. James's Street. Lord and Lady Patterson agreed with the duke that yes, they probably *were* saints to have given up a morning to watch children flying a kite, but it had been worth every minute. Susan confessed to her great-grandmama that she had eaten *three* of the cakes but that she was not feeling even the slightest bit sick.

"Yet," her father added.

"And *someone's* manners have been misplaced somewhere," His Grace said at last, when the first hubbub of questions and answers had died down. He was seated beside Lucas and was peering directly across the table. "Present Her Grace and me, Luc."

Lady Philippa was gazing back, a becoming flush of color in her cheeks.

"My grandparents, the Duke and Duchess of Wilby," Lucas said. "Lady Philippa Ware, Grandmama and Grandpapa. And Lady Stephanie Ware, her sister." He indicated the latter to their left.

His grandfather nodded to Lady Stephanie, frowning in thought. "Ware," he said. "*Ware.* Stratton's girls? No, he passed on a few years ago, I recall. I was sorry to hear of it. I have not met the new Stratton. Or not-so-new by now, I suppose. Your brother?" He was addressing Lady Philippa.

"Yes, Your Grace," she said. "My mother and sister and I are expecting him and my sister-in-law at Stratton House any day now. They have been in Wales for a wedding."

"I knew your father," he said. "A jolly good fellow. He used to keep us laughing whenever he gave a speech in the House of Lords. Some members thought it inappropriate to desecrate such hallowed halls with mirth. I found it kept me from falling asleep. I do not recall meeting your mother."

"I do, though it must have been a long time ago," the duchess said. "How do you do, Lady Philippa? And Lady Stephanie? I do remember that your mother and Kitty were dear friends. Your mama was beautiful and charming but with a far darker coloring than either of you. Your father was closer to blond, however."

"This is your first Season, Lady Philippa?" the duke asked.

"It is, Your Grace," she said.

"I daresay you are being mobbed by all the young bucks," he observed. "It would be surprising if you were not. You certainly would have been in *my* day, though that was long before you were even thought of."

She laughed. "I was presented to the queen only a few days ago," she said. "I have not been to any really grand entertainments yet. But I do not expect to be *mobbed* when I do."

"Then you are in for a surprise," he said. "I daresay your mother is well prepared to discourage any impertinence, however. She and Stratton, when he gets here, will see to it that you are married eligibly, according to your rank in society."

"Papa," Aunt Kitty said, signaling the butler to set the plate of cold roast beef and wafer-thin slices of bread and butter he carried before her father. "You are embarrassing Lady Philippa."

"Embarrassing her by telling her she is lovely enough to attract an army of suitors even if she were *not* the daughter and sister of an earl?" His Grace asked.

"I am not embarrassed, Your Grace," Lady Philippa said, though the deepened color in her cheeks gave the lie to her words. "I am flattered."

"My dear young lady," he said, picking up his knife and fork. "I am not given to flattery. And I am pleased to welcome you and your sister into my home."

"Thank you," she said while Lady Stephanie beamed.

Lucas's stomach was feeling a bit queasy, *not* because of the one cake he had eaten—actually, it had been more icing than cake—but because it was as clear as day to him where his grandfather's thoughts were trending. It must be equally clear to everyone else at the table too—including Lady Philippa Ware herself. Fortunately Lady Patterson had the presence of mind to suggest to her husband just audibly enough for everyone else to hear that it was high time they took their leave with Roger after enjoying a thoroughly agreeable morning in good company.

It was the signal for everyone else to get to their feet too. There was one other awkward moment when Gerald informed Lady Philippa and her sister that it would be his pleasure to escort them home if they did not mind walking as he had only his horse with him at Arden House.

"Or you can come with us," Charlotte said to them rather unrealistically. "Provided you do not mind being rather squashed in the carriage, that is, and having one or more of the children talking your ear off."

"Luc will escort them," His Grace announced. "Our carriage is probably still standing outside the door."

For the moment that seemed to be the end of the matter.

"No," Lady Philippa said quite firmly after glancing at her sister. "That will be quite unnecessary, though we are very grateful for the offer, Your Grace. We will enjoy walking back to Grosvenor Square. It is not far, and we have each other for company."

"Perfect," Gerald said. "I have two arms."

Aunt Kitty went to see everyone on their way, leaving Lucas and Jenny alone in the breakfast parlor with their grandparents.

"Poor Grandmama," Jenny said. "You look exceedingly weary. I suppose the last thing you expected was to find a children's tea party in progress in your breakfast parlor."

"It was a delightful welcome to London," Grandmama said.

"Lucas," the duke said sharply. "Gerald is also my grandson, and he is every bit as dear to me as you are. But the fact remains that you are my heir and he is not. If you are not very careful, he is going to snatch that young lady right from under your nose. I believe Her Grace and I have arrived in the nick of time."

It was customary for young ladies to wear white evening gowns to social events during their first Season. It would be wise, the Dowager Countess of Stratton had advised her daughter, not to flout that unwritten rule entirely despite the fact that many ladies her age were already matrons. Her modiste had agreed with her ladyship, but she had suggested that Lady Philippa could look distinctive and quite ravishing if she incorporated some silver or gold into a few of her evening gowns and chose pale pastel shades for others—*and* if she avoided frills and flounces on her dresses and ribbons in her hair, all much favored by young girls. She said the word *girls* rather disparagingly.

Tonight, for her first grand ball at Lord and Lady Abingdon's mansion, Philippa was wearing a silver net tunic over a white muslin gown with silver jewelry that would sparkle under the chandeliers. Her long gloves and dancing slippers were also silver. She looked both delicate and beautiful, her maid had just told her after taking a step back to look critically at the elaborate hairstyle she had created with its high topknot and cascading curls and wavy tendrils over her neck and temples.

"She looks *gorgeous*, Madeline," Stephanie said. "Everyone else will fade into bland insignificance in contrast, Pippa."

Philippa laughed. "I do hope that is not true," she said. "I would feel wretchedly conspicuous and would not have a friend in London."

"But *that* is not so," Stephanie told her. "Lady Jenny Arden likes you exceedingly well. And you have told me of other ladies your age who are amiable and will surely become your friends or close acquaintances at the very least as the Season progresses."

Philippa's maid was tidying up and preparing to leave her dressing room.

"Are you nervous?" Stephanie asked. "I would be a mass of quivering jelly if I were in your shoes."

"It would be foolish to pretend I am not," Philippa admitted. "It would not take much to cause me to tear off all this finery and climb into my bed with a book to read beneath the covers. But Mama would be disappointed. So would Dev and Gwyneth when they get here. So would you, I daresay. And I would be *extremely* disappointed with myself. It is a relief to know that at least I will not be a total wallflower tonight."

When Sir Gerald Emmett had escorted them home from Arden House yesterday, he had waited for Stephanie to go inside first, and then had asked Philippa if she would reserve the opening set for him at tonight's ball. It had been a bit like having one's dearest dream come true. That all-important first set at one's very first grand ball with half the *ton* looking on was something she no longer needed to face with stomach-churning anxiety. She had a partner, a distinguished, good-looking, personable gentleman. A man she knew and with whom she felt comfortable. A titled gentleman too.

Stephanie made her lips vibrate as she blew out through them with a sound of scorn that was peculiar to her. "You, a wallflower!" she exclaimed. "How absurd you can be sometimes, Pippa. Sir Gerald Emmett admires you greatly and would fall in love with you with just the slightest encouragement—or maybe even without. I do like him too. He actually talked to me yesterday when we were in Hyde Park as though I were a real person."

"I do not know what else you would be but real," Philippa said with a smile.

But her sister was not to be deterred. "And there is the Marquess of Roath too," she said, picking up Philippa's white and silver fan and twirling it absently in her hands. "I think he does a bit more than just admire you, Pippa. He looks at you quite intently sometimes when you are not looking at him, and his eyes . . . *smolder.* Well, that is perhaps a bit of an exaggeration, but he definitely *likes* you, as I so disastrously said aloud in the hearing of his sister when we had tea with her. I could have *died.* Anyway, he is *gorgeous,* just as you are. He would be gorgeous even without the red hair, but with it . . . Though it is not really red, is it? It is not gingery as red hair very often is. It is more like . . . burnished copper. But even apart from his looks, he is going to be a *duke* one day. And the present duke is a very old man. He looks as if he must be at least ninety. I like him, though, even if he *does* frown a great deal. I believe he likes to be thought of as ferocious."

"You like him because he liked Papa?" Philippa asked with a smile. They had all loved Papa, but she knew that Stephanie had adored him perhaps more than any of them.

"Do you *like* the Marquess of Roath?" Stephanie asked. "Or Sir Gerald Emmett? I mean, enough to be courted by either one of them? How can you fear being a wallflower, Pippa, when even before your first ball you have two such eligible and handsome gentleman dangling after you—or willing to dangle if you would just hint that you are interested. Are you in love with either of them?"

Philippa forced herself to laugh. *And his eyes . . . smolder.* The very idea! "Too many questions, Steph," she said. "I am about to attend my first ball and my head is already buzzing. I hope to make some new acquaintances tonight. I hope to dance at least a few sets so I will not feel too terribly awkward and embarrassed. I have no intention of falling in love with anyone just yet. Perhaps not at all this Season. I—"

But she was saved from having to flounder onward when a tap on her door preceded the appearance of her mother, who was looking very striking and elegant in a shimmering gown of emerald satin. Her dark hair gleamed.

"Pippa," she said, stopping to look her daughter over from head to foot. "You are perfection. Is she not, Steph?"

"Yes," Stephanie said, beaming at her sister.

"It is frustrating to be sixteen, is it not?" their mother said, turning her gaze upon her younger daughter. "No longer a child but not quite a woman? But your turn will come sooner than you think. I promise."

"Oh, but I really do not want a turn, Mama, as I keep telling you," Stephanie said as she handed Philippa her fan. "I will come downstairs to see the two of you on your way. And tomorrow I will come to your room, Pippa, early but not *too* early, to rub salve on all the blisters your poor feet are about to acquire from dancing all night. And I will listen to an account of all your conquests."

Philippa laughed, rapped her sister lightly over the knuckles with the fan, and followed their mother from the room. The butterflies that had been threatening her stomach all day were dancing away there now at full flutter.

CHAPTER TEN

Lucas went early to the Abingdon ball, something he would not normally have dreamed of doing. However, Jenny had announced at breakfast that she was going to attend the ball herself.

"I love dancing," she had explained. "Why should I not go to watch even if I cannot dance myself? I was included in Aunt Kitty's invitation when it came a couple of weeks or so ago. I will not be a bother to anyone or get in anyone's way."

"You are never a bother, my love," her grandmother had assured her. "I do hope you have a pretty new gown to wear."

"It is a rather bright shade of pink, Grandmama," Jenny had told her. "I was afraid it might clash with my hair, but both Aunt Kitty and the dressmaker assured me it did not. If I see everyone at the ball wincing whenever they glance in my direction, I will know never to trust Aunt Kitty's judgment or that particular dressmaker's ever again."

"Jenny!" Aunt Kitty had protested, pressing a hand theatrically to her bosom. "I have always had a reputation for impeccable taste in fashion."

Jenny would see to it that she was not a bother to anyone, even her family, Lucas had thought fondly. And sure enough, she had arranged that Bruce, the hefty footman whose primary duty for many years had been to convey her from place to place, would carry first her wheeled chair and then Jenny herself upstairs to the ballroom, and her brother knew she would sit in a quiet corner all evening if allowed to, making demands upon no one. She would not be left alone, of course, or in any corner. She had a number of acquaintances in town and a few definite friends, even apart from family. Everyone would keep an eye on her even though she would do nothing to demand it—or perhaps because of that.

Lucas insisted anyway upon accompanying her when she and his aunt left early for the ball so she would arrive before most of the other guests and avoid having to make any sort of conspicuous entrance. The arrival of a wheeled chair in a ballroom might indeed be remarked upon if there were enough spectators to do the remarking.

Lucas did not mind arriving early anyway. He wanted to watch the guests as they entered the ballroom and learn who they were if he could. Lady Abingdon, he knew, was bringing out her eldest daughter, Miss Thorpe, this year. She might possibly be considered worthy to be added to Grandmama's list since the baronial title was an old, prestigious one. The young lady would probably be in the receiving line with her parents. He knew Lady Morgan Bedwyn, having been introduced to her at an earlier ball. He had no idea if she would be at tonight's. He knew Lady Philippa Ware. And that was almost the extent of his acquaintance with eligible ladies. He had been introduced to other young women since the day of his arrival in town, it was true, but he doubted any of them would meet his grandparents' exacting standards as a possible wife. He very much hoped to meet others tonight without the direct intervention of the duke and duchess. The least he could do for the bride he must choose this year was convince her somehow that he was offering for her *because he liked her.*

His grandparents were coming to the ball. Grandmama had sent a note to Lady Abingdon this morning as well as to other socially prominent hostesses, and of course an invitation to tonight's ball had arrived at Arden House within the hour.

Lucas wheeled his sister along the receiving line, pausing for an exchange of greetings with Lord and Lady Abingdon and an introduction to Miss Thorpe, who looked flushed and pretty and almost painfully young in her white, frilly gown. He settled Jenny in a convenient space between rows of chairs that had been set up about the perimeter of the room for chaperons and other nondancers. It was halfway along the ballroom and would afford Jenny a perfect view of the dancing.

He left her with their aunt as the ballroom began to fill with guests, and strolled about, greeting people he knew and being introduced to others. They included a few young ladies he had not met before. They were dressed almost exclusively in white, as was Miss Thorpe, as though it were some sort of signal to the single male guests that they were young, new on the market, and available. Horrid thought. He was only twenty-six himself. Nevertheless, most of them looked very young to him. All of them, however, would have been raised and educated to acquire the knowledge and accomplishments they would need as heads of their own households when they married, fitting partners and hostesses to gentlemen of good birth and—they would all hope—of comfortable fortune too.

It was really quite ghastly to know that he was an active participant in the marriage mart this year.

There were other single men in the ballroom too. At least, Lucas assumed they were single since they were there alone, as he was at the moment, or in company with one another. They were looking over the young women, most of whom were pretending not to notice. Some even pretended to be feeling slightly bored. A number of fans waved languidly before unsmiling faces to complete the impression. Perhaps it was an amusing, even exciting game for some. Lucas hated it. He wanted someone to love, damn it all, and he wanted the leisure in which to find that someone and court her properly until they were both as sure as anyone could be that they might expect some happiness together. Some real companionship. Some pleasure in the marriage bed.

He went to stand beside Jenny's chair again as the ballroom filled and it became obvious that Lady Abingdon was going to be able to boast tomorrow of what a grand squeeze her ball had been. Newly arrived guests were still moving along the receiving line. Aunt Kitty stood at the other side of Jenny's chair, talking with two couples with whom she had an acquaintance.

Lucas's eyes focused upon a man who was approaching him, a smile on his face. "The Marquess of Roath?" he said. "Arnold Jamieson, son of Baron Russell, at your service."

Lucas assured him with an inclination of his head that he was delighted to make his acquaintance.

"May I have the pleasure of an introduction to Lady Jennifer Arden?" Jamieson asked.

Jenny was smiling up at them. Her dressmaker and Aunt Kitty had been quite correct about the color of her gown. The brightness of the pink did suit her. It added color to her face and went very well indeed with her hair, which was dressed in intricate coils at the back of her head and was smooth and shining over the crown. Her face was probably not conventionally pretty, but there was surely something rather handsome about it. It was hard to tell, though, when one had known and been fond of someone all one's life.

"Jenny," he said. "Allow me to present Mr. Jamieson, son of Baron Russell."

"*Elder* son," the young man said, bowing and offering her his right hand. "How do you do, Lady Jennifer?"

"I am very well, thank you," she said, setting her hand in his but not allowing it to linger there. "I am pleased to make your acquaintance, Mr. Jamieson."

"I am hoping," he said, "that you will grant me the honor of the first set of dances."

She raised her eyebrows and Aunt Kitty turned away from her conversation in order to look at Jamieson. "I am unable to dance— or to walk," Jenny said. "But thank you for the invitation."

"Ah," Jamieson said. "I did notice the wheels on your chair and deduced your inability to walk. However, some dance partners do not take to the floor at all but use the half hour of a set to sit and converse. Will you allow me to sit and talk with you during the opening set?"

Fortune hunter? The thought flashed through Lucas's mind as he looked the man over. He was elegantly, though not ostentatiously, dressed. He appeared to have polished manners. He had a smile women would be sure to find charming. He was goodlooking. He sounded to be of decent pedigree. But . . . an impoverished pedigree, maybe? Or perhaps he had expensive habits? It was totally unfair to jump to negative conclusions, of course, without even a jot of evidence upon which to base them. Why, after all, should someone *not* wish to seek an acquaintance with Jenny and sit talking with her for half an hour at a ball?

"Thank you, Mr. Jamieson," she said. "I would like that."

Jamieson bowed and strolled away.

"Do be careful, Jenny," Aunt Kitty said, her brows knitting in a frown. "I shall remain here beside you to see to it that Mr. Jamieson offers you no impertinence."

"Would you stand beside me if I were able to dance, Aunt Kitty?" Jenny asked, sounding amused. "To make sure that my partner offered no impertinence? At a ball hosted by Lord and Lady Abingdon and therefore of the utmost respectability?"

Aunt Kitty sighed. "I take your point," she said. "Sometimes I can be overprotective merely because you cannot walk. Forgive me."

Jenny reached out a hand and patted her arm. "I am well aware of the possible motive of any man showing an interest in me," she said. "As I would be even if I could walk. I am the granddaughter of a duke, after all, and sister of the duke's heir. I am wealthy in my own right. I am therefore a matrimonial prize. I will not allow myself to be duped, Aunt."

But Lucas's attention had been diverted. For here she came. She was moving along the receiving line, poised and smiling, and looking like a fairy queen, though that was a strange, even silly comparison to make. She was dressed in white like the other, mostly younger women making their debut in society this year. But in contrast to them, she shimmered. Her close-fitting, high-waisted white gown had some sort of silver overlay. Her slippers and gloves were silver too, as were her earrings and the fine bracelets that glittered at her wrist. Her hair gleamed pure blond in the candlelight. Her face was sheer beauty.

Lady Philippa Ware.

Accompanied by her mother, the Dowager Countess of Stratton, a dark, mature beauty, clad elegantly and vividly in emerald green.

He felt his heart turn over and land with a thud back in the middle of his chest. He was half aware that almost all eyes in the ballroom were upon her. Many, particularly male eyes, lingered.

Yet she was the one woman of superior rank who was not for him, Lucas thought. This, her first grand ball, ought to have happened four years ago. He was the man who had prevented it from happening either then or in the three years since. He had never thought of himself as villainous—until he met her at Arden House on the day of his arrival in town.

She had made a villain of him. Or, rather, since she had played no active role in the matter and was in fact quite innocent, he had made an unconscious villain of himself that night when he had made the fateful decision to accompany James Rutledge to a maypole dancing practice, of all unlikely absurdities. Fate sometimes had a very odd sense of humor. No sense of humor at all, in fact.

He turned away to greet Gerald, who had arrived a short while ago but had stopped to exchange greetings with a group of acquaintances. Gerald too was looking toward the doorway.

"Ah," he said. "Lady Philippa Ware, looking rather divine. I doubt anyone would disagree that I am the luckiest man at the ball. I have reserved the opening set with her."

No, Lucas would not disagree.

Jenny was smiling brightly in the same direction and trying to catch the lady's eye, which she did after a few moments. Lady Philippa smiled back and came toward them with her mother. There was a flush of color in her cheeks. Lucas wished he had had the presence of mind to move away as soon as he caught sight of her, but it was too late now. There was a flurry of greetings.

"You *did* come," Lady Philippa said to Jenny. "I am so proud of you."

"I could not resist your challenge," Jenny said. "And you are not the only one with a partner for the opening set, Pippa. I have one too, I am pleased to inform you. How do you like that?"

"I like it very well indeed," Lady Philippa said, laughing. "Is he tall, dark, and handsome?"

"Actually he is," Jenny said.

It seemed almost inevitable, Lucas thought, that these two were going to remain close friends, probably even after they both returned home at the end of the Season. Just as the dowager countess and Aunt Kitty had been for many years.

Laughter still lingered in Lady Philippa's eyes when she turned to bid first him and then Gerald a good evening.

But they were not allowed to remain for long in a group together. The dancing was about to begin, and Lady Abingdon was making sure those young men who did not already have a partner found one. No hostess liked it to be said on the morning after a ball that there had been wallflowers who had not been invited to dance even though there were unattached males propping up doorways and pillars or huddled together in groups for self-defense.

Lucas found himself leading a Miss Legge into the lines and performing the steps of a stately country dance with her while she gazed at him with what looked like frightened awe. He smiled and set about the task of setting her at ease. He had already reserved the second set with Miss Thorpe, Lady Abingdon having informed him pointedly in the receiving line that the girl would open the ball with a second cousin but had not yet reserved any other set for the evening.

Jamieson, he could see, was seated beside Jenny, focusing all his attention upon her. They seemed to be deep in conversation. Lady Philippa was dancing with Gerald and looking very happy about it, though Lucas tried not to notice.

Between the first and second sets he talked with Jeremy and Laura Bonham, Sylvester's brother and sister-in-law.

"Do look at Lady Philippa Ware," Laura said after a couple of minutes. "She is being mobbed."

And it was not much of an exaggeration. She had a cluster of men about her, all of them presumably having passed her mother's inspection and been properly presented to her. She was still shimmering. She was also looking flushed and animated. Her dance card was no doubt full or soon would be.

"A very modest young lady," Jeremy said. "The Duke of Wilby, your grandfather, seemed very interested in her at your tea party, Luc, when he discovered that she is the Earl of Stratton's sister. Are you under orders yet to do your duty as his heir?" He was grinning.

"One might say so," Lucas admitted with a grimace. "And speaking of the devil . . ."

His grandparents were arriving, looking very elderly and very stately. Although there was no longer a receiving line at the door to greet late-arriving guests, a kind of hush fell on the ballroom as the majordomo announced the Duke and Duchess of Wilby, and Lord and Lady Abingdon hurried toward them to greet them and find them comfortable chairs together in a place from which they would have an unimpeded view of the dancing.

"I had better go and pay homage," Lucas said, and strode across the floor to greet them. At almost the same moment, Lady Abingdon brought her daughter to make her curtsy to them, and Lucas found himself leading her onto the floor for the second set with almost every eye in the room upon them.

Including the critical, assessing eyes of his grandmother and grandfather.

The campaign, it seemed, had begun in earnest. The days of his freedom—of person and of choice—were numbered.

———————

Jenny always had company, Philippa was glad to see each time she glanced her way. She had been a bit anxious about it, for she was the one who had more or less dared Jenny to come and enjoy herself even if she could not dance. Most of her friend's companions were members of her family and other close acquaintances, it was true. But one had been Mr. Jamieson, the tall, dark, handsome gentleman who had solicited the first dance with her. He also smiled a great deal and gave Jenny the whole of his attention during that set. Between it and the next set her chair was flanked by two other young men until a third joined them after fetching Jenny a glass of lemonade from the refreshment room. There was a great deal of laughter from the whole group before the young men left to claim their partners for the next set.

Philippa joined her the next time there was a break in the dancing. Jenny was flushed and bright-eyed.

"You were quite right, Pippa," she said. "I am loving the music and the spectacle of people dancing in all their evening finery. And I have certainly not been neglected. Did you see the men who were with me half an hour ago? Lady Abingdon introduced them to me as a group. I suspect they stay together between dances to give one another courage. They are recently down from Cambridge, though I would swear they have not a whole brain among the three of them. Their conversation was utterly trivial and terribly diverting. I have not laughed so hard in a long while."

"It is indeed a wonderful evening," Philippa said, fanning her face in a vain attempt to cool herself after the dancing. "I cannot believe so many gentlemen wish to make my acquaintance and dance with me."

"You are very funny," Jenny said. "You have no idea of your beauty and charm, do you? You outshine all other ladies at the ball, Pippa. By far." But her eyes had moved beyond Philippa and she smiled warmly. "Grandmama. Grandpapa. Are you enjoying the ball?"

The Duke and Duchess of Wilby had risen from their chairs to come and greet their granddaughter. Philippa would have slipped away to give them more room, but the duchess caught her by the hand and squeezed it.

"Are we *enjoying* a ball?" the duke said. "Is that not a contradiction in terms, Jenny? Are *you* enjoying it? That is more to the point."

"I am, Grandpapa," she assured him. "Immensely."

"Lady Philippa," the duchess said. "Your mama will be very gratified by the impression you are making tonight. This is your debut ball, I believe?"

"In London, yes, Your Grace," Philippa said. "Though we have quite frequent assemblies at Ravenswood and occasionally a more formal ball."

"There must be a story behind the lateness of your debut," the duchess said. "I would love to hear it sometime. But this year you have arrived in town with poise as well as beauty. Perhaps the delay was prearranged by some kindly fate."

"Thank you." Philippa was embarrassed and longed to get away. She wished her next partner would come soon to claim her for the upcoming set.

The Duke of Wilby meanwhile had turned to face the ballroom and was beckoning someone imperiously. His grandson, the Marquess of Roath, appeared at his side within moments.

"Grandpapa," he said. "May I fetch you something? A drink, perhaps? Grandmama?"

His grandfather ignored the offer. "You have reserved a dance with Lady Philippa Ware?" he asked abruptly.

Oh.

"I have not yet had the opportunity," Lord Roath said, not looking at her.

"You have one now," the duke told him.

"I am afraid I have already promised every set," Philippa said quickly, horribly embarrassed, though at least she did not have to lie. "Except for the waltzes, of course."

The duke harrumphed.

The duchess squeezed Philippa's hand again. "Because of that absurd rule that a young lady may not waltz in a London ballroom until she has been given the nod of approval by one of the patronesses of Almack's?" she said. "That is *very* absurd in your case, my dear. However, I can understand that you would wish to avoid putting a foot wrong at your very first ball. Leave this to me."

And she turned to look purposefully about the ballroom.

"Sally Jersey to your right, May," His Grace said, addressing his duchess.

"Horrible woman," the duchess said. "But she will do."

The duke offered her his arm.

"I do believe, Lady Philippa," the Marquess of Roath said, his eyes looking as hard as steel, "you are about to be permitted to waltz. And if I do not then reserve the first set of waltzes with you, I will probably find myself excommunicated from my family before the night is over."

Jenny laughed. "Our grandparents are *benevolent* tyrants," she explained to Philippa. "But they are tyrants nonetheless. They will *not* be pleased if Luc does not dance with you. It is a good thing you already know and like each other."

Philippa was saved from answering when someone touched her shoulder and she turned to find her next partner bowing to her and extending a hand to lead her into the set that was about to begin.

F or some reason no one could quite explain, Sally Jersey wielded great power in the world of the *ton*. She could make or break a young lady's hopes of success and the acquisition of an eligible husband simply by denying her a voucher to attend the weekly dances at Almack's assembly rooms. She could humiliate even princes by denying them entry to Almack's if they arrived improperly clad—without knee breeches, that was—or even one minute past eleven o' clock in the evening. Even she, however, could be cowed by one very elderly and determined duchess and a small, equally elderly and imperious duke at her side. She smiled graciously, as though conferring a great favor upon the couple, who had probably made her quail in her dancing slippers, and informed them that *of course* Lady Philippa Ware, sister of the Earl of Stratton, who was taking the *ton* by storm tonight despite the presence of several other acclaimed beauties, was permitted to waltz with the Marquess of Roath or any other partner of her choice.

She swept across the ballroom in the midst of the set in progress, cutting past dancers as though it were they who were getting in her way, not the other way around. She tapped Lady Philippa on the shoulder and graciously conferred upon her the coveted permission for everyone in the room to see and even hear.

Including Lucas himself.

Why the devil could she not be plain and dull and ordinary? Lady Philippa Ware, that was. Though he had the feeling that even then she would have taken his grandparents' eye and got onto Grandmama's list. As it was, she was almost certainly at the very head of the list, her name written in large capitals. Lady Morgan Bedwyn was not here tonight. She would very probably appear on the list too. And perhaps Lady Abingdon's daughter and one or two others who were here tonight.

Between sets he went to ask Lady Philippa formally for the first set of waltzes, which, he realized even as he was approaching her, came next on the program. Perhaps she would refuse him. He was quite certain she would wish to do so. But the Duke and Duchess of Wilby were a formidable pair, and it was quickly obvious that she had been cowed or at least awed by them. Perhaps by Lady Jersey too.

"Thank you, Lord Roath," she said. "That would be pleasant."

It was unclear what she meant by *pleasant*, for her words were spoken without enthusiasm. However, they *had* been spoken.

So he found himself a few minutes later leading her onto the floor, where he stood facing her, willing the orchestra to stop fiddling around with their instruments and get on with playing a waltz tune. She stood before him, her face unsmiling and quite expressionless, but very beautiful nonetheless. And he had a memory of that night in the barn, when he was being coaxed into trying to dance about the maypole and had been about to capitulate—but *only* if his partner could be the blond beauty. Even then . . .

But the memory could not hold him. For he was becoming uncomfortably aware that he and his partner were the focus of much interested attention. Gossip was like manna in the desert to the *ton*, who searched it out wherever they went. Large numbers no doubt had watched the Duke and Duchess of Wilby make their stately way around the edge of the ballroom to confer with Lady Jersey. There was probably not a single soul here present who had not then watched Lady Jersey's progress across the ballroom floor to tap Lady Philippa on the shoulder, like a queen conferring a knighthood. And here was the culmination of those two events for the *ton*'s delight—the duke and duchess's grandson and heir about to waltz with the most beautiful and probably the most eligible lady at the ball.

To many it must seem like a moment of high romance, the prince dancing face-to-face with his intended princess. It was excruciatingly embarrassing.

"Will it never begin?" she asked.

It was a rhetorical question, of course. "Nervous?" he asked, and smiled at her.

"Coerced," she replied, looking into his face. "The Duke and Duchess of Wilby are a menace to the world."

He laughed, and so, surprisingly, did she.

There was an almost audible sigh from those who stood watching.

Then the orchestra struck a chord and he slid one hand about her waist and raised his other hand to take hers. She set her free hand on his shoulder, and even though he stood a respectable distance from her, he could feel the heat of her body and smell the delicate perfume that clung about her.

The music began. He said nothing for the first moment or two while they found their footing and adjusted it to the rhythm of the music. He led her into a simple twirl about the first corner to make sure their feet did not become entangled. And he felt her gradually relax, physically at least, as she followed his lead. She looked up into his face, saw that he was gazing back, and let her own gaze slip to his mouth before bringing it hastily back up.

"They are determined, you see," he said, "that I will marry this year. Not just anyone, however. She has to be someone of superior rank and breeding, someone who will fit one day into the role of duchess as easily as her hand would into a well-made glove."

She smiled at him. "She will not be me," she said.

"No, no," he agreed. "I understand that, not having been born stupid. However, I must beg leave to point out that I have not asked you."

"If that was intended as a setdown, Lord Roath," she said, "it has missed its mark."

"I am twenty-six years old," he told her. "Most gentlemen my age would be looking forward to at least four or five more years of kicking their heels and sowing some wild oats before considering the more sober responsibilities of marriage and fatherhood. I am not, alas, of their number. There is a missing generation in my family and a dearth of heirs of the direct line. I am it, in fact. Gerald is the duke's grandson as surely as I am, and he is quite as much beloved. He would make a superb duke. However, he has the misfortune—or perhaps the good fortune—of being the son of the duke's *daughter* and cannot therefore inherit. Only I can. And it may be soon. It would appear that my grandfather has been given notice by his physician."

"Oh," Lady Philippa said. "I am so sorry."

"So am I," he said. "Selfishly, I am sorry for me. More important, I am sorry for his sake. His consuming desire is to see me married. He has promised—though I am not at all sure he will be able to keep the vow—to live until he sees my first son in his cradle. He will not even consider the possibility that my first child may be a daughter, of course. No child in the womb would dare thwart his will."

He watched her swallow. "Lord Roath," she said, "you *are* proposing marriage to me."

"Am I?" he asked her. And was he really? Her of all people? The one woman on earth with whom he could never even flirt, let alone court? Why the devil had he told her all these things—while he was waltzing with her, half the *ton* looking on? *No child in the womb . . .* Good God. She must be made of stern stuff. Many ladies would have swooned right away.

"You expect me to be filled with pity for the Duke of Wilby," she protested. "And I *am*. You expect me to volunteer to help grant his dying wish. Though he does not look as though he were dying. He is at a *ball*, not on his deathbed. You are hoping I will say yes without your having to go to the bother of asking the question directly."

"On bended knee? With red rosebud clutched in one fist?" he said. "I must confess I would do almost anything to avoid such a colossal embarrassment."

He twirled her once about, and she tipped back her head and laughed while he smiled at her.

"You waltz very well," she said.

"So do you."

For a few moments, until the first tune of the set came to an end and they stopped dancing, they gave themselves up to an enjoyment of the moment—to lilting music; to the gleaming dance floor beneath their feet and the candlelight creating a prism of colors amid the crystal of the chandeliers overhead and along the upper halves of the walls; to the swirling colors of the ladies' gowns and the more sober elegance of their partners; to the banks of flowers and greenery with which the ballroom had been decked; to the sounds of conversation and laughter beyond the music; to the touch of their hands and the heat and shared rhythm of their bodies as they waltzed.

Then they stood, recovering their breath and waiting for the next dance of the set to begin.

"Well?" he asked.

"*Well?*" She looked back at him with raised eyebrows.

"*Are* you going to volunteer?" he asked her.

He watched indignation harden her eyes and tighten her lips.

"Never, Lord Roath," she said. "Not in a million years."

"As I expected." He grinned at her.

This was all a little bizarre, he thought. Or surreal. Or, at the very least, improper.

"*Volunteer,*" she said contemptuously. "The very idea! If you wish to propose marriage to me, *my lord*, you may do it on bended knee after conferring with my brother. And then you may get to your feet while I blister your ears with my refusal."

"What is your favorite color rose?" he asked her.

CHAPTER ELEVEN

It was by far the most exhilarating set of the evening so far. Indeed, if she were perfectly honest with herself, Philippa would have to admit this was the most wonderful night of her life. How could it not be? She was in London at the start of her come-out Season. She was at her first grand *ton* ball, and all her fears had been put to rest even before she danced the opening set with Sir Gerald Emmett. An astonishingly large number of gentlemen had sought to be presented to her, had bowed over her hand and gazed upon her with admiration, and had paid her lavish, foolish compliments, which had caused her to laugh and fan her heated cheeks. Her dance card had begun to fill up. It was quite full before the second set began. She was not going to be a wallflower. Stephanie would enjoy saying *I told you so* tomorrow.

But now . . .

She was not even going to have to sit out all the waltzes. Against all her expectations, permission had been granted her at her very first London ball. It was astounding, to say the least. For there was no dance in the world more exhilarating, more purely *romantic* than the waltz. She wished this set would never end. Though there would be others after supper, and surely it was not too much to hope that someone else would ask to partner her for at least one of them. It was even possible that she would end up dancing every set of the evening. It would be success beyond her most extravagant dreams.

She could not deceive herself, however, into believing that this intense happiness she was feeling was attributable only to the fullness of her dance card and the fact that she was waltzing when she had not expected to do so for at least the next few weeks. Would she be feeling quite this exuberant if, for example, she were waltzing with Sir Gerald? Or with any of the other gentlemen who had signed her dance card or would have done if it had not been full? She knew she would not, much as she liked Sir Gerald. She ought to be ashamed of herself. She was reacting to the Marquess of Roath tonight just as she had upon her first sight of him when she was eighteen—before he had spoken and revealed himself to be a heartless, cruel man.

Though . . . was he *really*? Did a few unguarded words define a person for all time? He *had* assured her more recently that his words had been unjustified and that she had misunderstood. None of which had been a real explanation, of course.

In the week or so since she had met him again, he had not once given her a proper explanation of those words. Merely saying they had been unjustified and she had misunderstood was really not saying anything at all. It was easy to deny. It was far harder to explain.

They danced the second waltz of the set to a somewhat slower, more lilting rhythm than the first. And if she was not much mistaken, he was holding her a little closer, though there was no suggestion of impropriety. They touched each other only with their hands. But his body heat mingled with her own, and it seemed she could almost feel his heartbeat. They danced without talking, their eyes roaming over each other's face and only occasionally looking away.

She was aware of Jenny, smiling happily at them. Mr. Jamieson was beside her again. She saw her mother conversing with a silver-haired gentleman, and caught her eye. Mama nodded with obvious approval. The Duke and Duchess of Wilby, seated side by side, somehow made their plush velvet chairs look like thrones. They were both looking directly at their grandson and Philippa. His Grace was frowning, while Her Grace looked speculative, her head nodding slowly, just like Mama's.

Philippa suspected that she was already under serious consideration as the Marquess of Roath's bride. They had come to London in order to see him married. To set his feet on the path to getting the next heir of the direct line. All as soon as could decently be accomplished. There was some urgency because the duke was dying, or at least in questionable health. There must be any number of other women they were considering too, of course, but she was undoubtedly one of them. Which suggested that whatever issue Lord Roath had had with her father had not also involved them.

"Peach," she murmured, and winced slightly when she realized she had spoken aloud. He would think she had taken leave of her senses. Ten minutes must have passed since he asked the question.

He understood her, however. "A peach rose it will be, then," he said, and she looked back into his face and wondered if he really would have the gall to come to Stratton House to make an offer for her. She must surely be the last woman on earth he would want as a wife, just as *he* was the last man on earth . . .

He would never get by Devlin, anyway. For Devlin *knew*. And he had promised to confront the Marquess of Roath one day if their paths should ever cross. He had been furious when he said it and had looked every inch the ruthless infantry officer he must have been for six years during the Peninsular War.

"To match your cheeks," the marquess said.

Her eyes dipped to his mouth, which she could only describe to herself as sensuous, and she wondered what it would feel like on her own. But allowing such wayward and improper thoughts to seep into her mind caused an uncomfortable throbbing low in her abdomen and a weakness in her knees. Was it pathetic that in twenty-two years she had never been kissed? Except by family members, that was. But that did not count. It was not *that* sort of kiss for which she sometimes found herself yearning.

But *not* with the Marquess of Roath.

The music came to an end. There was one more waltz in the set.

"Have you realized that this is the supper dance?" he asked her.

She looked inquiringly at him.

"A gentleman is expected to lead his partner into the dining room, fetch her a plate of food, sit beside her, and converse with her until it is time to return to the ballroom," he said.

Assemblies at home had never been like that. Not even the formal balls they had at Christmas and at the summer fete.

"I believe," she said, "you have made that up on the spot, Lord Roath."

"I do assure you," he said with raised eyebrows, "that you would humiliate me beyond hope of recovery if you were to walk away when the waltz is over. I may be handing you a deadly weapon by telling you that, of course, but you might also cause scandal for yourself from which it would be hard to recover."

"You exaggerate," she said. "At the very least."

"We will take Jenny with us as chaperon," he said. "Will that soothe your misgivings?"

She drew breath to speak, but the orchestra, after a brief pause, struck up another, more spirited waltz tune. And this was, she thought as he twirled her about the floor, the loveliest of all. She was waltzing on the most magical night of her life with surely the most handsome man at the ball. It would be foolish not to enjoy it all to the full. But it seemed it would not be over even when the set was done, for he was to escort her in to supper and sit with her and converse with her—*and* Jenny.

She was not committing herself to anything by smiling at him and twirling with him, laughing as she did so, and feeling happy. *Was* she? For one was supposed to do those things at a ball. No one, after all, had the power to force her into marrying against her will. Even that very formidable duke and his duchess. *He* might feel an obligation to them. She had none, even if they *had* made it possible for her to waltz. And it was very much against her will even to *consider* marrying Lucas Arden, Marquess of Roath.

Jamieson was wheeling Jenny in the direction of the dining room as Lucas and Lady Philippa approached them. Aunt Kitty, Lucas saw, was gazing after them and must have given her blessing. There was no reason why she would not have done, of course. It was quite unfair to assume that any man who showed the smallest interest in his sister must be a fortune hunter. It was even insulting to her to assume such a thing. Not much harm could come to her, anyway, in the Abingdon dining room with half the *ton* squeezed in there with her.

"May we join you?" Lucas asked.

"But of course." Jenny smiled at both of them, but was there an edge of disappointment in her voice?

Ah, Jenny.

"Thank you," he said.

"I have never before seen the waltz performed," Jenny said to Lady Philippa as they walked. "I do not wonder that it has taken the Continent and London by storm. It is divine."

"I learned the steps last year so that I could waltz at a local assembly," Lady Philippa told her.

In the dining room two long tables had been arranged parallel to each other down the length of the room, with a number of smaller tables set against the walls on either side. His grandmother, Lucas saw, was already seated at the end of one long table, her hand on the back of the vacant chair beside her to reserve it. The intended occupant of that seat, the Duke of Wilby himself, was standing a short distance away guarding one small table in a corner of the room. It had been set for two. He was frowning ferociously, an expression that no doubt deterred any would-be occupants of that table, a pair of lovers, for example, who would be only too delighted to spend the following half hour tête-à-tête without the necessity of making polite conversation with fellow guests.

The duchess beckoned. "Your chair will fit here very nicely, Jenny," she called, indicating the corner of the table. "Thank you, Mr. Jamieson. Yes, just here. Very kind of you. And there is room for you beside her at the head of the table. A servant will bring another chair and another setting."

Which a pair of servants promptly did.

"Lady Philippa," His Grace said while Jamieson was maneuvering Jenny's chair into position and taking his own seat. "The main table is a little too crowded at this end for you to squeeze in comfortably. I beg your pardon for that, but Luc will keep you company here."

Lucas looked steadily at his grandfather, but the old gentleman, after pulling back a chair for the lady and indicating it with one hand, acted as though his grandson were invisible. He turned to make his way to his own place, where he seated himself after bowing graciously to a large-bosomed matron in the place next to his. The preposterously tall plumes on her headdress nodded back at him.

Lucas pushed in the chair as Lady Philippa sat upon it and he took his place across from her. He looked ruefully at her. "That was not even subtle," he said. "I do apologize. You are obviously at the very head of the list my grandmother came here to compile. It is even possible that no one else's name is even on that list yet. They came and saw you in their own home and decided that you would do very well indeed. Unfortunately the world has never given them much of an argument when their minds are set upon a certain course. Would you like me to have a stern talk with them tomorrow and inform them that you must be struck from the list since you are quite adamantly opposed to marrying me?"

She surprised him by laughing. "I cannot help liking them," she said. "Though it is obvious even without your saying so that they are very accustomed to having their own way. Is your grandfather *really* dying?"

"Who knows?" he said. "Even his physician cannot predict such an event with any great accuracy, I suppose. His Grace can be a very stubborn man. He may give Death one of his looks when it comes calling, and Death may go slinking away and not dare return until a more convenient time."

"Or is he perhaps—your grandfather, that is—manipulating you?" she asked.

"By hinting that his physician has given him bad news?" He sat back in his chair while one servant set two large plates of food in the middle of the table and another poured their tea. He had not even considered that possibility. Manipulative his grandfather could undoubtedly be. But . . . a liar? "Anything is possible with him. But I believe him to be telling the truth about this. I do not know why else there would be this sudden haste to get me married. I am only twenty-six, and I have always enjoyed good health."

She had not answered his question about that stern talk with his grandparents. At the very least, though, he must sit down with them tomorrow—*both* of them—and insist quite firmly that they were not to harass Lady Philippa Ware. She was under no obligation whatsoever to marry him just because they had decided she was perfect for him. Perhaps they assumed she must be over the moon with delight to find herself in the running to be the bride of the heir to a dukedom—*and* with the full approval of the duke and the duchess. In their minds, any single woman with half a brain in her head would be.

"When did your father die, Lord Roath?" she asked him as she set a lobster patty and two other savory delicacies on her plate and looked across the table at him.

"Eleven years ago," he said. "I was fifteen. Jenny was twelve and Charlotte was nineteen and betrothed to Sylvester Bonham. They had already been forced to postpone their wedding once while we were in mourning for our mother. But then it had to be postponed for another year. I was taken out of my school and away from my home at Amberwell to live at Greystone Court. My education for a few years after that consisted almost exclusively of training to become the Duke of Wilby one day. I had the best of tutors, though my main teacher was always my grandfather himself. He was a stern taskmaster. If he set me to learn the names and titles of every peer of the realm and how they ranked in order from top to bottom, for example, he expected perfection. If he tested me and I made one small mistake, I would be sent to my room and ordered to remain there until I could be sure to get it right next time. I was

not starved on those occasions. But the meals sent to my room were as bland and unappetizing as they could be without actually being inedible. Salt, apparently—or rather its lack—is a great inducer to boys to perfect their knowledge. Those meals were quite ingenious. Also they were cool if they were meant to be hot and tepid if they were meant to be cold. Poor Cook. It must have been a severe blow to her pride to be forced to send them up to me." He chuckled.

"But you learned," she said.

"But I learned."

"And you were separated from your sisters while you did it after the blow of losing both your parents within a year or so."

"I had been away at school during term times before that," he told her. "But there were the holidays. There were scarcely any of those after our father's death. We missed one another, my sisters and I."

"And had to grieve apart from one another," she said.

"Yes." He did not want to go there. Not into that terrible, lonely darkness from which at one time he had thought he would never emerge. "But my grandparents grieved too, you know. They had lost their only son and they had loved him. My grandmother used to tell me stories about him when he was a boy. I think it comforted her a little. And me."

Lady Philippa had lost her father too, he thought. But he could not ask her about that. Or tell her how viciously glad he was that the man was dead.

"Tell me about your family," he said as she dabbed her lips with her napkin after eating a small sausage roll. "I know very little. You have just the one sister?"

"Stephanie, yes," she said. "She is six years younger than I am. It is strange how that age gap seems to shrink as we grow older, though. For a long time she was just the child in the house, of

whom I was largely unaware most of the time, though sometimes she induced me to play with her when there were other activities I would far prefer to have been doing. Now I love being with her, though she has her own life and never clings to any of us. I am not sure if that is a good thing or not. She spends a lot of time at the church—not from an excess of piety but because Sir Ifor Rhys, our neighbor, is the organist there and conducts a few different choirs and Steph loves to sing. Sir Ifor is very talented musically. He is Welsh," she added, as though that fact explained everything. "She is the sweetest person in the world. But her expectations for her future seem to have been set very low. I wish I could do something about that, but we cannot organize someone else's life, can we? Sometimes love hurts."

"Why are they low?" he asked. Though he could guess. The girl was overweight, and while she was not exactly plain, neither was she obviously pretty. She had lovely hair, but she wore it in an unbecoming style. Every day of her life she saw her older sister, who was uncommonly lovely. It must seem very unfair to her. Perhaps it *was* unfair. But that was the nature of life.

"She loved our father very dearly," Lady Philippa told him. "And our older brothers too. Yet they had all left her by the time she was twelve. Ben and Devlin and Nicholas went to war when she was nine, all within a couple of months of one another, and Papa died of a sudden heart seizure three years later. Also, Steph sees herself as less than . . . lovely. But a mirror is not always the best conveyor of beauty, is it?"

He smiled. She was quite right. But it must not be easy for a girl of fifteen or sixteen to understand that.

"Ben, Devlin, and Nicholas are your brothers?" he asked. "You did tell me a little about Ben on another occasion. Ben *Ellis*, that is."

"And there is Owen too," she said. "He is the youngest. He is

in his first year at Oxford. When he was born, he was intended for a career in the church just as Nicholas was intended for the military. But Owen quickly became the mischief of the family, and Mama and Papa abandoned their plans for him. Now I am not so sure they were right to do so."

"He may end up in the church after all?" he asked.

"It does seem unlikely," she said, smiling. "He is still full of fun and energy. For the past year Mama has been in daily expectation that he will be sent down from Oxford over some foolish prank. He is also intelligent and serious about his studies, however. He is a complex character. It is hard to predict what he will make of his life."

"And Ben?" he asked. "How does he fit in?"

"For a number of years after he grew up he was my father's steward at Ravenswood," she said. "He did not have to do it. He was treated just as the rest of us were, as a full member of the family. It was a career entirely of his own choosing. After he returned from the wars with Devlin, he did not resume his duties. He had recently been widowed and brought a young daughter home with him. His mind was set upon making a home and life of his own with her. He is still officially living at Ravenswood, but he does have a new home, Penallen, on the coast not terribly far from Ravenswood. He is having it renovated before he moves there later this year. We will miss both of them dreadfully."

But perhaps she would not be living at Ravenswood herself by that time, Lucas thought. Surely she would be betrothed before the Season was over and married by the end of the year. She had been besieged tonight.

"Nicholas is still a military officer?" he asked.

"Yes," she said. "He is a major in a cavalry regiment. I am worried about him. So are Mama and Stephanie, though we do not talk much about it. It was such a *huge* relief last year when we heard that

Napoleon Bonaparte had surrendered and been exiled to the island of Elba. We thought the wars were finally over and the three of them were safe. But now Nicholas is *not* safe. There is almost bound to be war again."

He might have pointed out to her that there was always war somewhere in the world, and that much of it would inevitably involve England. She would not be consoled. She and her family were never going to be able to relax and stop worrying about the military brother. But they must know that. He reached across the table and set a comforting hand over hers before realizing what he was doing. He gave it a quick squeeze and withdrew his hand.

"The Duke of Wellington is in charge over there," he said. "He is a brilliant general, though many people here would argue that point, I know. The whole of Britain needs to trust him, however, and the Prussian general Von Blücher too. Though that is easy for me to say, I know. I have no one close to me fighting over there. You have a brother."

"So do thousands of other women," she said. "And fathers and sons and husbands."

"And you have the one other brother," he said. "Stratton."

"Devlin, yes," she said. "We had a letter this morning from his wife—Gwyneth. They are on their way here from Wales at last. They could arrive any day now. I was unhappy with him for most of the six years he was away at war. For he never once wrote to any of us, even Stephanie, who pined for him and had done nothing to offend him. As I had not. Or Owen. And he did not return or write even after Papa died. Not for two years. I was determined not to forgive him after he did come home—with a scarred face and a heart of granite. Or so it seemed. But love does not die, I think. It may lie dormant, and it may leave wounds and scars. But it never goes away."

She was staring down at her plate, though she seemed not to notice that the lobster patty was still on it, waiting to be eaten. She had drunk only half her tea. What remained in her cup would be cold by now.

She did not explain what had happened to cause all that disruption within her family, and he did not ask. But it sounded as though they had once been a close family and perhaps were again—now that Stratton was dead. Was there a connection? He would wager there was.

"Love is not love . . ." he said. "Do you know the sonnet?"

"It is an ever-fixed mark . . ." she said, quoting from a different part of the poem as she looked up and smiled at him. "But I think Shakespeare was talking about romantic love."

"Love is love," he said.

"Love is not love . . . Love is love. I am feeling a little dizzy." She laughed softly. "Some people are going back to the ballroom. I think we should go too, Lord Roath. I have promised the next set of dances and would not like to be late."

Lucas had the horrible feeling as he got to his feet and offered her his arm that he was falling a bit in love with Lady Philippa Ware, who was not only beautiful but also likable. For perhaps the dozenth time in as many days he cursed the fate that had taken him into the neighborhood of Ravenswood Hall for Easter four years ago.

And for the dozenth time he reminded himself that if he had not done so, she would doubtless be married by now. And probably happy.

Perhaps he would be happy too, for he would never have met her.

CHAPTER TWELVE

*H*arassed?" the Duke of Wilby said. "Lady Philippa Ware is under consideration to be offered marriage to the heir to a duke's title and vast properties and fortune besides, yet she is being *harassed*, Lucas? She is, according to my observations and Her Grace's, the most beautiful, the most charming, modest, poised, and eligible young lady now present in London. She is amiable in your company and converses with you and smiles at you without in any way giving the impression that she is intent merely upon snaring you. She has become Jenny's friend. Kitty likes her, as do Charlotte and Sylvester. She lives up to and even exceeds every expectation Her Grace and I had when we came to town this year. We have indicated our approval by treating her kindly. Yet you accuse us of *harassing* her?"

Whenever His Grace referred to him as *Lucas*, his grandson knew he was in trouble.

"Well, there is Lady Morgan Bedwyn, Bewcastle's sister," the duchess reminded the duke. "We have heard that she is in London, Percy. She was not at last night's ball, however."

"She is not in search of a husband," Lucas said. "She made that abundantly clear on the one occasion when I met her. She was haughty in manner and very, very bored with the whole social scene around her. I do not believe it was an affected boredom. I was not attracted to her."

"What has attraction to do with anything?" His Grace snapped, signaling for the butler to refill his coffee cup now that he had finished eating his breakfast.

"That is your second cup, Percy," the duchess reminded him.

"And the next one will be my third, May, should I decide to have my cup filled again," he said testily. "They are an odd family, the Bedwyns. Especially Bewcastle himself. A cold fish if ever I knew one, though actually more like a wolf than a fish with those silver eyes of his. Let someone else take on Lady Morgan Bedwyn. I daresay she will grow to resemble her aunt Rochester in time anyway, and that would not be a happy prospect for whoever marries her. I still say Lady Philippa Ware is the one for you, Luc."

"You were by far the most handsome couple on the floor when you waltzed together last evening," the duchess said. "You would have lovely babies, Luc."

Lucas winced.

His Grace stared at his wife, speechless for a moment. "Babies are not *lovely*. They resemble nothing more than bald eggs, which cry noisily and incessantly at one end and wet themselves or worse endlessly at the other," he said. "But babies are a necessary means to an end, Lucas. Male babies. *Not* that I have anything against female ones. But for you, a male one first and preferably second as well and then as many daughters as you want."

The thread of this conversation had somehow begun to unravel, Lucas thought.

"Unfortunately, Grandpapa," he said, "you have a measure of control only upon me. *Not* upon Lady Philippa Ware or any other prospective bride who may win your approval and Grandmama's. I promised Lady Philippa last evening that I would have a word with you today and make it clear that she is not to be harassed."

"You *promised* her?" The duke grabbed his cup and downed his coffee in what looked to be a single gulp. "Did she say she felt bullied, then?"

Lucas sighed. "She actually said she could not help liking you both," he said. "But—"

His grandfather slammed the flat of his hand down on the table, rattling the dishes and cutlery upon it.

"But *nothing*," he said. "It appears to me, Lucas, that I have a poor apology for a grandson, who is afraid to court a beautiful woman when he sees one for fear she may reject his suit. Court her. Make sure she has no reason to reject you and every reason to accept. Is that harassment? Is that bullying? She will still have the freedom to say no when you make your offer. See to it that she does *not* say no."

"Jenny has told me she would love to have Lady Philippa as a sister-in-law," the duchess said, smiling at her grandson, as though she thought that would be encouragement enough for him to force his attentions upon a woman who simply would not have him. "Have you sent her flowers yet today, Luc?"

"It is only breakfast time, Grandmama," he reminded her. His grandparents were almost always up at first cockcrow in the mornings—not that there were any roosters in close proximity to Arden House. It did not matter, though. Neither did the late night they had had after a busy evening at the ball. They were up anyway.

His aunt and his sister, on the other hand, were still sensibly asleep in their beds, as doubtless were nine-tenths of everyone else who had attended last evening's ball.

"The largest bouquet you can find," His Grace said. "And then have it doubled in size. Every other young buck who was there last night will be sending her flowers. Make sure yours stand out."

It was hopeless. There was no point in continuing to argue. For Lucas's definition of *harassment* would never match that of his grandparents. In their minds they were conferring a great favor upon Lady Philippa Ware by making it clear they would welcome her as a bride for their grandson and heir.

"I will do my best," he said weakly. "But even my best efforts may not induce her to say yes, you know. And if I ask her and she says no, then there will be an end of the matter. I hope, Grandmama, you have a few other names on your list of eligible brides."

"I do," she said. "Including Miss Thorpe, who seems a sweet enough girl and is prettily behaved. But Lady Philippa does appear to be outstanding. Now, I am to go shopping with Kitty this morning, if she should decide to get up before the clock strikes noon. According to her, all my hats are antiquated and she is embarrassed to be seen with me—*not* that she has said that last quite so bluntly, of course. I must go and get ready."

The two men rose with her and watched her leave the breakfast parlor.

"I am off to the House to see to the business of the nation," the duke announced. "Make sure you send those flowers, Luc. And get busy on that courtship. This is important to Her Grace, and Her Grace is important to me."

A low blow indeed, Lucas thought as he tossed his napkin onto the table and followed his grandfather from the room. The duke was not above a bit of blackmail when it suited his purpose.

———

Philippa returned home that afternoon from a walk in the park with her mother and sister to the discovery that no fewer than four gentlemen with whom she had danced last evening had left their calling cards in her absence. The cards were spread upon a silver salver in the hallway beside a small pile of what looked like fresh invitations. They must have been delivered by hand after the day's post arrived earlier.

Then, when they went into the library at the suggestion of the butler before going upstairs to divest themselves of their outdoor garments, it was to the discovery that the room looked and smelled like a particularly lavish flower garden because of all the bouquets that had been delivered since they left to add to those that had arrived during the morning. They had all been arranged in bowls and vases and even a few larger urns.

It was not the flowers that took their immediate attention, however, or accounted for the butler's urging that they come here before they did anything else. For there, examining the floral offerings and the messages and signatures upon the cards that accompanied them, were Gwyneth and Devlin. The Earl and Countess of Stratton themselves.

"*Someone,*" Devlin said, turning toward the door, "is taking the *ton* by storm. I believe that is the correct term, is it not? Could it be *you*, by any chance, Pippa?"

But Stephanie had given a quite unladylike whoop of delight and hurled herself into her brother's arms, and Mama had hurried forward with an exclamation of joy to hug Gwyneth. Philippa meanwhile stood beaming at them both, her hands clasped to her bosom, feeling a rush of pure happiness. All would be well now. She did not stop to consider how all had *not* been well before they came.

Last night and today had been a great triumph for her, after all, though she was trying hard not to let it all go to her head. She had been launched upon society, and society, it seemed, had opened its arms to welcome her.

"You are here," she said.

"At last," Devlin said, releasing Stephanie and turning to hug Philippa. "I hope I am not merely dreaming it and am about to wake up to discover I am still in the carriage with a hundred miles yet to go. Having seen all these flowers, Pippa, and having read about the number of devoted servants you appear to have collected if the accompanying cards are to be believed, I feel impelled to say *I told you so.* Expect me to gloat."

Stephanie had said it before him this morning.

"You must be very weary, Gwyneth," Mama said.

"We thought you would *never* come," Stephanie added, beaming from one to the other of them.

"We would have been here two days sooner, perhaps even three, if your brother had not insisted that we make the journey in *very* short stages, Steph," Gwyneth said.

"Well, pardon me for being a considerate husband," Devlin said while Gwyneth laughed at him. "Go on, then. Tell them. We had planned to keep it for tonight, after dinner, but what is wrong with this afternoon? Especially when we are surrounded by flowers and the room is looking very festive."

"It seems I am in a delicate way," Gwyneth said, and blushed.

Stephanie shrieked again and rushed at her sister-in-law, Philippa hugged her brother, and this time it was Mama's turn to clasp her hands to her bosom and beam at them all.

"Oh," she said. "My second grandchild. How very well blessed I am going to be."

For which words Philippa loved her. For Joy was not really her grandchild. Ben was not really her son. He was the illegitimate offspring of one of Papa's mistresses. But Mama had always behaved as though both Ben and Joy were her own.

"He or she should be putting in an appearance around or about November," Devlin said. "Maybe sooner. Gwyneth suspected before we went to Idris's wedding, but she did not say a word, even to me—*especially* to me—lest she be forbidden to travel."

"We are very happy," Gwyneth said. "So are Mama and Papa, as you may imagine. And so is Ben. We made a short detour to Penallen on the way here so we could let him know. He is coming here soon—ah, and now I have spoiled his surprise. Joy has outgrown all her prettiest clothes and I have promised to go shopping with him. But enough of all that. You are all looking very well indeed. You are not sorry you came to London, Steph, instead of staying at home with Miss Field?"

"I am not," Stephanie assured her. "I have walked all around the Whispering Gallery of St. Paul's Cathedral even though my knees were knocking, and I have watched the launch of a homemade kite in Hyde Park. I have explored every corner of Westminster Abbey and been to Hampton Court by boat. I have met a real, live duke—the Duke of Wilby—and his duchess, and they looked upon me kindly and even spoke to me. And Pippa already has so many beaux that soon she will not know what to do with all the flowers. She did not have to sit out a single set last evening at Lady Abingdon's ball. She even danced the *waltzes*. Lady Jersey gave her permission. The *famous* Lady Jersey."

"Yes, we have been reading the cards that came with the bouquets," Devlin reminded her. "Including the anonymous one with the single rose."

"It is on the mantel," Gwyneth said when she saw Philippa looking about the room. "A very clever gentleman, I would say.

Instead of trying to impress you by going larger than all the rivals he must have known he would have, he went small and exquisite."

"Here," Devlin said, and reached up to take down the card that had been propped against a narrow crystal rose vase. He handed it to her and she read it.

Neither red nor pink. Just a perfect peach rose.

She raised her eyebrows.

"It *is* perfect too," her mother said, reading the card over her shoulder and looking at her curiously.

"Yes." Philippa handed the card back to Devlin and turned to look about the room. "So are all these other flowers. People are very kind. It is all a bit overwhelming."

"I think you had better grow accustomed to it," her brother said. "And I doubt kindness has much to do with the flower garden that has blossomed in the library here."

"Come," Mama said, slipping a hand through Gwyneth's arm. "Let us go up to the drawing room. I am parched and simply longing for a cup of tea. I daresay we all are."

Philippa, taking one of Devlin's arms while he offered the other to Stephanie, was *so* glad the card that had come with the single rose—the *peach* rose—was unsigned. She was going to have to tell her brother, of course, about the identity of the sender. But not just yet.

That same day, Lucas took Jenny to call upon their sister and stayed for a late luncheon. He met an old friend from his Oxford days during the afternoon and spent an agreeable hour fencing with him under the instruction of a skilled swordsman, who declared that the marquess was improving despite the fact that he lost every bout. He rode in the park at the fashionable hour with the same friend and was pleased to discover that his circle of acquaintances was expanding. He conversed with a number of people and made his bow to others, including several young ladies to whom he had been introduced at last night's ball. He had even danced with a few of them. He dined with the friend at White's and went with him to the theater in the evening.

On the following day he went to White's and then to Jackson's boxing saloon. He spent the afternoon on a picnic excursion to Richmond Park with a party Lady Abingdon had put together for the amusement of her daughter. It was obvious from the first moment that he was the suitor most favored for Miss Thorpe's hand. He found himself seated in a carriage with her, her mother, and a male cousin. He had accepted the invitation with the approval of his grandmother, who had listened to his assertion that Lady Philippa was feeling harassed, and had decided rather reluctantly that Lucas ought to widen his net a little while being cautious not to allow himself to get trapped into a marriage that was not entirely to his liking.

Trapped! Not entirely to his liking!

He had not protested. What was the point?

He spent the evening at a soiree hosted by Lord and Lady Patterson, Charlotte's in-laws. They had been disappointed, Lady Patterson told him at one point in the evening, that the Dowager Countess of Stratton and her daughter had been obliged to excuse themselves because Mr. Charles Ware, the late earl's brother, and his wife had arranged a dinner to welcome the Earl and Countess of Stratton to town. The earl had apparently been admitted to the House of Lords during the day.

So Lucas now knew that Stratton had arrived in town. The present Stratton, that was. He wondered how long it would be before his grandfather hurried along the next stage of the campaign.

It all felt horribly out of control. It was quite impossible to tell His Grace exactly why Lady Philippa Ware would not marry him if he were the last man on earth. It was equally impossible to explain why *he* would not marry *her*. Even though, of course, he had toyed with the idea in some of his madder moments.

He did not have long to wait for the next step to unfold.

Late the following afternoon, when he returned home from a lengthy session with his tailor, hoping for some time to relax before a private card party he had agreed to attend during the evening, Lucas was summoned to the study. His Grace awaited him there, seated behind the ornate oak desk, though there was nothing upon it apart from a blotter and a bottle of ink and some quill pens. This was to be a formal meeting, then, not a friendly chat by the fire about how their day was going.

"Sit down, Luc." His grandfather indicated the chair that had been positioned on the far side of the desk, across from him.

Lucas sat.

"Stratton has finally taken his seat in the House of Lords," the duke said. "He is a former military chap. With the scar to show for it." He slashed one finger diagonally across his forehead and cheek. "Not the sort of fellow one would want to cross, from the look of him. He seems decent enough, however. We had luncheon together."

Of course they had. At His Grace's invitation, no doubt.

"He has been in Wales for the wedding of his wife's brother," the duke said. "He has agreed to receive you privately at Stratton House at ten o'clock tomorrow morning."

Good God! *Already?*

"I explained to him," his grandfather said, "that you have decided this year in light of my advanced age and the unfortunate fact that your father is deceased that it is time to seek a bride of eligible birth and breeding. I explained that Her Grace and I have come to town to support you in your search. I informed him that you have an acquaintance with Lady Philippa Ware and that Her Grace has observed that you seem much taken with each other."

How expert His Grace was at bending the truth, Lucas thought, without ever actually breaking it and outright lying.

"And he explained to me," the duke continued, "that unavoidable circumstances, including the passing of their father and their grandmother one year apart, prevented his sister from taking her place in society until this year, when she is already twenty-two years of age. She is eager to marry, he informed me, but only to a man of good, steady character who also touches her heart. Stratton does not know you or anything about you except what he heard from me. He does not know if Her Grace's impression that his sister seems to be taken with you is true or not. He is willing to receive you, however, though he very properly intends to talk first with Lady Philippa to ascertain whether she is open to receiving your addresses. The decision must be hers, he informed me, since he ceased being her guardian, even nominally, when she reached her twenty-first birthday."

Oh good God, Lucas thought, this was a disaster in the making. There was no way he could now escape this encounter, though. His grandfather had made arrangements with Stratton himself, and the man would be expecting him—unless, that was, Lady Philippa flatly refused to speak with him, as she very possibly would. Perhaps she would even give her brother a good reason for doing so. The truth, for example.

"I will go there tomorrow morning," he said with an inward sigh.

"I shall expect a betrothal to be imminent, then," His Grace said, "even if for sheer pride's sake the lady hesitates over your first proposal and asks for more time. You must see to it that the delay is only days long rather than weeks, though. You are a handsome man, Luc, and a fine figure of a man. You have no known vices. You love your sisters and your niece and nephews. You love your grandmother and treat her with unfailing courtesy. You are capable of great charm when you exert yourself. You did so a few evenings ago when you were waltzing with Lady Philippa, and she was visibly captivated. She is the one, Luc. Never mind about the others Her Grace is keeping in reserve should an alternative become necessary. I expect you *not to need any alternative.*"

"Unless," Lucas said, holding open the door of the library to allow His Grace to precede him from the room, "she outright refuses to have me, Grandpapa, and it becomes clear that she is not merely being coy. Or unless her brother expressly withholds his approval of the match after talking with me and refuses even to let me speak with her."

"Neither is an outcome you will allow to happen," the duke said. "Always keep in mind that you are my *grandson.*"

Yes, that arrogant certainty of his superior place in society had been part of his training, Lucas remembered as he followed his grandfather from the room.

G wyneth wished to shop for a bonnet to replace a favorite of hers that had been so sodden by a sudden downpour of rain while she was walking along an exposed beach in Wales, far from any shelter, that it had been irretrievable and had to be thrown out. Stephanie wished to exchange the books she had on loan from Hookham's Library for some different ones. Philippa needed nothing, but she was very happy to accompany her sister and sister-in-law and promised to give her honest opinion of any bonnets under consideration. They spent a pleasant afternoon together while the dowager countess went to call upon Aunt Elise, who had been suffering from a migraine the evening before and had been unable to join the rest of the family at the dinner Uncle Charles and Aunt Marian had arranged in celebration of Devlin's becoming an official member of the House of Lords.

It was rather lovely not to have any social event to attend. It was rare, Philippa was discovering, to have a free afternoon. A free evening was even more rare.

"So of course," Gwyneth said, laughing as they entered the hall of Stratton House on their return to find that Devlin was there, almost as though he had been waiting for them, "Pippa has come home with a ravishing new bonnet, and I have come with none. I was born a ditherer, it seems. Though I may go back for the chip straw tomorrow. Both Pippa and Steph liked it."

"And I came with six books," Stephanie said. "I could hardly lift them to carry to the carriage. One of them is eight hundred pages long."

Devlin kissed Gwyneth on the cheek and smiled at his sisters. "I have given directions for tea to be brought to the drawing room fifteen minutes after your return," he said. "Mama said not to wait for her. She will probably have tea with Aunt Elise if her migraine has gone away. But before you go up to your room, Pippa, may I have a quick word with you in the library?"

She looked inquiringly at him.

"That sounds ominous," Stephanie said cheerfully. "I think Dev is about to crack the whip, Pippa. You had better examine your conscience before you go in. *What have you done?*"

"We will see you both in no more than fifteen minutes," Gwyneth said, smiling at them before linking her arm through Stephanie's. "I am parched."

The library was still laden with flowers, though some wilted blooms had been pulled out and the slim vase had been removed from the mantel and taken up to Philippa's room—*because it is sort of lost among the large bouquets in here,* she had explained vaguely when she took it. Though in fact the opposite had been true.

"I was invited to take luncheon with the Duke of Wilby at the House today," Devlin said after closing the door. "It was, I would guess, a considerable honor. He is very elderly and autocratic, and most of the other members appear to stand in awe of him. I understand you have met him."

Oh.

"Yes," she said. "I was at Arden House when he and the duchess arrived from the country. It was the day of the kite flying Steph told you about. Both the duke and the duchess were kind enough to speak to me again at Lady Abingdon's ball the night before you arrived. It was Her Grace, in fact, who persuaded Lady Jersey to grant me permission to waltz."

"Wilby gave me to understand that he wishes to set his house in order," Devlin said. "He must surely be close to eighty, a prodigious old age. He had only one son, now deceased, who himself had just one son. Luke Arden."

"Short for Lucas," Philippa told him, going to sit on the edge of the chair beside the fireplace.

"Ah," he said. "It was he with whom the Duchess of Wilby wished you to waltz?"

"Y-yes," she said. "Though I waltzed with other gentlemen too after that."

"It would seem," Devlin said, "that the duke and duchess have come to London this year, for the first time in a while, for the specific purpose of helping their grandson find an eligible bride and of seeing him married. They appear to have fixed their choice upon you."

Philippa licked her lips. "Me among several others, no doubt," she said. "I have given him absolutely no encouragement, Dev. Quite the opposite, in fact. They will soon see that he is not pursuing any courtship with me and that I am not encouraging him to do so."

"They have not seen it yet," he said. "The grandson is to call upon me here tomorrow morning, presumably to rattle off his credentials and make an offer for your hand. I have agreed to receive him, though I did make it clear to Wilby that I would speak with you first to discover your feelings on the matter. You are under no obligation to receive his addresses if you are as adamantly opposed to doing so as you say you are. You cannot have met him more than a handful of times, after all. The Duke of Wilby may feel in a rush to see his grandson married, but the Earl of Stratton feels no such haste to marry off his sister. It has been abundantly clear from all I have heard and seen"—he gestured about the room—"that you have attracted considerable attention since your arrival in town and will almost certainly accumulate an abundance of suitors. This would, however, be an excellent match for you. Unless you have a real aversion to Lucas Arden, I would suggest that at least you listen to what he has to say. But I have been doing all the talking. What do you wish me to say to him?"

She gazed at him, a frown between her brows. "Dev," she said, "do you not know who he *is*?"

"I do indeed," he said, looking puzzled. "I understand the dukedom to be one of the richest in England in property and income and investments. I do not know the details, of course, but I will be sure to find out if this offer should lead to a serious discussion of a marriage contract."

"Dev," she said and paused to lick her lips again. "He has a courtesy title. He is the Marquess of Roath."

CHAPTER THIRTEEN

Though the Duke of Wilby had conducted his interview with his grandson privately, behind closed doors, he had obviously not kept quiet about it afterward. Lucas came downstairs at twenty minutes to ten the following morning, looking, in his own estimation, like a damned dandy, though his valet had been both shocked and hurt when Lucas had used those exact words to him and had assured his lordship that he would deserve to be sacked without a letter of recommendation and to live the rest of his life in abject penury if those words could ever be accurately associated with his handiwork. Any hope, though, that Lucas could slip from the house unnoticed by anyone, including servants, was quickly dashed.

The hall was half filled with a gathering of his relatives come to bid him farewell. Even Jenny was there in her chair, which must have been carried down specifically for the occasion. Even *Cousin Gerald* was there, for God's sake. Was it a rule at the building where he had his bachelor rooms—a very exclusive building, it might be added—that residents had to be out at the crack of dawn? A couple of footmen were in the hall, imitating wooden soldiers, as well as the butler, who was looking like a benevolent uncle instead of his usual dignified, impassive self.

Only the Duke of Wilby himself, the traitor, seemed to be absent.

"Ah," Aunt Kitty said, clasping her hands to her bosom. "Does he look impossibly handsome? Or does he look impossibly handsome?"

To which asinine questions Gerald offered no reply but merely smirked and asked if his cousin's cravat was feeling a bit on the tight side.

"Oh, he *does*," Jenny said. "You look gorgeous, Luc."

"You must not be late, Luc," his grandmother advised. "It would give the Earl of Stratton a very poor first impression."

Who was *making* him late, for the love of all that was wonderful?

The butler opened the door and bowed him out with an inward beam of encouragement that did not quite transform itself into a smile. That might have damaged his dignity.

Precisely fourteen minutes later, Stratton's butler received him in a far more correct manner, bowing formally as he took Lucas's hat and gloves, leaving him only with a package containing a peach rosebud in his hand and a fervent desire for a great black hole to open at his feet so that he could drop both himself and the rose into it. The butler conducted him to the library he had visited before when he had come to invite Lady Philippa Ware to drive in the park with him—where they had met Charlotte and Sylvester, and the children had invited her to the kite flying, an event that had led to her being in the breakfast parlor at Arden House when the duke and duchess had arrived from Greystone in time to be introduced to her, a meeting that had led to . . . this.

The man who was standing in a forbidding manner before the fireplace, his booted feet planted slightly apart, his hands clasped at his back, looked rather formidable. He was not as tall as Lucas, but he was solidly built and held himself with upright military bearing. He was dark haired, unlike his sister—for this was presumably Stratton himself. His face might have been handsome were it not for the diagonal scar the duke had spoken of. The wound that had caused it must have come very close to taking off the top of his head or at least depriving him of his left eye. As it was, his face was merely memorable and perhaps attractive to women.

"Stratton, I presume?" Lucas said with an inclination of his head when the man did not rush forward with a smile of welcome and an outstretched hand.

"For many months," the Earl of Stratton said without confirming his identity, "I have thought it would give me the greatest satisfaction to relieve you of your life, *Roath*. I still think it. Alas, Lady Philippa Ware has forbidden me to . . . *make a fuss,* as she puts it. It would cause a scandal, she tells me, and be an embarrassment to her as well as to my mother and my wife and younger sister. I must bow to her wishes since they are of greater importance than my personal gratification. To me my sister is very *precious* goods, you see. Even *priceless* goods. Have a seat."

He indicated the armchair on one side of the fireplace and took the other himself.

Well, this was a colossal embarrassment, Lucas thought. For obviously Stratton *knew* and had known for some time. *For many months . . .* He must have known yesterday when he had luncheon with Grandpapa. He must have known when he agreed to this meeting. He must have . . . Oh, the devil! Bizarrely, Lucas was hideously aware of the peach rosebud clutched in his fist. Had the package swelled to three times its size since he stepped into the room, or was that just his imagination? He was embarrassingly aware again too of looking like a dandy—despite his valet's almost tearful denials.

His first inclination after recovering some of his wits was to turn and walk out without saying another word. But that, he realized just in time, would be the coward's way out and something he would long regret.

He sat. He even made the effort to move back in the chair in order to give the appearance of relaxation.

"I had no idea until two weeks ago," he said, "that Lady Philippa Ware overheard those impulsive, ill-considered words I spoke in the hearing of a number of her—and *your*—male neighbors several years ago. She was some distance away with all the ladies, who were chatting and laughing among themselves. They were words I regretted immediately and *have* regretted ever since. Discourtesy is not a normal part of my behavior. Neither are insults or cruelty. Begging your pardon would be pointless. Begging *hers* would be inadequate, as I have already told her. I am nevertheless quite sincerely sorry."

"I will hear an explanation of those words," Stratton said as Lucas set down his package on the table beside him. "They were spoken, I believe, immediately after you discovered that James Rutledge, the man with whom you had come to spend Easter, was a close neighbor of the Earl of Stratton—my father."

"I have given Lady Philippa a very incomplete explanation," Lucas told him. "She is entitled to a full one even though it will half kill me to give it. I *will* explain to her, whether that be this morning if you will permit me to speak with her or she will permit me to do so, or at some other time, or eventually by letter if she will never again allow me speech with her. But it is to *her* I must make the explanation. Not to you or anyone else. What she does with the information when she has it will be up to her."

Stratton gazed steadily at him across the distance between them, saying nothing.

"It would be inappropriate," Lucas said, "to ask now for your blessing upon a proposal of marriage to your sister. I will not be making her an offer this morning—or perhaps ever. I do ask, though, that you allow me to speak with her. Unless, that is, she has already informed you that she does not wish to speak to me."

Stratton set one elbow on the arm of his chair and propped his jaw upon his clenched fist. He had not once removed his eyes from Lucas's.

"She does not," he said. "*Wish* to speak with you, that is. She will do so, however. She wishes to inform you that an offer of marriage from you is abhorrent to her and that she will not tolerate hearing it now or anytime in the future. She is of age, however, and quite capable of speaking for herself. Get to your feet, Roath, and pull on the bell rope beside the mantel."

Lucas did as he was bidden.

"I will leave you alone with her," Stratton said after instructing the butler to ask Lady Philippa if she would be so good as to step down to the library. "However, my butler will remain in the hall and I will remove myself only as far as my secretary's office through that adjoining door." He pointed to it. "Any sound of distress from my sister will bring instant assistance through both doors."

He was not even trying to avoid being insulting. Quite the opposite, in fact. But Lucas had a younger sister of his own and knew what it was to be protective of her. When that Jamieson fellow had come to take Jenny for a drive in the park a couple of days ago, Lucas had watched them go after advising the man not to stray from the well-traveled paths. Jenny had even taken him to task for it afterward and reminded him that she was *twenty-three* years old.

Lucas was still on his feet when the door opened again to admit

Lady Philippa Ware, who was dressed simply in a high-waisted, high-necked, long-sleeved dress of pale green, with her hair styled in an equally simple knot at the back of her head. Instead of appearing plain and severe, however, as perhaps she had intended to do, she looked delicate and very, very lovely. He was powerfully reminded of his own elaborate appearance—like a damned Bond Street beau.

Their eyes met. Neither of them smiled.

"Pippa," Stratton said. "The Marquess of Roath wishes to have a word with you. Do you wish to have a word with him?"

"Yes," she said. "Thank you, Dev."

"I will be in the office if you should need me," he said, nodding toward the other door. "Richards will be in the hall."

"Thank you," she said again, and waited until her brother had gone into the study and shut the door behind him before crossing the room and seating herself on the chair he had just vacated.

"Please sit down, Lord Roath," she said.

A veritable storm of conflicting thoughts and emotions had kept Philippa tossing and turning on her bed throughout the night. She would have sworn she had not slept at all if she had not kept remembering bizarre events that had certainly not happened to her waking self. A dozen or more times during the night she had made the definite decision not to see the Marquess of Roath today when he came to Stratton House. And a dozen or more times she had decided that yes, she would. She would put an end to this . . . this *thing* once and for all. She could not think of another word by which to call it. *Obsession*, maybe? But that was far too exaggerated.

She had been horrified to see him again a couple of weeks ago. He had been equally aghast when he had realized who she was and what she had once overheard him say of her. He was the last man on earth she could ever think of marrying, she had told herself repeatedly. Yet she was doing just that. She was the last woman on earth *he* would ever dream of marrying. Yet he was coming to Stratton House on a formal call, presumably to make her an offer.

The autocratic nature of the Duke of Wilby was no excuse for either of them, especially her. They were thinking, reasonably intelligent adults, she and the Marquess of Roath. If he must marry and she wished to marry, there was no reason on earth why it should be to each other. He was extremely eligible, probably more so than any other single gentleman in London this spring. The same might be said of her among the ladies, though there *was* that duke's daughter, Lady Morgan Bedwyn. Why did the Duke of Wilby not insist that he marry *her*? The success of her own debut had assured Philippa that she would almost certainly have marriage offers, some of them eligible, one or two of them—*surely*—attractive to her.

But the marquess was coming to confer with Devlin, to make an offer for her hand—though Dev had suggested that he kill him for her instead. Not quite literally, of course, but as near as he lawfully could. At the very least he had wanted to send the Marquess of Roath on his way with a flea in his ear and perhaps a boot to his backside.

She had told him that no, it would not do. She would not have her brother fight her battles, literally or otherwise. She had a few things of her own to say to Lord Roath before *she* sent him away. She would make it clear to him that he must never come back, never again broach the subject of marriage with her, never deliberately seek her out at any social event they were both attending. And this time she would make it clear that she meant it. If necessary, she would have a similar conversation with the Duke of Wilby. If he felt it imperative that his grandson marry soon, then he must look elsewhere. *She* was not going to marry him, in haste or at leisure.

So there had been her restless night. And there had been the six different dresses she had tried on and rejected after breakfast before fixing upon one she had had for three years and had always considered rather plain even for the country. It was one in which she felt comfortable, however. Hence the fact that it had been packed and brought to town with her. Her maid had looked a bit dubious but had held her tongue after one glance at Philippa's face. She *had* suggested leaving some tendrils of hair loose, though, and curling them becomingly about Lady Philippa's face and along her neck after she had been instructed to confine the hair in a simple knot at the back of her head.

"That would be an *un*simple knot, Madeline," Philippa had told her. "It is not what I asked for."

All the servants, of course, down to the lowliest scullery maid and boot boy, would know that she was in expectation of a marriage offer this morning. They would know too who was to make that offer. How servants found out such things was a mystery, since one never actually saw any of them with an ear pressed to a keyhole.

Mama and Gwyneth and even Stephanie—*ought she not to be in the schoolroom with Miss Field?*—had looked her over critically when she joined them in the morning room.

"I have always loved that dress on you," Stephanie had said, beaming. "It is the perfect color for you, and you absolutely do not need any fussiness to enhance your beauty."

"My mother would agree with you, Steph," Gwyneth had said. "She once observed that Pippa could wear a brown sack and still outshine every other woman in a room. I begin to think she was right."

"But you do have some very smart and pretty new dresses," her mother had said ruefully.

The three of them had returned to their various activities without saying anything more. They must have realized that Philippa was not in the mood to talk. Perhaps they thought she was just nervous. They had looked at her again only when the butler came to ask her to join his lordship in the library.

"Just remember, Pippa," her mother had said, "that no woman is under an obligation to accept the first proposal of marriage that comes her way. Or the second or twenty-second for that matter."

"Go with your heart, Pippa," Gwyneth had said with a radiant smile. "Somehow nothing else seems to work."

Gwyneth had been almost betrothed last year to a Welshman, a rather famous musician, who had seemed suited to her in every possible way. She had broken off the connection in order to marry Devlin. No one doubted that it was a love match on both their parts.

"Pippa will do the right thing," Stephanie had said, closing her book with a snap—it looked like the eight-hundred-page one. She had beamed again at her sister.

Pippa will do the right thing, Philippa thought as she made her way downstairs behind the butler. But *would* she? Perhaps it would help if she knew what the right thing *was*. Well, she *did* know. At least, the sane, rational part of her did. Alas, there were other, more unruly parts of herself that did not react rationally to anything. It was all very confusing. *Go with your heart . . .*

He was dressed with immaculate elegance, she saw as soon as she stepped into the library. He was standing to one side of the fireplace while Devlin was seated at the other side. His dark green tailed coat, surely made by the famous Weston himself, molded his powerful frame. His shirt points beneath it were crisply starched and fashionably high, cupping his cheekbones but not threatening to poke out his eyeballs, as they did on some of the more ridiculous dandies, who took fashion to extremes. His neckcloth had been tied with artistic but not ostentatious precision. Buff breeches hugged his muscled thighs. His boots were of supple black leather and were highly polished. His dark red hair was shining and fashionably disheveled.

Well, she had never doubted that he was perfect to look upon, had she? His outer appearance had nothing to say to anything, however, except that villainy really ought not to look like that.

And then, just a minute or so later, she was alone with him and seated on the chair from which Devlin had just risen. She would not be put at a disadvantage of height, though, and have him looming over her while they talked.

"Please sit down, Lord Roath," she said.

He sat across from her and they gazed at each other. Neither rushed into speech. She was the first to break the silence.

"I loved my father very dearly," she heard herself say. She had not even tried to plan ahead of time what she would say to him. She would have forgotten the thread of any rehearsed speech and got herself all tied up in knots. She had not even been sure she would say *anything* until he did, and then she would merely respond to his lead.

"Yes," he said.

"He always seemed wonderful and perfect to me," she said. "Perhaps all daughters feel that way about their fathers. But everyone appeared to think the same of mine. You have said you did not know him. He was large and handsome and always cheerful and smiling and generous. He was . . . charming, though that is not quite a strong enough word. He drew people to him like a magnet. He talked to everyone. He visited everyone. Not just people of our own class, but *everyone*. He loved to talk and he loved to entertain. It seemed to me that everyone loved him in return. We were a very happy family. We were a happy neighborhood, very largely due to him. I realize that my memories are those of a child and young girl. There are things a child does not see or understand or think about critically. But I believe even the adults of our acquaintance would have largely agreed with me."

"I believe you," he said.

She frowned. "He had a strong sense of duty and responsibility," she said. "He always came here to London in the spring to attend Parliament as a member of the House of Lords. He came even though Mama chose to stay at Ravenswood with us. He often wept as he hugged us all goodbye and wept again with happiness as he hugged us on his return. I never doubted his sincerity. I still do not."

He did not say anything though she paused. His eyes searched her face and she wondered if she was about to dissolve into tears herself. But she would not allow it. Goodness, there was nothing new about this story. She had lived with it all her life.

"And then, when I was fifteen," she said, "he brought a . . . woman with him from London and set her up in a cottage in Boscombe. Oh, not openly, of course. They did not arrive together. She was a supposed widow whose husband, a military man, had been killed in some skirmish in India. She had chosen Boscombe sight unseen because she had heard it was a quiet place where she could do her mourning in peace. Except that she did not dress or behave like a grief-stricken widow. Inevitably the truth came out that she was no random stranger who had arrived out of the blue in our midst. Devlin caught her and my father alone together in a temple pavilion close to our house while a ball for the whole neighborhood was in progress. He made a very public fuss about it. The bubble of our happiness burst, and life changed for all of us in various ways. Even for our neighbors. Ravenswood had always been the center of the universe for people for miles around—or so I believed. It was the focus of numerous grand social events and innumerable more minor ones throughout the year. They all came to an abrupt end. And my brothers went away to war. All except Owen, who went off to school."

She paused for a few moments, her eyes upon her hands in her lap.

"Mama did not collapse outwardly," she continued when he said nothing. "But she did suffer some sort of emotional . . . shutdown, if there is such a word. Like a candle being snuffed. My father was no longer perfect in my eyes. He was human. He was flawed. I was fifteen and ought to have been old enough to realize that even before the great collapse. But I did not. I was still living in the dream world of happy children who have not yet been nudged out of the nest to experience the harsher realities of life."

"I know just what you mean," he said.

Did he? Was not the process of growing up and maturing far more gradual and therefore far more gentle for most people?

"Then, a few years later, he died," she said. "Suddenly. Of a heart seizure. It happened at the village tavern, which added a horrible element of farce to the whole tragedy. I had never stopped loving him, Lord Roath, though I had been dreadfully disillusioned when I was confronted with his flaws. I still have not stopped. I loved him and I love him."

"That is the hard part, is it not?" he said. "Even while one hates with a terrible intensity, sometimes one comes to realize that hate and love are just two sides of the same coin. Hatred is impossible to sustain. For love is more powerful. And more enduring."

She gazed mutely at him. How did he *know* that? How was it he understood?

"I did hate him for what he had done to our family," she said. "Mama blamed Devlin for making such a public scene over Papa and his mistress when he caught them together. She told him—Devlin, that is—to go away. That was why he went, and Ben went with him for reasons of his own. They were gone for six years. I hated Papa for what he had done to my mother, for it was clear she had always *known* and had lived with the knowledge that she had a faithless husband. I hated him—selfishly—for what he had done to *me*. I was fifteen years old and bubbling over with happy dreams of parties and balls and beaux in the near future. But the dreams all faded away in one single night. I hated him. As time went on, though, I could not keep on hating. You are right. He was the same person I had known and adored all my life. The only change was that my eyes had been opened to his imperfections. For the last three years of his life I saw him as he was. I did not like everything I saw, but there were other things . . . He was still my father. He was still warm with affection for us and for everyone else, and . . . Well." She shrugged.

"I am sorry," he said. He held up a staying hand when she drew breath to speak again. "I am sorry you had to suffer that way. I am sorry you had to grow up so abruptly."

"Did you come here this morning to make me a marriage offer, Lord Roath?" she asked him.

He sighed audibly. "I was not sure of the answer to that question even as I was knocking upon the door," he said. "I came because my grandfather had arranged it—*without my knowledge*—and the Earl of Stratton had agreed to it. It would have been a terrible discourtesy to both of them—and to you—if I had refused to come. I did not know if your brother was aware of what once happened between you and me. I did not know if I would tell him if he was not. I rather thought I might, though I was not sure. It occurred to me that if you had kept it secret from everyone all these years, you might wish it to remain that way. If Stratton *did* know, as it turned out he did, then I did not know what to expect. I did not know if I would be given the chance to speak to you. I was certainly not sure either way that I would make you an offer if I were given the chance. In other words, Lady Philippa, my mind was abuzz with contradictory thoughts as I came here this morning. There was one thing I knew with absolute certainty, however. If I had the opportunity at least to speak with you, I was going to tell you a story I have never told a living soul before and believed I never would."

They gazed at each other. His face looked pale and troubled. Philippa wondered if hers looked similar.

"About my father?" she asked.

He nodded. "About your father."

CHAPTER FOURTEEN

Lucas's thoughts touched upon his grandparents, who at this very moment were probably imagining that he had worked out an amicable marriage settlement with Stratton, shaken him by the hand, and made his offer to Lady Philippa herself, complete with bended knee and lavish floral bouquet. Despite his warnings to the contrary, they were probably convinced that all was now smiles and celebration at Stratton House. They would be persuading themselves and each other that they were not at all anxious or impatient as they awaited his return.

It would seem extremely unlikely, to his grandfather at least, that she might actually refuse him. It would seem impossible that he would not even make an offer.

But here they were, he and Lady Philippa Ware, seated on opposite sides of the fireplace with its unlit coals, as unloverlike as any two people could be, frowning at each other. *Not* in anger, it was true. But frowning nonetheless.

And he realized, even more than he had before, the enormity of what he had done. Those words he had spoken, which would have been cruel and hurtful at any time, had destroyed what had already been fragile and extremely vulnerable—her belief in any possibility of a happy future.

After he had told her his story, he was going to feel that he was suspended over an abyss, just waiting for the inevitable drop. Silence on the matter had become a part of his very being for the past eleven years. Now he must break that silence. He owed her that much. *Her* and no one else. But what she did with the knowledge, as he had told her brother, would be up to her. He could not— *would* not—force an oath of silence upon her.

"I was fourteen years old," he said, "and on holiday from school. It was late summer, but we were not having summer weather. The sky was heavy with gray clouds, the wind was blowing, it was raining—mostly drizzle rather than heavy stuff. It was chilly and downright miserable and had been that way for several days. I had gone to the study at Amberwell to read, but I knew there was no fire in there. I had brought a big pillow and a blanket from my room and made a warm nest for myself on the wide sill of one of the windows and made sure there was no gap between the curtains after I had settled there. The curtains were always kept drawn in that room because it was south facing and sunlight would damage the books on their shelves. When I heard someone come into the room after a while, I stayed very quiet in the hope that whoever it was would choose a book or find what else they needed and leave. There *was* a fire in the drawing room. But it was actually two people, I soon realized—my mother and father."

He paused for a moment at the sound of voices in the hall beyond the door, but silence was restored within a few moments and no one came to disturb them.

"I kept quiet anyway," he said, "for I knew that if I revealed my hiding place, they would accuse me of being antisocial and send me to find my sisters. For the past twelve years I have bitterly regretted that I did *not* reveal myself. Within minutes it was impossible to do so."

"Being an eavesdropper rarely turns out well, I suspect," Lady Philippa said softly. She was thinking, no doubt, of the evening in that barn, when she had very probably been trying to overhear what he and the other men were saying some distance away from where the women were gathered.

"The doctor had been to the house to see my mother," he said. "It was at my father's insistence because she had been unwell for some time, though she had kept insisting there was nothing wrong with her. *'So,'* my father said within moments of my hearing the library door close. *'You are with child. And are showing it already. The doctor's considered opinion is that you are four months along.' 'Yes,'* she said. She did not sound thrilled. Neither did he. I was simply open-mouthed with shock. Jenny was already eleven. Like boys everywhere, I suppose, I thought of my parents as old and past anything as embarrassing as the sort of activity that produced babies. Pardon me for such plain speaking. It was a bit horrifying to think of my mother having another child at her age. She was not far off forty. I can remember wondering how I would tell my friends at school, or if I would tell them at all. If only that personal embarrassment had been the worst of it."

Lady Philippa had moved back in her chair. Her hands were gripping the arms, though not to the extent of turning her knuckles white.

"It is strange," he said, "how some words spoken years ago can be seared upon one's memory while others spoken yesterday are already forgotten."

"Yes," she said.

"My father spoke one word: *'April.'* My mother spoke six: *'It must have happened in March.'* But it could not have happened in March, my father pointed out. She had had her courses the week before she left for London. I beg your pardon again for speaking so bluntly. At the time I did not even know what he was talking about. And then he went on to remind her that she had gone to London without him at the invitation of a cousin whose home was in Scotland but who was making a rare visit to town for the six weeks following Easter. It was the middle of May before my father went there himself."

He watched Lady Philippa stretch her fingers before they gripped the arms of the chair again.

"There was a horrible quarrel," he said, "while I battled with the almost overpowering urge to sneeze. I have probably forgotten most of what was said, though I remember the gist of it all too well. My father stated the obvious conclusion—that the child my mother was expecting was not his. She denied the accusation over and over but finally gave in and turned to defiance. What was he going to do about it? She sounded frightened as well as angry when she asked the question. My father sounded like a dead man. He demanded to know who the father was. It seemed for a while that she would hold out and refuse to tell him. But she did in the end."

"My father," Lady Philippa Ware said. Her face was chalk white. Her lips looked almost blue in contrast.

"Yes," he said.

She closed her eyes and swayed. He got to his feet to go to her.

"No!" she said sharply, holding up one hand, palm out. "I will be fine."

He sat down and waited for her to open her eyes again and gaze across the space between them and into his own eyes.

"I have always . . . consoled myself," she said, "with the belief that at least he amused himself with women whose profession it was to give pleasure and be very well paid in exchange. Though even that was scant comfort, for I daresay many if not most of those women are forced into what they do by penury or other dire circumstances. But at least I believed he had never destroyed another family as he had ours."

"Stratton," he said. "The name became synonymous to me with all that is irredeemably evil. I would have killed him if I had ever come face-to-face with him—or so I believed as a fourteen-year-old boy. In reality, of course, I would have done no such thing, just as my father did not kill him or even confront him with his perfidy. At least, there was never any evidence that he did so. It seemed like cowardice to my boyhood self, but as I grew older I came to understand the hopeless complexity of his dilemma. He had two possible courses of action. He could denounce my mother, disown her child, put her away from him and us, perhaps even divorce her, and thus destroy our family and bring terrible and lasting scandal and suffering upon us all. Or he could keep his knowledge to himself, pretend he did not know, continue with his marriage, and accept the new child as his own. It was a choice made more terrible, I am sure, by the knowledge that if the child were a boy, he would be the spare to the heir—to myself, that is—that my father and my grandfather had always craved. We are all brought up to believe that we ought always to speak the truth openly to the world and do what is right and just, even when it is painful to do so. When we grow up, though, we quickly learn that concealing the truth and doing nothing is sometimes the wiser option to avoid a devastating impact upon other, innocent people."

"Yes," she said. "I know."

And he realized, too late, that she did indeed know. According to her story, her brother had spoken the truth about their father and his paramour and done it publicly before everyone in their family and neighborhood, whereas their mother had kept it to herself for years before that. Who had been right and who wrong? There was no obvious answer, was there?

"My mother went into labor prematurely a few months later," he said, "and gave birth to a stillborn son. She died herself a few hours later. My father's grief was profound and doubtless many layers deep. Less than a year later, when I was still only fifteen, he set his horse's head at a hedge that was far too high and wide and unnecessary. There was an open gate a mere few yards away. His horse had to be put down, and he broke his neck and died instantly. I would not say it was deliberately done, but I do believe he had grown reckless and did not care what happened to him—or us. Our world changed, Lady Philippa, just as yours did at the same age."

Her hands were now clasped tightly in her lap and she was gazing down at them. He watched as one tear fell onto the back of one hand. She brushed it away with a finger of the other. A short while later another tear fell, though she was not openly weeping.

"My brother and yours," she said so softly that he scarcely heard. She was referring to his mother's dead child, he realized. His mother's and Stratton's.

"Yes," he said. "My hatred was for your father alone, Lady Philippa, though I realize that in all probability my mother was equally to blame. I doubt he forced her. What I said of you that night was totally unconsidered and untrue and wicked. But I understand why you can never marry me anyway—especially now, after hearing my story. You will understand why I can never marry you. But let us . . . Please let us not hate each other."

Another tear plopped onto her hand.

Lucas got abruptly to his feet, strode across in front of the fireplace, grasped her upper arms, and half lifted her to her feet and into his arms. He held her close, his cheek against the top of her head, feeling her slim, supple warmth as she collapsed against him and her arms came about his waist. He closed his eyes, concentrating upon giving her comfort even as he realized it was impossible. He drew comfort, however, from the way she arched into him when she might well have shrunk away from him.

She did not weep, but for a long while she rested the side of her face against his neckcloth, no doubt crushing the folds upon which his valet had expended such care a few hours ago. She kept her arms about him. She sighed at last, deeply and audibly, and tipped back her head to look into his face. Her own was still pale. Her eyes were large and as blue as an early summer sky.

He lowered his head and kissed her.

He was not without experience. His years at Oxford had provided him with a valuable education in both academics and sexual matters. He had kissed a number of women and bedded a few. Compared with most men his age, though, he did not doubt he was a veritable novice. He had never kissed a woman with less experience than he had. Nevertheless . . .

He thought it altogether possible that Lady Philippa Ware had never been kissed before. Her lips pouted and then trembled and then relaxed against his own. When he parted his lips, she allowed her own to part too. But it was all wrong, he thought after a few self-indulgent moments. She ought not to be stuck with the memory that her first kiss had been with him of all people. It was happening nevertheless. A kiss of comfort. A kiss of hopeless longing—on his part anyway. Of unwilling affection. A kiss he must not prolong.

He raised his head. "Phil."

Those blue eyes gazed into his again. "You must not fear that I will tell anyone else," she said. "Ever."

"Thank you," he said, though he realized that she would surely wish to keep his secret as much for her own family's sake as for his.

There was a brisk knock upon the inner door of the library at that moment, and it opened abruptly before they could move apart.

"Ah," Stratton said curtly. "I am to wish you happy, then, am I?"

Lady Philippa removed her arms from about his waist, and he dropped his own arms to his sides as he turned to face the door.

"Not yet, Dev," she said. "And perhaps never."

Stratton's eyes, as hard as granite, moved to Lucas.

"We have agreed that it is too soon," Lucas said. "For me to ask. For Lady Philippa to answer."

Which was not strictly accurate, but it was all he was prepared to say.

"You have taken the devil of a long time to come to that conclusion," Stratton said. "I beg your pardon for my language, Pippa."

"Yes," Lucas said. "It did. It took a long time because it *needed* a long time." He suddenly noticed the rose lying in its packaging on the table next to where he had been sitting and picked it up rather than allow it to be found by someone after he left. "Please accept this, Lady Philippa. My grandfather suggested a dozen red roses times two, on the assumption that you might be so impressed you would not even consider refusing my offer."

She came close to smiling as she took the package from his hand and peeped in at the peach rosebud.

"Thank you," she said. "A single rose need never be multiplied. Indeed, it *ought* not. It is perfection in itself."

He bowed to her and inclined his head to Stratton, who looked back at him with a hard, unreadable expression.

"I thank you for allowing me this time with your sister," Lucas said to Stratton. "And I thank you for listening to me, Lady Philippa. I will take no more of your time."

And he strode from the room and from the house rather as though he had the hounds of hell on his heels. Though no doubt there were a couple more of them awaiting him at Arden House.

W hat am I missing?" Devlin asked after the door had closed behind the Marquess of Roath. He frowned at Philippa in obvious perplexity as she folded back the paper from her rose and breathed in its sweet perfume.

She looked up at him and smiled ruefully. "He explained to me," she said. "He told me the story behind those words he spoke, never intending to speak them aloud, never meaning to be overheard. It is a story he had never told before and one I will never repeat. I am sorry, Dev, for you listened to *my* story last year, and you made all the difference in my life. I would not be here now if you had not listened and comforted me and given me the courage to claim my life back. But I cannot share this."

"All is forgiven, then?" he asked. "When he wrecked your life for years at a very crucial time for you? Merely because he told you a story?"

"Y-yes," she said. "All is forgiven. But that does not mean I will ever marry him. It does not mean that he will ever wish to marry me. That is all in the head of the Duke of Wilby, who came to London to see his grandson and heir married to someone eminently eligible and met me almost at the very moment of his arrival. I was sitting at the table in the breakfast parlor at Arden House with his family members and Steph. And with the Marquess of Roath, of course. My presence there must have seemed like fate to the duchess and him."

"But not to you?" he said.

"No," she told him. "And not to the marquess either."

"What are you going to tell Mama and Steph and Gwyneth?"

he asked, raising his eyes to the ceiling and the drawing room above them.

"That he came here to talk to me rather than to offer me marriage," she said. "That we did talk, quite amicably, but that we agreed we are not ready to marry each other and perhaps—probably—never will be. I have been in London for only a very short while, Dev. I have just begun to mingle with the *ton* and meet people. I have met several single gentlemen I like and who I think may like me. I believe it would be a mistake to try to press the issue of marrying anyone too soon, however—assuming two or three of them have enough interest to court me seriously, that is. I may be twenty-two, but I am not *desperate*. I will explain everything when I go upstairs. Shall we go? They must be in suspense."

But he did not immediately move toward the door. He had still not stopped frowning. "Pippa," he said. "Was he *kissing* you?"

She sighed. "And I was kissing him," she said. "Dev, it is complicated. *Life* is complicated. We do not hate each other."

"One more question, then," he said. "Do you *love* each other?"

She laughed and sniffed her rose again. "Well, that I *can* answer," she said. "Absolutely, unequivocally *not*."

The lady doth protest too much. Where had she read those words or some very like them?

He went ahead of her to open the door and hold it for her. He was *still* frowning.

"I think I should just have killed him and been done with it," he said as she passed him.

So let me be clear on this," the Duke of Wilby said with an ominous calm of voice that was starkly contradicted by his nearly purple face. "I went to all the trouble of inviting Stratton, a man with whom I had no previous acquaintance, to join me for luncheon at the House. I condescended to make clear to him that a marriage between his sister and my grandson, an eligible and advantageous connection for both of them, would have my blessing and that of Her Grace. He was good enough to indicate his approval of the proposed match by inviting you to wait upon him at Stratton House at an appointed hour this morning. The idea was that you would discuss a marriage contract with him and then make a formal offer to Lady Philippa Ware herself. I am correct so far, I believe? Set me right if I am wrong. I am an old man with an old brain and a memory that is perhaps playing tricks on me."

He paused for someone to answer. There were only three of them in the vast drawing room at Arden House, the duke and duchess seated like bookends on either side of the fireplace, and Lucas himself. Her Grace clearly felt no need to assure the duke that he was not falling into senility. Obviously she had learned a thing or two about rhetorical questions in her many years with Grandpapa.

"You are correct, Grandpapa," Lucas said—and there was no point in continuing with a sentence that would begin with the word *but*. He had already explained himself perfectly clearly.

"A woman of great beauty and charm and impeccable lineage," his grandfather continued. Lucas was standing, like a schoolboy hauled before the headmaster for a tongue-lashing preceding a caning. "A woman moreover who bestows the warmest of her smiles upon you whenever you are in company together. Yet *you did not ask her to marry you?*"

There was no more wrong with his grandfather's hearing, Lucas thought, than there was with his mind. He had already told his grandparents that he and the Earl of Stratton had not discussed a marriage contract but had talked of other things, and that he had not offered marriage to Lady Philippa but had talked of other things with her too. Admittedly, it must all seem very vague. If not odd.

"I did not," he said. "She has no wish to marry me, and I will not embarrass or harass her by forcing the question upon her. Unlike me, Grandpapa, Lady Philippa Ware feels no great urgency to marry the first man who asks her."

"Were you the first, Luc?" his grandmother asked.

"Of course he was not," the duke barked. *"He did not even ask her."*

"Do remember what the physician warned you about being too excitable, Percy," Her Grace said. "And do not allow yourself to get even more so now by jumping down my throat, which I see you are about to do. Remember that it is I who would be left behind if you were to bring a heart seizure and a premature demise upon yourself. I have always told you I wish to be the first to go."

Lucas closed his eyes briefly. His grandfather drummed his fingers on the arms of his chair but did not explode into further wrath. He gazed broodingly at the duchess instead.

"What did you talk with her about?" he asked, addressing Lucas though he was not looking at him. "Did she say specifically that she will not marry you? It seems hard to believe if you did not even ask her. Did she say what it is about you to which she is averse? How could any woman in her right mind say no to you?"

"Perhaps, Percy," Her Grace said, "she has an attachment to someone else."

"If she does," he said, "her brother certainly knows nothing of it."

"She has waited a long time for a Season in London," Lucas said. "At first she was held back by the death of her father. Then, just when her family was coming out of mourning for him, her grandmother died. She is here at last, and she is attracting a great deal of admiring attention. She cannot be blamed for wanting to enjoy herself for a while and for choosing to take her time before she favors one potential suitor over all others. You do not wish me to delay in my choice, Grandpapa. If I am as eligible as you say I am, then there must be plenty of other ladies who *would* welcome my addresses. I have been invited by Lady Abingdon to join an evening party to Vauxhall next week. I have not yet sent an answer."

"I will arrange for a few more introductions," Her Grace said. "Jenny and Kitty will be disappointed."

There was nothing to say to that. Lucas did not even attempt an answer.

"Did you take roses?" his grandfather asked abruptly, apparently unwilling to let go of the idea of Lady Philippa Ware as his grandson's bride.

"She called it perfect," Lucas said.

"It?" His grandfather picked up immediately on the singular pronoun and looked at his grandson with a frown. *"It?"*

"A single rosebud," Lucas said. "Peach. Her favorite color."

"A single rosebud," Her Grace said. "How very romantic."

"Hmph," His Grace said.

"Are you quite, quite sure you have no feelings for her, Luc?" his grandmother asked.

Ah, but he had never said he had no feelings for her. His emotions were still feeling raw from that kiss. A laughably *chaste* kiss. But it had shaken him to the roots of his being. For he had tasted beauty and sweetness and had felt a yearning deep in his very bones, or perhaps in his *soul*, that he did not know quite how he was going to shake off. It was the irony of ironies, perhaps, that he had fallen hard for the very woman he had once insulted quite unforgivably.

Perhaps this was a just punishment, this feeling he would describe as emptiness if only it were not so very painful.

"I like her sufficiently, Grandmama," he said carefully, "to choose not to pester her and risk distressing her."

"Ah," she said, and smiled rather sadly at him.

"You had better go break the news to Jenny and Kitty," his grandfather told him.

He supposed, Lucas thought as he left the room and closed the door behind him, that at least part of the heavy depression he was feeling was caused by the fact that he had told the story of what had happened twelve years ago for the first time and, he fervently hoped, the last time. It was all fresh in his mind again, as though it had happened yesterday. Except that then he had been a boy of fourteen and now he was a man of twenty-six. He had been little more than a child and quite unequipped to handle the enormity of what he had overheard. Pure emotion had overcome his judgment, and all the blame had been heaped upon Stratton. *Stratton. Satan.* The names had become interchangeable in his mind so that even eight years or so later he had believed that the children of Stratton must be the spawn of Satan, or at least *soiled goods.*

She—Lady Philippa Ware, that was—had been the victim of her father's promiscuity just as much as he had. The man had actually taken a mistress home to the country with him one summer, titillated, no doubt, by the danger involved, hoping to get away with it. He had brought disaster and humiliation upon his family instead. Lady Philippa had suffered. And then, just perhaps when she was recovering her spirits and her hopes for the future, along had come the Marquess of Roath—*himself,* that was—and with a few ill-chosen words, which ought never to have been spoken aloud even if he had thought them, had destroyed any vestiges that had remained to her of confidence in herself and her own worth. And then the final blow—the sudden death of her father.

Lucas knew just how *that* felt.

His own part in her tragedy was all too terrible to bear. But bear it he must. And he must do the only thing he *could* to atone. He must stay away from her.

Yet that had not been an unrequited kiss. Inexperienced though she undoubtedly was, she had very definitely kissed him back.

He paused outside his sister's sitting room and then resolutely opened the door and stepped inside.

"Well?" Aunt Kitty asked, her hands clasped to her bosom.

CHAPTER FIFTEEN

I t had not seemed possible to Philippa during the first couple of
weeks of her come-out Season that her life could be any busier
than it already was. She was wrong. Entertainments multiplied and
were presented on a far grander scale as the stragglers of the *ton*
came to town at last and settled in. A pile of invitations was delivered daily to Stratton House by the morning post, addressed now
to the earl and countess as well as to his mother and sister. More
were delivered by hand later in the day. Sometimes it was difficult
to decide which should be accepted and which refused—with re-
grets. It was hard to decide how many could reasonably be fit into
each day. There was little time left over for simple relaxation or for
ordinary daily activities like letter writing and leisure reading and
even just family conversations. Sometimes there was too little time
even for sleep since balls and even many parties continued long into
the night and sometimes intruded upon the dawn.

Philippa attended everything she could, sometimes with her
mother, sometimes with Gwyneth and Devlin, a few times with

one of her cousins or a newly made friend. She often went for a drive in Hyde Park at the fashionable hour with one of the young men who vied for the privilege of being seen there with her. For she had apparently become all the rage, if that was the correct term. She attracted men about her, Uncle George had commented when he came to dine one evening, as a flower bed attracts bees. Her dance card at balls almost always filled up before the start of the second set, sometimes sooner.

There was even the morning when a gentleman with whom she had danced and conversed several times presented himself at Stratton House, requested a private word with Devlin, and then stammered out a marriage proposal to *her*. She was taken totally by surprise, since he had given no indication that his interest in her was amorous or that his intentions were serious. She felt quite dreadful as she refused his offer as tactfully as she could and vowed to herself that she would be more careful in the future.

"*Careful*, Pippa?" Gwyneth said when she reported back to the family. "Can you possibly make yourself less beautiful? Or less sweet and charming? And let me add that I have *never* seen you either flirt or encourage any man to believe that you harbor tender feelings for him."

Apart from that one rather upsetting incident—for he was a very likable gentleman—Philippa was enjoying herself enormously. She never had to fear being a wallflower at a ball or finding herself standing alone at a party. She had women friends and men friends, some of whom liked to sigh soulfully over her and pay her lavish compliments, but she did not take them seriously—not, at least, until after that painful proposal. There was no one with whom she felt she could fall in love and no one she could imagine herself marrying. She doubted she would ever accept a marriage offer unless she could feel something more than just affection and respect for the man concerned. Her favorites were Sir Gerald Emmett and Lord Edward Denton, the tall, cheerful, rather gangly fourth son of a duke, to whom her uncle had introduced her at Almack's on her first visit there. She felt quite sure that neither man was really angling for a wife, but both consistently singled her out for attention, were easy conversationalists, and had a good sense of humor. Perhaps they both enjoyed her company because they sensed that she was not angling for a husband.

She saw the Marquess of Roath quite frequently. How could she not? Though they did not always attend the same entertainments, very often they did. Sometimes they came close enough to each other to exchange pleasantries. But there was never more than that, and Philippa was glad of it. It would become easier as time went on, she told herself, to look upon him with no stronger emotion than she felt for any number of men to whom she had been introduced and with whom she had danced or conversed a time or two. It was not happening yet, but she enjoined patience upon herself.

Her mother, Stephanie, and Gwyneth had all quizzed her on that day of the nonproposal, after she had given them a very vague account of her interview with the marquess. They had all been disappointed and a bit puzzled, for apparently Lord Roath seemed perfect to all of them. With his good looks and charm of manner, of course, that was not really surprising. But after she had told them, with a slight bending of the truth, that she had said a very definite no and that he had seemed disinclined to press the issue, they had said no more. Lady Catherine Emmett and Jenny had also been kind and tactful.

Both had told her they had been very much hoping she and Luc would make a match of it, but neither had belabored the point. Perhaps he had asked them not to?

———————

A couple of weeks after the Marquess of Roath's infamous visit to Stratton House, Philippa went to a garden party in Richmond with her mother. Devlin and Gwyneth were taking Stephanie to Kew Gardens, specifically to see the pagoda there.

It was a beautiful day. The long stretch of lawn between the house and the river Thames had been carefully scythed to look almost like a bowling green. The numerous flower beds were ablaze with color. The water was blue and calm so that all but the most skittish were eager to take a turn rowing or being rowed in one of six small boats. Comfortable chairs were set in groupings out on the grass and along the riverbank for the comfort of those who wished to relax while soaking up the heat of the sun. On the paved terrace outside the house, long tables covered with crisply starched white cloths were laden with a wide variety of savory and sweet foods and beverages both hot and cold. Small tables had been arranged on either end of the terrace for the convenience of those who preferred to sit in the shade as they took refreshments.

Philippa did not remain for long with her mother, who was whisked away by friends to view the flowers. Philippa meanwhile was borne off for an early turn on the river with Lord Edward Denton. She walked through the hothouses with another of her admirers afterward and conversed for a while with a lively group of young people, with all of whom she had an acquaintance. She was beginning to feel, in fact, that she knew almost everyone who frequented *ton* events, even if only by sight. She was starting to find it easier to put names to faces and sometimes given and family names to their accompanying titles. She had a sense of belonging, and she liked it.

She went to talk with Jenny and her sister and aunt. They were sitting on the lawn, alone together for the moment, Viscount May-berry and Mr. Jamieson, who had been with them a few minutes before, having wandered away together.

"The grass is remarkably smooth underfoot," Philippa said after greeting the three ladies. "I do not believe the wheels of your chair would get stuck on it, Jenny. Shall we go for a stroll?"

"Perhaps," Lady Catherine suggested, "we should hail one of the men to push the chair."

"I believe I can manage," Philippa assured her. "And there are plenty of men upon whom to call if we should need help."

"Oh, yes, please, Pippa," Jenny said eagerly. "I would love to go down by the water's edge. There is a footpath there. That will be easier for you."

They walked and talked and stopped to exchange greetings with other guests for all of half an hour before agreeing that they were hungry and thirsty and in need of the shade the terrace of-fered. But there was no empty table there, alas. There was one with only two occupants, however, an elderly couple, who both raised an arm to attract their attention and point to the empty places.

"Grandmama and Grandpapa," Jenny said. "They told Aunt Kitty they might come later, but I did not see them arrive. I am amazed that they do not find all the socializing they do a drain upon their energies."

"I shall wheel you up to the table," Philippa said, "and then go to—"

"Oh, please do not," Jenny said, interrupting. "They will be hurt. Though perhaps you—"

"—fetch us some food," Philippa said, completing her sentence, though not in quite the way she had planned.

She had managed to avoid the Duke and Duchess of Wilby since their grandson called upon her at Stratton House, though she had glimpsed one or both of them from a distance a few times. She did not know how they felt about her. The duke had arranged a formal marriage offer for his grandson to make her and had almost without a doubt expected that she would accept it. It must have been a severe blow to his pride that she had not. She wondered if the marquess had admitted that he had not even made the offer.

"Lady Philippa," the duke said, getting gallantly to his feet in order to draw out a chair for her. "Do please give Her Grace and me the pleasure of your company."

The duchess was patting Jenny's hand. "Yes, do, Lady Philippa," she said, indicating the chair.

"I will go and fetch a plate of food for the table before I sit," she said. "Would you like tea or—"

"You will do no such thing," the duke said. "That is what we brought Luc for."

And sure enough, Philippa saw when she turned her head sharply in the direction of the food tables, he was on his way back with a tray bearing plates of food and cups of tea.

She sat. It was too late now to insist upon moving away. Her reason for doing so would be too obvious.

"Lady Philippa?" the Marquess of Roath said by way of greeting. "Jenny? Are you having a good afternoon?"

"I certainly am," his sister said. "Pippa and I have been down by the river. It is lovely there. Very peaceful despite all the people."

"Yes, I saw you," he said. "Grandpapa wanted me to dash down there to push your chair. But Lady Philippa did not look close to collapse, and no doubt I would have inhibited your conversation if I had joined you. I shall go and fetch more food. Tea to accompany it? Or lemonade?"

"Tea, please," Philippa said.

"Lemonade, please, Luc," Jenny said.

And of course, Philippa thought, he would join them at the table. There was, after all, still one spare chair. She had seen him a few times in the past few weeks with other women—dancing with them at balls, strolling arm in arm with them at various parties, driving them in the park. Miss Thorpe, Lord and Lady Abingdon's daughter, seemed a particular favorite, her mother always hovering close by, a look of complacency upon her face. Surely his grandfather was pressing upon him a match with one of those ladies since *she* had put herself firmly out of the running.

"And so you are enjoying your first Season, Lady Philippa," the duchess said, smiling upon her with what seemed like genuine warmth.

"I am," Philippa said as Lord Roath returned with food and drink for her and Jenny. "I have made the acquaintance of many interesting people and have even made a few lifelong friends, I believe."

"Of whom I am one, I hope," Jenny said, laughing. "Indeed, I insist upon it."

"Of whom you are one," Philippa said. She wished it were not so. It would be very much easier to remain at a distance from three of the people at this table if she did not have a friendship with Jenny and if her mother were not so close to Lady Catherine Emmett. They were sitting together now out on the lawn with Lord and Lady Mayberry and Uncle George.

"You have a brother out in northern Europe somewhere with Wellington's forces," the duke said abruptly. "A cavalry major?"

Her laughter died. "I do," she said. "Nicholas. And war, or at least one more battle, seems inevitable. He almost died in the Peninsula. Devlin believes he would certainly have done so if Ben, our older brother, had not gone to him and bullied the medical people and coaxed him into living. I daresay he was wounded other times too without telling us. Devlin did not tell us about his own wound, which almost took his head off and left him with a permanent facial scar. I beg your pardon. I ought not to talk of such matters."

"I am the one who introduced the topic," the duke said. "You seem to be a close family. It must have been a great blow to you when your father died young. It was sudden, I understand?"

"Yes," she said without glancing Lord Roath's way. "It was devastating for us all."

"He was a jovial fellow," His Grace said. "Well liked."

The Marquess of Roath really had kept his secret very close, Philippa thought. His grandfather obviously had no inkling of what havoc her father had wreaked upon his own family.

"And your mama," the duchess added, glancing across the lawn in her direction. "She is still a very beautiful woman, Lady Philippa. Time has been kind to her despite the heartbreaking loss of your father."

"I have come to realize that having to endure loss is an unavoidable part of living," Philippa said. "But how lovely it is to be alive on a day like today and in such beautiful surroundings."

"It is indeed," the duchess agreed.

"Have you been out on the river, Lady Philippa?" the duchess asked after a while.

"I have," she said. "It was almost the first thing I did upon my arrival earlier. Lord Edward Denton was obliging enough to take me out in one of the boats."

"And you, Jenny?" her grandfather asked.

"Oh no, Grandpapa," she said. "Mr. Jamieson did offer to take me, but I declined."

"Because you were afraid he would drop you in the water?" the marquess asked.

"That was part of it," she admitted. "I also chose not to make a spectacle of myself before so many people, or him."

"Do you trust me?" he asked.

"To take me rowing in a boat?" she said, grimacing and then laughing. "I do not know. Do I, Luc?"

"You do," he said, tossing his napkin onto the table beside his plate and getting to his feet. "With your life. If I drop you in while lifting you from your chair to a boat and you sink like a stone, I shall dive down and haul you up even though doing so will cause the ruin of one of my favorite coats."

"We are not really going out there, are we?" she asked. "What if—"

"What if you trust your favorite brother?" he asked her, drawing her chair back clear of the table before turning it.

"As far as I recall, Luc," she said, "you are my *only* brother."

"Get someone to hold the boat steady for you while you lift her in," the duke advised. "And again while you lift her out."

"Do be careful, Luc," the duchess advised. "Boats have a habit of *wobbling.*"

"So do I when I am standing in them," Lord Roath said, winking at her and waggling his eyebrows and looking suddenly boyish. And very handsome.

Jenny was laughing helplessly as he wheeled her away.

Philippa made to get to her feet, but the duke set a hand on her wrist.

"Stay awhile if you will," he said. "Keep an old couple company for a few more minutes."

Philippa settled back into her seat and looked warily from one to the other of them. It sounded like a bit of a pathetic request, but she doubted it was any such thing.

"Tell me, Lady Philippa," the duke began. "Was it something he said? Or did? Like bringing you a single rose when I had advised at least two dozen? All of them *red?*"

He could not possibly believe she had rejected a marriage offer for such a trivial reason, of course. But both he and the duchess were looking intently at her.

"You very kindly gave me your blessing when you spoke with my brother at the House of Lords and arranged to send the Marquess of Roath to call upon him to discuss a marriage contract," she said. "Believe me, please, Your Grace, when I say I was touched and honored. I know he is the only heir of your direct line and is therefore very precious to you. I have seen also that you are very fond of him. But I am differently situated. I am not ready yet to think of marriage."

"I believe you must be lying to me," he said with what sounded like a sorrowful sort of gentleness. "Why else does a young woman come to town in the springtime? Especially when she is several years past her days in the schoolroom. Young men like to sow a few wild oats before they settle down. Young women wish to establish themselves far sooner as wives and mothers and heads of their own households."

"You generalize, Percy," the duchess said.

"I do," he admitted. "Generalities are largely true, though, are they not? I look at my grandson through partial eyes, Lady Philippa. Even so, I believe he is a more than normally attractive prize for any young lady currently on the market. I have seen you waltz with him and look upon him as though you were attracted to him. I have seen him waltz with you and look at least equally attracted. He came to town this spring knowing that his duty is to choose a bride and marry her—even though he is only twenty-six, on the young side for a man. For several reasons you are far and away the most eligible, most obvious choice for him. As I see it, from the outside looking in, a match between you and Luc might even have the supreme attraction of being a love match. Am I way off the mark?"

"We agreed not to harass the poor lady, Percy," the duchess said.

"Harass?" His bushy eyebrows met across the bridge of his nose as he frowned at her. "Always that word. Is it harassing a young woman to plead with her to explain why she will not be my granddaughter?"

Was he deliberately attempting to make her break down in sentimental tears? Philippa did not suppose so, but she suspected he was a wily old man. If he could not get his way by one method, then he would try another. But she had a feeling deep down that he was sincerely puzzled and upset. So was *she.* There were other women, of equal or similar rank to her own, who would be only too happy to receive the Marquess of Roath's addresses. A few of them were here this afternoon. Why was the duke still so interested in *her?*

"Come, my dear," the duchess said, patting Philippa's hand, onto which a tear had just dropped, she realized with some mortification. "Walk with us to join Kitty and your mama out in the sunshine. It is a pity to waste it, is it not, when it may rain tomorrow?"

She linked an arm through Philippa's as they walked, though she did not lean upon it. She remarked upon the flowers and the sun sparkling on the river. The duke walked on Philippa's other side, his hands clasped behind his back. He did not sit, though, when they came up to her mother and Lady Catherine, though there were empty chairs and Uncle George Greenfield got to his feet to draw one closer for the duchess. Lord and Lady Mayberry had gone down to the river to watch Jenny have her boat ride, Lady Catherine told them.

"I will go and watch too," His Grace said, "if Lady Philippa will be kind enough to offer me her arm."

She offered it. What choice did she have?

"I do not intend to lean heavily upon you," he told her as they walked away together. "But the lawn slopes downward very slightly, if you have noticed, and I would hate to find myself breaking into a gallop and running right into the water. Someone would have to fish me out and ruin his boots."

Philippa laughed.

"I must beg your pardon if you were given the impression that I was . . . *harassing* you at the tea table, Lady Philippa," he said. "That was not my intention."

Why, then, had he chosen to walk with her when Uncle George would have been happy to supply a far stronger arm?

"Oh yes, it was," she said. "And it is."

For a moment she thought his temper was about to explode all over her. Instead he uttered a short bark of laughter.

"I like you, Lady Philippa," he said.

"I like you too, Your Grace," she said, smiling at him despite herself.

"The thing is," he said, "that I cannot get it out of this old head of mine—Her Grace calls me a stubborn old fool—that you and Luc like each other too."

"The trouble with you," she said, "is that you have had your way all your life, and now you cannot believe that one young woman would dare to thwart your will."

"Ah," he said with a sigh. "You remind me of my dear May when we were young and she would sometimes step up close to me, tower over me, and invite me to go find someone else to bully since she was beginning to find my tantrums tedious. Those were the days, Lady Philippa. I thought the good Lord had stopped making women like her. But then he made you."

"I doubt I could ever find you tedious," Philippa said, laughing again.

"And here comes my girl," he said with desperate fondness, stopping not far from the bank and nodding toward one of the boats, which was already returning from downriver. "As happy as the summertime. As though she had not suffered a day in her life. That girl is pluck to the backbone."

His eyes were upon Jenny, who was in the boat, laughing at something her brother was saying and twirling her parasol over her head to keep off the direct rays of the sun. And he was smiling as he talked—and pulling strongly on the oars. He had removed both his hat and his coat, as a few other gentlemen had who were rowing a boat. It must be warm out there on the water. The sunlight gleamed on his dark red hair. The muscles of his shoulders and upper arms rippled against the white linen of his shirt.

"Grandpapa!" Lady Mayberry had come up on the duke's other side. "What on earth are you doing all the way down here?"

Lord Mayberry smiled at Philippa.

"Standing on my own two feet, minding my own business, and conversing with a pretty young lady," the duke said. "I need your permission to move from place to place, do I, Charlotte?"

"If you look behind you," she said, "you will see that the return walk to the house is all uphill."

"If I should suffer a heart seizure halfway there," he said, "Sylvester will no doubt carry me the rest of the way."

She tutted but said no more.

"Here they come," her husband said, stepping forward to where the wheeled chair had been left by the bank. "I will help Luc lift Jenny safely to shore."

"It is *wonderful* out there," Jenny called. "Grandpapa, did you come to watch?"

"Thank you, Sylvester. Hold it steady, will you?" the Marquess of Roath said before stepping out onto the bank, pulling his coat on hastily as he did so, and turning to lift his sister out.

He was thwarted, however, by the arrival upon the scene of Mr. Jamieson, who was smiling warmly at Jenny. "You see?" he said. "You were not frightened in the boat after all, Lady Jennifer. And if you do not now come back out there with me, I will believe it is my skill at the oars you distrust rather than the sturdiness of the boat."

"Oh dear," she said, smiling brightly at him. "I cannot do that to you, can I?"

The marquess straightened up and put on his hat. "You can swim, Jamieson?" he asked.

"Like a fish," Mr. Jamieson said, and stepped into the boat and took up the oars. "Though I have no intention of putting on a demonstration this afternoon. Not when I have such a precious cargo."

"If he breaks her heart," the duke murmured as the boat moved away from the bank again, "I will break *him*."

"His father has a gambling habit, and his properties are mortgaged to the hilt," the marquess said. "But I have yet to uncover any great vice in Jamieson himself."

"He smiles too much," the duke observed. "Sylvester, I will borrow your arm for the return walk to the house. Luc will wish to stay to lift Jenny from the boat when it returns. And Lady Philippa likes being close to the water. She finds it peaceful. Charlotte, take my other arm."

He was as subtle as a sledgehammer, Philippa thought. Besides, it was Jenny, not she, who had claimed to find proximity to the water peaceful.

"There is one thing you should know about my grandfather, Lady Philippa," the Marquess of Roath said, squinting after him as he moved away between his granddaughter and grandson-in-law. "He never admits defeat. *Ever*. Not in my experience, anyway."

CHAPTER SIXTEEN

W hy?" she asked him. She was frowning and looking genuinely puzzled. "What is so special about me? His Grace
must have seen you with Miss Thorpe as much as he has seen you
with me, perhaps more, and there must be other women on your
grandmother's list he has seen. Surely there is at least one of them
who would meet with his approval and yours. I have not even been
particularly polite to him. When he told me on the way down here
that it had never been his intention to harass me, I told him that
indeed it had been. I also told him that the trouble with him
was that he had had his own way all his life. But all he would say
in return was that he *liked* me and that I reminded him of Her
Grace."

Lucas turned to look along the river. Every boat was in use, but
he could pick out Jenny, a distant speck downriver in one of them
with Jamieson. He had looked away in order to hide a grin, though
he was not feeling entirely amused.

"Then that is one thing he finds special about you," he said.

"My grandfather likes people who stand up to him, though very few ever do and it is not easy to prevail with him even when one tries. You would have had better luck if you had simpered at him and flattered him and flattered *me* to him. But now you have sealed your own doom in his mind. If he is comparing you favorably with my grandmother, then he likes you indeed. He positively adores her, though he never stops complaining about her superior height."

"Perhaps he favors me just because I do not favor *you*," she said. "I suppose every other single woman below the age of twenty-five or so *does* and makes no bones about it, whether she is on your grandmother's list or not."

"It is the red hair," he said, turning his head to look at her over his shoulder. She was frowning. "The fact that I will be a duke one day, an almost indecently *wealthy* duke, possibly has something to do with it too."

"I have never liked red hair on men," she said, and he grinned again. "I am going back up to the house. There is no need for you to accompany me."

"Good," he said. "I am going to be right here when the boat returns to lift Jenny out. I am not letting anyone who is not related to her do it."

She gazed off to the distant boat. "I believe she likes him," she said.

"I am sure she does," he agreed. "My sister has a very sensible head on her shoulders. However, most of us slip once or twice in our lives and do—or say—something that is quite out of character and has a long-lasting and sometimes disastrous effect upon ourselves and others."

She neither looked at him nor said anything for a while. She seemed to have forgotten that she was going back up to the house.

"You are afraid she will fall in love with him?" she asked.

"Afraid?" he said. "Yes, perhaps I am. Afraid that she will fall for him but that he will not fall for her. That is not quite it, though. I am afraid that he will pretend to fall for her. Is it insulting to harbor such a fear just because she is crippled? *She* would say it is, and I daresay she would be right. I suppose I would not be quite so protective of her if she had not suffered that illness when she was a child. Love rips at the heart sometimes, Lady Philippa."

Neither of them spoke for a while, and he realized with some surprise that the garden party was still proceeding around them with a great deal of noise and merriment and activity. For a few minutes he had seemed to be quite alone with her—and they had spoken about his grandparents and about Jenny and his fears for her very much as though they were friends. He wished they were.

And that, he realized, was what was wrong with all the other women to whom he had been introduced since he came to London, including the few he knew his grandparents would consider acceptable as his bride. All of them were young and pretty and personable. All behaved with perfect good manners and modest demeanor. All would make satisfactory wives and duchesses. None had shown any reluctance to be in his company—or any unseemly eagerness either. He was reasonably sure that any one of them would receive his addresses with some pleasure and agree to an instant betrothal. None of the parents involved would object to his paying those addresses. Quite the contrary. Lady Abingdon, for example, was openly eager to see her daughter so well settled. But . . .

Well, there was a *but*. For none of those ladies was a friend. It was a bit unfair to come to such a conclusion, perhaps, when he really had very little acquaintance with them. But he could not even imagine having a close friendship with any of them. He had very little acquaintance with Lady Philippa Ware either. She would seem to be the last woman with whom he would feel able to talk about anything that was close to his heart—including the fear that his sister would fall prey to a fortune hunter and be miserable for the rest of her life. But she felt like a friend. Perhaps it was because they both knew something about deep suffering and about holding it all inside in the form of a secret they could not divulge without hurting those who were nearest and dearest to them.

Or perhaps . . .

Perhaps the attraction had been there from the start. The *very* start. Why had she been straining her ears in that barn to hear what he and the other men were saying? Why had he singled her out as a possible partner when James Rutledge and the owner of the barn had tried to persuade him to dance about the maypole?

"What did you think the very first time you set eyes on me?" he asked, and then felt idiotic since the question must seem to have come from nowhere. He squinted off into the distance. The dot that was Jenny and Jamieson's boat was getting larger, he was relieved to see. They were on their way back.

She surprised him by laughing softly. "I fell head over heels in love with you," she said. "I daresay it was the red hair."

"I thought you did not like red hair on men," he said.

"There are exceptions to every rule," she said. "Or so some people claim when they cannot explain why they have broken one."

"Hmm," he said.

"Of course," she added, "I fell out of love a mere few minutes later. There is nothing so sure to kill one's dizzy flights of fancy as to be called *soiled goods*."

"No," he said with a sigh. "I suppose not."

Oddly, they seemed almost to be *joking* with each other. But they were no longer to be left alone together. A group of young people had come up to them and stopped to chat. Cousin Gerald was one of their number. He must have arrived late at the party. Lucas had not seen him before now.

"That is Jenny out there in the boat?" he asked, nodding down-river. "If it is not, I will wonder why you are standing here guarding an empty wheeled chair. She is a plucky one. She is with Jamieson?"

"She went out with me first," Lucas told him. "But Jamieson came along before I could lift her out. She loves the boat."

"I hope he can swim," Gerald said, frowning.

"He can," Lucas told him. "Like a fish apparently."

Gerald grunted. "I'll wait and help you get her back into her chair," he said. "Grandmama is up close to the terrace reminding Grandpapa that he is no longer two years old or even twenty. Apparently he came down here a while ago and gave everyone heart palpitations."

"*Not* including himself, it is to be hoped," Lucas said, listening to Lady Philippa laughing with the rest of the group over something he had not heard. She had a distinctive laugh—merry and genuine and infectious. He felt himself smiling though he had not heard the joke.

"He was looking pretty red in the face," Gerald said.

The boat was pulling to shore and Jenny, Lucas thought, was looking a bit weary. Perhaps two turns on the river had been too much for her. Gerald held the boat steady while Jamieson jumped ashore and turned with his usual smile to lift her out. But Lucas was there ahead of him. She wrapped her arms about his neck as he swung her over to her chair and settled her in it.

"I am guessing," she said, smiling at him, "that none of us will have any trouble sleeping tonight after all this fresh air."

"You have not overdone it?" he asked, looking down at her with some concern.

She shook her head. "It is lovely being close to the water," she said. "Trailing one's fingers in it. Watching the sunlight sparkle on it."

"Shall I push you back up to the house?" he asked her. Jamieson was still hovering on the bank.

"Yes, please," she said. It looked to Lucas as though Lady Philippa was about to move away with the group that had joined them a few minutes ago, but Jenny, perhaps not noticing, stretched out a hand toward her. "Come with us, Pippa?"

"Of course," Lady Philippa said, and set her hand in Jenny's.

There was something not quite right here, Lucas thought as he pushed the chair up the slope. Jamieson had been dismissed out of hand, had he? But there was no chance for private conversation. There were fellow guests to greet as they went and, in a few cases, to converse with at somewhat greater length before they proceeded.

The sun beamed down from a clear blue sky, and it was actually better than a summer day, which might have been oppressively hot. There was still a spring freshness to the air today.

The Marquess of Roath offered to take Jenny home and come back later for their aunt if necessary. But Jenny smiled warmly at him and told him not to be silly, she was not an invalid. All she needed, she told him, was a big glass of lemonade, a place in the shade to drink it, and Pippa to keep her company. He fetched them each a glass, found an unoccupied couple of chairs with a small table between them in the shade of a willow tree, pushed his sister's chair up close to them, positioned one of the chairs for Philippa, and then left them together there. He strode away to join a group of men, including their host, at the far side of the terrace.

"That was all very imperious of me," Jenny said apologetically.

"You will be thinking I have been taking lessons from Grandpapa, Pippa. I have presumed upon a friendship I insisted upon. Perhaps you would—"

"Perhaps I am quite contented to be right where I am with you," Philippa said. "You have not presumed upon anything. I believe we are friends. I *hope* we are."

There was something a little desperate about Jenny, though, it seemed to Philippa.

"He asked me to marry him," she said abruptly.

"Mr. Jamieson?" Philippa said. "Without speaking first with your brother? Or your grandfather? Though perhaps that was not strictly necessary since—"

"He told me he was aware I am of age," Jenny said, cutting her off. "How could he *not* be?"

"Ah," Philippa said. "And?"

"And I asked him," Jenny said, "if it was my fortune that was the main attraction. He did not deny it."

What? Philippa set her glass on the table. He had *admitted* it?

"He told me he could not deny it," Jenny said. "It would become too clear to me when a marriage contract was discussed. He told me that his father is in deep financial straits and that he himself has no more than a modest income from investments his grandmother left him. He admitted to needing to repair his fortunes by marrying money. I must commend him on his honesty. Many men in his situation would have been hot in their denials."

"But?" Philippa said.

"But nothing really," Jenny said after pausing to drink some of her lemonade. She held the glass with both hands, neither of which looked quite steady. "He followed that candid admission with more or less what one would expect. He has a deep regard for me. A profound respect. It would be the greatest honor of his life to call me wife. Et cetera *and* et cetera. I must commend him again for not claiming to feel any great passion for me."

"What answer did you give him?" Philippa held her breath.

"Oh, I was tempted," Jenny admitted. "For his honesty is something, is it not? Though I do wonder if it faltered a bit with his claim of *deep regard* and *profound respect.* I am realistic enough to understand that I can never expect a declaration of undying love from any aspirant to my hand. *Regard* and *respect* are good things, though perhaps more meaningful without the lavish adjectives. They would last and very possibly grow into affection over time. Affection is a *very* good thing. Yes, I was very tempted, Pippa. And of course he is good-looking and very charming. And I suppose he cannot help his father's extravagance."

"You said no?" Philippa said. Oh, poor Jenny. She clearly liked Mr. Jamieson, and he had been very attentive to her.

"I did not," Jenny said with a sigh. "I told him I needed some time to consider my answer."

"Do you love him?" Philippa asked.

"Ah. Now, *there* is a question," Jenny said, lowering her glass to the table. "Probably not. But I have never actually wanted to fall in love. I have always thought it would be too painful. For I could never expect to marry. I have always known that if I ever did have an offer, it would almost certainly be from someone who wanted or needed my fortune but had to marry me in order to get it. I have always believed that I could never . . . marry such a man just because I wanted marriage. I have always believed that I would want to be . . . valued at least as much as my fortune. Not necessarily loved but *valued.* I would also want to *value,* to like and respect, any husband I took. That was an impossible dream, of course, and I have never wasted much time on it. I am not in love with Mr. Jamieson, Pippa. But for a while . . . Well, I was tempted."

She was speaking in the past tense, Philippa noticed, though she had told Mr. Jamieson she needed more time to think.

"There is no chance, then," she said, "that he was telling the full truth? That he really does honor and respect you?"

"I do not know." Jenny's voice sounded bleak. "Or perhaps I do and just need a little time to steel myself to admit it. Does he smile too much, Pippa? I have rarely seen him with any other expression on his face. Sometimes it looks to me very like a mask."

Jenny might indeed not be in love with Mr. Jamieson, Philippa thought, but she was clearly upset by whatever feelings she did have for him.

"I told him," Jenny said, "that he must talk with Luc before I give him any definite answer. He said he would."

"That was good," Philippa said.

But Jenny looked at her with eyes that had lost none of their bleakness. "I wonder if he will," she said. "But even if he does . . . Luc does not like him. He has never actually said so any more than Aunt Kitty has. But I know that neither of them likes him."

"Jenny." Philippa leaned closer to her friend and touched a hand to her arm. "The Marquess of Roath *loves* you. There can be no doubt whatsoever about that. He will not destroy anything he believes might bring you happiness. He might have doubts. He might give advice. But he will not dismiss Mr. Jamieson singlehandedly or ride roughshod over your feelings. He will allow you to make the final decision, and he will support you in whatever that is. You must surely believe that. I believe it, yet I know him far less than you do."

"Pippa, I *do* wish you were my sister," Jenny said. But she looked instantly contrite. "Oh. I did not mean that the way it sounded. I do *not* want to put any pressure on you. I promised Luc I would not, though the promise was not necessary."

"We are friends," Philippa said, smiling. "That is as good as sisters. I do believe we are about to have company."

A group of three ladies and two men, all of them young, all of them acquaintances of both her and Jenny, were coming to join them, bringing chatter and laughter with them.

"*May* we join you?" one of the young ladies asked rhetorically as she sat upon the vacant chair. "This looks like a lovely shady spot. Who would have known it would be so warm today when it is still supposed to be springtime?"

One of the others sat upon the arm of her chair and one came to sit upon the arm of Philippa's. The two men sat cross-legged on the grass, and soon Jenny and Philippa were chatting and laughing along with them.

B oth Philippa and her mother were feeling weary as they rode home in the carriage. They were agreed that the garden party had been a delightful event, but both were thankful they had no engagement for the evening. They looked at each other in some dismay, then, when the carriage turned onto Grosvenor Square and they could see a post chaise drawn up outside Stratton House.

"Visitors," Philippa said, pulling a face and then smiling ruefully. "How very ungracious of me."

But her mother was looking more intently through the window on her side, and Philippa soon saw why. One of their footmen was climbing the steps to the open door of the house, a bulging valise in each hand. Suddenly her tiredness was forgotten.

"*Ben,*" her mother said.

"And Joy!"

Oh, how she had missed them, Philippa thought as their carriage drew to a halt behind the chaise and their coachman came to open the door and set down the steps. And how she would miss them when they moved permanently to Penallen. Thank heaven it was no more than a few hours' journey from Ravenswood.

She hurried up the steps and into the hall. Devlin and Gwyneth were there, as well as Stephanie. They were back from Kew Gardens, then. Beside Devlin stood a tall, broad-shouldered, muscular, blond-haired man in the somewhat faded uniform of a cavalry officer.

"Nicholas," the dowager countess murmured before dropping her gloves and reticule to the floor despite the proximity of the butler and hurrying toward her second son with both hands extended.

"Mama." Major Nicholas Ware was grinning at her and opening his arms to receive her. He ignored her own arms and swept her up and about in a complete circle before setting her back on her feet. "Looking more and more every day as though you must be my sister."

He was still grinning when he turned to Philippa, and she hurried toward him to be subjected to the same treatment.

"Pippa," he said. "Almost the first thing Steph said to me when I walked through the door a few minutes ago was that you are taking the *ton* by storm and that you have already had two proposals of marriage, one from a marquess and one from a baronet. Damn their presumption. They had better be worthy of you. I can only say I am not surprised, though. Just *look* at you."

"Nick," she said while he made a production of looking her over. "Nick, you are home."

"For five minutes," he said, lifting his head to address them all. "Which is not too much of an exaggeration. I have to get back as soon as I can. *Yesterday*, if possible, and even that might be too slow to satisfy the Duke of Wellington. The cavalry is desperately short of mounts. Horses have been gathered here in large numbers. But the powers that be in their dark, plush offices at the Horse Guards cannot seem to work out how to get them within the next year or five to where they are desperately needed. I have been sent to use my charm on them, and if that does not work, to throw my weight around." He grinned.

It was so *good* to see him, just when they were most worried about him. Not that that would change. He had come to hurry along the process of transporting more horses across the channel so that the cavalry would be able to ride into battle in larger numbers. There *would be* a battle, and probably fairly soon if the Duke of Wellington wanted those horses *yesterday*. But at least Nicholas was here now—and looking impossibly handsome in his uniform. He had been home on leave twice since beginning his military career seven years ago. Both times he had come to Ravenswood but had left his uniform behind. He had been there last Christmas in time to attend Devlin's wedding, though it had not been planned that way.

"Gwyn wrote to me when she was at Penallen with Dev a few weeks ago," Nicholas was saying. "She mentioned that Ben was coming to London soon. He is not here yet, though, is he? He had better come during the five minutes I will be here. I want to see that niece of mine. I wrote to Owen when I knew I was coming. I suggested that maybe he could slip away from Oxford for a few days without anyone noticing and getting the idea of sending him down permanently for truancy."

"We thought you *were* Ben when we saw the post chaise outside the door," Philippa said. "We did not dream of seeing you, Nick."

He walked with a slight limp, she knew, the result of a wound that had almost taken his life in the Peninsula a few years ago. Yet looking at him now, she saw a man of great vitality and power and confidence. A man whose weathered face radiated good humor and great charm. His fair hair was longer, more tousled than it had been at Christmas. He looked, she thought, very like their father. Yet there was something about the hard line of his jaw that suggested a greater firmness of purpose than Papa had possessed.

"Why are we standing here?" Gwyneth asked, laughing. "We have all had a busy afternoon. Come upstairs, Nick, and Dev will pour you a drink while I have a tea tray brought in, late in the afternoon though it is."

"Yes," Nicholas said, grinning at her. "I can see that you in particular ought not to be standing about too much, Gwyn. And Dev hinted at the reason when he wrote to me the day after you arrived in town. I received it just before I left to come here."

Stephanie slid a hand through his arm, beaming up at him, and Philippa took his other as they all made their way upstairs to the drawing room.

CHAPTER SEVENTEEN

Lady Abingdon made the mistake of calling upon Her Grace, the Duchess of Wilby, two days after the garden party in Richmond. She came, Lucas heard later when his grandmother was giving an account of the visit upon His Grace's return from a day at the House of Lords, in order to smile and simper and congratulate the duchess upon the closer ties between their families they could surely expect in the near future. She had hinted that Lord Abingdon was in daily expectation of a certain *visit* from Her Grace's grandson—she had apparently looked archly at Grandmama as she said this. Indeed, it seemed to Lady Abingdon that his visit was overdue, that soon the *ton* was going to begin to murmur about the dear boy raising expectations he did not mean to fulfill.

"Her very words, Percy," the duchess said while his bushy eyebrows snapped together above his nose. "But she and I, mothers both—a grandmother too, in my case—know how young men sometimes drag their feet, perhaps because they are simply bashful, perhaps because they fear disappointment."

"She *threatened* you, Mama?" Aunt Kitty asked, sounding incredulous.

Lucas, standing by the window in the vast drawing room, lifted his eyebrows. He had *raised expectations*? Not merely hopes, but expectations?

"If she did, Kitty," the duchess said, "she soon regretted it. I rarely use my lorgnette. I find it blurs my vision rather than enhancing it. But I was very glad I had it beside me on the table. I raised it to my eyes and looked at her through it. I find that words are rarely necessary when I use it thus."

"You said nothing, Mama?" Aunt Kitty asked. "When she had been so presumptuous and so offensive? You merely *looked* at her?"

The duke laughed with a short barking sound. "You are fortunate, Kitty," he said, "if you have never found yourself on the receiving end of your mother's lorgnette. How soon did she leave after you looked at her, May?"

"I did not consult the clock," the duchess said. "No longer than two minutes, though, I daresay. She left. With every appearance of great confusion. I hope, Luc, you did not have your heart set upon marrying Miss Thorpe. Neither your grandpapa nor I could possibly approve of your connecting yourself with a young lady who has such a vulgar mother. The woman's father, of course, made his fortune in trade. Abingdon would not have honored her with a second glance if he had not needed to marry a fortune. She had no brothers or sisters, it might be added."

"Luc with his heart set on *that* chit?" his grandfather said, just as though Miss Thorpe's name and Grandmama's list had never had an encounter with each other. His face had turned a shade of purple. "His *heart* is set upon Lady Philippa Ware, no matter what he says to the contrary. There is nothing vulgar about *her* family even if the Greenfields are not actually nobility. I do not know why you even waste your time on the likes of the Miss Thorpes of this world, May."

Lucas said nothing, though he was not sorry Lady Abingdon had overreached herself. He and Miss Thorpe had attended the same private concert last evening, and everywhere he had turned, there she was. He had sat beside her for every musical item except one even though he had excused himself and strolled away and then found a different seat every time there was a change of artist. He had somehow been coaxed into filling a plate for her during the intermission and then standing beside her while they ate. He also inexplicably found himself escorting her out to her carriage afterward. He had stood by the open door after she seated herself within, conversing with her while her mother hurried back inside to fetch something she had left behind. It had taken her the devil of a long time to find whatever it was. Every other carriage had driven away by the time she came back out and scolded him for not getting into the carriage out of the cold while he waited.

He had been growing more and more uneasy about the possibility that he would find himself one of these days accidentally making Miss Thorpe an offer of marriage. It was one he knew he did not want to make, even if his grandparents encouraged it. He might be able to tolerate the young lady as a wife. The mother-in-law he most certainly would not.

"Jenny," His Grace said. "Is Lady Philippa going to be at Almack's tomorrow evening? You probably know. The two of you have grown as thick as thieves."

Jenny had sat silently through Grandmama's account of Lady Abingdon's visit.

"Aunt Kitty has secured vouchers for me and a ticket for tomorrow night's assembly after discovering that I would love to go there at least once," Jenny said. "And yes, Grandpapa, Pippa will be there too. I sent a note to Stratton House this afternoon to ask her. She is bubbling over with excitement because two more of her brothers have come to town, including her military brother, who is making a lightning visit to England on official business. She is hoping to persuade him to accompany her and the Earl and Countess of Stratton to Almack's. Their other brother, Mr. Ellis, will not come, though. He is a widower with a young child."

He was also, Lucas thought, the illegitimate son of the late Earl of Stratton and, presumably, some courtesan.

"Lucas," His Grace said, frowning ferociously at his grandson as though he were expecting some defiant opposition. "You will escort your sister and aunt to Almack's tomorrow evening. Her Grace and I will look in there later."

"You had better be sure to arrive before eleven," Lucas warned him. "I do not believe the patronesses would bend the rules even for you, Grandpapa."

"Hmph," the duke said.

N icholas looked very splendid when he went off each day in his dress uniform to carry out the business for which he had been sent to England—to ensure that his regiment had sufficient horses for the battle that was surely inevitable in the next month or so.

"Not that there is *sufficient* of anything when the military heads, who know what is needed, have to appeal to politicians here, who know nothing and either do not believe them or else set wheels in motion that turn so slowly we just *might* get half of what we need by the time the next war comes along," he explained to his family at dinner on the night of the dance at Almack's. "I would not be in Wellington's shoes for all the money in the world."

But he was making progress, he reported cheerfully in the next breath. His men would not have to march into battle on foot.

He was looking almost as splendid this evening, Philippa thought, dressed in the regulation knee breeches required for admission to Almack's because, as far as any of them knew, military uniforms were not acceptable there. Nick would, of course, look gorgeous no matter what he wore.

He could remember the steps to all the dances, including the waltz, he assured Stephanie after she asked. He had heard that waltzing was now allowed at Almack's. He kept in practice because there were any number of military balls to attend wherever he went. They were sometimes a little thin on ladies, it was true, but he did not usually have any great trouble finding a partner. He grinned and winked at his young sister, who had one arm linked through Ben's.

"Yes, I believe you," she said.

"Indeed," he said when Ben mentioned a neighbor of his at Penallen who had gone to Brussels recently to be closer to his son, an ensign in an artillery regiment. "Brussels is bursting at the seams with visitors, most of them Englishmen, and many of them with their families too. It is somewhat surprising there are enough people left here in London to attend all the balls and whatnot during the Season. All is bustle and gaiety there, with parades and picnics by day and parties and balls by night. Often we fall into bed at dawn, having danced our feet off, only to have to rise a few hours later to go on parade again. Do you miss the life, Dev?"

"Not for a moment," Devlin assured him.

"Perhaps," Stephanie said, "there will be no fighting after all. Men can be so *silly*."

"What else would we do with our time?" Nicholas asked, winking at her.

But Philippa knew he was not nearly as carefree, even careless, as he sometimes appeared to be. She had seen him look serious to the point of grimness as he returned from his duties. But then he put on his family face almost as though he were donning a mask.

She was looking forward to the evening at Almack's. She had been there once before with her mother and had enjoyed herself greatly despite dire warnings about the barnlike appearance of the assembly rooms and the insipid nature of the entertainment and the blandness of the refreshments. Some of those stories, she suspected, were spread by people who had never been granted one of the coveted vouchers and therefore had never actually been there. Or by those who found fault wherever they went and were determined to be miserable.

The patronesses of the famous assembly rooms took their duties seriously and made sure everyone had a partner for the dances. They introduced young ladies to gentlemen they deemed eligible for them. Indeed, Almack's was often referred to as the marriage mart, a sort of miniature within the larger one that encompassed the whole of fashionable London during the spring months. One never had to fear being a wallflower at Almack's. It could almost be said that one did not have to fear not finding a husband either if one had been approved to attend the weekly dances there.

Almack's was where Philippa had been introduced to Lord Edward Denton, one of her favorites, though she was not at all sure he was in search of a wife. It was where she had met several other ladies in her own age range who had since become close acquaintances. It was where she had met several other young men who danced with her regularly at balls, conversed with her at parties, and drove her in the park.

Tonight she was greatly looking forward to going again. Her mother was going to the opera with Uncle Charles and Aunt Marian, Aunt Eloise and Uncle Vincent. Ben was going to stay at home with Stephanie. They would play with Joy and read her stories before putting her to bed. But Gwyneth and Devlin and Nicholas were coming to Almack's with her. And Jenny was going to be there with Lady Catherine Emmett—and perhaps the Marquess of Roath?

She tried to tell herself that she hoped not. She had felt herself weakening at the garden party. Since hearing his story, she understood why he had said what he had in Sid Johnson's barn after he learned her identity. It had still been a horrid thing to say and certainly not easy to excuse. But . . . Well, had it really been an unforgivable sin? Even after more than four years? Despite all the havoc his words had wreaked in her life?

They could not possibly have a close relationship, however. That incident would always hang like a cloud between them. And there would always be the awareness that her father and his mother had dishonored their marriage vows with each other and conceived a child. It would always be a dark secret neither of them could share with their families.

He was the first person she saw at Almack's as she followed Gwyneth and Devlin into the assembly rooms on Nicholas's arm. He was standing at the opposite side of the room beside Jenny's chair. It was Jenny's waving arm that had drawn Philippa's attention their way.

"Lady in green across the room in a wheeled chair," Nicholas said. "The friend you have spoken of, Pippa? It seems to be you at whom she is waving."

"Yes," Philippa said. "Come." And fortunately he came with her, a sort of bulwark against the effect of having to come face-to-face with the marquess so early in the evening.

"Jenny." Philippa leaned over her friend to hug her. She was wearing a shimmering gown in a shade of pale moss green. It complemented her hair, which was dressed smoothly at the front and in a cascade of curls at the back. "I am so glad you really did come. May I present my brother Major Nicholas Ware? Lady Jennifer Arden, Nick. And the Marquess of Roath, her brother."

Nicholas bowed to Jenny and shook hands with the marquess. There was a brief exchange of pleasantries before one of the patronesses came to take Nicholas off to introduce to a young lady she described as the eldest daughter of a retired colonel. She looked inquiringly from Philippa to the Marquess of Roath.

"Yes," the marquess said. "I am about to ask Lady Philippa for the opening set."

Well, Philippa thought as she watched her brother walk away, his slight limp hardly noticeable, his most charming smile directed ahead to the colonel's daughter. *Well!*

"You must be very happy to have Major Ware with you, even if it is for but a short while," Jenny said.

"Yes, we all are," Philippa said. "I just wish he did not have to go back."

"It will be soon?" Jenny asked.

"Yes." Philippa nodded. "Within the week, I am almost certain."

"I daresay he is eager to be back with his men," the Marquess of Roath said.

"He is," she said. "He would never forgive himself if the battle was fought while he was still away."

Jenny was smiling at Sir Gerald Emmett and two other young men who were approaching.

"*Will* you dance the opening set with me?" the marquess asked Philippa.

"I will," she said. What choice did she have? "Thank you."

The three men were chatting with Jenny—all at once, it

seemed—until one of them asked her if he might sit with her during the first set since he was wearing new dancing shoes and feared he might already have blisters on his toes.

"Not to mention my heels," he added.

"And not to mention the fact that he has two left feet when he *does* dance, Lady Jenny," one of the other men said.

Lines were forming for the opening set of dances, and the marquess led Philippa onto the floor to join the ladies before he stepped back into the line of men facing them. Nicholas and his partner were a little farther along, Philippa could see, and Devlin and Gwyneth were just beyond them. She was going to enjoy the evening, she told herself. The Marquess of Roath was a good dancer, after all, and why should she not enjoy dancing with him? She smiled at him and he raised his eyebrows. Were his eyes smiling? She thought they might be.

The orchestra played a chord, and the dancing began.

T he Duke and Duchess of Wilby were not late arriving. They came just before the opening set finished and were shown to a couple of vacant chairs at one end of the room. Lucas could have wished they had waited a little longer, for now they would see that he was dancing with Lady Philippa Ware, and that would put ideas in their heads again—*if* those ideas had ever left their heads, that was.

Actually he wished they had not come at all. His grandfather had been complaining all day of an upset stomach and shortness of breath, but when Aunt Kitty had suggested that he spend the rest of the day quietly at home, he had snapped at her and reminded her that he was not going to Almack's in order to dance and frolic. He could sit quietly there as easily as he could at home. They had come here, of course, to see what eligible young ladies were in attendance and to make sure Luc was introduced to any he had not already met. Though Lucas was perfectly sure Lady Philippa remained their clear favorite.

"Shall I take you to Jenny?" he asked when the set ended. "Or would you prefer to join Lord and Lady Stratton? I must go and pay my respects to my grandparents even though I saw them at dinner a few hours ago."

She was not given a chance to answer him. His Grace had raised an arm and was beckoning imperiously—to both of them, it seemed.

"I will come with you and bid them a good evening," Lady Philippa said, smiling at them. "I cannot help but like them, you know."

So Lucas led her across the ballroom, which was already largely clear of dancers, in full view of everyone gathered there, to meet his grandparents, the Duke and Duchess of Wilby. The apparent implication could not have been more glaring.

It got worse.

When Lady Philippa offered them a slight curtsy, Grandmama reached out a hand to take hers and turned her cheek so that Lady Philippa had no choice but to bend and kiss it. And then Grandpapa moved over one chair and indicated the seat between him and Her Grace, and she was obliged to sit on it.

His grandparents had a way of depriving people of choice without ever having to be obnoxious about it. Quite the contrary in this particular case. Grandmama beamed upon Lady Philippa from one side, and Grandpapa gazed upon her from the other with an expression that was almost genial.

The bride they had approved for their grandson.

It was a picture that would surely remain with half the *ton* after the evening was over and provide the main headline for tomorrow's gossip columns. Without a word being spoken.

And they knew how to lay it on thick, like fruit preserves on toast.

"Fetch Lady Philippa a glass of lemonade, Luc," his grandfather said. "She has been dancing."

As had nine-tenths of the other people in the room. *At least* nine-tenths. Lucas went to fetch the lemonade.

P hilippa was feeling amused rather than annoyed. She was not at all sure why she liked the duke and duchess. They wielded power quite ruthlessly even when they said very little. Even when they smiled and looked benevolent, as they did now. And for the past few weeks she had been their chosen victim. It was puzzling since she had made her feelings perfectly clear to both them and their grandson. It was hard to understand their persistence. But they wanted her to marry the Marquess of Roath, and they were not prepared to take no for an answer.

It was entirely her own fault that she was sitting here now, between the two of them, looking along the length of the assembly room, like a king, queen, and princess holding court while the prince dashed off to fetch a glass of lemonade. She might have merely smiled at them and raised a hand in greeting at the end of the set and gone to join Jenny or one of her brothers—or any of a dozen or more other acquaintances. She was no longer a novice in society, after all. She knew and felt comfortable with any number of people of all ages. But Jenny had had a cluster of people around her at the time, Nicholas had been returning his partner to her chaperon—presumably her mother, the colonel's wife—and Devlin and Gwyneth had joined a group of people with whom Philippa did not have a close acquaintance.

Besides, the duke's beckoning arm and the duchess's warm smile had drawn her. And now she was sitting here, on the edge of laughter even though these two people spelled danger to her.

"Stratton is a man of sense and firm principle," the duke said, "as he has shown at the House of Lords. He looks nothing like your father. The dark-haired beauty with him is the countess, I suppose?"

"Gwyneth, yes," Philippa said.

"And another of your brothers was coming here tonight, according to Jenny," he said. "No, do not point him out to me. His rugged looks and military bearing would be a powerful enough clue even if he were not your father all over again in looks. I assume the young man now heading toward Jenny really *is* Major Ware?"

"Major *Nicholas* Ware," the duchess said, patting Philippa's hand. "He is indeed an extraordinarily handsome young man."

"He *does* look like Papa," Philippa said. *But please, please, Nick,* she thought as she gazed at him conversing cheerfully with Jenny and the group around her while all of them looked at him with smiles on their faces, *if and when you marry, do not be like Papa.*

The Marquess of Roath had been held up by a couple who had something to say to him. He had a full glass in each hand. He must be bringing one for his grandmother.

The Countess of Lieven, one of the patronesses of Almack's, was approaching with a young man Philippa had never seen before. He must be new to town. The countess introduced him as Mr. Maurice Wiseman, middle son of Viscount Trollope. Philippa smiled at him as he made his bow to them all and then concentrated his attention upon her.

"I would be honored if you would dance the upcoming set with me, Lady Philippa," he said.

But even as she drew breath to accept, the Duke of Wilby cut in ahead of her.

"Lady Philippa Ware has granted the next set to me," he said. "Perhaps the next one after it, Wiseman?"

"I would be delighted," the young man said. "Lady Philippa?"

"I will look forward to it," she said. She waited until he had turned away with the countess before addressing the duke. "I hope this coming set is a vigorous jig, Your Grace. Perhaps we should take our places on the floor?"

"You asked for that, Percy," the duchess said as she fanned her face. "I would greatly enjoy watching if I did not feel it my duty to remind you of what Dr. Arnold has said about vigorous exercise."

"Hang the physician," His Grace said, but he was actually chuckling as Philippa turned her head to laugh too.

But suddenly he was no longer laughing. He was gasping instead, and one hand was clawing at his chest, trying feebly to pull off his neckcloth and to push his evening coat to one side. He sagged forward and Philippa clutched his arm.

"Percy!" The duchess's voice sounded loud and unfamiliar.

"Grandpapa?" The marquess was there suddenly, minus the glasses he had been carrying, crouched before his grandfather's chair and holding him firmly by both shoulders.

The old man's face had turned gray, Philippa saw. His eyes were closed. His gasps had taken on a rasping sound. She looked around frantically for help. Sir Gerald Emmett was hurrying toward them. So was Lady Catherine. Bright conversations were being replaced throughout the room with concerned murmurings. The dancers who had already taken their places on the floor had turned, wide-eyed, to watch the drama.

"Is he . . . ?" There was a quaver now in the duchess's voice.

Philippa squeezed her arm but then got to her feet to move to the duchess's other side and make room for Sir Gerald.

The marquess had torn off the duke's neckcloth and collar and opened his shirt at the neck. Lady Catherine was plying her fan before his face.

"Here, Gerald," the marquess said. "Help me get him out of here so he can get some air."

"Would someone please have the Duke of Wilby's carriage brought up to the doors?" Sir Gerald said, raising his voice.

Nicholas, Philippa could see, was wheeling Jenny in her chair across the floor.

They lifted him between them, the marquess and Sir Gerald, and Philippa stepped in behind them to hold his head and stop it from tipping back too far. He was still gasping for air. His eyelids were fluttering.

"If you will tell me who his physician is, Roath, and where he is to be found, I will fetch him to Arden House without delay," a crisp voice said. It was Devlin's.

The marquess told him, and the Duke of Wilby was carried out while everyone in the assembly rooms made a path for him and watched in silent concern.

"We ought to have summoned a physician to Almack's," Lady Catherine said when they were all huddled outside the doors while a few of the guests who had come out ahead of them were beckoning the two carriages that were approaching. "We ought not to be moving him."

"My main concern was to get him outside, Aunt Kitty," the marquess said. "The air is fresh out here. How is Grandmama?"

"I have her," Lady Catherine said. "Set him down for a moment, Gerald. Dr. Arnold really ought to be coming *here*."

But the fresh air seemed to have revived the duke somewhat.

"Take me home," he said. "May?"

"I am here, Percy," the duchess said. "And a precious fright you are giving me."

"I suppose I made a precious spectacle of myself in there too," he said, and gasped in some air.

"Stop talking, Grandpapa," the marquess said. "Gerald and I are going to lift you into the carriage. Just let us do the work. Thank you, Lady Philippa. I will take his head and shoulders now."

Philippa stepped back and pressed the fingers of both hands to her mouth. In the light of a lantern someone was holding aloft, the Duke of Wilby looked ghastly indeed. She watched his grandsons maneuver him into the carriage and lay him along one of the seats. Lady Catherine helped her mother in after them.

"I will follow with Jenny, Mama," she said.

The coachman was about to shut the door.

"Wait a moment," the duchess said, holding up one hand. "*What* is that you are saying, Percy? Ah. Lady Philippa, you are to come with Kitty and Jenny, if you will be so good."

And the door slammed, the coachman vaulted up to the box with unexpected agility, and the horses moved off at a trot.

"I really think I ought not," Philippa said, turning to Lady Catherine.

"A ducal decree," she said. She was looking very distressed. "Which you have every right to ignore. But please come. I believe Jenny needs you."

Jenny, sitting silently in her chair with Nicholas standing behind her, was looking almost as ghastly as her grandfather.

"Please, Pippa?" she said.

The burly footman who always lifted her from place to place and conveyed her chair whenever she was going to need it came striding toward them at that moment. The second carriage had moved forward and the door had been opened and the steps set down.

"I'll hold the chair steady while you lift her in," Nicholas said. "What shall I do with—"

"I'll see to it, sir, thank you," the footman said, lifting Jenny into the carriage with practiced ease.

Lady Catherine climbed in after her. The footman was already hurrying away with the chair, presumably to another conveyance, so that he could be at Arden House right behind Jenny's carriage.

"You will tell Mama where I am?" Philippa said to Nicholas as he offered his hand to help her into the carriage.

"Of course," he said, and kissed her cheek.

"Thank you, Major Ware," Jenny said, looking out at him. "And thank you, Pippa."

"One is never quite prepared, is one?" Lady Catherine said, clasping her niece's hand as Philippa took her seat opposite them and the door closed mere moments before the carriage lurched into motion.

Chapter Eighteen

Philippa felt very awkward about intruding upon a family in crisis, even though it was the Duke of Wilby himself who had asked her to come. However, it was soon obvious to her that Jenny really did need her. Her footman carried first her chair and then Jenny herself up to the bedchamber floor so that she could sit in the private sitting room next to her bedchamber and be close to her grandparents if there should be any sudden need of her presence. She was not forgotten in the meanwhile. Various members of the family came in at frequent intervals, including Viscount and Viscountess Mayberry, who had been fetched from wherever they had been spending the evening. But no one stayed for long—except Philippa.

"One always understands," Jenny said after she had tried and failed to drink a cup of tea, "that elderly grandparents are going to die sometime, as indeed we all are. But then suddenly one is confronted with the reality of it and realizes one is not prepared at all. It has been obvious to us all since he came to London that Grandpapa is in failing health. But I suppose we have not been ready to admit it."

Philippa thought of Grandmama and Grandpapa Greenfield. And of Grandmama Ware. She had no clear memory of her paternal grandfather. But oh dear. At times like this it was so easy to sink deep into gloom, to believe that life was nothing but one loss and disaster upon another.

"His Grace is comfortable now in his own bed," she said. "Your brother-in-law told us so a few minutes ago. He has even revived sufficiently to talk. And his physician is with him. Lady Catherine said your grandparents have known and trusted him for years."

"Dr. Arnold. Grandpapa summons him all the way from here to Greystone twice each year," Jenny said. "And then he does not believe a word the man says. Or he pretends not to." She smiled before her face crumpled and she set the back of one hand over her mouth and shut her eyes for a few moments. "It is so difficult, Pippa, to imagine a world without that giant . . . *presence.* To imagine my life without it—without *him.* Poor Grandmama."

Philippa remembered that she had been teasing the duke about dancing a jig with her as the heart seizure caught him. She patted her friend's hand. The door opened and Lady Mayberry came in, followed by Sir Gerald Emmett.

"The doctor has left," Lady Mayberry said, "though we are to summon him back here if there should be any change. He has given Grandpapa some medicine and says his condition is stable for now. The medicine should help him sleep."

"O-o-oh," Jenny said. "Does he still look as bad as he did outside Almack's, Gerald? I really thought he was going to d-d-die before he even got home. And Aunt Kitty was so insistent that he ought not to be moved."

"He looks much the same," Sir Gerald said. "But his breathing is easier now and he has stopped plucking at his clothing and at the bedcovers."

"May I see him?" Jenny asked. "Grandmama and Aunt Kitty are still with him?"

"And Luc," her sister said. "Gerald will push your chair in there, Jen. I do not believe you will disturb him."

She ought to leave now, Philippa thought. But how? She could not simply exit the house and walk home alone at this time of the night. Sir Gerald was behind Jenny's chair. Before he could move it, however, and before Philippa could feel the awkwardness of her situation even more, the door opened again to admit Lady Catherine and the viscount. The small room was getting crowded.

"Grandpapa is asleep, Sylvester?" his wife asked.

"Not quite yet," her aunt replied. "He is as stubborn as ever, Charlotte. Pippa, he wants a word with you. *Will* you oblige him? It was extraordinarily kind of you to come here at all when the burden of our family grief ought to be none of your concern."

Five pairs of eyes fixed themselves upon her.

"I will go," Philippa said, getting to her feet. "I will stay just a moment."

Lady Catherine took her to her father's room but did not go inside with her. The butler opened the door, murmured, "Lady Philippa Ware, Your Grace," and stood aside for her to enter.

The room was dimly lit with one lamp on a table beside the head of the four-poster bed and another in a corner to the right of the door, where a servant, probably the duke's valet, stood beside a table upon which Philippa could see bottles and small boxes and a glass and spoons. The Duke of Wilby was lying in the bed, his head and shoulders propped up on a bank of pillows, one arm flung out to the side. The duchess, still dressed as she had been at Almack's, sat on a chair beside the bed, holding his hand. There was no one else in the room.

"This is very good of you, my dear," the duchess said, beckoning Philippa closer. "He will not sleep until he has spoken to you."

"I am happy to have been able to give my company to Jenny, Your Grace," Philippa said softly as she moved up beside the duchess. The duke was lying with closed eyes. If it had not been for the gray hair and bushy eyebrows, it might have been difficult to see him. His complexion in the dim light almost matched the white pillows. He looked small, somewhat diminished, though his eyes were keen enough when he opened them and fixed them upon her.

"Just one question, Lady Philippa," he said, his voice quiet but firm enough.

"Yes, Your Grace?" She leaned closer.

"Do you love him?" he asked, and his eyes did not waver from hers.

She understood immediately the enormity of the question. If she said no, she knew there would be the end of it, whether he lived on or not. An end to all the harassment—if that was the right word. All the *persistence.* If she said no . . . It was a simple question with a one-word answer. But what was that word to be? What was the truth? It was a time for truth, not merely an answer she knew he wanted to hear. Or one she felt she ought to give. That one word he wanted might comfort a dying man, but she had to live on. And she owed him nothing. She could not ask for time. He might not have time. But what was there to ponder when she was being asked to choose between two extremes? The answer could not be both.

"Yes," she said.

He looked at her for a second or two longer before closing his eyes again, and the duchess inhaled slowly and audibly.

"Thank you, my dear," she said. "May we impose upon you to stay a little longer before the carriage takes you home? It is getting late, I know."

"I will stay as long as I am needed," Philippa said, and she turned and left the room. The butler closed the door behind her and escorted her back to Jenny's room, where Lady Catherine, Sir Gerald, and Jenny's sister and brother-in-law were still keeping her company. They all gazed at her with expressions of avid inquiry.

"Pippa?" Jenny looked alarmed, and Philippa realized there were tears in her eyes. One was actually running down her cheek. She brushed it away.

"I believe he may be sleeping," she said. "Her Grace asked if I would remain with you a little longer, Jenny, before going home. But I do not wish to intrude. Perhaps—" Oh dear, this *was* awkward. Jenny was surrounded by her family and no longer needed the presence of a mere friend. A recently made friend at that.

"Please stay," Lady Catherine said. "Though the imposition is on our side, Pippa, not yours. Sit down with us, and we will have a fresh pot of tea brought up. When we know for sure that my father is asleep and my mother has settled for the night, then Gerald will see to it that you are conveyed safely home. He will escort you. We will be in your debt for this for a long time."

"We will indeed," Lady Mayberry said with a smile. "I am sorry you had to be dragged away from Almack's so early in the evening, Pippa."

"I will wait until tomorrow morning, then, to see Grandpapa," Jenny said with a sigh. "But poor Pippa. You danced only the opening set. What were you and Grandpapa talking about before he had his attack? You both looked quite merry."

"He had just informed the Countess of Lieven that he had reserved the second set with me and I could not therefore dance with

Mr. Wiseman," Philippa explained. "I was telling him that it would serve him right if the set consisted of some vigorous reels."

Viscount Mayberry laughed, and they all joined him. It actually felt good, Philippa thought. At least it would be a lighthearted memory for them all to carry forward into the future, no matter what happened in the next few hours or days.

"The gall of the man," Lady Catherine said. "To prevent you from dancing with a man who must be at least fifty years younger than he. He really can be quite outrageous. Yes, do ring for a tea tray if you will, Charlotte."

The duke's daughter and his grandchildren recalled similar stories about him while they all waited for the tray to arrive. They laughed a great deal. There was nothing unfeeling or irreverent about it, though, Philippa thought. Quite the contrary. They were all on the edge of tears too.

"Ah, here comes the tea," Lady Catherine said at last when there was a tap on the door. It was not a maid or footman who appeared, though, but the butler himself. He bowed to Lady Catherine.

"The presence of Lady Philippa Ware is requested, my lady," he said.

What? *Again?* But how very embarrassing.

"Really?" There was an edge of something in Lady Catherine's voice, and Sir Gerald Emmett was frowning. She ought to have gone home as soon as she left the duke's room, Philippa thought. This was really an embarrassment. "Then you must go, Pippa. I am so sorry about this."

The butler did not speak again while Philippa stepped out of the room and he closed the door behind her. He led the way, but not to the duke's bedchamber this time. He stopped outside a room two doors down from it, tapped on the door, and opened it.

"Lady Philippa Ware, my lord," he said, and she stepped inside a sumptuously furnished sitting room she guessed to be the duchess's. The duchess was not in there, though, despite the cheerful crackling of a fire and the light shed by numerous candles in branches on the mantel and in wall sconces about the room. The only occupant was the Marquess of Roath, who turned away from the fire as she came and gazed at her. His face was as parchment white as his grandfather's, she noticed.

She gazed back at him. She did not step away from the door when it closed but actually took a step back so that she could clutch the doorknob behind her with both hands.

Seconds passed. They felt more like minutes.

"My grandfather is capable of wielding enormous power," he said then. "I have no idea how he does it. It must be a combination of rank and character and reputation, I suppose. He never expects his will to be crossed and therefore it never is. With one word he can send forth his secretary in the middle of the night, and the man will return before the night is over with a special marriage license issued by the Archbishop of Canterbury, though it is doubtful that the archbishop himself will be required to rise from his bed to issue it. It will allow the couple named on the license to marry at a time and place of their choosing, not necessarily a church."

He paused and set an elbow on the mantel. Philippa clutched the doorknob more tightly.

"All this my grandfather can do," he continued. "He can obtain the services of a clergyman and he can arrange for the recitation of the wedding vows in the drawing room below here at two o'clock tomorrow afternoon. He can even command the presence of the prospective bridegroom. He *believes* he can command that of the prospective bride too. That, however, is *not* within his power if the lady herself should utter the one word that will prevent this whole series of events from happening."

His face was grim and set. His eyes, expressionless and perhaps cold, bored into hers.

"Lady Philippa," he said. "Will you do me the great honor of marrying me tomorrow?"

Tomorrow.

She felt as though a great ball of ice had lodged in her stomach.

Tomorrow?

She had already made a hugely consequential choice of answer once tonight. Now she was going to have to do it all over again. But the finality of this one was so . . . *enormous* that her mind was threatening to shut down altogether.

Tomorrow?

She had said in the hearing of the duke and duchess no more than half an hour ago that she loved him. She still did not know if it was the truth, though she could not in all good conscience have said no. But admitting to loving a man—or thinking that perhaps maybe one just might love him—was a far different thing from agreeing to marry him. Marriage was forever. For better or worse. Getting married was something she wanted to feel *good* about. Her wedding, that once-in-a-lifetime event, was something she wanted to plan with meticulous care. It was something for which she wanted her family about her. Her wedding day ought to be the happiest of her life.

Tomorrow? At two o'clock in the afternoon? Less than twenty-four hours from now? With *the Marquess of Roath* as her bridegroom and then as her husband for the rest of her life? The man she had hated above all others for four long years?

All because a dying man was to be placated?

She *loved* that old man, she realized. And the duchess. And Jenny and Lady Catherine. Even Jenny's sister and her family. From the first day she had been drawn to them all as she never had been to any other family except her own.

But not to *him.*

It had seemed the irony of all ironies that all these people she had come to love were *his* family.

Tomorrow?

She had no idea how much time had passed since he had asked the question. But he had not moved—or removed his gaze from hers. She had not moved either. It would be surprising if there were not ten dents in the doorknob at her back by the time she finally let go, so hard was she gripping it.

Tomorrow?

"Yes," she said.

And she felt that the one small word was like a physical thing, expanding to fill the room and seal her fate and his.

He moved then. He removed his elbow from the mantel and made her what looked like a curt bow. His expression did not change.

"Thank you," he said. "I shall devote my life to ensuring that you never regret your decision. Allow me to escort you back to Jenny's sitting room. I must go and report to my grandfather."

He took her upper arm in a firm grasp, almost as though he were leading a prisoner away, and opened the door. He did not abandon her outside Jenny's room, however. He opened the door, paused to look into the five expectant faces turned his way, and spoke.

"Lady Philippa Ware has done me the honor of agreeing to marry me tomorrow at two o'clock downstairs in the drawing room," he said. "Excuse me now, please. I must return to Grandpapa's room. There are arrangements to be made."

And Philippa was left standing in the doorway, staring mutely at five people who stared mutely back.

W hen she awoke the following morning, Philippa yawned and stretched beneath the covers, considered turning onto her side and allowing herself to slip back into slumber for a little while longer, and . . . shot up into a full sitting position.

Good heavens, she had *slept*! She had not expected to sleep ever again.

The events of last evening flooded into her mind in all their jumbled intensity. There had been enough of them, not to mention emotions, to fill a month of days and nights. But they had all happened within a few hours.

Today was her wedding day. If, that was . . .

There was a huge and heavy *if.*

She was almost not surprised when she realized her mother was sitting quietly by the window, half turned toward a narrow opening in the curtains. A band of sunlight was beaming through it.

"Did the Duke of Wilby live through the night?" Philippa asked. Foolish question. How was her mother supposed to know?

"He did," her mother said. "He was awake when Kitty wrote me an hour ago and was demanding coffee, which he had been strictly forbidden to have."

An hour ago. *What time is it?* She looked at the clock on the mantel.

"Half past *nine?*" she said, pushing back her tangled hair from her face with both hands. It had been almost half past two when she blew out the candle beside her bed. She had tossed and turned for an hour or more after that. But she must have slept soundly for at least five hours. She could not even recall any dreams.

"You needed the sleep," her mother said. "I am to let you know that all is arranged at *that* end, Pippa, though how everything could have been done during the night and very early morning hours I do not know. We are all to attend the ceremony, of course. Any other relatives we have in London are welcome to attend too. Ben has gone to Eloise and Vincent's to invite them, and Nicholas and Owen have gone to invite Charles and Marian and will then call upon George."

Owen? But yes, of course. Owen. He had come to London on a lightning visit from Oxford. He had even been granted official permission since he had given the reason that his brother, an officer with Wellington's armies as they prepared to face Napoleon Bonaparte and his newly gathered forces, was in London for a few days and wished to see him. He had arrived last evening, when only Ben and Stephanie were at home, though Devlin, Gwyneth, and Nick had not been far behind him, home early from Almack's. Mama had returned from the opera much later.

"Oh, Pippa." Her mother stood and opened the curtains so that the sunlight streamed into the room. "My mind is still grappling with the reality of what is happening. You are *really* going to marry the Marquess of Roath? Today? By special license? And not even in a church, but in the drawing room at Arden House?"

Philippa's stomach growled, though whether with hunger or something else she did not know.

"It is the Duke of Wilby's dying wish," she said.

Her mother was frowning. "With all due respect to the Duke of Wilby, Pippa," she said, "he has had altogether too much of his own way all his life, or so I have understood from knowing Kitty all these years. And how do you know it is his *dying* wish? He is still alive this morning. He may live for another year—or ten years. Is every wish of his from now on going to be his *dying* wish and therefore to be granted without question? Not that it would make much difference. His family have *always* jumped to his tune anyway. Or *danced* to his tune, I believe is the correct idiom. We are not his family, Pippa. You were not even betrothed to the Marquess of Roath . . . But then he came into the house with you last night after bringing you home and announced that you had accepted the offer of his hand . . . and that the wedding would be today."

"It must have been a great shock to you all," Philippa said.

"A *shock*?" Her mother laughed, though she did not sound the slightest bit amused. "When he came here to discuss a marriage contract with Devlin a while ago and to propose marriage to you, you said a quite firm no. Though, actually, that whole incident was somewhat more bizarre than that. Apparently no contract *was* even discussed, and no offer was made. No refusal was given. There was *no betrothal*. And no real explanation by either you or Devlin. Sometimes I think I must be losing my mind. But, Pippa, this is *not* something you ought to be doing in such a hurry. I can understand that all must have been grief and worry and heightened emotion at Arden House last evening. I can understand—*just*—why the proposal was made and even why you accepted. One does not think rationally in times of crisis. One tends to react emotionally. But it is not too late. The hurried plans can be canceled or at least postponed. Give yourself time to know your own mind and your own heart. Let me send Devlin to Arden House."

Philippa raised her knees beneath the covers, wrapped her arms about them, and lowered her forehead to rest on them.

She thought about marrying for love. She was not at all sure she loved the Marquess of Roath. How could she? She was even less certain that he loved her. He had never said anything to suggest that he did. She thought about a wedding at St. George's on Hanover Square, with members of the *ton* crowding every pew, organ music filling the church—perhaps played by Sir Ifor Rhys—bells pealing from the church tower outside. She thought of a flower-bedecked carriage and showers of petals as she made a dash for it from the church doors with her bridegroom. She thought of a lavish wedding breakfast at Stratton House and speeches and cake and champagne. She thought of all the shopping that would precede such a wedding, of choosing designs and fabrics for her own gown and Stephanie's and perhaps Joy's. She thought of walking along the nave of the church on Devlin's arm while the Marquess of Roath watched her come, the light of—

Even in that scenario was the Marquess of Roath to be her bridegroom, then? Not the man of her dreams, the love of her heart, and all the other commonplaces she might think of if she gave herself a bit more time?

She raised her head and looked at her mother.

"This is the wedding I want, Mama," she said. "The Marquess of Roath is the man I want."

Her mother heaved a deep sigh. But she did smile, albeit somewhat ruefully. "Then it is time you got out of that bed," she said. "There is *so* much to do, Pippa, that my head is about to spin on my shoulders."

Philippa threw back the covers and swung her legs over the side of the bed, actually smiling at her mother.

CHAPTER NINETEEN

The Duke of Wilby had been denied his morning coffee. He was inclined to be grumpy about it and bark at anyone who came within his line of vision. Until, that was, the duchess reminded him of two facts that should make him ashamed of himself. First, he was still alive this morning, when last evening at Almack's it had looked as though it was all over for him. Second, Lady Philippa Ware was going to marry Luc today.

"A day is still better worth living when it begins with coffee," he muttered peevishly.

"You are an ingrate, Percy," she said. "You might have been just a memory to me this morning."

He brooded upon her words.

"I did not *harass* that young woman, did I, May?" he asked.

"You did your very best, Percy," she said. "But I do not believe she allows herself to be bullied."

"Hmph," he said. "All is in readiness, I assume?"

"It will be by two o'clock," she told him. "One great advantage to my being old, Percy, is that no one expects me to exert myself any longer. More than that, no one *wants* me to exert myself."

"I daresay you did not get more than a wink of sleep last night," he said, squeezing her hand. "Either go to your bed right now, May, and lie down, or climb in here beside me. Am I right in the middle of the bed? Is there room?"

"There is room. You do not need to move," she said, looking toward the corner of the bedchamber, where His Grace's valet had been standing quietly through most of the night lest his services be needed. He was already letting himself quietly into the duke's dressing room and closing the door softly behind him.

The duchess drew back the covers and lay down beside her husband, her head on his outstretched arm. She sighed and relaxed.

"Percy," she said. "Try not to give me any more frights like the one you gave me last night."

"Not until at least nine months from tonight," he said. "It is a promise, May. I intend seeing my great-grandson before I set out on my final journey. And I always get my way—or so say some people who shall remain nameless."

They were both sleeping before many more minutes had passed.

Lucas stood in the doorway of the drawing room, remembering another quite recent occasion when he had been doing the same thing. He had been looking in then upon a roomful of guests at one of Aunt Kitty's tea parties. He had stood here, gathering his courage to step inside and begin circulating—that dreaded word when one was not particularly sociable, especially when one knew hardly anyone. Then he had spotted his aunt just before Jenny's waving arm had caught his attention. A moment later so had the woman who was seated beside her.

Lady Philippa Ware.

Today he would be marrying her.

"Ah, you are back, Luc," his sister Charlotte said, coming briskly toward him, bright-eyed and rosy-cheeked though she could not have had much sleep last night. Her hair was disheveled and the sleeves of her dress were rolled up above her elbows. "Did you get everything you need?"

"I did," he said.

"The *ring*, Luc?" Aunt Kitty called from across the room. She was balanced on a stool, rearranging vases on the high mantel. "Did you get the *ring*?"

"I did," he said.

"The right *size*?" she asked him.

"The right size," he assured her. She had sent Gerald to Stratton House early this morning with a note for the Dowager Countess of Stratton and a verbal request for Lady Philippa's ring size. Lucas had purchased a plain gold wedding band and another set with a single large diamond. It would have been a betrothal ring if there had *been* a betrothal of longer duration than fourteen hours or so. As it was, he would present her with both rings today.

"You have given it to Gerald?" his aunt asked.

"Not yet," he said. "I sent him home to bed after he returned from Stratton House, if you will remember."

Gerald had been up all night, and he had been busy. He had accompanied His Grace's secretary as they dashed about London achieving the impossible. They had returned before breakfast with a special license and an assurance that a clergyman designated for the task by the archbishop himself would perform the nuptials at Arden House at precisely two o'clock this afternoon.

The drawing room, Lucas could see, had been transformed into a flower garden. There were vases and epergnes everywhere, cover-

ing every available surface that was above floor level and encroach-
ing even upon the floor itself. A linen-and-lace-draped table stood
before the window at the far end of the room. A branch of candles,
as yet unlit, stood upon it, along with a silver cross. A few rows of
chairs had been set up to face it. Not very many chairs, but more
than Lucas had expected. Were they all going to be occupied with
his family and hers? It occurred to him, though, that at least she
would have all her immediate family about her, as would he. When
he had taken her home last night, he had met the eldest brother—
half brother, actually. Ben Ellis, that was. And he had met the
young student, Owen Ware, who had somehow been spirited from
Oxford to London.

"You are going to have to move out of the doorway, Luc," Charlotte said, waving her arms at him in a shooing gesture.

He turned to see a couple of footmen behind him. They were
carrying a large roll of . . . *carpet*? *Red*? It was indeed carpet, but it
was white. He watched them set it down across the doorway and
unroll it all the way across the room and between the rows of chairs
to the table so that anyone attending the wedding would not have
to set their feet upon anything so mundane as the Persian carpet
beneath it. The footmen even managed to turn a corner skillfully
with it without leaving behind them treacherous folds or lumps for
someone to trip over. Charlotte was busy directing them, though it
was clear they did not need any direction. Aunt Kitty, still perched
on the stool, added a few contradictory suggestions. Jenny, seated
in her wheeled chair, was making some adjustments to one of
the enormous bouquets of roses—red, of course—that flanked
the table.

There was a *harp* in the room by the fireplace, Lucas noticed
suddenly. It had not been there yesterday or any day before that.
Dared he ask? He decided against doing so. He would only distract

his female relatives from what was clearly a very busy time for them. And he was, after all, only the bridegroom.

All of this was not at all what he had expected last night when he had been sent by his grandfather—with the silent acquiescence of his grandmother—to make his offer to Lady Philippa, who, His Grace had assured him, would accept it. She had capitulated to their bullying, then, he had thought, half sympathetic to her, half annoyed that she had not after all held firm. He had expected a dour, chilling, very private nuptial ceremony this afternoon in this huge, normally barren room. It had not occurred to him that anyone would try to make a *wedding* out of it.

What *had* occupied his mind through much of the night was the very real possibility that his grandfather would not survive it. His Grace had very definitely suffered a rather severe heart seizure, Dr. Arnold had reported to the family. But his condition had stabilized during the night and might improve if he was kept very quiet in his bed and in a darkened room and if he avoided company and any sort of excitement.

None of them who had been present when he gave his report this morning—Aunt Kitty, Charlotte, Sylvester, Jenny, Gerald, or Lucas himself—had informed the physician that there was to be a wedding at the house today. None of them had promised to keep the duke from attending it. How could they have done so in all good faith? Trying to stop Grandpapa from doing what he had set his mind upon was akin to King Canute trying to order the tide to stop coming in to wet his feet and the legs of his throne.

One of the chairs that had been set out, Lucas noticed now, the one just to the right of the white carpet in the front row, was his grandfather's favorite wing chair. The one next to it was his grandmother's more modest armchair. All the others were upright chairs not specifically designed for comfort.

"I really must dash home," Charlotte said as she rolled down her sleeves and patted her hair ineffectually. "Will you have a carriage summoned, Luc? I must make sure the children are getting ready. Goodness, is that the time? After eleven o'clock?"

It was indeed. Lucas went to do his sister's bidding. Three hours from now he was going to be a married man.

It was a stomach-churning realization.

Unless Lady Philippa Ware came to her senses before then, that was.

P hilippa traveled to Arden House in a carriage with her mother, Devlin, and Stephanie. Her mother alternately patted her hand and lightly rubbed it the whole way from Grosvenor Square while Stephanie nodded and smiled encouragingly and Devlin gazed out of the window, his expression blank and stern—if an expression could be both at the same time.

Philippa appreciated his silence and the way he did not look at her. She appreciated too the wordless reassurances her mother and her sister were beaming her way. She was not feeling nervous, however. Or if she was, then it was an anticipatory sort of nervousness, not a doubtful one. Mama had suggested this morning that it was not too late to call off her wedding or at least postpone it until she had given herself more time to consider. Devlin had suggested the same thing an hour later. He had offered to go in person to Arden House to tell the marquess so. Nicholas, half an hour after that, had made the same offer. He had reminded her of other times when she had acted impulsively and regretted it afterward. *Not* that he had anything against the Marquess of Roath, he had assured her. Far from it, in fact. He seemed a fine sort of chap and there could be no doubting his eligibility. And he could understand, Nicholas had said, why they all wanted to please the old duke, who had looked for a few moments at Almack's as though he were beyond being pleased or displeased by anything more in this life.

"But when all is said and done, Pippa," he had said cheerfully, "it is your life and your happiness at stake. Love him, do you?"

"Yes, Nick," she had said, because it had been the easiest thing to say and he had been looking at her with such kindness and anxiety that she had simply wanted to hug him and maybe shed a tear or two on his broad shoulder.

She was committed to the decision she had made last night. She was not going to start having second and third thoughts until she did not know which direction was up and which was down. She loved the Duke and Duchess of Wilby and their family. Perhaps she even loved . . . But her feelings for the Marquess of Roath were far too complex for any neat label. Not that there was anything neat about love. Had anyone ever defined the word to encompass all its many meanings and manifestations? She was beginning to believe there *was* no definition. Love was too vast a thing. It was not even a thing, in fact, but what else did one call it? And the word *vast* must itself have limits. She did not believe love had any.

It was such thoughts during the morning that had calmed her—surprisingly, perhaps. For there was no point in trying to think of something no one could even define. One could only live one's life day by day, minute by minute, holding true to the choices and decisions one made and hope that somehow one would find . . . what? Love? But she refused to allow her thoughts and emotions to spin in endless circles.

She set her hand in Devlin's as she descended from the carriage and looked up the steps to the open doors of Arden House. The butler, looking both stately and avuncular, awaited them. She did not know what to expect inside. One great blessing, though, was that somehow or other—certainly not by prearrangement—all her immediate family would be present at her wedding. She might have wept over Owen last night if by the time she arrived home and saw him she had not been numb to all feeling.

As the butler bowed them into the hall, Viscount Mayberry was coming downstairs, a warm smile on his face, a twinkle in his eye.

"I am to hand you this," he said to Philippa after greeting them all. He picked up a long package from the hall table, unwound the white cloth in which it had been loosely rolled, and handed her a perfect peach rosebud. The long stem had been ingeniously wrapped about with golden gauze to protect her hand from the thorns.

"Thank you," she said, raising the flower to her nose and inhaling its sweet perfume.

The gold would complement her gown. It was one of her new ballgowns. She had not worn it before because it had seemed too gorgeous even for a grand *ton* ball. Perhaps she would keep it for a ball at Stratton House if Gwyneth and Devlin chose to host one, she had thought. But then along had come today—her wedding day. It was pure white, with fine lace wafting over soft silk. It was high-waisted, low-necked, short-sleeved. It fell in straight folds from beneath her bosom to give her a narrow, Grecian profile, but it billowed a bit as she moved—to add femininity and draw attention to her slender figure, Mama's modiste had explained before suggesting gold sequins to catch the light and add distinction to the gown. They encrusted the bodice and sleeves quite thickly and were dotted sparingly over the skirt, almost unnoticeable until she moved and they caught the light. She was wearing gold slippers and long white gloves. Her hair, dressed simply with only a few fine, wavy ringlets, was unadorned.

"Ma'am?" Viscount Mayberry was bowing to the dowager countess and offering his arm. "Allow me to escort you up to the drawing room. You may follow as soon as you are ready, Stratton, with your sisters. All is in order, and His Grace sets great store by punctuality. Having said which, I will add, since he is not present to overhear me, that it ought to be a bride's privilege to be late by a minute or two or even ten if she so chooses." He winked at Philippa.

Her mother, elegant as always, dressed in blue, ascended the stairs on his arm, and Stephanie fussed with the hem of Philippa's gown though there was no need to do so. She was wearing her pretty sprigged muslin dress, one of the few new garments to which she had consented. Her hair was dressed in its usual thick braids wrapped over the top of her head.

Joy might have been a bridesmaid too, as she had been for Gwyneth and Devlin's wedding before Christmas. But when Philippa had asked her this morning, she had shaken her head vigorously, moving all her soft curls and her whole body with it, and checked to see that her papa was not far away.

"Not even with Aunt Steph as your fellow bridesmaid to hold your hand?" Stephanie had asked.

Stephanie was perhaps Joy's favorite person after her papa, with the possible exception of Owen. But she was not to be moved and had shaken her head again and gone to wrap her arms about one of Ben's legs. The weeks she had spent at Penallen with him seemed to have brought back some of the early shyness she had shown when Ben first brought her to England and Ravenswood with him after the Battle of Toulouse.

"You look gorgeous, Pippa," Stephanie said now.

"You do indeed," Devlin agreed, and at last there was a smile in his eyes. "Ready?"

Yes, she was ready. She ascended the stairs, her hand through his arm. Stephanie came behind them. Philippa could hear the soft murmur of voices coming from the drawing room. Viscount May-

berry stood in the doorway and waited for them to cross the landing from the top of the stairs before smiling warmly at them and
turning to give a signal to a person Philippa could not see.

Someone played a sweeping chord on a harp, and Devlin turned
his head to smile fully down at Philippa. He patted her hand on
his arm.

"Gwyneth's little surprise," he murmured.

Gwyneth was sitting across the room beside the fireplace—just
where she, Philippa, had been sitting with Jenny one afternoon not
long ago when she turned her head to see the Marquess of Roath
standing in this very doorway. It was Gwyneth who had played the
run on the harp, though it was not her own instrument.

The murmur of voices from the other end of the room had
stopped. And Gwyneth played and sang in her lovely contralto
voice. She sang the very hymn the choir had sung at the start of her
own wedding in the church at Boscombe before Christmas. The
choir had sung unaccompanied because Gwyneth was the bride
and Sir Ifor Rhys, her father and the organist at the church, was
leading her in, just as Devlin was now leading Philippa into the
drawing room.

Now Philippa felt the breath catch in her throat. They had
stepped onto a white strip of carpet. She could see people standing
in neat rows to one side of the fireplace—the servants of the house,
all clad in what were surely their best uniforms, starched and ironed
for the occasion. The carpet turned in the middle of the room and
led them toward the far window and banks of flowers and rows of
chairs, all of them occupied, and a stately, white-haired clergyman
in full clerical vestments standing before a table upon which a
branch of candles burned. He held a leather-bound book clasped to
his bosom with both hands crossed over it.

And . . .

And the Marquess of Roath stood straight before a great wing chair, his hands clasped at his back, his cousin at his side, his eyes upon Philippa.

The room smelled like all the beauty of summer.

The music, played softly, sung softly, nevertheless filled the room and made perfectly clear to all those gathered there, though they were in a private drawing room rather than a church, that this was a holy occasion, one of the most solemn of anyone's lifetime.

"Blest be the tie that binds
Our hearts in Christian love
The fellowship of kindred minds
Is like to that above"

Philippa swallowed, and Devlin hugged her arm more tightly to his side.

She had not expected to feel any great emotion. She had not expected to want to weep. She had not expected to feel such a rush of . . . *something* for the man who waited for her. Last night she had thought these nuptials would be brief, passionless, and colorless. A mere means to an end. If they happened at all, that was. She had been more than half convinced that the Duke of Wilby would not survive the night. And then what? Would they marry anyway? She had had no idea.

He had survived the night. And he had come to the drawing room with the duchess to see his grandson and heir wed the woman they had chosen for him and been quite determined he *would* marry. They were seated in the large chairs at the front, across the white carpet from her mother and her brothers.

But though she saw the scene around her, as though with a sharpened vision, it was upon one figure that Philippa's eyes focused. And they did not waver, even as his did not waver from her. She gazed at him when she and Devlin stopped walking and the music faded to silence. She removed her gaze only long enough to draw off her gloves and hand them, with the rosebud, to Stephanie.

She gazed at him again. Into those dark, sometimes green-flecked eyes. Steady, unsmiling eyes.

"Dearly beloved," the clergyman said.

Lucas had suggested that he would bring his bride up to his grandfather's room immediately after the wedding. They would sit with him awhile, and he would know that the first step had been taken to secure the succession. Then he could sleep again, relax, concentrate upon recovering his health.

"Balderdash," the Duke of Wilby had said, as Lucas had known he would. He had said it, after all, or something similar, to everyone else who had tried to reason with him today. Lucas had been the last hope of his family.

By ten minutes to two His Grace was seated in his wing chair, a mere few feet from what would be the main action, looking like a pale, crotchety gnome, gripping the arms of his chair. Her Grace beside him looked regal in purple gown and turban.

Gerald had the rings. Plural.

"Nobody told me I was going to have to worry about dropping *two* rings and having to chase them as they roll on the floor," he had complained. "Which one should I chase down first if they should roll in different directions, Luc?"

Lucas had ignored him.

Everyone came despite the shortness of the notice. Even Sylvester's mother and her husband and his grandson and Sylvester's brother and sister-in-law and their family came, though none of them were blood relations of the Ardens. The niece of a second cousin of Grandmama's had been invited to come with her husband since they had called at Arden House a couple of weeks or so ago to pay their respects to their illustrious relative. They were here. The Ware siblings had come, of course, as well as the brother and sister of the late Stratton, with their spouses and children and the be-trothed of one of them. The dowager countess's brother had come.

It was almost like a normal wedding.

There was even music. Very superior music, as it turned out. Aunt Kitty had discovered from the dowager countess that the new Countess of Stratton was Welsh and therefore a good singer and therefore too an accomplished harpist—it seemed the three went hand in hand. She had won contests at festivals whose Welsh name Aunt Kitty could neither pronounce nor spell, but her dear Clarissa was going to ask the countess to volunteer her services at the wed-ding if a harp could be found. A harp had been found—Lucas had not asked where or how.

Perhaps it really *was* a normal wedding, he thought at approxi-mately one minute after two as his bride joined him at the end of the white carpet and he forgot his discomfort at having his grand-father gazing fixedly upon him, just like the picture of an eagle Lucas had seen staring downward at its prey. Eagle, gnome—could one man look like both? He forgot the discomfort of having his own family and hers nodding benevolently his way as though they could sense the fact that his valet had tied his neckcloth as though he were fashioning a noose.

It *was* a normal wedding, he thought as the clergyman intoned those age-old words, *Dearly beloved*... and he found himself in the middle of his own wedding service, making vows, listening to vows, sliding two rings onto the slender finger of his bride, and becoming, before he could quite comprehend what was happening, a married man. A husband gazing at his wife. At Lady Philippa Arden, Marchioness of Roath. And realizing, quite unexpectedly, that it *mattered*, this ceremony. This marriage. He was not just a duke's heir, allying himself to an eligible bridal candidate because his grandfather had decided it would be so. He was Lucas Arden, marrying Philippa Ware, who would be his wife until death parted them.

It mattered.

She had not smiled even once since she stepped onto the white carpet on her brother's arm. But there was something in her eyes. Something in her expression. Some intensity. And he wondered if it mattered to her too, or if her resolve had merely crumbled last night in light of the dire condition of his grandfather's health. She had been seated between him and Grandmama at Almack's. She had been *laughing* with him. The Duke of Wilby, who rarely laughed, had been laughing with the young woman he had set his heart upon his grandson marrying.

Lucas did not know if this marriage mattered to her. But it would. It must. It was the relationship in which she would remain for the rest of her life. She might have married almost any single man of her choice now present in London. He was not even sure if she was aware of her power to captivate male hearts with her loveliness, her smiles, her laughter, and her charm. But it was too late for her to discover it now if she had not already done so. She was his. He would see to it that their marriage mattered to her.

She was his indeed. The clergyman was saying so.

"Forasmuch as Lucas and Philippa have consented together in holy wedlock, and have witnessed the same before God and this company, and thereto have given and pledged their troth to each other, and have declared the same by giving and receiving of a ring, and by joining of hands: I pronounce that they be man and wife together in the name of the Father, and of the Son, and of the Holy Ghost. Amen."

They gazed at each other while there was a faintly audible sigh from their gathered relatives.

The clergyman continued with prayers and a psalm. But the deed was done.

They were man and wife together.

And it mattered.

CHAPTER TWENTY

The Duke of Wilby was still breathing. That was probably about the best he could say about his condition. But he had come down to the drawing room. Well, to be more accurate, he had allowed himself to be carried down by two burly footmen, who had made no eye contact with either him or each other during the process. But the result was the same. Here he sat on the only chair in the London home worth sitting upon. He had been present for Luc's wedding. He had, by God, achieved the penultimate goal of his life, which had been devoted since the death of his own father when he himself was sixteen to the performance of his duty.

To achieve his ultimate goal, of course, he was going to have to keep on breathing for at least another nine months. He was perfectly well aware that babies did not get implanted just because a man was having marital relations with his wife. For reasons known only to some jokester of a deity it sometimes took a month or two or six of such marital encounters. Some women, apparently perfectly healthy specimens, continued barren. Some suffered miscarriage after miscarriage. Others produced girl after girl, with annual regularity. His Grace had nothing whatsoever against girls. His daughter and his granddaughters were among his favorite people. Not to mention his duchess, who was soul of his soul. But girls, damn it all, could not inherit dukedoms or entailed property. They could not carry forward one's name and one's legacy and all for which one had spent a lifetime of hard work.

And some women, bless their hearts, gave birth to healthy sons. Plural. The first of them nine months from the nights of their weddings.

One could only trust that Lucas's bride was such a woman. The Duke of Wilby believed she was. He had a feeling about her. He had had it since he first set eyes upon her sitting on the far side of the round table in the breakfast parlor in this very house, directly across from Luc, who had been looking smitten. He had been looking smitten ever since, though he was too stubborn to admit it, even to himself, His Grace suspected. Lucas had given him more sleepless nights than anyone else since the death of poor Franklin. He was a good boy in almost every conceivable way, and his grandfather loved him to distraction. But there was *something* that had always blocked him from being the happy man he ought to be. That was why His Grace, with the full blessing of his duchess, had decided soon after their arrival in London that more important even than eligibility in their selection of a wife for his heir was *love*.

His Grace did not dare contemplate what his own life might have been like without his May. It was as plain as the nose on his face that Lady Philippa Ware was to Lucas what May had been to him—after he had got over his irritation with her for being a whole head taller than he when he stood in his stockinged feet, that was.

Why Lucas had denied the obvious from the start, and why the lady had denied it too, the duke had no idea whatsoever. They were a handsome enough couple, by God. And Lucas was a good half head taller than she. The way things ought to be in a perfect universe.

They would learn. Perhaps they would begin to learn tonight. There was nothing like a good, vigorous bedding to begin turning a couple's thoughts in the direction of love. Not that even the best of beddings equated love, of course, but they could certainly help.

He gazed broodingly at the couple while the clergyman, his interminable prayers and psalm readings and even a sermon on the duties and blessings of marriage, for God's sake, having come to an end, turned to the table behind him and opened the register for the bride and groom to sign and Stratton and Gerald to witness.

To sew everything up right and tight.

Her Grace sniffed, and the duke reached out a hand—his arm still worked, he was pleased to discover—to cover hers. May never sniffed and never wept. Except on the most momentous of occasions, that was. Kitty's wedding, and Franklin's. Now Luc's.

The two witnesses hugged the bride and shook the groom's hand. The clergyman bowed solemnly to both and shook their hands. There was a murmuring among the family members gathered behind the duke and hidden from his sight by the wings of his chair. One tiny voice spoke up.

"Aunty Pippa."

Another voice—young Susan's—whispered so audibly that she might as well have shouted aloud. "Aww. Isn't she *sweet*, Mama?"

The duke assumed she was referring to the owner of the tiny voice rather than to Aunty Pippa.

And then the newly married couple turned from the table and the bridal party. The groom offered a hand to his bride, she set her own upon it, and he led her forward the few steps to the wing chair and the one next to it. Luc's eyes were burning in his head, the duke saw with approval. His bride's were bright as though lit from within. Her cheeks matched the color of the rosebud she had taken from her sister's hand.

Luc bowed. His bride curtsied.

"Grandmama, Grandpapa," he said. "May I present the Marchioness of Roath. My wife."

Her Grace's hand turned beneath the duke's and she squeezed it tightly enough, it seemed to him, to break bones—it would not take much.

"Oh. My dears," she said.

"I am content," the duke told them. And if it sounded a bit of an anticlimactic comment to them, what did they expect? That he would leap from his chair and cut a caper?

Then he almost did just that. For the marchioness leaned over May's chair and kissed her gently on the cheek before doing the same thing to him.

"And *now* are you happy?" she murmured to him, and he would swear there was laughter in her voice even though he had not seen her crack a smile yet today.

"Ecstatic," he said gruffly. And frowned.

That harp was playing again. Quietly, in the background. The duke had never thought too highly of the Welsh and the Irish, even when his granddaughter had married one of the latter. They tended to have emotions that were too volatile for his taste. But heaven had certainly singled them out for particular favor when it had dropped that instrument in their midst.

Philippa found herself enfolded in the arms of her own family and then the marquess's. But oh goodness, could she continue to think of him by his title? He was her *husband*. They all hugged her and kissed her cheek and told her how lovely she looked and wished her many years of happiness. All except him. Both families hugged him too and congratulated him and wished him well. Everyone except her.

They had been drawn apart by their families. They had not spoken a word to each other since her arrival except what had been required of them by the wedding service.

The servants had left the drawing room while the register was being signed. Gwyneth played the harp for a while and then stood it upright and got to her feet to shake the outstretched hand of Lord Patterson. She crossed the room to hug Philippa and tell her what a very beautiful bride she was and what a handsome husband she had.

"Marriage is *wonderful*," she said, holding both of Philippa's hands tightly. "Take it from an old veteran. You are going to be *so* happy, Pippa."

"Is my wife saying things to make me blush?" Devlin asked, stepping up to them and setting an arm loosely about Gwyneth's shoulders. "It was a very lovely service, Pippa."

"It was," she said. "Thank you for your surprise, Gwyneth. The music made me want to weep."

"Thank heaven you did not," Gwyneth said, laughing. "Imagine my embarrassment if you had. And imagine what it would have looked like to poor Lord Roath if he had seen you coming toward him with tears streaming down your cheeks."

All was bustle and celebration after that. Cake and champagne were being carried in and set out on a table at the other end of the room. Susan, her hands on her knees, was bending over Joy and talking to her in a baby voice, inviting her to come and play with her cousins Matthew and Patty. Joy was bouncing up and down on both feet and reaching for Susan's hand, her papa forgotten for the moment. Roger Quick, blushing hotly, was talking with Stephanie.

Sir Gerald Emmett, Viscount Mayberry, and his brother were turning the Duke of Wilby's chair, with the duke still in it, to face the room instead of the window. His Grace, not surprisingly, had refused to retire to his bedchamber, which he ought not to have left in the first place. He still looked far from well. Devlin went to talk to the clergyman and then shook his hand and walked with him to the door, where the marquess was waiting to escort him downstairs. It seemed the man had declined any invitation to stay for refreshments.

The duchess stood while her chair was turned and then reached for Mama's hand, Philippa saw, held it in both her own while they spoke, and then kissed her cheek. Lady Catherine and Mama were then hugging each other and making sounds that were suspiciously like girlish squeals. They were celebrating the fact, perhaps, of the new connection between their families. Owen and Nicholas and then Ben were talking with Jenny, who was smiling happily and waved at Philippa when she caught her eye. She said something that caused Philippa's brothers to turn their heads her way and beam at her. Uncle George was deep in conversation with Timothy and Raymond Bonham. Uncle Charles was chatting with Lady Patterson, Aunt Marian and Cousin Angeline with Charlotte and Laura Bonham.

Everyone appeared to be in high spirits. No one seemed to be mourning the fact that this marriage had been a rushed, passionless affair.

Philippa drank in the scene around her, so unexpected before her hasty agreement last evening to marry the Marquess of Roath because she wanted to grant an old man his dying wish. Though that was not quite the truth, was it? Surely she would not have agreed to marry a man she was quite adamantly opposed to marrying. Was it that she had just needed an excuse to change her mind, then?

But she really had not anticipated *this*. She had expected something quiet and subdued, something almost dreary. She breathed in the heady scent of all the flowers and noticed how the light from the window was winking off the dozens of sequins on the skirt of her gown.

"It is time to cut the cake and serve it to our guests." The marquess had come up behind her when she was for the moment standing alone. He must have just returned from seeing the clergyman on his way. He set one hand lightly behind her waist. "Lady Stephanie will carry the platter, and young Roger Quick will distribute napkins. Gerald and Sylvester will carry around trays of champagne. Everything has been organized down to the last detail by my female relatives."

Sir Gerald Emmett was standing by the large table, waiting for them. He silenced the room with a piercing whistle, which caused Lady Catherine to look quite horrified for a moment. And he delivered a short speech fully intended to embarrass his cousin. He soon had everyone laughing—and then applauding as Philippa took up the big cake knife, her husband covered the back of her hand with his own, and together they cut through icing and marzipan and fruit cake. How the duke's cook had managed to produce it on such very short notice, Philippa could not imagine.

Lady Catherine took over then and cut generous slices of cake while Philippa's mother arranged them on a platter. Stephanie carried it and Philippa placed individual pieces onto the small plates her husband handed to the wedding guests. Roger gave everyone a linen napkin. Sir Gerald and Viscount Mayberry made sure each adult—as well as Steph and Roger—had a glass of champagne.

Before anyone drank, however, the Marquess of Roath gave a brief speech, thanking everyone for coming at such short notice to make this a very special day for his bride and him, and thanking *her* for doing him the great honor of marrying him. He raised his glass and asked everyone to join him in a toast to the bride. He did not smile. He had not done so all afternoon. But, oh, surely there was something in his eyes, Philippa thought as he looked directly at her. Something suggesting that perhaps this marriage had not been entirely forced upon him.

It felt like a wedding, even though there had been no formal wedding breakfast, and the dozens of guests she might have expected at a grand *ton* wedding at St. George's had been reduced to those members of their immediate families who happened to be in town. The smallness of the gathering did not matter. These were the people who were really important to them, after all.

Devlin made a speech after everyone had drunk to her. He proposed a toast to both of them.

The little girls and Matthew continued to play in a corner of the room, oblivious to all the boring things that kept the adults occupied. Everyone else continued to mingle and talk and laugh. There was a bit of a stir when the Duke of Wilby, finally persuaded to retire to his own apartments with the duchess, insisted upon walking across the room to the door without the help of anyone's arm. He even stopped in the doorway in order to have a word with his grandson and to bow over the hand of his new granddaughter and raise it to his lips. Then he caused renewed consternation when he refused to allow anyone to follow them from the room and insisted that someone close the door behind him.

"There is no cause to worry," the marquess said to all those who were obviously doing just that, including Philippa. "His pride will not allow him to let any of us see two of his footmen carry him up the stairs."

The small reception continued for a while longer. No one was in any hurry to leave. Philippa sat chatting with Jenny and Charlotte and Gwyneth for a while and then joined her brothers and Sir Gerald Emmett. Soon after, she was drawn into a group with her uncles and aunts and the duchess's niece and her husband.

And suddenly it was no longer afternoon but early evening. The heart-wrenching moment had come when Philippa's family must go home—but leave her behind. For Stratton House was no longer where she lived. Her maid had packed her belongings as soon as she left for her wedding and had then accompanied them to Arden House, where she had unpacked them and put everything away in her mistress's new dressing room, next to that of her new husband.

Arden House was now Philippa's home when in London. She was no longer a Ware of Ravenswood. She was an Arden of Amberwell in Leicestershire. She was the Marchioness of Roath. This was her wedding day. Her wedding evening.

She clung to her mother in the hall and then to Stephanie and Gwyneth and each of her brothers, holding back tears as she did so. She hugged them as though she expected never to see them again. She would, of course, and no doubt very soon, even tomorrow. But nothing would be the same, for she would never again belong with them. She belonged here. With her husband, who was shaking her brothers by the hand and kissing Mama and Gwyneth and Stephanie on the cheek. Joy roared by him, bright-cheeked and very obviously overtired. She stopped briefly in order to point at him.

"Uncle Luc," she said.

Ben scooped her up when she came within arm's length of him. Philippa's husband stayed just behind her, giving her space as she stood in the doorway, watching the carriages drive away with her family, one hand raised in farewell.

And they were gone.

He set a hand against the back of her neck.

"It is time we went up to change for dinner, Phil," he said.

Phil. He had called her that before. No one else ever had. She shivered slightly, though not with revulsion.

"Dinner," she said, and remembered that, apart from a few bites of cake, she had not eaten since the meal back at Stratton House that had been too late for breakfast, too early for luncheon. Though actually . . . had she eaten even then?

"Yes," he said. "Aunt Kitty is going to dine with Jenny in her sitting room. You and I will dine alone. It will be good to be quiet together."

Would it? She turned to look into his face. But it was as essentially unreadable as it had been all day. He was offering her his arm. She slid her own through it and they ascended the stairs together.

L ucas took the chair at the head of the dining room table and seated his wife to his right. Her gown this evening was blue, a few shades darker than her eyes. He was beginning to recognize her clothing style—excellently fitted, perfectly fashionable, but simple and virtually unadorned. He doubted he would ever see her in frills and flounces and bows. He wondered if she did it deliberately because she knew that her own beauty needed no enhancement. He doubted it, though. He had seen no sign of vanity in her.

"I hope your grandfather did not overtax his strength by leaving his bed this afternoon and insisting upon remaining in the drawing room even after the service was over," she said.

"My grandfather's strength has always been as much a mental

as a physical thing," he said. "He was determined to see me married and he did so. I believe he might have done himself more harm than good if he had remained in his room."

She did not comment immediately. She waited until the footman who was serving their soup had moved back to take his place beside the butler at the sideboard.

"Will he slip away, then, now that he has seen you safely married?" she asked, frowning as she picked up her spoon.

"Not if he can help it," he said. "For *safely* to him means married with a son. He will try to live another nine months."

Her spoon paused halfway to her mouth. She returned it to the bowl.

"But you knew this," he said, keeping his voice low, as she was doing so that the butler and the footman would not overhear more than the odd word or two of their conversation. "You knew that as soon as you married me your primary duty—and mine—would be to provide the dukedom with an heir to come after me."

"It is always so with men of property and fortune," she said. "It is even more urgent for men with hereditary titles. But I do not like to think of marriage as being solely for the production of heirs. And I do not like to think of having children for that reason alone. What would be the point? Where would be the happiness?"

He looked at her bent head as she drank her soup noiselessly—and with a perfectly steady hand.

"Duty and happiness cannot coexist?" he asked her.

"I keep remembering your telling me that you were taken away from your home and your sisters when you had so recently lost both your mother and your father," she said. "You were taken to Greystone—what an apt name that must have seemed to you at the time—to *learn to be a duke*. I am not sure if those were your exact words. You must have learned then, though you were only fifteen at the time, that your foremost duty was going to be to marry and secure the thin thread of your grandfather's line."

"I did," he said. "Though, to his credit, my grandfather did not insist upon my marrying as soon as I was of age—as had happened even sooner for him, by the way. He became Duke of Wilby when he was sixteen. He had no brothers and only one male first cousin."

She set down her spoon, having finished the soup, and looked fully at him. "Have you ever been happy, Lord Roath?" she asked him.

"Luc," he said, irritated. "Or Lucas if you must. I am your *husband*, Phil."

"Yes." She was still gazing at him. "I know. Lucas. I prefer to use your full name. Everyone calls you Luc."

Just as everyone called her Pippa. *Pippa* sounded bouncy and pretty, a little girl's name. *Philippa*, though lovely, was too long. It had not occurred to him until now that names were actually important to those who used them.

"*Have* you ever been happy?" she asked again. "Since you were fourteen, that is."

Oh, he thought, this was so like women. Everything had to be about feelings. Well, he would confound her. Maybe silence her.

"Yes," he said, gazing back at her. "I was happy this afternoon."

She was both confounded and silenced. She sat back in her chair for the footman to remove her soup bowl and bring on the next course. And then, dash it all, when the servant had moved back more or less out of earshot, *she* confounded *him*.

"So was I," she told him.

"You were not wishing like hell that you could go back to last night and give a different answer to the question I asked you?" he said.

"*Like hell?*" She was frowning.

"I beg your pardon," he said.

"You are pardoned," she told him, and for the merest moment he thought he saw laughter in her eyes. "I do *not* wish to go back. It could not be done anyway. We cannot change last night. Or this afternoon. Or four years ago in Sidney Johnson's barn. Or . . . anything that is in the past. As you observed a few moments ago, you are my husband. Lucas."

"It is a little difficult to comprehend, is it not?" he said. "That the brief service in the drawing room this afternoon completely changed the course of our lives."

"Yes," she said.

"It must be more difficult for you than it is for me," he said, frowning. He could remember Charlotte saying so a few months after she married Sylvester, even though she had also said she was more blissfully happy than she had ever imagined was possible— Charlotte had always been a bit given to hyperbole. "You have had to leave your home and family behind today. Your home from now on will always be with me. I, on the other hand, remain in my home with my family."

"But you have a wife in your home too from now on," she said. "Perhaps it is easier to adjust to everything being new than just one thing."

"Shall we admit, then," he said, "that growing accustomed to our new state will require effort? And patience."

It sounded very dull. He had not meant it that way.

"Patience." She smiled—one of the few smiles he had seen on her face today. "I wonder how much patience your grandmother had to practice when she married your grandfather."

He sat back in his chair and laughed.

"The patience of Job, I would wager," he said. "Multiplied by two and then doubled. It may have helped that by his own admission he fell in love with her almost immediately, while it took her a year to fall in love with him."

She laughed too, and it was a good moment. Though he felt a bit of a pang at the thought that neither he nor his wife was in love and perhaps never would be.

Or would they?

Or *were* they?

Was he?

They ate their way through five courses. Lucas was surprised to find that he was hungry. He was gratified to see that his wife had a good appetite too. They conversed on a variety of topics—with some ease, he was happy to discover. It was so strange, this—all of it. The whole day. The frantic preparations this morning while his grandfather clung stubbornly to life in his own room with Grandmama in attendance on him. The brief nuptial service in the familiar surroundings of the drawing room rather than in a church. The busy, noisy hours afterward with a surprisingly large number of their relatives about them. His grandparents withdrawing to their own apartments and Aunt Kitty informing him that she and Jenny would dine quietly together in Jenny's sitting room. Everyone else leaving within fifteen minutes of one another. His realization when he was alone with his wife that they belonged together now and for all time while they both lived. And now this quiet meal alone together, far less awkward than he had feared it would be.

It was his wedding day. He was a married man. He had wed Lady Philippa Ware, of all people. Daughter of the late Earl of Stratton. It was enough to make his head spin on his shoulders.

"Shall I go to the drawing room and leave you to your port?" she asked when the covers from the last course had been removed and both their wineglasses were empty.

"I think not," he said, getting to his feet and offering her his hand. "The drawing room is really not a cozy place unless there is company. It is not late, but it is not early either. Shall we go up?"

Their wedding day was not over, after all. The part of it that was still to come was at least as important as what had been accomplished this afternoon. And he was ready for it, by God. For there had not been a moment all afternoon or now, during dinner, when he had not been aware of her as a woman. Whom he desired quite acutely.

"As you wish." She set her hand in his. Slender, long-fingered, smooth-skinned. He could feel her rings with his thumb. For a moment their eyes met and he saw in hers . . . Not desire, surely. But not revulsion either, or even just mute acceptance.

He closed his fingers about hers.

CHAPTER TWENTY-ONE

He understood that there was one very basic difference between what marriage meant to a woman and what it meant to a man, Philippa realized. A bride must relinquish both her family and her home in order to live in the midst of a new family in a strange home. It was a huge difference. Did all men know that? She doubted it.

He had accompanied her downstairs to the hall this afternoon when her immediate family was returning home to Stratton House. He had shaken hands with her brothers, kissed the women on the cheek, and tousled Joy's hair as she dashed by. He had stood in the doorway, not beside Philippa but slightly behind her. His presence had given support, but he had not intruded upon what was an emotional moment for all of them. He had given her space and the time to hug everyone at some length. At dinner this evening he had acknowledged that today must be more difficult for her than it was for him.

In fact, since meeting him in London, she had seen no evidence at all that he was a man capable of arrogance or disdain or cruelty. And the story he had told her when he came to Stratton House to speak with Devlin and then her had really quite adequately explained his behavior on that notorious evening just before Easter four years ago.

Philippa stood at the window of an unfamiliar bedchamber, which would be hers while they remained in London. Behind her, candles burned on the dressing table. Before and below her was the garden at the center of Berkeley Square, visible in the light shed by the lamps about its perimeter. It never seemed to be quite dark in London as it was in the country whenever clouds hid the moon and stars. There was a couple walking arm in arm diagonally across the garden. It was really not very late, of course. There were probably balls and parties somewhere tonight that were just nicely getting started.

It seemed strange that he had kissed her only once. At Stratton House after he had told his story and just before Devlin came back into the library and interrupted them. He had kissed her only that once. Yet this was her wedding day. Her wedding night.

It was as though the thought brought him to her. There was a tap upon her dressing room door, which was not quite shut, and it opened as soon as she answered. He must have performed some sort of juggling act in order to tap on the door, though. He was carrying a glass of wine in each hand.

"I toasted you with our families and guests," he said, approaching to hand her one of the glasses. "Then they toasted us. We did not toast each other."

"It is champagne?" she asked, noting the bubbles in her glass.

"It is," he said. He was wearing a burgundy-colored dressing gown and slippers. He was clean-shaven. She could smell what must be his shaving cream—a musky, masculine scent. His hair had been brushed to a smooth sheen.

"Do you have mistresses?" she asked abruptly, and was instantly appalled that she had spoken aloud. She did not know where the question had come from. She had not been *thinking* it.

He recoiled, rather as though she had punched him on the chin. He looked down to make sure he had not spilled any of his champagne.

"Plural?" he said. "No. Not singular either. And if I did, they— assuming the number to be plural—would have been dismissed early today and for all time."

"I would not remain silent about it, you know," she told him. "Even though ladies are taught that they must acquiesce with dignity and silence when necessary to the way their husbands choose to live their lives. I would not keep silent. I would make noise."

"I could almost wish to hear it," he said. "Alas, it will never be necessary. I have a wife. I made promises to her before a clergyman and both our families a few hours ago. There is no time limit on those promises, only *until death do us part*."

He spoke quietly, though his tone was a bit grim.

"I did not intend to ask," she told him. "The question seemed to ask itself. But I will not apologize for it. I will not tolerate a marriage like my mother's."

"You will never be expected to," he said. "But it is as well you asked your question so that I can now ask mine. Will you ever take lovers? After you have presented me with a son, perhaps? It is done, you know, and far more frequently than you might think. Or so I have heard—and believe. *Discretion* seems to be the guiding principle of many in the *ton*, both men and women. Almost any transgression can be forgiven except *indiscretion*."

She had angered him, Philippa could see. But she was still not sorry. It was a question she ought to have asked last night before it was too late. But even now, after she had married him, she would not allow him his conjugal rights if he kept mistresses. Or even *one* mistress. She *would not* be like her mother, despite all the admirable dignity Mama had maintained throughout her marriage.

"I will have no lovers except you," she told him.

"Except me," he said softly. "How is it you can defy superlatives, Phil? How can you look even lovelier tonight than you did this afternoon—with your hair down and your feet bare and a loose nightgown that merely hints at the curves beneath?"

How could he look more gorgeous in his dressing gown?

He answered his own question, saving her from having to do so. "Perhaps because tonight there is no need to quell the desire that comes along with the appreciation," he said.

Yes. Perhaps so. *Probably* so. She did not say it aloud.

He raised his glass. "To us, Phil," he said. "To a marriage of honesty and respect. To a marriage of fidelity to each other. To a marriage of companionship and friendship and—I sincerely hope—affection."

She raised her own glass. "To us, Lucas," she said. "To loyalty and always doing our best." She hoped, more than she had hoped for anything else in her life, that their best would be enough. For it was a mutual best of which she spoke, not an individual one. She could speak for herself but never really for him too. It was a matter of trust.

He touched the rim of his glass to hers and they drank. She had not got to join in either toast this afternoon. But she liked champagne. She liked the way the bubbles tickled her nose and sprayed her upper lip.

He took the glass from her hand even though there was still champagne in it and set it with his own on the windowsill.

"And to Grandpapa's great-grandson nine months from tonight," he said, and smiled at her. No, it was not a smile. It was more of a *grin*.

Philippa had a choice between blushing and laughing. She chose the latter, though her cheeks felt as though they might burst into flames at any moment.

"And if it is a great-granddaughter?" she asked.

"Then we will have to try again," he said. "And yes, you may well blush. You walked straight into that one."

She had stopped laughing. And he stopped grinning—and smiling. He cupped both her cheeks with his hands and kissed her. Softly, almost lazily, as though he had all night—which, of course, he did. He raised his head for a moment and reached out with one hand to close the gap in the curtains she had opened when she came into the room earlier.

He kissed her again, a little more deeply. His tongue pressed lightly against the seam of her lips, somehow sending sensation right through her body. His tongue came right into her mouth when she opened it and caressed inner surfaces and stroked the roof of her mouth so that she sagged against him, her hands gripping his elbows.

He raised his head and gazed into her eyes. "We need a bed for the rest of this," he said.

"Yes."

"And nakedness," he added.

Oh. She had not expected that. She was not at all sure . . .

"Come," he said, and he moved her backward to the bed, which was ready for them, the covers turned back. He took hold of the sides of her nightgown and lifted it until she raised her arms. He removed it entirely and dropped it to the floor before laying her on the bed and gazing down at her while he undid the knot of his belt at the waist and his dressing down fell open. He shrugged out of it and let it fall to join her nightgown. He was not wearing a nightshirt. He lay down beside her as she moved farther to the center.

She was not going to be nervous or missish, she thought, even though she had not expected that they would be completely un-clothed and he made no move to pull the covers over them. They were husband and wife. If this was what happened . . . But *the candles.* They were burning steadily in the holders on the dressing table. They must have been newly placed there today. They had hours' worth of light left in them.

"I do not want to make you nervous," he said as he turned toward her and raised himself on one elbow. "I have *some* experience, though not much. Enough to know what I am doing, though. I know you have none. It does not matter. It is the way it is supposed to be. I will try not to hurt you. Trust me?"

"I will," she said. "Kiss me again."

He did. He did a great deal more than just that, though. His hands moved down her arms and along her back while she got her breathing under control and tried to relax and tell herself that this was just the first of many, many such nights and was not to be feared. But then his hands moved inward to roam and caress. They circled her breasts, and his thumbs stroked lightly over her nipples, causing raw sensation to engulf her and fill her with a longing to which she could not put a name.

His mouth had been on hers, his tongue engaging her own. But he moved his head downward now, and he suckled first one nipple and then the other, his tongue at play, his breath alternately warm on her sensitive skin as he exhaled and then cold as he inhaled. Her fingers found his thick hair and twined into it. And his hand moved lower and found private places and parted and caressed lightly un-til she thought she would not be able to stand the unnamable yearning any longer. She lifted herself toward his hand and one finger slid inside her, shocking her into gasping aloud. She could feel and hear wetness.

He raised his head again then and moved over her and brought his weight down on her. His hands slid beneath her as his knees pushed her legs wide, and he looked into her eyes, his own heavy-lidded, while he came into her. Slowly. Stretching her. Not hurting her, as she had expected he would. Until . . . ah, until there was no room left but he kept entering her anyway. Just before she could panic, there was a sharp pain and he came all the way into her and she wondered if it had been pain or intense pleasure she had felt.

"I am so sorry," he murmured, his lips against hers.

Then he moved his head to the side, held her firmly, and began to move in her with what brought both pain and pleasure. And shock too. The ultimate intimacy of marriage. Something with which she would become very familiar in the days and months and years ahead. And she was glad. So very glad that it would be an integral part of their marriage and that it was beautiful.

She must learn, she thought, to please him as he was pleasing her. But she had a lifetime in which to learn.

It went on for a long time. She did not want it to end. When it did, she was faintly disappointed. But there would be more times. Many more times. The rhythm of his thrusts and withdrawals had broken, and he held deep inside her until she felt the hot gush of his release. He exhaled with an audible sigh against the side of her head and relaxed more of his weight onto her for a few moments.

"That was self-indulgent of me," he said then as he moved to her side. "I ought to have ended it sooner. I hope I did not cause you unnecessary pain."

"No," she said. There ought to have been more to say, but she could not think of anything.

"You must sleep now, Lady Roath," he said. "You have done your duty for one day."

She could not tell from his tone if he was serious or if he was somehow joking with her. And she could hardly ask. She wished he had kept his arms about her, maybe drawn her against him. She felt suddenly chilly. He leaned down almost as though she had told him so and pulled the covers over them. He did not touch her. But he did not go away to his own bedchamber either. She knew he had one. It was beyond his dressing room, which adjoined hers.

Perhaps duty did not allow him to sleep alone until he had got her with child. But oh dear, it sounded very calculating. Very chilling. As though human emotions and relationships were of no real importance when set against duty.

He was sleeping, she realized after a few minutes. She turned toward him and gazed into his face in the candlelight.

She saw the Marquess of Roath.

Her husband. In every conceivable way.

D awn was graying the room when Lucas awoke. He had slept deeply for a number of hours, he was surprised to discover. This was a strange room and a strange bed. He was unaccustomed to sharing either. Nevertheless, he was totally comfortable. Philippa was still fast asleep beside him, turned slightly away from him, naked and warm, blond hair covering her shoulder and hiding her face.

He thought of last night, of how thoroughly enjoyable it had been. Though *enjoyable* was rather a tame word to describe just how good it had been. She was a beautiful woman, as lovely without her clothes as she was with them. Lovelier, in fact. They had had satisfactory sex. Though why were words not superlative enough when one wanted them to be? It had been far more than just satisfactory. Best of all, she was *his wife*. His for the rest of their lives—as he was hers. It made a difference—marriage, that was. What had happened had not been just about desire and passion. It had been about commitment and the rest of their lives.

He wondered if it would be selfish to wake her and have her again now, before it was time to get up. Getting her with child was his primary duty as a new husband, after all. Yet it seemed a chilling thought. She had, of course, been a virgin—he had felt her flinch while he was mounting her. Would she be sore this morning? Had *she also* found the consummation of their marriage *enjoyable* and *satisfactory*? He really was not sure.

She had not said much at all last night, in fact. Except, that was, when she had asked him if he had mistresses and told him she would not tolerate them if he did. When he had proposed a toast to them, she had said, *"To us, Lucas. To loyalty and always doing our best."*

Loyalty.

Always doing our best.

She had said it just after he had spoken of his hope for friendship and affection between them. Ought he to have mentioned love too? But love was not something one mentioned as a future possibility, surely, not when one was speaking to the person one might perhaps love at some future date. Ought he to have said it anyway, as something he already felt for her? He would not have been lying.

It would not have seemed fair, though. She had already been bullied into marrying him—and maybe that was not too strong a word. His grandparents, particularly his grandfather, had pursued her relentlessly—by *liking* her, by making her like them. He believed she was genuinely fond of them. It had seemed to him that the evening before last—had it really happened so recently?—she had been as upset by Grandpapa's heart seizure as his own family had been. She had been bullied by circumstances. The Duke of Wilby was dying. She had it in her power to let him die in peace, knowing that she, His Grace's own personal choice, would marry his grandson. What Grandpapa had said to her in his bedchamber when he had her summoned there Lucas did not know, but whatever it was, it had persuaded her to say yes without any time for consideration. She had been bullied, benign as the coercion may have been.

And *he*, God damn it, had bullied her too. By agreeing to make her his offer in Grandmama's sitting room. By throwing the whole weight of the decision upon her shoulders, instead of asserting himself and telling his grandparents for once in his life that no, *no,* it was not right and he would not put that burden upon her at a time of heightened emotion, which really ought not to concern her at all.

Would she *ever* have listened to a proposal of marriage from him if Grandpapa had not suffered that near-fatal heart seizure at Almack's? Would she ever have accepted it even if he had tried? She had every reason to keep her distance from him, to want as little to do with him as possible, even though he had told her the whole story and she surely did not think as badly of him as she had done quite justifiably for the past four years.

No, he thought, turning away from her on the bed and staring at the window, she would not have married him in the natural course of events. It was his grandfather who had courted her, but it was he, Lucas, to whom she was married for the rest of her life.

She could have married *anyone.* She seemed largely unaware of the effect she had had upon the male half of the *ton*—married men and single, young, middle-aged, and elderly. *He* was aware of it. She could have held out for love and happily ever after. She would surely have found them. And she would have deserved them after four years of what sounded to him like severe lowness of spirits, believing herself to be *soiled goods* on account of her father's transgressions.

Now this was a pretty kettle of fish he found himself holding. He was married and could not go back to do what he surely ought to have done the night before last—refusing to put pressure upon Lady Philippa Ware, that was, when she was away from her own family, embroiled in *his* family's drama, and surely unable to think straight. He was married, and nothing could change that. *She* was married, rushed into making a hasty decision because an old man of whom she had grown fond was dying. She would now do her duty as his wife because she had been well brought up and had a strong sense of what was right and proper. She had said it last night.

To loyalty and always doing our best.

But it would not be a passive loyalty. She would not tolerate any misbehavior on his part. His wife was sweet and loyal by nature. She did not, however, lack resolve and firmness of character. Those facts at least made him smile.

He would *not* wake her, he decided. She was not a *vessel for reproduction.* Nor was she just a convenient female to cater to his lust. The fact that he was feeling lusty both annoyed and shamed him.

He got out of bed as carefully as he could, picked up his dressing gown from the floor, and made his way quietly through her dressing room into his.

Ten minutes later he was in the stables in the mews behind the house, saddling his horse despite the protestations of a sleepy groom, who put in a sudden appearance and was told to go back to bed. Five minutes after that Lucas was riding into Hyde Park and making his way toward Rotten Row, where he could give the horse its head and feel the wind in his face. The fact that it was a chilly morning, which threatened rain at any moment, suited him well.

CHAPTER TWENTY-TWO

Philippa was not for a moment disoriented when she awoke. She remembered everything as clearly as the daylight brightening the insides of her eyelids. She smiled and stretched and reached out a tentative hand to touch him.

He was not there. And the mattress where he had lain was cold beneath her hand. She opened her eyes, horribly disappointed, but telling herself not to be. Perhaps he had woken early and, not wanting to disturb her, had eased himself off the bed and out of the room. Maybe he was waiting to tease her for being a sleepyhead.

What time *was* it? She opened her eyes and looked around the room for a clock. There was none. She had not noticed last night. Her room was fully light, however, and there was a cup of chocolate on the small table beside the bed—with a gray film covering the top of it. It must have been there for at least half an hour. How excruciatingly embarrassing. She threw back the covers and swung her legs over the side of the bed—only to realize that she was not wear-

ing anything. She blushed just as though there were someone else
in the room to notice.

She could only imagine how everyone would look knowingly at
her when she finally appeared in the breakfast parlor. *If* there was
anyone left there, that was. It was altogether possible that everyone
was halfway through their busy morning activities by now. She
hurried around the bed, pulled on her nightgown, went through to
her dressing room, and rang for her maid.

It was not as late as she had feared it might be. When she entered the breakfast parlor twenty minutes later, Lady Catherine and
Jenny were still eating at the round table. No one else was there,
though. Goodness, where was Lucas? She hoped no one asked, for
she surely ought to know. He was her *husband*.

"I am so sorry to be late, Lady Catherine," she said. "There is
no clock in my bedchamber."

"That is inconvenient," Jenny said. "You must have one taken
there today, Pippa."

Lady Catherine had got to her feet to come and kiss Philippa
on the cheek. "It must be *Aunt Kitty* now that you are my niece,"
she said. "No, do not sit down, Pippa. You are under strict orders to
take breakfast in my mother's dressing room. You are privileged
today. I, who am merely her daughter, must eat here with Jenny,
who is merely her granddaughter." But her eyes twinkled to show
that she was not at all offended.

"Oh dear," Philippa said. "Am I dreadfully late?"

"Not at all," Aunt Kitty said. "Mama would not have expected
you any earlier this morning."

Philippa drew a few deep breaths as she followed the butler
back upstairs and then waited for him to knock upon the duchess's
door and open it to announce her arrival. The Duke of Wilby was

there too, she saw as she stepped into the room, fully aware that this was the very place where Lucas had proposed marriage to her just the night before last. Despite the instant sense of reality she had felt when she woke earlier, everything now felt just the opposite.

"You will forgive me, perhaps, Granddaughter," His Grace said, "for not getting to my feet to bid you good morning. I must beg you to come here to kiss my cheek."

He was seated in a large armchair, looking gray in the face but sharp-eyed nonetheless. And those eyes saw what they were looking for, Philippa believed as she felt her face grow hot. She bent and kissed his cheek, and he took one of her hands in both of his and raised it to his lips.

"How are you this morning, Your Grace?" she asked him.

"All the better for seeing you looking rosy-cheeked and bright-eyed," he said. "I will feel even better if you will call me Grandpapa."

"Grandpapa," she said, smiling. "Release my hand, if you please. I have not yet greeted—"

"Grandmama. You must call me that now," the duchess said. She was on her feet to greet her, both hands extended. "But, my dear Pippa, you must not allow His Grace to embarrass you. Come and sit here and tell me if you will have tea or coffee while we wait for the food to be brought up."

"Coffee, please," Philippa said. "Shall I pour?"

"I will do it this morning," the duchess said. "You are our guest here, though not in the rest of the house. I hope you understand that even if it takes you a few days to accustom yourself to the change. You are a valued member of our family as of yesterday."

"Thank you." Philippa smiled and remembered Lucas telling her that he understood adjusting to marriage must be far more difficult for a woman than for a man. She no longer quite belonged in the home that had always been hers, not in the same way, at least, he had said, yet she surely must feel an awkwardness with her new family in her new home.

"Now, when do you expect that grandson of mine back from his early morning ride in the park?" the duke asked.

Oh. Had he really gone out? Without a word to her? The morning after their wedding night? Had it all meant nothing to him after all except duty, then? He had said all the right things last night—most of them, anyway—and he had consummated their marriage. He had taken his time over it and had presumably got pleasure from it, but he had not said anything meaningful afterward. He had gone to sleep. Had he merely done what he needed to do in order to accomplish that for which he had married her? What was it he had said to her last night . . . ? *To us, Phil. To a marriage of honesty and respect. To a marriage of fidelity to each other. To a marriage of companionship and friendship and—I sincerely hope—affection.*

No, she was being silly. Everything he had said and done had been neither chilling nor a mere formality. He hoped for friendship and affection between them. She must not now start imagining that he was going to be cold in the performance of his duty. She would not allow herself to fear that she had made a dreadful mistake.

You have done your duty for one day. He had said that too. And he had called her *Lady Roath* rather than *Phil*, the shortened form of her name that had warmed her through to the heart when he had used it because no one else ever had.

"I will not expect him to tell me the exact hour and minute of his return whenever he steps out, Grandpapa," she said in answer to his question. "Any more than I would expect him to demand it of me. But I do not suppose he will be long."

But it was the morning after their wedding night.

She had no idea how long he would be. Perhaps he was taking breakfast at one of the gentlemen's clubs. White's was the one she knew about. Devlin was a member there. But oh dear, she hoped not. Not this morning. She would feel it as a great humiliation.

It was a huge relief a moment later when a tap upon the door heralded Lucas's arrival in the room. He was not wearing riding clothes or smelling of horse, Philippa noticed. He had changed and washed and shaved. His eyes alit on her and he smiled.

"My love," he said as he closed the distance between them, took her hand in his, and raised it to his lips as his grandfather had done a short while ago. "I tried not to wake you when I left your bed. You were sleeping peacefully after what was a very long and busy day yesterday. I took myself off riding. I ought to have left word for your maid to pass on to you when you awoke, however. Did you know where I had gone? I have much to learn about being an attentive husband, I fear."

My love? His smile held a touch of . . . roguery? He was speaking to an audience, she thought. Not really to her. She wondered how long it had taken him to compose that little speech and to practice just the expression he would don when he delivered it. But perhaps she was being unfair. They *both* had much to learn. They had not had the usual betrothal period in which to prepare themselves for being married.

"Thank you, Lucas," she said, returning his smile. "I appreciated a little extra sleep this morning."

His eyebrows rose before he turned away to kiss the duchess and bend over his grandfather to inquire after his health.

"Everyone who has come near me wants me to remain in bed and not exert myself," His Grace said gruffly. "It is not going to happen. I intend to live at least another nine months from last night, and I am not going to do it from my bed. Sit down, Lucas. You are *looming*. Her Grace and I wanted this private time with the two of you this morning. Though you might have felt that we— that *I*—harassed and bullied you into marrying our grandson, Philippa, we did it in the conviction that you belong together. Just as our son belonged to our daughter-in-law. Both their lives ended early and tragically, along with that of our grandson in our daughter-in-law's case. But while they lived, Luc's parents, they were devoted to each other and happy. Just as Her Grace and I have been for almost sixty years, though I still sometimes find it hard to forgive her for being half a head taller than I am."

"A full head, Percy," the duchess murmured.

"I daresay your parents were just as devoted to each other and just as happy, Philippa," the duke said. "May remembers that your mama was a lovely and charming young wife. I remember your papa as a handsome, vigorous, good-humored young man, whom everyone liked. They raised children any parents would be proud of. It is our dearest wish that you and Luc will be just another such couple. Our happy families have been united in the two of you, and we are contented."

Philippa sat very still on her chair. Lucas stood very still in the middle of the room.

"We—" he began. But another tap on the door interrupted him and preceded the arrival of a trolley laden with breakfast foods.

Philippa realized with some surprise that she was ravenously hungry.

T wo of his wife's brothers were in London for just a few more days, Lucas had remembered while he was riding in the park. One of the two would very soon be rejoining his regiment and facing the grand battle that was almost certainly going to be fought within the next month or so, possibly sooner. Her whole family must be painfully aware that the farewells they were about to say might very possibly be goodbyes. Another brother—Ben—would probably be returning to the country soon too. He apparently did not participate in *ton* events, or so he had told Lucas when the two of them had talked for a while yesterday. He had come to purchase new clothes for his daughter with the help of his sisters and sister-in-law.

Philippa needed to spend time with her brothers while she could.

In addition, Lucas needed to get to know them all better too. He needed to reassure them, if it was possible after that very abrupt wedding yesterday, that he would treat their sister—and daughter in the case of the dowager countess—with respect and affection, that she had not made a mistake she would live to regret. He certainly needed to have another private talk with the Earl of Stratton. The fact that he was already married to Philippa did not excuse him from discussing a proper marriage contract with his brother-in-law.

"And how are you intending to spend the first day of your married life?" Her Grace asked when they had all finished their breakfast and Grandpapa had just admitted, before any of them could risk his wrath by suggesting it, that perhaps he would lie down upon his bed for a short while before going into the drawing room. Lucas had got to his feet to help his grandfather rise from his chair.

"I—" Philippa began.

"We are going to spend it at Stratton House," Lucas said before leaving the room with the duke. "I sent word there after I returned from my ride. Philippa's family will be expecting us."

"Oh," Philippa said. She sounded surprised. "Thank you. I was hoping to see Nicholas and Owen sometime today."

"You will give them our very best wishes, Philippa," the duchess said. "Especially Major Ware, who I expect is quite eager to return to his regiment."

"Thank you," Philippa said again.

They walked to Stratton House since there was so sign of rain clouds and no appreciable wind and it was really not far. Lucas liked having his wife on his arm, he discovered, her slender gloved hand resting upon his sleeve, her step light, the brim of her bonnet hiding her face from his view except when she tipped back her head to speak to him. Every time she did so, her face looked slightly flushed and animated and happy. He knew the happiness was there because she was about to see her family. Even so, that was happening because he had decided to take her there without having to be asked.

"I intend to have a private talk with Stratton if it is convenient to him," he told her. "We need to discuss a marriage contract, even though it will be after the fact."

"Will you?" she said, smiling. "I am sure Devlin will be delighted to talk with you."

He hesitated a moment. "I would like to tell him the story I told you a few weeks ago," he said. "You gave him your account of that incident some time ago, but he has not heard my explanation. *Not* my excuse, I hasten to add. There is no excuse for what I said that evening. But he must be feeling very uneasy about our marriage. Perhaps I can allay some of his fears by telling him the full story of what led me to say those words. Doing so, however, will show your father and his in a poor light. I will remain quiet if you would prefer."

She thought about it for a few moments. "I almost told him myself the night before last," she said. "He was indeed disturbed that I had agreed to marry you. He tried to talk me out of it. I did not tell him, though. It is a story that defames your mother, and I decided I had no right to tell it without your knowing."

His grandfather had embarrassed him, and surely Philippa too, just before breakfast when he had talked about how it was his dearest wish and Grandmama's that they would be as happy and devoted a couple as their respective parents had been. Grandpapa had also made his comment about their two happy families having been united by this new marriage, as though there was now the double likelihood that their union would be a perfect one. Perhaps, though, Lucas thought, they really could heal old wounds, even though no one but the two of them knew they existed.

They did not have to allow themselves to be dragged down forever by an ill-considered and ultimately tragic affair between his mother and her father. It had had terrible effects upon him as he grew up, keeping a heavy secret buried inside him instead of sharing it with his family. It had had even worse effects upon Philippa, though she had not known of the affair, because of what he had said one evening, quite unaware that she had overheard him. She too had bottled up her secret knowledge inside until she had told her brother last year.

They did not have to be defined by the past, however. He was *not* his mother, just as she was not her father. The present was theirs as was however much of the future was allotted to them. Perhaps they really *could* be as devoted and happy as his grandparents expected them to be. The present Stratton and his countess seemed happy enough. *This* Stratton certainly seemed nothing like what Lucas knew of his father.

"Yes, tell Devlin your story," Philippa said as they turned onto Grosvenor Square. "I do not believe you will be destroying any illusions. He has none. But this is something he ought to know. He loves me very dearly. He wants more than anything to see me happy."

She believed, then, that they could be happy? Lucas was beginning to understand the great disadvantage of their having rushed so headlong into marriage—though really he at least had had no choice. They had been given no chance to become betrothed, to get to know each other more gradually and more fully, to prepare themselves for the changes marriage would bring to their lives. He had not made a good start this morning. By doubting himself and feeling unworthy of the great sacrifice she had made for his sake and his grandfather's, he had almost certainly given the impression that he did not care very deeply for her. He had gone off riding in Hyde Park when he might have stayed in bed with her and gathered her in his arms, perhaps made love to her again if she had felt up to it. Or he could simply have let her sleep until she woke on her own and then talked for a while before they got up together. They could have planned their day together.

He had *so* much to learn.

Their approach to Stratton House must have been observed. The front doors were being thrown open even before they reached the steps.

She turned her face toward him. "It was thoughtful of you to arrange for me to come here today," she said. "And it was kind of you to come too. It matters to me."

It was strange how already home felt different—a place she was visiting rather than one where she belonged.

Everyone was there, and they had all come downstairs to greet them, as though they were visiting royalty. Philippa did not know if some at least of them would have been out doing other things if

Lucas had not sent notice of their coming, but perhaps not, for Nicholas and Owen would be leaving soon. So would Ben and Joy.

The fleeting nature of happiness struck Philippa as she hugged everyone and Lucas shook hands with the men and kissed the women on the cheek and all of them, it seemed, tried to talk at once. Today, for a few hours at least, they would be together here, all her immediate family, enjoying one another's company. Tomorrow they would begin to disperse. Stephanie lost no time in informing them that Nicholas would be returning to Brussels, his mission here in England completed, and that Owen would be going back to Oxford. Even later today they would no longer be all together as a family, for she would be returning to Arden House with her husband.

Where she belonged.

Strangely, even after less than a full day, it no longer seemed an alien concept. Or even an unwelcome one. For she already loved her new family as though she had known them all for a long time. And there was her marriage to which to grow accustomed. It had had a slightly shaky start this morning, perhaps, but Lucas had redeemed himself with that somewhat theatrical speech, in which he had addressed her as *my love*, and then announced that he had already sent word to Stratton House that they would be coming later. He had known how she must long to be here today while all her brothers were still here. And tonight she could surely expect a repetition of last night. It was his reason for marrying her, after all. Her breath quickened at the very thought that she had *that* to look forward to all over again.

Gwyneth took Lucas's arm and led the way up to the drawing room with him, talking the whole way. Nicholas drew one of Philippa's arms through his while Owen took her other arm.

"It is a good thing you have two arms, Pippa," Owen said, "or Nick and I would have to fight each other."

"But she does not have three," Ben grumbled from behind them.

"I hold your hand, Papa," Joy offered.

Lucas mingled well with her family, Philippa was pleased to see during the next hour before luncheon was announced. He seemed relaxed and in good humor. Devlin treated him with a certain stiff reserve, it was true, but her other brothers did not. Nor did Gwyneth or Mama or Stephanie, who had liked him as soon as they met him earlier this spring.

Even Joy, after eyeing him warily from some distance at first, finally pointed a finger at him in that characteristic way of hers and announced in her precise little voice that he was Uncle Luc. She was not talking a great deal yet, but she did seem to have a knack for learning names.

Lucas pointed right back at her. "Niece Joy Ellis," he said.

She chuckled and looked up at Owen, who was sitting on the floor, building a tower of painted wooden blocks for her to push over as soon as it was almost finished.

Gwyneth meanwhile had drawn everyone's attention her way. "Before Devlin and I came to London," she said, "we planned to host some sort of party here at Stratton House. It is the first time we have been to London together and we do need to do more than just attend everyone else's entertainments. Mother agrees with us and so does Stephanie. We are going to invite everyone who *is* anyone in the *ton* to a special ball in celebration of your wedding, Pippa and Lucas. There was no time to arrange either a big wedding or a lavish wedding breakfast for a large number of guests yesterday. So there will be a ball instead. It must, however, have your approval."

"I am holding my breath," Stephanie said. "Please, Pippa? *Please*, Lucas?"

A wedding ball. Oh goodness.

And Philippa realized in a rush how much she had been suppressing a certain disappointment at having had to sacrifice the large wedding she had always dreamed of—except during those dark years when she had not dreamed at all. She knew she would always remember yesterday as a day that had been very nearly perfect in every way. But . . . Oh, was she really going to have *a ball* in honor of her wedding after all? In *London* during the *Season*?

Her eyes flew to Lucas's face. She half expected to see him wincing at the very prospect. But he was looking steadily back at her with no discernible expression.

"What is your wish, Phil?" he asked her.

She smiled at him. "I say yes."

"Then yes it is." He looked as though he were smiling, but just for her. "On condition that there be at least one waltz and you promise it to me—now, before witnesses."

"I will." She laughed, and he smiled for everyone to see. "But"— she turned her gaze upon her mother and Gwyneth—"everything will be dependent upon the Duke of Wilby's health. He is still very weak."

"Of course," Gwyneth said.

"It would be unwise ever to underestimate my grandfather," Lucas said. "He has promised to live to see *my* heir, and I fully expect that he will."

Luncheon was announced then, to Philippa's relief. She could feel her cheeks turn hot. After the meal, Lucas disappeared with Devlin while the rest of them adjourned to the drawing room, where the ladies were soon in a huddle, discussing plans for the ball while the men talked politics.

Gwyneth ordered a tea tray to be brought in when Devlin and Lucas joined them about an hour later. But Devlin did not sit down. He asked for a word with Philippa and took her down to the library.

He closed the door and reached immediately for her. He held her in a wordless hug for a full minute before he spoke.

"Lucas will tell you, Pippa," he said, "that he wants nothing to do with your dowry, which is considerable, as you probably know. It will be held in trust for you and your children. It is no less than I would expect of any man who has the means to support you for the rest of your life in the manner to which you are accustomed. You are a wealthy woman in your own right, a fact that must give you comfort."

"Yes," she said. "But I trust my husband, Dev."

"As it seems you ought," he said. He drew a deep breath. "We really did not know our father very well at all, did we, Pippa? That he would consort with courtesans seemed like the end of the world when we first knew of it. But that he would ruin someone else's marriage as well as his own . . . Well. There are no words."

"The Marchioness of Roath was equally responsible for what happened," Philippa said. "But we are privy only to the bare facts, Dev. We do not know all that lies behind them. I would really rather not stand in judgment."

"I would," he said. "The marchioness destroyed more than just her own life. She permanently scarred the life of her fourteen-year-old son. It was really no excuse that she did not know he was aware of the truth. Our father, who perhaps assumed that what he did during the spring months here in London while he was away from Mama and all of us would do us no harm, was actually wreaking future havoc upon all of us. It is no excuse that we might never have known had he not grown reckless that one year and brought a woman to Boscombe and right into our home. It is hard to forgive either our father or Lucas's mother. I am not sure I ought to do it."

"I loved Papa," she said. "I love him. But I cannot deny his faults. I can only leave them with him and recognize that they are ultimately nothing to do with me."

"You can be happy with Lucas, then?" he asked her, frowning.

"I believe I can," she said.

"I think after all," he said, "he is a decent sort, Pippa. I think he is genuinely fond of you."

"And I am fond of him, Dev," she said.

"Are you?"

She nodded and he hugged her tightly again.

"This being head of the family can be pretty daunting," he said. "I want to make the world and life perfect for all of you. Including Mama. But that is not within my power, is it?"

"No." She shook her head. "It is enough that you love us all, Dev."

"One thing I can tell you," he said. "No matter how many sons Gwyneth and I are blessed with, I will *never* designate any of them for a military career."

"Ah, but I think Nick might have chosen it anyway," she said.

He set an arm loosely about her shoulders and sighed as he opened the door and led her back out into the hall. "We had better go up and spend as much time with him as we can," he said. "I believe you are right, though. He is very different from me. Which is just as well. Who would want two of me in one family?"

Philippa laughed and rested her cheek against his shoulder for a moment.

It was late in the afternoon when Lucas and Philippa took their leave of her family and walked back home to Arden House. It was not an easy parting, for Philippa did not know when she would see three of her brothers again. Owen would be at Oxford until he returned home to Ravenswood at the end of term. Ben would soon be moving permanently to Penallen. And Nicholas . . .

She hugged him, and he rocked her in his arms and kissed her forehead beneath the brim of her bonnet.

"It will take more than Napoleon Bonaparte and his ragtag army to put me down, Pippa," he murmured to her. "But whatever happens, remember that I will be doing what I want to do. And that I want you to be happy. You and Steph. My favorite sisters."

She smiled at him, a bit watery-eyed. "The usual answer," she said.

"You are my *only* sisters?" he said, grinning at her. "I must think of a new one by the next time I see you."

. . . *his ragtag army.*

Napoleon Bonaparte had never had ragtag armies. They had always been the most efficient and fearsome fighting forces the world had known.

Then she was walking home with her husband, leaning a little more heavily on his arm than she had when they came. And he was setting his hand over hers and drawing her a little closer to his side. And it did seem lovely, she thought, not to feel all alone in the world, to have someone to whom she belonged exclusively. *Not* that she intended ever to be a clinging sort of wife. But his arm felt very steady and reassuring, and his hand over hers was warm.

She was very glad she had said yes the night before last, when if she had had an ounce of sense she would have said no.

One word could make all the difference to one's life.

CHAPTER TWENTY-THREE

The Duke of Wilby suffered no deterioration of his health during the three weeks following his grandson's wedding. According to him, though, eager as he was to get his life back to normal, there was no real improvement either. It irked him that he felt obliged to take to his bed several times each day and had to be carried up and down the stairs when he insisted upon establishing himself in the drawing room.

He was improving, nevertheless. His complexion lost its chalky quality. His speech became firmer, and his appetite more robust. He talked of returning home to Greystone. He also talked of attending the Earl and Countess of Stratton's ball. His family frowned upon both ideas as utter madness, but none of them were foolish enough to argue with him. It would have been pointless. They merely hoped that when the time came he would realize he was not strong enough either to attend a ball or to take to the king's highway for what would have to be several days of travel before he reached the comfort of Greystone.

Major Nicholas Ware had returned to his regiment, now stationed near Brussels in Belgium, part of the Kingdom of the Netherlands. The news coming across the channel, usually in unofficial word-of-mouth reports and therefore of dubious accuracy, was grim indeed. Yet every single piece of it pointed to a grand battle being both inevitable and imminent. Members of the British upper classes, both men and women, went in droves to Brussels to see for themselves, to offer support to sons and husbands and brothers enlisted in various regiments, and to attend parties as though there were no tomorrow—as soon there would not be for large numbers of those who would be involved in the fight. George Greenfield, younger brother of the Dowager Countess of Stratton, was one of their number. He would send daily word of the situation and of Nicholas, he had promised his sister and his nieces and nephews before he left.

Owen Ware and Ben Ellis had left London, the one to return to Oxford, the other to return to Penallen, despite the anxiety they felt for their brother. Stephanie resumed her studies with Miss Field as well as their educational excursions. She also consented to the tedium of being measured for a new evening gown since her mother and Gwyneth had both deemed it unexceptionable for her to attend at least the first few hours of Philippa's wedding ball. She would not dance, of course—she protested quite firmly that she would not wish to do so even if she could—and she would remain by her mother's side or her sister-in-law's or perhaps Jenny Arden's throughout. But she would be *there* to hear the music, to watch the dancing, to see Devlin waltz with Gwyneth and Pippa with Lucas. She would be happy.

The friendship between Clarissa and Kitty held firm. They attended the theater and the opera, garden parties and soirees and private concerts, together. And on the rare occasion when there was nothing else to do, they went shopping. They were both agreed that they must not go so long without seeing each other in the future. Kitty must come to Ravenswood to stay, Clarissa said. She must bring Jenny with her to enjoy the spaciousness of the house and park—perhaps to coincide with the summer fete Devlin and Gwyneth intended to resume and make an annual event again.

Jenny herself was determinedly cheerful during those three weeks. Mr. Jamieson had called upon Lucas, by appointment, three mornings after the wedding, in order to make a formal application for her hand. Lucas took her aside before she went to the visitors' salon to listen to his proposal, and explained to her that Jamieson had admitted his father's financial situation had gone from bad to worse recently. But one must not necessarily blame the son for the father's deeds. Jenny did not need the warning. She listened to the marriage proposal, thanked Mr. Jamieson for his kind offer, and refused him. She spent the rest of the day in her own rooms, supposedly nursing a headache though no one doubted the true reason. She reappeared the following day, as cheerful and even-tempered as ever.

Philippa asked her about her decision when they were alone together a few days later.

"Do you love him, Jenny?" she asked gently.

"I have considered the possibility, of course," Jenny told her, snatching up a cushion to hold to her bosom. "I think I *could* love him if he loved me. He does not, however. He loves my money. He is not a villain. Many men find themselves forced to look for wives with fortunes. It works the other way too. That fact does not necessarily mean the marriage will be an unhappy one. But I do believe that under such circumstances there should be no pretense of love. It is not a necessary element in a marriage, after all—is it?— provided there is honesty and respect and some affection. He told me he loved me when I asked him. And he *smiled.* Poor man. I ought perhaps to have told him that someone who smiles incessantly is not really smiling at all. But I did not wish to be cruel. I was tempted to accept him, Pippa, for he is very good-looking and very charming. But I do not believe I was ever in danger of saying yes. I doubt I ever will be. It is even to be hoped I will never again be asked. I do not like upheavals to my emotions. There. Enough of me. One thing I am *very* happy about. I hoped for you as a friend as soon as I met you, but I have got far more than that. You are my *sister,* and I am over the moon with delight."

"So am I," Philippa assured her. "One is always aware that when one marries one takes on not just a husband or wife but a whole family too. That must cause a great deal of anguish in many cases, must it not? I am very fortunate. I love all my new family."

"Even Grandpapa?" Jenny's eyes twinkled.

"Perhaps *especially* Grandpapa," Philippa said, and they both laughed.

As for Philippa's marriage, she was cautiously hopeful. It had been rushed and forced upon them partly by the indomitable will of the Duke of Wilby and partly by the heart seizure he had suffered at Almack's. Would Lucas ever have asked her to marry him if his grandparents had not been so set upon promoting a match between them? Or if she and Stephanie had gone straight home from Hyde Park after the kite flying that morning instead of going to Arden House for cakes and lemonade? Would she have accepted if she had not grown so inexplicably fond of the duke? Or if she had not gone to Arden House from Almack's that night but had returned home with her brothers and Gwyneth? However it was, he *had* asked and she had said yes.

He had never said he loved her.

She had never said she loved him.

But she remembered what Jenny had said—*I do believe that under such circumstances there should be no pretense of love. It is not a necessary element in a marriage, after all—is it?—provided there is honesty and respect and some affection.* It was very much what Lucas had said himself on their wedding night. And Philippa asked herself if she would prefer that he profess a love he did not really feel—and that he smile incessantly.

Oh, she would far prefer honesty, she decided.

And really she had very little of which to complain. They did not spend all their time together—which was a *good* thing. But they did go walking and riding together and attended some private dinners and parties. They both agreed to avoid any of the grander entertainments of the Season, especially balls, until after the one Devlin and Gwyneth were organizing in their honor. They spent some time at Stratton House and went to the Tower of London one day with Ben and Joy and Stephanie. And they spent more time at home than they might otherwise have done in order to give their company to the duke and duchess—and to Jenny, who was obviously mourning her lost love even though she had made what was almost undoubtedly a wise decision.

And there were the nights of lovemaking, and often the early mornings too—and occasionally an afternoon. Her husband was a considerate lover and probably a skilled one too, though Philippa had no one with whom to compare him, of course. She *loved* the nights. And if he was still beside her when she awoke in the mornings, she always turned toward him and hoped he would love her again before they got up. He almost always did. He was, of course, doing his duty. His grandfather very much hoped for a child at the end of nine months.

It never felt like *just* duty, however.

It was never duty on her part. At first she found it merely very, very pleasant and assumed that it would never mean any more than that to her. It was men, after all, who were assumed to get all the pleasure from such activity. She soon learned how wrong she had been, however. The physical part of her marriage became deliriously, even passionately pleasurable. And as for the rest . . . she was satisfied. She might hope for more, but even if it never happened, he *liked* her, she believed. He was *fond* of her. He was kind and considerate.

If there was never any more than that, she would consider herself fortunate indeed.

She loved him, of course. She did not know just when she had fallen in love, but she had. She could live without telling him, though, and embarrassing him. She could live her love. She did not need to put it into words.

She was having a new gown made for the ball. She no longer needed to keep to white. She also no longer presented her bills to her mother or Devlin. Her husband would pay for her ball gown and all the accessories to go with it. How strange that seemed. But he insisted. The *only* time since their wedding he had frowned at her and even spoken rather sharply to her happened when she had suggested that she use her own money for at least a part of the expense. It was an extravagance, after all. She had other gowns she might have worn.

"Phil," he had said. "Please do not be ridiculous." There had been no humor in his voice or in his face. There had been no invitation to discuss the matter. Quite the contrary.

She had not repeated the offer.

It was perhaps foolish to be looking forward so much to the Stratton House ball when she had already experienced *ton* balls and

in many ways they were all much alike. And when she had had
what she considered a very nearly perfect wedding day.

But she was.

L ucas wished the wedding ball had been set for any other week
but this particular one. For while Philippa was very obviously
excited about it, as were Aunt Kitty and Jenny and the ladies from
Stratton House, there was also a vastly contrasting air of anxiety
and foreboding hanging over them all. It hung over the whole of
London, in fact.

During the past week conflicting snippets of news had been
coming from the Continent. Nothing could be fully verified or
relied upon, however. Some reported a massive battle having already been fought somewhere in the vicinity of Brussels. A few
people close to the southern coast of England claimed to have heard
the pounding of cannon, which had continued for hours on end.
Others spoke of a massive defeat for the Duke of Wellington's
forces, and panic spread among those who believed them and were
convinced that Napoleon Bonaparte and his fearsome columns of
French infantry were about to march into London and either mas-
sacre all its citizens or lead them into captivity. There were a few
feeble calls to burn the bridges spanning the river Thames.

There were those too who had heard of a decisive victory and
had expected no less. For was not Wellington himself at the head
of the British armies and Field Marshal von Blücher at the head of
the Prussian forces? Had they not proved themselves invincible in
previous battles?

But no one *knew*. No official dispatches had arrived in England, or, if they had, no public announcement had been made.
Hard facts were in remarkably short supply. Stories abounded, and,

as is ever the case with rumor, there was an endless supply of persons willing to embellish and sensationalize them and add lurid details that proceeded purely from their imaginations.

All of Wellington's great military victories seemed to have come on a Sunday, people remembered. That was *fact*, and many used it to declare with some certainty that the battle had been fought *last* Sunday, on the eighteenth of June. But the skeptics were quick to point out that Sunday came once every week. Perhaps battle would be engaged *next* Sunday or the Sunday after. Or not on a Sunday at all.

Lucas spent all morning and the early part of the afternoon on the day of the ball going from place to place, most notably White's Club, in the hope that by now someone had heard something definite. And of course many men had. Some had heard quite definitely of a defeat. Others had heard just as definitely of a victory.

He went home before midafternoon to accompany his grandparents to Stratton House. The Duke of Wilby had insisted, of course, against the advice of everyone foolish enough to offer it, that he and Her Grace would attend the ball. Everyone's anxieties had been allayed slightly, however, when the Countess of Stratton sent a letter to say she and her husband would be delighted to receive the duke and duchess during the afternoon of the ball and to assign them a suite of rooms on the same floor as the ballroom, where they might rest whenever they wished during the day and evening and remain to spend the night.

Lucas went with his grandparents and their personal servants and enough baggage for a month's stay. They were received at Stratton House like visiting royalty. Lucas stood in the hall watching his mother-in-law lead Her Grace slowly upstairs while His Grace followed between Stratton and the countess. Each of them had one of his arms, but he had insisted upon making the ascent upon his own feet.

"Do you think I will be just as stubborn an old man as my grandfather if I should live as long?" Lucas asked young Stephanie, who had remained at his side instead of following the procession.

"Oh, I hope so," she said, turning her head to smile brightly at him. "I adore your grandpapa. So does Pippa."

"She takes no nonsense from him," he said. "And he loves it."

They both laughed.

Somehow His Grace had enough breath remaining when he reached the first landing to call down the stairs. "Go home to your bride, Luc," he said. "I do not need either a jailer or a nursemaid. This is a big day for her. Make a fuss of her. Tell her how lovely she looks. Take her flowers. Roses. At least two dozen. Red. How many more stairs?" That last question was directed to the Strattons.

"I have been given my orders," Lucas said, setting a hand on Stephanie's shoulder and kissing her cheek. "We will see you later."

"You will not recognize me," she said. "I have the most *gorgeous* gown."

"But the golden coronet will remain?" he asked, glancing at her hair. "You will be gorgeous from head to foot, then, and I *will* recognize you."

"Flatterer." She laughed with girlish glee.

He hurried home, though he did stop along the way to purchase a single rose for his wife. He had not seen the gown she would wear tonight, but she had described its colors as a mixture of blues and turquoise and sea green. The rose was white.

CHAPTER TWENTY-FOUR

A dinner at Stratton House for the members of both families preceded the ball, though the Duke and Duchess of Wilby dined privately in their suite, which His Grace declared to be too spacious and too comfortable to be abandoned just yet. Indeed, he told the dowager countess and his daughter when they called there, he might even forget to go home for a few days after tonight's ball. The elderly were expected to be forgetful, after all.

It was an informal dinner in the sense that there were no speeches and no toasts.

"We got all that out of the way on your wedding day," the Earl of Stratton explained to Philippa and Lucas. "Tonight is for relaxation and enjoyment."

There probably had not been a great deal of relaxation in the household all day, though, Philippa thought. The dining room looked like a work of art, and the food and wine were sumptuous. There would be a lavish supper later for all the ball guests as well as light refreshments throughout the evening. The ballroom, which she had always considered a bit dark and gloomy and neglected and a waste of space, now looked breathtaking. She and Lucas had taken a quick look inside upon their arrival earlier. There was greenery everywhere. Who knew that nature was capable of providing so many shades and textures of the same color? There were a few pots of flowers too—all of them white. But predominantly it was a green paradise.

How very clever Gwyneth had been in thinking of a way for her ballroom to be distinguished from all others in London with their profusion of blooms and color. The chandeliers had been cleaned and filled with candles, and the floor had been polished to a high gloss. Velvet upholstered chairs had been arranged about the walls for the convenience of those who wished to sit and watch the dancing rather than participate in it. Two high-backed chairs with arms and footstools had been placed halfway along the wall inside the doors.

"For King Percy and Queen May, no doubt," Lucas had said for Philippa's ears only, nodding in their direction.

It was going to be a magical evening, Philippa thought as dinner ended and she turned her thoughts to the ball. Guests would begin to arrive within the hour. She and Lucas would stand in the receiving line with her mother and Devlin and Gwyneth. They would lead off the dancing. But tonight she was not wearing virginal white—how inappropriate it would be anyway. Tonight she was wearing the most beautiful gown she had ever seen. At first glance it was not very different from the fashionable gowns all women wore these days. It was high-waisted with a low neckline and short, puffed sleeves. The skirt fell straight from bosom to hem, in classical Grecian lines. It looked blue or green or turquoise, depending upon the light and the angle from which one looked at it. In reality, however, the lightweight silk and gauze of which it was made disguised the fullness of the skirts, which swirled and billowed about her when she moved, revealing too many shades of blending colors to enumerate.

Lucas had stood in the doorway of her dressing room earlier, one shoulder propped against the doorframe, his arms crossed over his chest. He had been looking gorgeous, of course, all in black and white, his hair glowing dark red. "That gown was designed for a woman who might not otherwise be noticed," he had said. "On you it has failed miserably, Phil. Your own beauty quite overpowers it."

His eyes had smiled at her when she burst out laughing.

"Do you lie awake at night composing these pretty compliments?" she had asked him.

"Er . . . *do* I lie awake at night?" he had asked her. "It seems to me that when I *am* awake, I am far too busy exerting myself to be mentally composing any compliments at all."

Philippa had been very glad she had already dismissed her maid.

She rose now from the dining table when Gwyneth did. The ladies would withdraw to make any minor repairs to their appearance that were necessary. The men would not linger at the table, Devlin promised.

But the ladies were fated not to leave the room so quickly after all. For someone else entered it unannounced. He was immaculately clad for the evening even though he had not been invited to either the dinner or the ball.

There was a loud scraping of chairs from those who were not already on their feet.

"*George!*" the Dowager Countess of Stratton exclaimed. She hurried toward her brother.

"Uncle George," Philippa murmured as Lucas's hand enclosed hers and squeezed tightly.

Noise surged and died away almost immediately.

"Victory," George Greenfield said. "And Nick is safe and unharmed."

He was merciful enough to give with terse brevity the two key pieces of news for which they had all waited seemingly forever. He went on to mention Waterloo, a small village south of Brussels, as the scene of the battle, and the fact that it had been no grand victory but what the Duke of Wellington himself had apparently described as a very near-run thing. But it was a victory nonetheless. Nick had been in the thick of the fighting all day long but had come through it with barely a scratch, though he had had a horse shot out from under him.

Philippa scarcely heard the details her uncle was giving to reassure his listeners. She had turned into Lucas's arms and was weeping uncontrollably on his shoulder. She had not even realized until that moment how very anxious she had been all week. She, along with her family. Yet here they all were this evening, preparing to dance the night away, as though they had no care in the world. How was it possible for people to *do* that? To carry on with the business of living even while the world was coming apart and their hearts were ready to shatter?

What if the news her uncle had brought in person had been different? It *would* be different for hundreds and thousands of other families, both in Britain and in France.

"How did we manage to retain our sanity during those years when Devlin and Ben as well as Nicholas were in the Peninsula and fighting battle after battle?" she asked, raising her head and gazing at her husband.

"Because it is what people do, Phil," he said, and kissed her on the lips. "People endure and carry on living."

And then she was hugging her mother and Stephanie and her brother and sister-in-law and the other Ware relatives, and everyone was talking at once. And laughing too. But not heartlessly, Philippa believed. They were very well aware that no battle was cause for rejoicing, whether it had been won or lost, for *so much* was lost on both sides when violence became the only answer to a problem.

Devlin managed to make himself heard after a while.

"Our first guests will be arriving soon," he said. "I believe a number of us need to wash away the marks of our tears before we greet them."

But, oh, there was something over which to rejoice with unalloyed happiness, Philippa thought as Lucas took her by the hand again. Nicholas was safe. And unharmed—though there were those words of Uncle George's: *with barely a scratch.*

England was safe from invasion.

She would dance tonight with her husband. The man she loved. And life would continue.

As he stood in the receiving line with his wife and her mother and brother and sister-in-law, Lucas could not suppress an inner tremor of laughter over the fact that he had ended up with *this* of all families. He had spent so many years, from the age of fourteen until very recently, hating the very name *Stratton*, making it sound in his mind very similar to *Satan*.

The former bearer of the title was dead. So was his own mother. The memory of the suffering they had caused themselves and their families had faded from his mind, never to be forgotten, of course, but never again to blight his own happiness. Or Philippa's, it was to be hoped. And he *was* happy. She was sparkling at his side, beautiful in that incredible gown, her blond hair, dressed in its usual smooth, simple style, gleaming in the light from the chandelier overhead. The marks of her tears had been sponged away. The damp patch on the shoulder of his new black evening coat had dried.

He could only imagine how she had felt earlier when she learned—from a firsthand account—that her brother had survived with *no more than a few scratches* the great battle that had been fought close to Brussels this past Sunday.

He remembered too, as he shook hands with male guests and bowed to the ladies and occasionally raised a gloved hand to his lips, that he had avoided London and all these people for years. Even this year he had been reluctant to come, knowing as he had that he would probably be married before the *ton* dispersed to their own homes for the summer. And he *was* married—to the woman his grandparents had picked out for him. He had never really had any choice. But he ought to have trusted them more than he had. He glanced at Philippa, who was laughing at something Lord Edward Denton and another young man were saying to her as they passed along the line. For of course his grandparents' choice would never have been made with a cold disregard for sentiment. They would only have chosen someone they loved, someone they assumed he must love too.

And dash it all, they were right.

"I believe it is time to begin the dancing, Dev," the Countess of Stratton said at last. "You will lead off the opening set with Pippa, Lucas. Oh, my first *ton* ball as hostess is beginning and I am consumed with excitement."

She was a total contrast to Philippa, dark haired and vivid in royal blue, the skirt of her gown carefully designed, he noticed, to disguise the rounding of her figure.

Stratton mounted the orchestra dais, though he did not immediately announce the opening set. He waited politely while the

Duke of Wilby made his entrance, the duchess on his arm, Cousin Gerald hovering on one side of them, Sylvester on the other, but neither one actually touching them. Lucas was amused again by the smattering of applause that rippled through the ballroom as they took their places on what he thought of as their thrones.

Jenny had a cluster of persons about her chair, Lucas saw, both male and female. One of the latter was young Stephanie, wearing a flattering gown—as she had informed him she would—of light muslin with narrow lemon and white vertical stripes. She was beaming happily, her round cheeks shining in the candlelight.

And then the dancing began, and for almost half an hour Lucas forgot everything and everyone except his wife, with whom he danced. The figures separated them and brought them together as they paced out stately measures and executed more vigorous twirls, acknowledging their fellow dancers as they were brought together but somehow never losing their focus upon each other.

They took other partners for the following two sets but came together again for the first waltz—which Lucas had made clear he would dance with no one else but Philippa. And yet again they discovered the magic of moving about a ballroom floor in each other's arms, dancing in sweeping twirls until the candles overhead and the gowns of the ladies and the sparkle of their jewels swirled into a kaleidoscope of light and color and sheer joy.

He smiled at Philippa and she smiled back, and for the moment all was right with their world. *For the moment.* Life was made up of moments, following endlessly upon one another throughout a lifetime. One must grasp those that were good and face those that were not as they came. It was the nature of the ebb and flow of life. Like a dance. This was one of the good moments. Ah, but no. This was one of the very best moments.

"I will always remember tonight," she said, echoing his thoughts, and he realized they were the first words either of them had spoken since the music began.

"For good reasons, I hope," he said.

"For the very best," she assured him. And she was not just smiling tonight, he realized. She was *glowing* from deep within.

"We will reminisce about it when we are old and gray," he said. "We will recall it as one of the happiest of many happy memories we will have accumulated over the years."

"Yes," she said.

"I do love you, Phil," he said. "It must be very obvious to you, of course, but I believe women like to be told, do they not?"

She laughed with what sounded like a gurgle of glee. "Oh yes," she said. "We do indeed like to be told. Don't men?"

He thought about it and grinned at her. "I suppose we do," he said.

"I love you too, Lucas," she said. "To the moon and the sun and the stars." She laughed again. But the laughter faded as he swept her into a wide twirl and another couple moved sharply out of their way.

"Lucas," she said more softly. "I do love you. With all my heart."

"Which is just exactly as much as I love you," he said. "How fortunate that our feelings for each other are in such harmony."

T he Duke and Duchess of Wilby did not stay for very long. They withdrew to their suite of rooms before the supper dance began, a move that was quietly applauded by all their family members, who from the start had feared a repetition of what had happened at Almack's, but perhaps with a different outcome this time.

Lucas and Philippa accompanied them, though they could not stay away long from the ball. They must be present for the supper since it was in their honor and would involve a few speeches and some cake cutting, Gwyneth had admitted when Philippa had questioned her closely.

But they did wait while His Grace settled in a comfortable chair in the sitting room of the suite and sighed with relief that the sound of the music was more distant from here and the noise of conversation and laughter quite obliterated.

"The time was," he said, and paused as Her Grace poured him a cup of tea, upon which he frowned with some disgust though he knew better now than to grumble and demand a glass of port or claret or ale or . . . *anything but tea, May.* "The time was when I would have danced the night away, but now I must leave that to the two of you. Come and kiss my cheek, Philippa, and tell me this is one of the happiest nights of your life, and then we will keep you no longer. I intend to be tucked up in my bed before another hour has gone by, after which Her Grace may sneak out to dance away what remains of the night if she chooses."

"I will be tucked up right beside you, Percy," the duchess said. "How very kind your brother and his wife and your mother are, Philippa dear, to make these rooms available for our comfort even though we live scarcely more than a stone's throw away."

Philippa sat down on a stool beside the duke's chair and took his hand in hers, though she did not immediately kiss his cheek.

"I was intending to wait until tomorrow," she said. "Until after I had talked with Lucas tonight. But somehow the time seems appropriate now, and why should not the three of you hear it from me at the same time?"

His Grace looked sharply down at her. The duchess sat down with her cup and saucer in her hands. Lucas, standing before the fireplace, raised his eyebrows.

"I am not perfectly sure," Philippa said. "I have not consulted a physician yet. But I do believe I am with child." She felt her cheeks flame with heat—and probably with color too.

The duke's hand closed more tightly about hers. "Well, of course you are, Granddaughter," he said. "You have been married to my grandson for almost a month, have you not?"

Lucas's eyes were very intent upon her.

"It might be a girl," she said.

The duchess had set aside her cup and saucer in order to clasp her hands to her bosom.

"It would not dare," His Grace said. "*He* would not dare."

"I would love her," Lucas said, "with everything that is in me."

"And so would we all," the duchess agreed. "Including Grandpapa, Philippa. We love Susan every bit as much as we love Timothy and Raymond, after all. Girls are in no way inferior or less welcome to a family despite the fact that they cannot inherit ducal titles and properties. You and Lucas have all the time in the world to produce a boy. There always has been one in this family for generations past. There will be another."

"I do not have all the time in the world, May," His Grace reminded her. "But I daresay if she comes out a girl, I will find her the most perfect thing ever created and send the two of you back to work. But you, my Lady Roath, must see a physician at your earliest convenience. Tomorrow. Luc will see to it."

"I will do so," Philippa promised, getting to her feet and bending over his chair to kiss his cheek. She did the same for the duchess.

"And now, my dear," Her Grace said, "you must get back to your brother and sister-in-law's guests, who have come to celebrate your wedding."

Lucas was offering his arm.

"Remember, though," the duke said as they were leaving the room. "I am fully expecting a boy."

Lucas led her out of the room and closed the door quietly behind them. He had not spoken a word since making his comment
about loving the child even if she turned out to be a daughter. He
had not even bidden his grandparents good night. Perhaps, Philippa
thought, she had made a mistake in not telling him her news privately first. It was certainly what she had intended to do. But . . .

"Should I have told you first?" she asked.

He had waited only for the door to be shut, however, before
turning her almost fiercely against the wall beside it, the weight of
his body holding her there. In the dim light of the candle burning
in a wall sconce on the other side of the door, she could see his eyes
burning into hers. Then his mouth found hers and ravished it while
one of his arms pushed behind her shoulders and the other came
about her waist and her own went about him.

"Phil," he murmured into her mouth. "Ah, Phil. It is almost too
soon. It has all happened just as it was planned. You were married
in haste, you were impregnated in haste, and now you are—or may
be—with child before our marriage is quite a month old. Just as
though you have no other function in our union. As though you
are not a person. As though I do not love you with every breath I
draw into my body."

She pressed her hands against his shoulders until there was a
little space between them.

"No one forced me into anything, Lucas," she said. "Least of all
you. I married you because I wanted to. I lay with you because I
wanted to. I love you because . . . Well, because I want to. And
because I just *do*. And I am so happy about being with child,
though I am not quite, quite certain, of course, that I do not know
quite what to do with all my happiness."

He cupped his hands about her cheeks and gazed intently into
her eyes again. "You are sure you forgive me?" he asked her. "Even

though I once called you soiled goods and robbed you of your youth and ruined your life for many years?"

It was hard to look back on those years, hard to believe they had even happened. But she would not belittle the suffering, just as she would not belittle what he had suffered after overhearing that very private argument between his parents when he was emotionally unfit to deal with what he learned. Sometimes life just happened, whether a person was ready for it or not.

"I am quite, quite sure," she said. "My life at this moment is everything I could ever want it to be."

He sighed and leaned into her again. He kissed her lips.

"I meant what I said," he told her. "I would love, love, *love* to have a daughter with you."

She smiled. "But a son first," she said. "*Very* first, though, Lucas, we have a supper to attend as the guests of honor at our own wedding ball. The music has just ended."

He kissed her again before stepping back and drawing her hand through his arm. "Let us attend what remains of it, then," he said.

CHAPTER TWENTY-FIVE

There was a lily pond to the west of the grand stone mansion that was Greystone. It was slightly below the level of the rose arbor, which had been built beside the house, and it could be viewed from there on a warm summer day while one relaxed on one of the wrought iron seats and breathed in the scent of the roses. Today was not such a day. There were no roses in late February. No lilies either. It was a sunny, chilly day with clouds scudding across the sky. The brisk wind that moved them was held at bay from the pond, however, by a band of trees to the north and west of it and the arbor and house to the east. Only to the south was there an open view of the park stretching into the distance. The prevailing winds did not blow from that direction.

Lucas was standing beside the pond, his hands clasped behind his back, his gaze upon the countryside, which would soon lose its faded winter look and brighten with the delicate colors of spring. He loved the changing of the seasons, but he always looked forward most to the coming of spring. Especially this year.

Philippa was heavy with child. Aunt Kitty had declared just yesterday that she must be carrying twins at the very least. But the dowager countess, who had come to spend the last weeks of the confinement with her daughter, had said that she herself had been more than usually large with all five of her own children.

"But I never did give birth to twins or triplets or more," she had added with a smile of reassurance for Philippa. "Though a cousin of mine had two sets of twins in little more than a year, poor thing."

Aunt Kitty had come to Greystone with the duke and duchess two weeks after the Strattons' wedding ball last year, though the journey home had stretched over a week and a half and had been one of the most tedious things ever, she had told Lucas privately. She had remained with them ever since and nursed Grandmama through a stubborn winter chill, which had settled on her chest and refused to budge. The duke had not caught it from her despite the fact that he had openly defied the advice of the local physician and the pleadings of his daughter to stay away from her.

"Nonsense," he had said, according to Aunt Kitty's report. "After almost sixty years with your mother, Kitty, I would not know how to stay away from her. Stop fussing."

Aunt Kitty had stopped.

Both grandparents were now in what Lucas would call middling health. They were apparently well, but he could see a difference even from last year. In *both* of them. He had spent a thoroughly agreeable summer and autumn at Amberwell with his wife and sister—and Stephanie. At the end of October they had arranged for a neighbor and friend to stay with Jenny for a few weeks and gone to Ravenswood in Hampshire for the christening of Gareth Ware, Viscount Mountford, son of Devlin and Gwyneth. They had left Stephanie there when they returned home. Lucas loved Amberwell, and fortunately Philippa loved it too and was quickly taken to the bosom of all their neighbors, whom he had known all his life. They had come to Greystone soon after Christmas, however, for His Grace was restless, Aunt Kitty had reported, and Grandmama too wanted them there for the birth of their first child.

Jenny had accompanied them.

His Grace was not the only restless member of the family. For the past few days Philippa had *prowled*, for want of a better word. She could not sit and she could not stand, yet lying down made her feel like a *lazy lump* or a *beached whale*. She could not read—and *forget* writing letters, usually one of her favorite activities. She could not get close enough to the escritoire to see what she was writing. Doing nothing was worst of all. She could not remain indoors, and she could not stay outdoors. At night she could not sleep—or stay awake. She could not lie on her back or on either side. Moving from one position to another was a major undertaking. She told Lucas that it would be better for both of them if he slept in the bed in the room that was nominally his though it had never been used. Yet when he asked her if that was what she really wanted, she informed him fretfully that if he did not *want* to sleep beside her, then fine. *She* did not care.

He stayed in their bed with her and cursed himself for being a man and putting the woman he loved above all others through such hell. It was not *fair*, damn it all. And it was dashed humbling. Not to mention irritating.

"Lucas," she said now from behind him. "Come and see."

He turned to look at her. She was on the far side of the pond, up against the trees, half bent over something at her feet. It was impossible, of course, for her to bend fully, poor Phil. He went to look. She had one arm stretched out toward him, though she did not remove her eyes from whatever she was gazing at.

"Look," she said when he came close and took her hand in his.

And he bent over to see a cluster of snowdrops blooming bravely in defiance of the lingering winter chill.

"Spring is coming," she said, straightening up to smile dazzlingly at him.

"As it does every year," he said, smiling back at her and watching as she frowned suddenly and briefly and spread a hand over her bulk, as he had noticed her doing a few times today.

"The heir is lively, is he?" he asked, and he moved behind her and spread his own hands lightly over her. The baby was indeed making his presence felt with little regard for the comfort of his mother. And as often happened, Lucas felt almost dizzy with the realization that a fully formed child was just beyond the touch of his hands, curled up inside his wife, awaiting birth. How was such a miracle even possible?

"I think we had better go back inside," she said. "I do not feel . . . right. But is that a peevish note I hear in my voice? I am so sorry, Lucas. I know I am very difficult to live with these days."

"My God, Phil," he said irreverently, setting an arm firmly about her and moving her in the direction of the front doors. "You are bearing *my child*. I believe you are entitled to some shortness of temper."

His mother-in-law and Aunt Kitty were both in the grand hall when they stepped inside, almost as though they had sensed that they might be needed.

"Philippa is not feeling quite the thing," he said.

Her mother hurried toward her. "Pains, Pippa?" she asked.

"Not really," Philippa said. "Are they not supposed to be bad? These are just . . . a nuisance. I am sorry. You must all be so tired of my complaining."

"I'll take you upstairs," Lucas said. "Perhaps if you lie down for a while, you will feel better. Will you come too, Mother?"

They were in Philippa's dressing room when she suddenly exclaimed and then wailed, "Mama-a-a."

"Oh dear," the dowager said, her voice quite calm. "Have your
waters broken?"

His wife, Lucas saw in some horror, was standing in a puddle
of wetness. Aunt Kitty, who had been hovering in the doorway,
stepped inside. Philippa's maid had appeared, as though from nowhere, and hurried toward her lady.

"Luc," Aunt Kitty said, taking command. "Out! Now! Go
away. Stay away. Make yourself useful and send for the physician.
This baby is on its way."

Lucas did not need any further urging. Like the craven coward
he was, he fled.

Everything was a blur of discomfort and clawing fear for
Philippa. Aunt Kitty prepared her bed and her mother and her
maid undressed her and cleaned her and laid her down. It was
strange, some remote part of her mind told her, that one had nine
months in which to prepare and brace oneself for what one knew
would happen, yet when the time came one thought in some panic
that one was not ready at all, that one did not know what to do or
how one was going to be able to bear the pain when it came.

She felt bloated and uncomfortable and quite unwell. But where
was the pain? Or rather, where were the pains, which she had been
told would be regularly spaced, the interval between gradually becoming less as the intensity of the pain grew more intense? She
waited for it all to start. Please, *please,* now that something had
happened, let it not be a false alarm. But how could it be when her
waters had broken?

The physician arrived in company with the midwife. The doctor examined her, announced that the birth was imminent, and sent her maid scurrying for hot water and clean towels and blankets. Mama and Aunt Kitty were both still in her room. Philippa could hear their voices. And then—

Oh, and then she felt the undeniable urge to push and did so while the midwife hastily positioned her and the physician appeared from wherever he had been a moment ago.

Her daughter was born all in a rush and squawking indignantly, and Philippa was weeping and holding out her arms. It had all been so quick, and without all the rumored horror of pain she had worried about.

A daughter! She had a child. She and Lucas.

Where was Lucas?

Lucas had been pacing outside Philippa's bedchamber even though everyone who had spoken to him had warned him that it would be hours yet before he could even begin to expect any news from within. But as a pulse pounded against his temples, almost deafening him, all the news he really wanted was that his wife was alive and not in unbearable agony. He tried not to think of his mother dying in childbirth. Hours of this would surely kill him. What, then, would those same hours do to her?

Did all expectant fathers go through this? He tried not to think of his own father.

But then, all those supposed hours of waiting be damned, he heard an unfamiliar squawking and stopped abruptly. A bird? *In the house?* The sound was repeated, and he knew it was coming from the bedchamber. He set a hand against the wall to stop himself from collapsing.

Not a bird. A baby.

It was a baby.

By the time Philippa wondered where he was, Lucas had been barred from the bedchamber until his wife was finished with the afterbirth process, whatever that was, and had been admitted to the dressing room instead. There he met his daughter, who was being sponged off by the midwife and then swaddled in a warm blanket. She was all large feet and hands and red, angry face, as far as Lucas could see. She was also the most beautiful creature he had ever set eyes upon. He lost his heart for the second time in a year.

But surely he ought to have met her for the first time when she was being held in his wife's arms?

"Philippa?" he asked his aunt.

"You must wait a little while yet, Luc," she told him. "She is still in a bit of discomfort and then will need to be cleaned up and made comfortable. Have patience for a little while longer." She smiled sympathetically at him. "I know this is all hard on the father."

"It is one of the quickest births I have ever encountered, my lord," the midwife said. "You and her ladyship must count yourselves fortunate. Here is your daughter."

And Lucas found himself holding a warm, soft bundle, which appeared to weigh less than nothing. The swaddling blanket seemed to be soothing his daughter. She had fallen quiet, though she was not asleep. She gazed at her new world through slitted eyelids. Her hair looked blond.

"Hello, little one," he said softly. "Welcome to the world."

"Take her to your grandparents," Aunt Kitty suggested, and Lucas looked up and met her eyes.

For the first time it struck him. Their child was *a girl*. Yet he was fiercely glad. His firstborn was not after all a boy, an heir. He loved her anyway with his whole being. There could be no question now of his rejoicing just because he had done his duty or because his wife had done hers. Their child had put their love to the test. She was a girl.

They were parents, he and Philippa. They had a daughter.

She is still in a bit of discomfort . . .

Was that normal?

"I will," he said. "Though just for a few minutes. I need to be near Philippa. It seems to me the most monstrous custom that a man is not allowed to be with his wife at such a time."

"She would not want you there to see her at her worst," Aunt Kitty said softly.

Her worst. Women had peculiar ideas about what constituted the best and the worst as far as a husband and lover was concerned.

He took his daughter to meet her great-grandparents.

"Stand your ground, little one," he told her as he made his way to their private rooms. "You do not have to answer for your gender. It is the absolute right and perfect one."

The butler, trying to look impersonal, trying not to show that he was taking a peep at the blanketed bundle, nevertheless looked like everyone's favorite uncle as he tapped on the door of the duchess's sitting room and opened it. Lucas stepped inside.

Jenny was with her grandparents. Her Grace was on her feet, holding up for Jenny's inspection a small crocheted blue and white blanket. Grandpapa was dozing in his chair, but he opened his eyes at the sound of the door shutting behind his grandson.

"What?" the duchess said, clasping the blanket to her bosom as she gazed at Lucas and his bundle. "Already?"

"Meet your great-granddaughter, Grandmama and Grandpapa," Lucas said. "Meet your niece, Jenny. She was very eager to be born. I believe she is going to be a force to be reckoned with."

"A girl," Grandmama said, sounding entranced. "Oh, Luc. A girl. Could anything be more perfect?"

He advanced farther into the room so that she and Jenny could see the child, who appeared to have lost interest in her new world for the moment. She was sleeping.

"I will not hand her to you," he said. "Philippa has not held her yet. The doctor is still with her. She is still in some discomfort."

"Oh, Luc," Jenny said. "She is *beautiful*."

Grandmama was dabbing a handkerchief to her eyes.

Lucas turned to his grandfather, whose eyes beneath his shaggy brows were fixed upon the bundle that was his great-granddaughter. He looked into her face when she was close.

"Well, little rascal," he said. "You have just doomed me to another year of staying alive, have you? You are going to be a strong and stubborn one, I suppose. Just like your great-grandmother. And your mother. Take her to your wife, Luc. And if they will not let you in to see her, go in anyway. Sometimes we men have to assert ourselves."

Lucas smiled and turned to the door. But His Grace spoke again before he could leave the room.

"Luc," he said. "Well done. Both you and my granddaughter-in-law. That little rascal is perfect."

Euphoria over the warm, living child he held in his arms warred with anxiety for his wife as Lucas made his way back to her rooms. The butler went before him.

"No, not there," Lucas said when the man stopped outside the dressing room door. "The bedchamber."

The butler tapped on the door, and Lucas gave him the signal to open it without waiting for an answer. He stepped firmly inside. Even without his grandfather's urging he would not be kept away any longer.

Aunt Kitty came hurrying toward him and scooped the baby from his arms. "Oh, Luc," she said. "You must leave. Quickly." She turned to lead the way to the dressing room, but he stood where he was, his eyes riveted upon the bed. His wife was lying upon it, moaning, her mother beside the bed, the physician at the foot.

God! Oh, God, she was dying.

"Phil." He whispered her name, but somehow she heard him. Her flushed face turned his way. Her hair was matted, her face drenched with sweat, her eyes heavy with pain.

"Lucas," she said. "Lucas."

With a few strides he was beside the bed and reaching for her hands on either side of her head. She panted and groaned and closed her eyes. Her hands gripped his as though intent upon breaking bones. He turned his head to look along her body.

And his eyes widened and his mouth fell open as her whole body tensed and their son was born.

I am just very glad that Emily was born first," Philippa said a little more than half an hour later. "She will forever be able to hold it over Christopher's head that he is her younger brother."

She smiled and closed her eyes, reveling in the feel of one warm bundle nestled in the bend of her left elbow and another in the crook of her right. Both babies were asleep, as she herself was very close to being.

She opened her eyes to see that Lucas was still standing close to the bed, gazing down at them with that special look he sometimes had—not quite smiling but bursting with happiness somewhere behind his eyes. It was always difficult to describe an expression that did not quite reach the face but lit it from within.

"Females can be formidable creatures, can they not?" he said.

"We can." She closed her eyes again and smiled. "Poor Aunt Kitty. You had better go and put her out of her misery, Lucas."

Aunt Kitty had gone to celebrate with her parents, though she had promised them both that she *would not say a word to them before Lucas could make a proper announcement himself.*

"I am afraid that if I leave the room again," he said, "I might come back to discover that we have triplets."

She groaned and laughed softly and opened her eyes to find that he was definitely smiling now.

"Phil," he said, "I had no idea. I thought I did, but I did not. Thank you, my love. For our surprise twins. For loving me. For forgiving me and marrying me."

"I had no idea either," she said. "But they are worth every moment of discomfort. I think I am about to fall asleep, Lucas. Take Christopher to meet Grandmama and Grandpapa. I wish I could be there to see their faces, but I am too tired. And I think Emily might be cross if I tried to move."

He leaned over the bed and kissed her softly on the lips before picking up their son and nestling him in the crook of his arm.

"We men know when we are no longer wanted," he said. "Sleep well, my love."

She was still smiling when the door closed behind him and her mother opened the dressing room door and came softly inside to make sure mother and daughter were comfortable.

The Duke and Duchess of Wilby had gone downstairs to the drawing room. It was the only place in which one could properly celebrate the birth of a great-granddaughter *with champagne,* His Grace had declared over the protests of his daughter. Jenny had been carried down too.

The champagne had been brought in, Her Grace had spoken again of her great pleasure in seeing her new great-granddaughter in Luc's arms, His Grace had declared—not for the first time—that he was *in no way* disappointed that she was not a boy and no one was even to think he was, and they waited only to see if the Dowager Countess of Stratton would join them for a toast to the new baby. A servant had been sent up to invite her to come down.

When the drawing room door opened again, however, it was not the dowager who joined them but Lucas himself—with the baby again.

"How lovely," his grandmother said, beaming and clasping her hands to her bosom. "You have brought her back, Luc. I suppose Philippa is sleeping. She has earned her rest."

"It is not Emily I have brought this time, Grandmama," Lucas said. "She is very contentedly sleeping beside her mama. I have brought Christopher instead. He lagged behind his sister by almost half an hour, but here he is to meet you all, though rather impolitely he is asleep. Here is your great-grandson."

Her Grace stared mutely, her hands still clasped to her bosom. The duke frowned ferociously.

"Hmmph," he said after a few moments of silence. "I daresay his sister will gloat for the rest of their lives and serve him right. However, it is said that slow and steady wins the race. Come here, Luc, and place my heir's heir in my arms. Let me have a look at him. Does he have red hair? His sister is going to be as blond as her mama."

"I believe he does," Lucas said as he laid his son carefully in his grandfather's arms, where the former continued to sleep quietly, quite unperturbed by the fierce frown being directed down upon him.

"Then he has fire in his blood," the duke said. "And all is well. Little rascal."

All was indeed well. Lucas could not imagine a happiness greater than this.

EPILOGUE

E aster came late that year, in the middle of April. Spring was already turning in the direction of summer as various members of the Ware and Arden families gathered at Greystone for the christening of the twins born to the Marquess and Marchioness of Roath in February.

Devlin and Gwyneth, Earl and Countess of Stratton, remained at Ravenswood, partly because they considered their own son still a bit too young to make the journey with them, though mainly because Gwyneth's brother, Idris Rhys, and his wife, Eluned, who lived on the neighboring estate, were themselves in imminent expectation of the birth of their first child. Major Nicholas Ware was still abroad with his regiment and unable to attend. Owen made the journey with Stephanie and their uncle George, however, and Ben came from Penallen with Joy. The dowager countess had remained at Greystone since the birth of her grandchildren.

Jenny had stayed too, thus allowing her aunt Kitty to remain close to her parents. Charlotte and Sylvester had arrived more recently with Timothy, Raymond, and Susan. Sir Gerald Emmett had come for Easter. So had his sister, Beatrice, with her husband and their two sons. They had planned a visit from Ireland during the summer but had changed the date in order to join the christening party.

The birth of another heir of the direct line was an occasion to be celebrated.

And so, both Lucas and Philippa insisted, was the birth of a firstborn, a daughter. Not that anyone argued the point. Indeed, the Duke of Wilby, despite what he had once said about the attractiveness of babies, was far more likely to be seen holding his great-granddaughter than his great-grandson. She had a way of gazing boldly back at him, frowning and blowing bubbles, while her twin was more inclined to fall asleep rather than endure the ducal stare.

"Little rascal," His Grace would mutter to both of them.

Two new and identical christening gowns had been fashioned, since the one that had been worn by Lucas and his father and grandfather before him had been made without any thought to the possibility of twins. The new gowns were splendid indeed and looked equally gorgeous on the blond-haired Emily and the red-haired Christopher. Both slept angelically on the way to the church in the village and through the first part of the service. But while Christopher merely wrinkled his nose when the holy water was poured over his brow, looked for a moment as though he might protest more loudly, but resumed his slumbers instead, his sister woke up with an indignant squawk, flapped her hands, and bawled lustily until she turned purple in the face. She was not to be pacified for some time after. Her mother's soothing murmurings and her father's steady hand patting her back merely gave her hiccups and made her crosser than ever.

"That is my girl," Lucas murmured, turning his head to grin at his wife.

"And that is my *boy*," she murmured back, chuckling softly as she nodded toward their son, sleeping peacefully in his aunt Stephanie's arms. It was amazing how two children, born of the same womb within half an hour of each other, could be so very different in temperament.

The two families celebrated and enjoyed one another's company for several days following the ceremony while the children played and tried not to be too disappointed that neither baby showed any real disposition to play with them. Smiles could be coaxed from Christopher, it was true, and Joy stood beside his crib for endless minutes cooing at him and patting his hands and pulling faces at him until he beamed at her. Emily *could* smile and did occasionally do so—usually for her father or her great-grandpapa—but she was more likely to bestow uncomprehending frowns upon the children, who clowned without all sense of dignity for her supposed entertainment.

The party was due to break up at last. The Wares would return to their respective homes. The dowager countess would accompany her younger daughter and youngest son. Ben and Joy would go to Penallen. Philippa and Lucas would go home to Amberwell with their babies and take Jenny with them. Kitty, all were agreed, would stay permanently with her parents at Greystone, and Gerald and Beatrice and her family would stay with her there too for a while longer.

They all sat down for a farewell dinner on the final evening, a warmly happy occasion, though it was cut a bit shorter than it might otherwise have been when the duchess announced she was going to retire early.

"You are feeling unwell, Mother?" Kitty asked, getting to her feet while everyone else stopped talking and looked with some concern at Her Grace.

"Not at all. Only very weary," her mother told her. "It has been a lovely day and a lovely week, but now I am tired. No, you need not come too, Percy. Stay and enjoy the final evening with all our family and guests. How blessed we have been. I apologize for not staying longer."

She left the dining room, leaning upon her daughter's arm, while His Grace frowned after her.

"It is a good thing summer is coming," he said, more to himself than to anyone in particular. "May has never fully recovered from that chill she had before Christmas."

"Greystone will be quieter when most of us have left," Clarissa said. "You will both enjoy some peace and quiet again, Your Grace."

But the celebratory air had gone from the gathering, and they did not remain at the table for much longer or for very long in the drawing room after that. Most of them would be leaving in the morning and would be glad of an early night. They climbed the stairs in a group together and stood on the upper landing, bidding one another good night in hushed voices so they would not disturb the duchess— or the children on the floor above. The Duke of Wilby leaned heavily upon Lucas's arm, looking a bit gray in the face again.

"Your Grace. My lord."

The voice did not belong to anyone from either family. It was quiet, respectful, a bit urgent, not fully steady—and it commanded instant attention from everyone. The duke's valet was standing a respectful distance from his master and Lucas, whom he had addressed.

Lucas looked inquiringly at him.

"Her Grace's maid sent me," the man said. "She thinks you ought to come."

"May," the duke said.

"My grandmother?" Lucas said. "She is unwell? She is in need of a physician?"

The valet did not speak with his usual tact, a sure sign that he was distracted.

"I believe she is dead, my lord," he said.

Her Grace's maid was distraught, though she was holding herself together and even managed to curtsy to the duke and Lucas as they entered the duchess's bedchamber while everyone else crowded the doorway or stood in the hallway outside. She answered the question Lucas put to her.

"She was terribly tired, my lord," the woman said. "She would not drink her tea. She wanted only to lie down, and she dismissed me and fell asleep immediately."

"Then why . . ." Lucas began.

"She sighed a bit funnily as I was leaving the room," the maid said. "It went rattling on and on and then . . . stopped. And when I tiptoed back to the bed, she was lying there so still. She—"

Yes. She was dead. That was very clear to Lucas, though he did not approach the bed as Grandpapa had done in order to take Grandmama's hand in both his own. She looked as though she were sleeping, but there was . . . an absence of something about her. A stillness beyond that of sleep. An emptiness. She had gone.

"Summon the physician from the village," Lucas said to his grandfather's valet. Nothing could be done, of course. But something needed to be made official. His head was buzzing, his heartbeat pounding in his ears and against his temples. "Grandpapa, come . . ."

But come where?

Aunt Kitty had moved to stand beside him. "Oh, Mama," she said. "Oh, Mama. Papa . . . ?"

There was a murmur of voices behind them. Lucas could not distinguish individual voices or words.

"Grandpapa, come," he said more firmly, taking a step forward. Someone needed to take charge. They must all go somewhere to wait. The full reality of this was going to hit them soon.

His Grace did not move away from the bed or turn his head.

"Go away, all of you," he said. "Leave us."

"Papa—" Aunt Kitty began.

"Go away," he said. "And do not return, any of you, until I summon you."

"Grandpapa—" That was Gerald from the doorway.

Someone—it might have been Charlotte or Beatrice—was weeping outside and trying to stifle the sounds.

"Leave us," the duke said again, and Lucas took his aunt's arm and drew her toward the door.

"My lord?" Her Grace's maid was looking toward Lucas for direction. So was the duke's valet, who had presumably sent someone else running to the village for the physician.

"Leave," Lucas said. "His Grace needs to be alone for a while with Her Grace."

And they all left the room. It was a measure of the strangeness of the situation that the butler, who was outside in the hallway with the housekeeper at his side, watched while Lucas shut the door of the bedchamber himself.

"He needs some privacy in which to say goodbye," Lucas said, and felt that buzzing in his head again, as though he was about to faint. Someone took his hand, and he turned his head to see his wife beside him, her face pale, as were the faces of almost everyone else gathered there.

"Poor Grandpapa," Philippa murmured.

"He must be left alone for a while," Lucas said. He was about to suggest Her Grace's sitting room as a gathering place, but it was too close. No other room up here was large enough.

"Let us all go down to the drawing room," Philippa suggested, raising her voice somewhat to address everyone. "We all need to sit down while we await the arrival of the physician. Perhaps we can have a tea tray brought there." She glanced at the housekeeper.

And so it was arranged. They all moved away, almost as though nothing momentous had happened, leaving behind them His Grace, who was saying goodbye to his duchess in her bedchamber.

Aunt Kitty, Lucas saw, was leaning heavily upon Gerald's arm. Sylvester was carrying Jenny downstairs while her usual footman was taking her wheeled chair. Philippa was resting one cheek against his shoulder and holding his hand in a tight, warm clasp.

W ell, May," the Duke of Wilby said, holding his wife's hand in both of his. "You have been granted your dearest wish. I have been able to hold on longer than you."

She did not answer him. But, gazing down into her face, it seemed to him that there was a distant, almost youthful twinkle there.

"You will never know how hard it is to be the survivor," he told her. "Or how glad I am that it is me, not you. Not for long, though, May. I am as weary as you were at dinner. Willpower has carried me through a great deal in my life. I do not want to exert any more of it, however. I am tired. And there are Luc and that rascal of a Christopher. I have done my duty."

She did not argue the point. She would not have done so even if she could. She would have agreed with him. And she would not expect him to live on after her through sheer effort of will. He wanted more than anything else to go with her, to be young again and spry and happy again, to shed the duties and responsibilities—and losses—that had weighed heavily upon him since he was sixteen, though he had borne them all without complaint. Well, without too much complaint.

"You made it all bearable," he murmured to her. "So did Kitty and Franklin while he lived and our grandchildren and great-grandchildren. You most of all, though. We have been tested, May. But we have been happy too. I am going to lie down beside you for a while. I will try not to disturb you. My love."

He climbed onto the bed, careful not to touch her. He even released her hand in order to pull the bedcovers over it and over all of her to her chin. Her hand was feeling a bit chilly. He covered himself and closed his eyes. He would sleep awhile and then deal with whatever was left over of his life. Pray God there would not be much more of it.

Not without his beloved helpmeet.

There were a few candles burning dimly in the room. But they did not account for the bright light that at first was a pinpoint behind his eyelids and then grew to engulf him, bringing warmth and a sense of joy and peace with it. And bringing May with it, looking young and old and everything in between. Looking her eternal self. And smiling and holding out both hands for his.

"Thank you, Percy," she was saying. "Thank you, my love. But come now. We will go the rest of the way together. I would not know how to go farther into that light tunnel without you. Come with me."

He was feeling a bit light-headed, he knew. A bit fanciful. Soon he would wake to the reality of a leftover life without his duchess. But for now . . .

"Is it my imagination, May," he asked her as he set his hand in her soft, warm one, "or am I taller than you?"

"By half a head," she told him. "By a full head if you were wearing your boots."

N o one left Greystone. No one except the late Duke and Duchess of Wilby, that was. Everyone stayed for the funeral, which took place in the village church and churchyard on a bright, sunny day in April, halfway between the freshness of spring and the warmth of summer.

The same venue where a christening had been celebrated just a week before.

It was a time of sadness, of course. All the mourners had lost parents or grandparents or great-grandparents or friends or neighbors, and it was hard not to feel great sorrow for one's own loss at such a time. It was always hard to grasp the fact that one would never see those beloved people again or hear their voices or feel their presence in the world. Goodbyes were never easy, especially when they were final.

But it was a time for rejoicing too. For two people who had spent almost sixty years of their lives together in a happy union had had the extraordinary good fortune to leave this life within an hour or two of each other, looking, when they had been discovered an hour after the arrival of the physician at Greystone, as though they were asleep, comfortable and contented side by side. All who saw them there agreed that there could be no doubt they still existed, on a plane or in a dimension indiscernible to human eyes, together, happy, no longer burdened by any of the cares they had borne in this life. Or by the trappings of old age.

It was impossible to see their deaths as a tragedy.

"Your Grace?" It was the vicar who was speaking, and Lucas turned his head to see that he and Philippa, hand in hand, were the only ones remaining by the graveside. Aunt Kitty was between Gerald and her friend, Philippa's mother, being helped back to the carriages.

"Yes. You will want to be finishing up here," Lucas said. "Thank you for a truly lovely service, both inside the church and out here. Thank you for lifting our spirits rather than dragging them down into gloom."

He strolled slowly away from the grave with his wife—his duchess—their hands still clasped.

"How is it possible, Phil," he asked her, "to be raw with grief and glowing with happiness at the same time?"

"Because it all comes from love," she said, squeezing his hand. "Because we loved them and miss them but know there was nothing so very sad about their passing. Quite the contrary. And because love continues here—with their blessing. We have each other, Lucas, and the twins. And your family and mine. We have an abundance of love, and we know it will never end. Ever."

They were walking into the sun, half blinded by it. Their families awaited them by the row of carriages. Villagers stood back, out of the way, quietly respectful. Awaiting them at Greystone were the children—their own and those of their siblings and cousins. The future. The endless turning of life.

And of love.